SPELLS OF IRON & BONE

BOOK ONE

Spells of Iron and Bone
Tarot Academy, Book One
Copyright © 2019 by Sarah Piper
SarahPiperBooks.com

Published by Two Gnomes Media

Cover design by Faera Lane

v13

E-book ISBN: 978-1-948455-46-6
Paperback ISBN: 978-1-948455-12-1
Audiobook ISBN: 978-1-977300-82-9

BOOK SERIES BY SARAH PIPER

* * *

Reverse Harem Romance Series

Claimed by Gargoyles

The Witch's Monsters

Tarot Academy

The Witch's Rebels

* * *

M/F Romance Series

Vampire Royals of New York

GET CONNECTED!

I love connecting with readers! There are a few different ways you can keep in touch:

Email: sarah@sarahpiperbooks.com

TikTok: @sarahpiperbooks

Facebook group: Sarah Piper's Sassy Witches

Twitter: @sarahpiperbooks

Newsletter: Never miss a new release or a sale! Sign up for the VIP Readers Club:
sarahpiperbooks.com/readers-club

ONE

STEVIE

There's no problem a proper cup of tea can't fix.

It says so right on my work apron, just beneath the Kettle Black logo Mom designed decades ago, back when the café only existed in her dreams and sketchbooks. It says so on our menus and the shirts we sell to tourists. And it says so on the Mother's Day mug I painted when I was six —a black-and-gold one that sits next to the cash register, holding all the pens.

There used to be a plaque on the wall too, but that came down years ago, buried in a box with the ashes of Connor and Melissa Milan, resting beneath a granite headstone in Los Piñones Cemetery.

Devoted parents and friends

May their eternal light shine as a beacon for all who loved them...

If you squint at that part of the wall now, you can still

make out the square of plum-colored wallpaper, slightly darker where the plaque used to hang.

Anyway, as far as truisms go, the tea thing always felt like a good one. For the first eighteen years of my life, the simple brew healed all manner of wounds, from scraped knees to bruised egos, from mean-girl dramas to the fathomless ache of unrequited love.

And later, when I lost my beloved parents, when even the shrinks and social workers had given up on me, when my days turned so dark I feared Death himself would come and snatch me right out of bed, two things brought me back from the abyss:

My best friend Jessa Velasquez and some good, hot, life-affirming tea.

There's no problem a proper cup of tea can't fix, my mother's voice echoes again now.

It's funny how badly I still want to believe it.

But there's another truism—bigger, all-encompassing—one my parents forgot to mention before the river swept them down the Lost Canyons of Arizona, dashing their skulls against the rocks before the water could even finish drowning them:

There's nothing the universe loves more than a chance to show us how truly breakable we really are.

TWO

STEVIE

I've never seen a sky as wicked as the one that just blew in over Tres Búhos.

It's a mean one all right, full of ire and vengeance. And while I love a bone-rattling Arizona storm as much as the next witch, I'd rather not be sitting on top of the tallest rock in the desert when Mother Nature goes balls-out ballistic.

She's kind of an asshole sometimes.

I'd also rather not be dressed like a human lightning rod, but considering I can't make the two-hundred-foot descent without some serious hardware, looks like that dream's dead on the vine too.

I glare up at the sky. All morning it was clear and calm, the perfect day for a climb. But the second I get settled on top, light the palo santo, and whisper a few words of my mother's magick...

"Message received," I grumble, keeping the *asshole* bit to myself.

In response, the oil-black clouds flicker with a preview of what's to come, and a burst of hot, gritty wind rifles through the old grimoire on my lap. The faint smolder of palo santo dies, its sweet fragrance replaced with the scent of ozone.

That sky is ready to burst.

I close the spellbook, resigned. My attempt at magick—if you can even call it that—was destined to flame out anyway. Sure, I can sense people's energies, and my body has an uncanny ability to heal itself quicker than most, but as far as active powers? Other than casting witchfire, my magick is basically nonexistent, just like my parents wanted it to be.

Just like I promised to keep it.

Guilt surges anew, making my skin itch.

"Forget magick, Stevie. It's a curse..."

They weren't Mom's *literal* last words—those would come in the hours that followed, high-pitched and panicked and mostly incoherent—but they're the ones that stand out now. The ones that twist a hot blade in my gut every time I open the forbidden grimoire, searching for a clue about her past. *Our* past. This unknowable thing inside me, crackling with a wild, potential energy that simultaneously terrifies and fascinates me.

The forest-green leather is warm beneath my palm, and I try to pick up a sense of Mom's gentle touch, her laugh, the scent of frankincense that always trailed in her wake...

Nothing comes.

Nothing *ever* comes.

They say time heals all wounds, but it's been five years since I buried my parents, and I still wake up every morning to the suffocating press of grief on my heart. As far as I can tell, the only thing time does is march onward; all that's left for the living to do is try not to get trampled beneath it.

Another gust of wind buffets the rock, and a spiny lizard skitters across my blanket, smartly tucking himself into a crevice. Tamping down the simmering guilt, I slip the book into my daypack with the rest of my stuff, hop to my feet, and gear up for the drop.

Climbing shoes. Harness. Ropes. Chalk bag. Knife. Carabiners and hexes and cams… Check, check, check.

Tightening my fingerless gloves, I blow out a breath and step to the edge.

Darkness smothers everything in sight, casting shadows as far down as I can see. A strange, gray mist blankets the desert floor, the tops of the saguaros floating like the masts of a hundred haunted ships.

It's a long way down. A lot longer than it's ever felt before.

El Búho Grande—the big owl—is the largest of the three owl-shaped sandstone formations that tower over the Santa Clarita Desert, marking the southern border of their namesake town—Tres Búhos, Arizona. Three Owls. It's the only place I've ever called home.

The other two "búhitos" flanking me are significantly smaller—and much steeper, thanks to the protection of the big guy. But here on the Grande, where time has worn the top of the owl's head into a slab the size of an Olympic swimming pool, I can see my death coming from miles away.

Off in the misty distance, a streak of lightning splits the sky. I count to five before I hear the thunder—still a ways off, but not for long.

Goddess, let me be on the ground before the rain starts...

But even that's too much to ask, and as the first few drops darken the dusty red rock to a deep brown, I shoulder my pack, triple-check my knots, and begin the descent.

The ropes and anchors I set on the climb up are still in place, and at first, I make good progress. But it's not long before the rain picks up, soaking me to the bone and making everything I touch impossibly slick. Ignoring the drumbeat of encroaching thunder, I focus on my footing, wishing for once I *hadn't* ignored the NO CLIMBING signs posted at the bottom.

Fifty feet down, slow and steady. Sixty. Seventy-five.

Another bolt of lightning flickers in my peripheral vision, the crack of thunder right on its heels, echoing across the eerie desert.

I need to hurry.

Shit. I hate the idea of leaving gear behind, especially since a lot of it belonged to my parents—some of the few possessions I wasn't forced to sell after they died—but Mother Nature clearly wants me off this rock, and I don't have time to remove everything as I go. I'll have to come back tomorrow, hope that some bored park ranger doesn't spot it and take it down first.

Right now, it's all I can do to clip in and work my way down without slipping and smashing my face.

Wedging my toes into a horizontal crack, I release the slippery rock and reach behind me for the chalk bag, knowing I'll find a pasty mess, hoping it'll help my grip anyway. But I don't even find any paste—just a small, thin card, completely out of place.

It's a Tarot card. I know it before I even look at it.

Fear prickles across my scalp.

I've never had my own deck, but Mom did—one of the few things she kept from her old life. Before I sold our house, I nearly tore up the floorboards searching for it, eventually concluding she had it with her on that fateful day, losing it in the tumult of the rushing water. But on the one-year anniversary of their death, the cards started appearing to me at random like this. Under my pillow, tucked into the spokes on my bicycle wheel, hidden in an old shoe. Last week, the King of Cups dropped out of my sealed electric bill. Yesterday I emptied the washing machine and found the Fool prancing around at the bottom, bright and undamaged.

I can't say for sure it's Mom, but the cards always bring me a message, and they're never wrong.

I hold it up to my face now, blinking away the stinging mix of rain, sweat, and sunscreen.

At the center of the ominous image, a stone tower rises from a rocky outcropping at the edge of the sea. A bolt of lightning decimates half the structure and sends two people jumping from the highest windows, presumably to their deaths.

The Tower.

Not the most encouraging visual, given the circumstances.

I try to feel into the energy, to decipher whatever message is trying to come through. Usually I pick up on a general impression or feeling, but this time the message is more sinister, more urgent. I sense it in the tightening of my muscles, hear it like a whisper on the wind, straining to reach me through the rain.

Danger ahead, Stevie. Trouble and treachery. You're not alone…

Seconds later, the card vanishes from my grasp, lost beneath the clatter of some new threat. The prickling across my scalp turns at once to sharp, stinging pain.

Rockslide.

Instinctively, I haul my pack over my head, shove one hand into a crevice, and tuck in close to the rock, toes still balanced in the crack. Dressed in a tank top and a pair of cargo shorts, I've got zero protection against the assault of tiny stones biting my bare shoulders and arms.

Stones? Scratch that.

Hail.

Lightning flickers behind me, making my shadow dance against the rock face as the wind surges with renewed force, whipping icy pellets at me from all directions. They clatter like gunfire.

Adrenaline shoots through my veins, my heart pounding so hard it hurts. Rappelling in this weather is much too dangerous, but I can't stay here. I'm totally exposed, and the storm is parked right on top of me now. It's only a matter of time before lightning zaps me like a bug, or a chunk of rock tumbles down from above and bashes my head, or my rope breaks and sends me careening into oblivion…

Come on, girl. Think. Think!

It's almost impossible not to picture the poor souls in that Tarot card, but I do my best to shove them out of my mind, refocusing on my own precarious predicament. I can't go back up—I'd be even more exposed up top. I'm better off descending, but I can't protect my head *and* manage the ropes and gear placements *and* mind my hand- and footholds. I can barely see a few inches in front of me.

I need shelter. And up here, there's only one possibility.

El Ala—The Wing.

It's a secondary route about twenty feet to my left, skirting the edge of the owl's "wing." It's the most dangerous route on the rock by far, but still bolted from when people used to climb here legally, back before a huge chunk of sandstone cracked off and killed three climbers in the early nineties.

Just inside the wing lies a deep fissure in the rock, big enough you can see it from the dirt road leading into town.

Big enough I can fit inside and wait out the storm.

Another bolt of lightning.

Another crack of thunder.

The hail intensifies, pinging off my pack. It's about the size of gumballs now, their stinging bite quickly becoming a bruising wallop.

El Ala? Here I come.

I re-settle the pack on my shoulders and lean back, propping my feet against the wall as the harness takes the bulk of my weight, providing momentary relief for my calves. My head and arms are prime targets for the hail and debris shooting down from above, but if I can't make the twenty-foot traverse climb to that cave, I'll have much bigger problems.

I lean close to the wall again, get a good grip, and gingerly step to the left, seeking a better toehold. But just as my foot finds purchase, the wind lashes out again, blasting me off the rock like a bug off a windshield.

Frantically, I scramble for the ropes, but it's too late. I drop hard and fast, bashing my knee on the way down.

There's no time to scream, no time for panic. Suddenly the rope tightens and the harness jerks me to a hard stop, gear clattering, stomach leaping into my throat.

Blood leaks from my throbbing knee. My lines are hopelessly tangled. I'm suspended from Death's eager grasp by a rope that's less than an inch thick, and now I'm *below* the position of the cave, which means I'll have to climb over *and* back up.

Unless…

Fighting against the relentless wind, I kick my legs out and back, harnessing the momentum into a pendulum swing, rocking harder and higher, closer... closer... almost there...

My fingers graze the bottom of the wing, just a few feet beneath the cave floor, but I can't get a good grip.

I try again on the next swing.

Miss.

Swing again.

Miss.

Again.

Again.

Again.

On what feels like the twentieth attempt, I finally hook it with the tip of my shoe, and I let out a victory cry bordering on mania. The toehold is precarious, gravity doing its damnedest to suck me back in the other direction.

No way, asshole. You can't have me.

With every muscle in my leg screaming in agony, I pull myself in by my toe, fighting the wind, fighting fatigue, fighting mental anguish until finally I reach out with my hand and feel the rough, wet rock beneath my fingertips.

And then, miracle of miracles, I touch one of the old bolts.

I quickly clip into it, sending a prayer of thanks to whoever put it there, and climb the final few feet up to the cave.

With the last bit of strength I've got left, I haul myself inside.

The clatter of the hail turns to a din, and a new warmth pulses all around me. Sprawled out on my belly, I give myself a moment to catch my breath, then slowly raise my head, peering inside the dark space of the cave.

I'm still here, mostly in one piece.

"Thank you," I exhale into the deep.

"You're welcome," comes an unexpected reply.

And there, from somewhere inside that gnawing blackness, a pair of glowing yellow eyes blinks to life, and a shadow in the shape of a man peels away from the wall and stalks toward the light.

Toward me.

THREE

STEVIE

"Shoulda known it was you, Stevie Milan." The shadow-man crouches down and extends a hand, his grin warm and familiar. "Only girl crazy enough in all of Arizona to summit the Grande on a day like this."

I take in the sight of his boyish dimples and the dark hair flopping into his eyes, which are thankfully not glowing at all. He's filled out a bit since high school, but beneath the new bulk, there's no mistaking my old friend.

"Luke Hernandez!"

Relief floods my body, erupting in a laugh that probably sounds insane. After the morning I've had, I don't care. I grab his hand and scramble up to my feet, crashing into his bear-hug. "Holy shit, it's good to see you."

As kids, Luke and I went on exactly one date—bonfire party, just after eighth-grade graduation. Our budding romance came to a spectacular end later that same night when he put a scorpion down his pants on a dare, earning himself a trip to the emergency room and the infamous nickname Scorpion King.

I dumped him on principle—even at fourteen, I knew any dude stupid enough to put a venomous creature near his dick was *not* boyfriend material—but we stayed friends. He was into climbing, just like me and Jessa, and while our classmates spent the next five years getting stoned and feeling each other up behind the Gas-N-Grab out on Route Nine, the three of us made the desert our domain, mapping out the most challenging routes up the Grande, hiking through the sagebrush, talking about all the mountains we wanted to scale and countries we wanted to visit—the bright, shiny dreams of three kids looking for their ultimate escape.

Luke was the only one who ever made it out, though.

"I thought you were in California building hotels or something?" I ask, trying to remember what I heard from his mother, who still lives in town and comes into Kettle Black to eat Jessa's scones and gossip our ears off.

Luke presses a kiss to the top of my head, crushing me against his chest. "I missed you too much to stay gone, baby girl."

Um… *Baby girl?*

Back up.

He's *never* called me that before. Or missed me, for that matter. We were peas in a pod for a while there, but halfway into junior year, he bounced to go live with his dad out on the coast. After a brief goodbye over pizza and a bucket of hot wings, Jessa and I never heard from him again

—not even when my parents died. No social media, no texts, no postcards.

Jessa and I were bummed when he left, and yeah, it stung that he lost touch. But I never held it against him. I was dealing with my own issues back then, struggling to understand the magick kindling inside me and the parents who wanted to talk about anything *but*, wondering if I'd be stuck working at Kettle Black the rest of my life, forever searching for my bigger, better "someday" on the horizon. I was glad Luke found his, even if it meant leaving me and our dusty-ass desert town behind.

But six-plus years later, he randomly pops out of a cave during this insane storm, tossing out terms like baby girl?

Seriously?

He's got me in a vice grip, and this whole thing is feeling weirder by the minute.

I fake a cough and finally disengage from his suffocating embrace, turning to peer out into the gloom and buy myself a second to think.

Outside, the sky continues to put on a show, flickering and shouting, lashing the rock with all its might. Hailstones pile up at the entrance, and I shiver, rubbing my bare arms.

"Storm came out of nowhere," I say. Then, turning back to Luke, "Where were you when it hit?"

Ignoring the question, Luke glances at my knee. "You're bleeding."

"Am I?" I crouch down and pretend to inspect the wound. I don't even feel it anymore; the bleeding has mostly stopped, the gash nearly healed. Go magickal me.

I close my eyes and take a deep breath, giving my brain a second to catch up. There's a whole mess of loose puzzle pieces here, and none of them fit together.

For one thing, Luke is bone dry, which means he got into the cave before the rain started. But I was only on top for about fifteen minutes before the weather shifted, and if he'd been that close behind me on my initial climb, I would've spotted him. And his scent? The man smells like sunshine and coconut oil—definitely not the athletic stink of a big dude who just scaled most of a two-hundred-foot rock.

I glance up at him again, taking in the sight of his clothes. T-shirt and board shorts, a pair of leather flip-flops on his feet, Aviators clipped casually outside his pocket. He's dressed for a stroll down the beach—not a climb.

And there's no freaking gear.

I peek into the space behind him. No backpack, no harness, no rope. Nothing.

The hairs on the back of my neck stand up.

"So you're free-soloing now?" I get to my feet, unable to keep the surprise from my voice. Even the old pros back in the day never free-soloed the Grande. It's too steep, with sharp, deadly rocks on the bottom and lots of smooth sandstone up top—notoriously unreliable, especially when there's moisture in the air. That's why they bolted it in the first place, and why they closed it off to us in the next place.

"Oh, I had to ditch my gear on the way up," he says coolly, but he's getting real twitchy all of a sudden, shifting his weight from one foot to the other, avoiding my gaze. "Got into a jam and cut it loose."

Why is he lying to me? How the fuck did he get up here?

"Luke, that doesn't—"

"Watch the edge, Stevie," he warns. He snatches my hand and tugs me away from the entrance. "It's a long way down."

"Hey! You're hurting me!"

His eyes flicker with regret, but he doesn't let go. Just shifts his grip, his thumb brushing the tattoo on the inside of my wrist.

Back and forth, back and forth.

"Remember when you got this?" he asks, as if I could forget.

"I wanted one, too," he continues. "But nope. I wasn't *special* enough. Not like you, witch-girl. You've always been special."

I glance down at the source of his fascination—a black pentacle the size of a dime, a nine-digit serial number inked below, courtesy of the state. "Careful what you wish for, Luke."

It's the same thing I said back then. Same thing I say to anyone who romanticizes the life of a witch.

Magick has only been public knowledge for about fifty years. And while it's more of a known quantity now—and Tres Búhos has become quite the mecca for the sage-burning, crystal-collecting set—that doesn't mean the general population is cool with real magick-users.

Far from it.

Natural-born witches and mages only represent one-tenth of a percent of humans worldwide, and in the minds of a lot of people, we simply don't count.

In the minds of a lot *more*, we're something to be feared, subdued, or worse—eradicated. Any public display or non-consensual private act of magick is punishable by imprisonment. Magickal assault, even in cases of self-defense? Forget it. Capital offense.

They say our magick makes us perpetually armed and dangerous. The law requires us to register and get the tattoo at age sixteen, for the "comfort and safety" of all.

Luke drove me to my appointment. Held my hand and told me corny jokes to distract me from the needle. After I was all done and patched up, he got his own tattoo. Not a magickal one like he'd initially wanted, but a scorpion. He said he just wanted to make me laugh.

After, he bought me takeout and drove me to the Grande, and we sat at the base throwing fries at each other until the moon rose and it was time to go home.

"Crazy girl," he says now, a cruel smile twisting his lips, and I wonder if he's thinking about the fries, too. Or the moon. Or the way he used to chase Jessa and me up this rock, the three of us competing for the fastest times, the hardest routes, the best techniques. "Crazy little witch-girl."

Warning flashes in my gut.

Whatever Luke is thinking about now, it's not our shared history.

Desperate for a read on his true intentions, I open myself up to his energy.

18

SPELLS OF IRON AND BONE

It washes over me like a wave—a strange, aggressive mix of guilt, fear, confusion, anger, and—strongest of all—revulsion. I've never felt anything like this from him before—not even when I broke up with him after the scorpion incident.

I blow out a breath. The hatred simmering inside him is nauseating... But it isn't his.

Someone—something—is hijacking his emotions, manipulating his every move. Some part of him is trying to fight it, but he's only human, no match for the dark magick at work.

Whoever's behind it, it's clearly meant for me.

My arms erupt in goosebumps. Outside, the hail has given way to torrential rains, a curtain of sheer water that can't be penetrated. Lightning flashes and refracts off the water, making it nearly impossible to tell how close it is.

Thunder rumbles through the rock, right through my chest.

How the hell am I going to get out of this?

I'm still roped in, clipped to the bolt just outside the wing, but climbing out now is a hell of a risk. I don't know what Luke's capable of in this state—only that I don't want to be scaling down a rock in a storm with him standing above me.

"Sorry, witch-girl," he says now, tightening his grip on my wrist. Then, as if he can read my intentions as clearly as I've read his, "You're not going *anywhere*."

He takes a step closer, eyes roving my body head to toe. I step back, but my shoulders hit the rock, and he's

19

crowding into my space like smoke. The Tarot card image of the people jumping from the tower floats into my mind.

Fuck this.

"Back off." I jerk my arm free, but he grabs me again, relentless.

His eyes flash, and a laugh slithers out of his mouth. Jamming his thumb hard into my wrist, he says, "Not until I see some of that Stevie Milan magick. Come on, witch-girl. Show me what you've got."

The flicker of warning inside me turns into a blaring alarm. He's asking me to commit a federal crime.

"Not happening, asshole," I say. "And I'd appreciate it if you'd leave my friend out of this and face me in your true form, like a *real* mage. Or are you so feeble and dickless you need to possess innocent humans to carry out your dirty work?"

The muscle near Luke's left eye twitches, but he doesn't say a word.

"Sticking with feeble and dickless then," I say. "Okay, works for me."

I'm still wearing my daypack, and now I reach my free hand around to the pocket where my knife is stashed.

But before I get a grip, Not-Luke jerks me forward, then spins me around and kicks my legs out from under me.

I go down hard, and from the corner of my eye, catch a flash of silver. He's got my knife. The tension in my rope vanishes.

He cut it, leaving me no safe exit.

I'm back on my feet in a heartbeat, twisting around to surprise him with a swift knee to the crotch.

He stumbles back for a second, but the pain that flashes through his eyes is all-too-brief, chased off by pure rage and the sickly yellow glow I saw when I first climbed up.

Guess it wasn't my eyes playing tricks.

"You're dangerous, witch-girl," he says, the voice no longer Luke's. This one is deep and cold, as ancient as the desert itself. "They won't come for you. They'll never come for you."

Something about his words makes my heart freeze. Not-Luke raises his arm before me, the knife glinting, and I catch sight of the scorpion tattoo on his wrist.

Scorpion… They won't come…

I gasp as the memories bowl into me, my mother's voice rising up against the rushing water, her face grim, her eyes determined…

"They'll come for you, Stevie. After the sky falls and the scorpion stings, after the star takes flight and the lightning burns… Flame and blood and blade and bone… Flame and blood and blade and bone they will come…"

Those were her final words. Cryptic and baffling. Nonsense, maybe—yet more impassioned than anything she'd ever said before.

Seconds later, she was gone, sucked away by the current while I watched helplessly from a cave above the waterline, her final prophecy burned forever on my heart.

I never told anyone what she said. Not Arizona Search and Rescue, when they finally saved me from that cold, dark cave three days later. Not the social workers and grief counselors that came after. Not even Jessa.

He can't be talking about my mother. No fucking way.

The monster presses the knife to my belly, the tip piercing my skin.

"Show me," he orders.

"Fuck off, dickless."

"Show me!" His yellow eyes blaze as the knife sinks into my gut.

A scarlet stain blooms on my shirt.

I don't feel any pain.

All I feel is rage. Like a living, breathing beast, it pulses inside me, hot and fiery. Hungry.

And not enjoying this little game one bit.

Not-Luke steps closer, crowding me, driving the blade deeper.

I peer into his yellow eyes. "Don't make me do this."

Clearly mistaking my warning for a plea, he grins and says, "You'll do what I—"

I slam the heel of my hand into his nose. Bone cracks. He stumbles backward, clutching his face. Red-black blood oozes through his fingers.

He charges me again, but in that moment, knife sticking out of my belly, my old friend possessed and covered in blood, the storm raging beyond the walls, my exits cut off, something inside me completely unravels.

My chest fills with a swirling heat, and I raise my palms. A burst of energy explodes outward, expelling the knife and encasing me in a protective shield of blinding white light. Magick drapes over my arms like gossamer curtains.

No, not curtains. Wings.

Even without seeing its full form, I know the energy around me is an owl—the legend and soul of the rock come to life. Luminescent and graceful, it fills me with a power and fearlessness that borders on predatory. I spread my arms wide, then bring them to my chest, making the great wings flap. The force of air slams Not-Luke into the wall. He hits the back of his head, then crashes down onto his ass.

His yellow gaze locks on mine, burning with new hatred even as a smile breaks across his bloody face. "You'll be executed for this, witch."

Before I can utter a single word, I feel a tug from the inside, almost like an undercurrent. I'm powerless to resist as the soul-force carries me backward, sucking me out into the storm. Rain continues to pound the sandstone, the desert below enshrouded in ghostly mist, but nothing can penetrate my protective shield.

The massive wings flap, spreading light all around me. It takes me a beat to realize I'm hovering outside the cave, feet no longer touching the ground.

Not-Luke scrambles to his feet. The energy of his murderous rage washes over me. He wants me to know he's going to kill me, and he's going to enjoy every torturous second.

It's the last thing I feel before I fall.

FOUR

STEVIE

I burst into Kettle Black, locking the door behind me and flipping the OPEN sign to BE BACK SOON. Thankfully, there aren't any customers, because holy shit, I need a minute.

Or maybe a month.

What the fuck just happened?

"Have a seat wherever you'd like!" Jessa calls from the kitchen behind the counter. "I'll be right with you!"

"It's just me," I call back.

"Stevie?" Her tone ices over in an instant. "You know I'm gonna beat your ass as soon as I've got a free hand, right?"

"I'm aware." I roll my eyes, but I totally deserve the ire. She doesn't climb much anymore and hates when I go alone —too dangerous, she says. On top of that, I'm late as hell—I was supposed to be here to help open the café hours ago. She had to manage on her own.

Still, my best friend's temporary anger is nothing compared to the morning I've had.

I drop onto a stool at the café counter and rest my head in my hands, taking a deep breath for the first time since I sailed off that rock.

Sailed is the only word for it, too. Through the storm, down the sheer drop, my magick protector glided along the air currents, deftly spiraling until we reached the misty desert below.

The moment my feet touched the ground, the owl energy vanished, taking that strange desert mist with it. Seconds later, a bolt of lightning struck one of the smaller owl rocks behind me. I leaped out of the way just before a huge slab smashed into the ground where I was standing, pulverizing instantly.

I couldn't help but think of the Tower card again.

Not knowing what the hell else to do, I sprinted up to the road and ran the two miles into town in my climbing shoes, my pack and gear slapping my thighs, not daring to slow down until I reached Guadalupe Street and the Kettle Black sign came into view.

Now, as I sit here in my parents' old café surrounded by the sweet, familiar scents of Jessa's baking and the pretty display of teacups behind the counter, the whole morning feels like a dream.

I press a hand to my chest, my heart still jackhammering. A faint glow pulses around my fingers—all that's left of the magick.

Magick.

How did I manage something so epic? I must've channeled it somehow, or conjured it... But how?

Hauling my pack onto the counter, I pull out the grimoire. The book is damp, but thankfully it survived the worst of the weather.

I flip open the cover just as Jessa emerges from the kitchen, balancing a tray of fresh maple-glazed scones on one shoulder and a chip the size of Arizona on the other. Her apron is covered in flour.

"You're two hours late," she snaps, fiery gaze raking me head to toe. "And you're bleeding, which is definitely a health code violation."

"I'm fine, though, thanks for asking."

To be fair, it's not the first time I've rolled into work late, muddy, and bloody. Spend enough time defying gravity in the Santa Clarita, and injuries are bound to happen. Fortunately, mine heal quickly.

"Is it yours?" she asks, and I know she means the blood staining my shirt.

"Half and half. Well, sixty-forty."

She sets her tray on top of the pastry case, a bit harder than necessary. "Who's the forty in this equation? Do I even want to know?"

Ignoring the question, I page through the grimoire, locating the section I was working on before the storm hit. This morning, I thought it was just a simple scrying spell—something Mom might've used to amplify her divining ability. But her spells are never straightforward, full of symbols and metaphors and Tarot references far beyond my limited understanding of the Arcana, so there's a good chance I got it wrong.

Why are you still hiding from me?

From the moment I found the book, stashed in a box of romance novels and cheesy sci-fi DVDs in the attic of our old house, I've been trying to decipher it. Not to recreate her magick—never. It's just... I want to understand it. To understand *her*.

"Are you seriously stonewalling me right now?" Jessa fumes. "Stevie, your freaking hands are glowing!"

"I know. I'll tell you everything. Just... just give me a minute. Please."

"You've got *two* minutes. I'm counting." Turning back to her task, she slides open the pastry case and sets the still-warm scones on a platter, arranging them just so. Like her sleek black bob and artfully applied eyeliner, her pastry game is always pure perfection, even in the midst of a crisis.

Goddess, I hate the taste of bad news. It's like the storm clouds outside; the longer it sits on my lips gathering strength, the more devastating it'll be when it finally lets loose.

I have to tell her. There's no way around it.

Closing the book, I take a deep breath and make my confession. "I fucked up today, Jess. Bad."

She slides the case closed and wipes her hands on the towel draped over her shoulder. When she meets my eyes again, the anger is all but gone from hers, replaced with worry. "Define bad."

"I sort of... accidentally... used magick on someone. A lot of it."

Jessa's eyes go as round as tea saucers. "Where? How? Who?"

"Up on the Grande. I got caught in the storm with Luke and—"

"Scorpion King Luke? I thought he was in California."

"He was. I'm not even sure he knows how he got here—or that he got here at all." I close my eyes, trying to make sense of the jumble of images in my head. "A dark mage got to him—it's the only explanation. He wanted me to do magick. Like, he kept pushing and pushing... Then he got a hold of my knife. He stabbed me, Jess."

"Stevie! Holy shit, we need to call the cops!"

"And tell them what?" I lift my shirt, showing her my unmarred skin, smooth and pale but for a splotch of dried blood. "It's already healed. Besides, Luke—*real* Luke—would never do that. I'm telling you, it wasn't him."

The rest of the story spills out—everything but the part about my mother's last words, which I can't bring myself to repeat.

The whole thing sounds so wild and impossible, I hardly believe my own tale.

But Jessa believes me. She always does.

Concern draws her eyebrows together. "What if this mage guy—posing as Luke—calls the cops on *you* for magickal assault?"

"Then I'm pretty much fucked, and I hope you *really* like

baking, because you're inheriting Kettle Black." I try to laugh, but it gets stuck in my throat.

Possessed or not, Luke is human. And unlike mine, his injuries won't spontaneously heal. His mother is also a prominent member of the community—an artist, a patron, a volunteer—you name it, Rita's got her hands in it. So if her son shows up at the police station with a busted nose and a story about the nasty little witch-girl who broke his face?

No way would the cops take my word over his.

"Protect and serve" doesn't apply to the magickal folk among us.

Jessa's not laughing at my stupid joke, either. She taps her fingers on the counter nervously, her gaze darting out the front windows, then back to me. "Do you want to close up shop and head back to the estate?"

The estate is what we call the double-wide we share—an old but perfectly serviceable mobile home situated at the edge of the Santa Clarita. And while I'd love nothing more than to camp out on our thrift store couch bingeing Netflix, it's not going to help.

"I'd only be crawling the walls there," I reply. "No, I need to work. Looks like we'll be pretty slow today, anyway—nothing I can't handle."

Jessa watches me a beat longer, then glances out front again. Sheets of rain blur the view, the street gutters already flooding. No one's crazy enough to be outside on a day like this.

"All right, *loca*. Go make yourself presentable." She grabs a Kettle Black T-shirt from the tourist stash and hands it over, then flips our sign back to OPEN. "I'll make us some tea. Then we'll figure out what to do about this dark mage situation."

Locked in the bathroom, I strip off my climbing gear, trash my ruined shirt, and do my best to wash up in the sink. I can't do anything about my shorts, but at least the Kettle Black shirt is clean and new.

Jessa's makeup bag is stashed in the cabinet over the sink, and I rummage through it for some eyeliner and lipgloss. There's not much hope for my crazy hair in this humidity—messy bun for the win.

I check my reflection in the mirror. I won't be entering the Miss Arizona competition today, but I'm no longer a walking health code violation.

No longer magickal, either. The glow is totally gone from my hands.

My shoulders slump. I know I should be relieved, but a twinge of sadness tightens my chest.

I try to remember the owl, the hot swirl of its energy in my chest, the powerful wings unfurling from my body, the cool snap of wind on my face as we soared through the sky, the desert floor rising to meet us.

I hold up my hands and try to call it back—even just a flicker of that intense white light.

But it's truly gone.

FIVE

STEVIE

The wind kicks up outside, the clouds I escaped on the Grande now unloading on Guadalupe Street. From my seat at the counter, I watch out the window as Luke's mother Rita scurries from Bruno's Bagel Shack into her adjacent pottery studio, losing her newspaper in the process. It catches on the current and flaps down the street like a drunken bird.

There's a quick flash in the distance, followed by an ominous rumble. The brunt of the storm hasn't hit this part of town yet, but it's coming.

"Just checked the news." Jessa's back, handing me a mug of soothing blackberry vanilla tea. "Storm's supposed to blow right by."

"And take Rita with it, apparently." I watch as the woman runs back outside for her newspaper. Now *she's* a drunken bird, too—arms flapping, obnoxious turquoise hair streaming out behind her, red dress billowing.

"Is Luke with her?"

"He's probably stuck on the rock, at least until the storm breaks." I sip my tea, grateful for the warmth. "Rita might not even know he's in town. Judging from his clothes, he was basically plucked off the beach and deposited in that cave."

"Dark mage possessions. Owl spirits. Flying." Jessa drops onto the adjacent stool and lets out a low whistle. "That's one hell of a magickal morning for a girl who doesn't even dabble."

Silence descends, rain pattering the windows. No hail here yet—maybe that's a good sign.

Absently I run my hand over Mom's grimoire. Jessa follows my gaze, her brow furrowed. She's terrified for me —I can feel it in her energy. The questions are already percolating in her mind.

But the words don't come.

I've known Jessa since Kindergarten, right after her family emigrated to Tres Búhos. She's not a witch, but her adoptive parents are. So when we were kids, she got all the bullying and fear-mongering that comes with being part of a witch family, but none of the magick. I had the magick, but wasn't allowed to learn about it, talk about it, or use it. The two of us bonded hard and fast, and we've been insep-arable ever since. Even when her parents decided to move back to Mexico our senior year, Jessa stayed here, moving in with my family so we could keep working at the café together until graduation, when we were supposed to figure out college stuff.

Plans changed after the accident. I deferred enrollment at Arizona State—no way was I shuttering Kettle Black, my deceased parents' lifelong dream. And Jessa? She stuck by my side through all of it. Still does.

In all the ways that count, she's my sister, and has been since the first day we met. We don't keep secrets between us—not on purpose.

But there's one thing we've simply never talked about.

My mother's magickal history.

It was always a forbidden topic of conversation in my house, and after my parents died, it felt wrong to open up the floodgates on our endless speculation. I was supposed to be forgetting about it, just like my parents wanted, and Jessa was eager to help me in whatever way she could.

But since those early days, she's seen me with the grimoire, sitting at the plastic patio table behind our estate, paging through it with a pen and journal at the ready as if deciphering my mother's cryptic words might bring her back to us.

She's always had the grace to keep quiet about it, let me figure it out on my own.

But a morning of dark mage possessions, owl spirits, and flying has a funny way of changing the rules—even the unspoken ones.

"Stevie," she finally says, "you can't keep doing this."

"It's the only connection I have to that part of her, Jess. I can't let it go."

"That's exactly what I'm talking about. You *can't* let it go. You *shouldn't* let it go. You're a full-blooded, natural-born witch. And you've never gotten the opportunity to explore your powers, or be around other witches, or even *talk* about magick."

"My parents—"

"Your parents are *gone*." Jessa rises from her stool, paces the floor before me. "Stevie, I'm sorry, but it has to be said. I understand you're trying to honor their memory, but all you're doing is living in the past."

"That's not true! I'm just—"

"Look around you!" She opens her arms, encompassing the entire café. "They've been dead for five years, and you're still following their rules. Managing their café. Living their life."

"I like working at Kettle Black!"

"Yeah, and so do I. But is this your dream? Your passion? Your true calling, like it was for your parents? If you say yes, I swear I'll shut up and never mention magick again."

I cross my arms over my chest. She's got me there. But still…

"That doesn't mean it's not worth something, Jess. This place, this life… It's their legacy. One I'm happy to uphold. They were right—we *don't* need magick. It's like Mom always said—it's nothing more than a curse. Today proved that."

The words burn my throat on the way out. Even *I* can hear the lie in my voice.

"Listen to yourself, girl." Jessa shakes her head, a bitter laugh escaping her lips. "You were attacked today—

targeted by a dark mage. Targeted precisely *because* you're a witch, and you know nothing about it, about how to defend yourself."

"I survived, didn't I?"

"On a fluke!"

"On my magick! Magick I shouldn't even be practicing!"

"But you *didn't* practice it. That owl thing—it just *happened*. And waiting around for things to just happen is a bullshit strategy—in magick, and in life." She storms behind the counter, but I'm out of my seat, close on her heels.

"Jessa, wait."

Ignoring me, she grabs a stack of those Kettle Black souvenir shirts, unfolding and refolding them, refusing to meet my eyes.

"*Jessa*." I yank a shirt from her hands, forcing her to look at me. "My parents spent the last eighteen years of their lives trying to put magick in the past. All they wanted—all they *ever* wanted—was for me to have a safe, mundane, normal life. They wanted that for you, too."

"But you're not normal!" She snatches the shirt back, resuming her frantic folding. "You're a witch! An amazing, beautiful, soulful witch. Pretending otherwise is only going to make you miserable, and possibly get you killed. And what happens to the Milan family legacy then? Spoiler alert: You all become memories—*my* memories. Game over, thanks for playing, have a nice afterlife."

Jessa turns her back on me, her whole body trembling. I don't even have to try to read her energy; it washes over me in great big waves. Anger and fear. A fierce protectiveness. Loyalty. Sisterhood.

The anger evaporates from my heart. She's coming from a good place. She's *always* coming from a good place.

And she's not wrong.

"So what am I supposed to do, then?" I ask softly.

She spins around to face me again, eyes still blazing with anger and frustration. "Learn your magick, for fuck's sake! Find a mentor, get some books, apply to that magick school—something!"

My stomach bottoms out at the mention of the school. She's talking about Arcana Academy, my parents' alma mater. The very place that trashed Mom's reputation, banished them from their coven, and basically destroyed their lives—and that's just the highlights reel I pieced together from years of hushed whispers and overheard arguments.

The Academy is the very place I begged them—naively, insolently—to send me.

It was the last argument we ever had.

Forget magick, Stevie. It's a curse...

I close my eyes. My anger might be gone, but the sadness isn't, all the old regrets resurfacing from the dark ocean constantly churning inside me, washing up on the shores of my heart like oily bits of trash.

When I speak again, my throat is tight. "It feels like... like you're asking me to shit on my parents' graves."

"No, Stevie." Jessa grabs my shoulders, her touch warm, her sugary scent enveloping me like a hug. I feel her love pulsing outward, overruling everything else. She puts her hand on my cheek, and I open my eyes, meeting her soft, copper-eyed gaze. "I'm just asking you to stop tending those graves."

"I don't know how," I whisper.

"Start by finding out about the Academy. From there, it's—oh." Her attention shifts to the windows, eyes narrowing. "We'll have to pick this up again later."

"What's wrong?"

"Apparently, the storm isn't enough to keep *everyone* away today." When she looks at me again, she's smiling like a master conspirator. "You've got company."

SIX

STEVIE

The man's steps are confident and quick as he plows through the deluge, a paperback tucked protectively inside his T-shirt.

Now my heart's pounding for an entirely different reason.

His hair falls in dark, wet waves in front of his glasses, but it doesn't matter. I know the intricate beauty of his eyes by heart—pale green irises surrounded by a burst of pure gold, like the sun setting behind the saguaros.

Kirin Weber isn't from around here, but he's been patronizing Kettle Black for months, camping out for a couple of hours every day, losing himself in an epic fantasy novel or the latest biography from Red Rocks Recycled Reads, the used bookshop around the corner. The book changes every few days, but his order is always the same: Two mini cinnamon buns and a small pot of tea, leaving the blend up to me.

"Mr. Cinnamon Buns," Jessa sing-songs, our magickal troubles fading in the wake of his complete hotness. "Braving the storm to get to his woman. Looks like true love to me."

"You *really* need to stop saying that."

"The buns part, or the love part?"

"Both parts! Jessa, you can't just—"

"*Anyway*, men like that shouldn't be allowed to exist. It makes the rest of us feel wholly inadequate."

A sigh escapes my lips. No, Kirin shouldn't exist. But like my magick owl and singing sand dunes and the fairy lights in the night sky over the Santa Clarita's Canyon of Ghosts, somehow, he does.

Plastering on my biggest customer-service grin, I head over to greet him, hoping he doesn't notice my lackluster hair and the slight whiff of *eau de hot mess* clinging to my skin.

I wonder if I look as nervous as I feel.

"Hey Kirin!" I blurt out as he walks through the door. "Hi! How are you? Crazy weather out there, right?"

Oh my Goddess, Stevie. Stop talking. Just stop.

Kirin pushes the wet hair from his forehead and raises a curious eyebrow, his fogged-up glasses sliding down his nose. Rain darkens the fabric stretched across his broad, take-no-prisoners shoulders, and he smells like storms in the summer, clean and electric.

The playful glint in his eyes makes me ache for something I've got no business even *thinking* about.

"I see you're dabbling in the highly caffeinated blends

today," he says in that deep, sultry voice of his, and I swear his eyes brighten when I laugh. The tingly touch of his magick whispers across my skin.

Okay, *fine*. I'm totally crushing on him. But that's irrelevant, especially after this morning's series of disastrous events. Me and mages? That can't happen. Ever.

Jessa might think I need to find my true calling or whatever, and I won't lie—the idea of learning my magick sends a forbidden thrill straight to my heart. But my parents made it clear that the Academy was off limits—the worst place imaginable. An institution that wrings every last drop of magick from your bones, then tosses you to the wolves as if you never belonged in their world at all.

No, getting involved with a mage isn't exactly the same thing as enrolling in the traitorous Academy, but it *is* one step closer to magick. One step farther from normal. And one step over a line I vowed not to cross the moment my parents died.

"Sooo," Kirin drawls.

"Sooo," I echo. His smile is mesmerizing. I'm already starting to forget my own name.

He rocks back on his heels, the smile never faltering.

I'm bouncing on my toes like an idiot.

"Hey, Stevie?" He leans in close, his sultry whisper sending a cascade of shivers down my spine. "Do you, ah, mind if I take a seat?"

"What? Oh. *Oh*! Sorry." I step aside, hoping to Goddess he isn't gifted with mind-reading.

Tamping down the awkward, I follow him to his favorite two-seater by the window.

He arranges himself in the chair, the soaked T-shirt clinging to every ripple in his muscled torso as he removes his book and tries not to drip all over the table. "Sorry about that."

"Don't be," I say. *Seeing you wet is the highlight of my decade.* "So, what are we drinking today?"

He removes his glasses and attempts to dry them on his shirt, giving me an unobstructed view of his eyes. "You tell me, queen of leaves."

I open myself up to his energy, trying desperately not to blush at the intimacy of his penetrating gaze. He feels off today—tired, maybe a little on edge.

"Something rejuvenating," I say. "With a little pep, but not so much you'll be vibrating all night. Sound good?"

"Stevie, I trust you implicitly." He puts his hand on his heart and smiles, just like always.

Goddess, those eyes…

"You'll regret that one day," I reply, just like always.

"Not a chance."

It's our thing, this banter. Yes, we have a *thing*. It's sickening, and it makes my insides fizzy, and no matter how off-limits he is, right now he's the only normal, predictable, routine thing about my entire day, and I desperately cling to it.

"Be right back." I head into the kitchen, ignoring the heat between my thighs and Jessa's know-it-all smirk.

"I'm warming up his buns," she teases. "Maybe one day you'll get to do the same. In bed. Naked."

I roll my eyes. How she can go from impassioned magickal life coach to middle-school pun master in less than two minutes is beyond me.

"Sorry, Miss Velasquez," I say. "Stevie can't indulge in your pervy little fantasies right now. She's busy working. You know, that thing we do here sometimes?"

"*I'm* working! I told you, I'm handling the buns."

"Then you'd better stay focused."

"Getting back to Kirin—"

"Buns, Jessa. Last time I checked, they don't warm themselves."

"The man looks good wet, is all I'm saying."

I spare a moment to chuck a pen at her, which she deftly dodges. She winks at me across the stainless-steel counter that separates us, and I smile; we've got a lot to talk about, but our earlier fight has been forgiven.

The pantry shelf is full of hundreds of jars, canisters, and herb and spice bottles, each one promising a different blend, a different healing magick all their own. I take down what I need, then get to work on Kirin's special brew.

"*A natural healer,*" Mom used to whisper, pressing a kiss to the top of my head as I made my blends. As much as my parents tried to downplay their magick, Mom could never truly hide her fascination when she saw my natural witch-craft at work, reading energies and concocting the perfect brew for every customer. She never shared much about her magick with me, but she once told me I was the first true empath in the family.

I blink back tears, refocusing on my task. I'm better at that now—coming back before grief takes hold. When my parents first died, it seemed like it was waiting for me around every corner, lurking in every shadow, ready to pounce at the slightest provocation—finding an old lipstick of Mom's in a bathroom drawer, seeing Dad's handwriting on a receipt, the smell of blueberry pancakes, some stupid song on the radio.

I didn't speak for three months after—not even to tell Search and Rescue what'd happened. Everyone thought it was the shock, or some survivor's guilt thing, but they were all wrong.

I was just afraid that if I opened my mouth, grief would reach a hand inside and stop my heart.

"I'm calling it Get Up and Go Green." I pour Kirin's first cup and set the teapot on his table. "Japanese green tea with dried pineapple and mango, a whisper of shredded coconut, and a pinch of coriander."

Like a true connoisseur, he lifts the cup and samples its scent, then takes a sip, savoring it for a long moment before taking another—a practice I find both mesmerizing and endearing. When he looks up at me, his glasses are all steamed up, his energy brighter than it was a moment ago. "You're amazing, Stevie. Beyond perfection."

"Thank you," I say, but my brain must be channeling Jessa, because all I really hear is...

You're amazing, Stevie. Allow me to tie you down and remove your clothing with my teeth, after which I'll read you dirty love poems and lick every inch of your skin until your legs are trembling and you're begging me to make you —

"So, there's something I've been dying to ask you," he says, drawing me back to the fully clothed present and gesturing for me to take the chair across from him. "It might be a little personal, though."

"Um. Okay?" A nervous giggle bubbles up.

I'm such a loon. Seriously. Two hours ago I was scaling a dangerous rock face, battling storms and dark mages and who knows what else. Now, a few words from Kirin reduce me to a puddle of insipid ridiculousness.

Not that I'm going to let *that* stop me.

I perch on the edge of the chair, still hoping he can't read minds.

"I've been wondering," he says. "Is it cheating if the queen of leaves drinks coffee?"

The genuine earnestness in his question makes me laugh.

"If I tell you something," I say, "you have to swear you won't tell a soul."

He draws an X over his heart, a gesture that only serves to underscore his complete adorableness and does absolutely nothing to cool the heat simmering in my core.

"I kind of have a thing for vanilla cinnamon lattes," I confess. "The ones they make at Froth? Two pumps vanilla, one pump cinnamon, a dollop of extra foam, finished off with a drizzle of honey and two shakes of cinnamon."

"Okay, that sounds like more than a *thing*. You're crossing into full-blown obsession territory. And I'm glad to hear that, because I was actually wondering if you might want to join me? I mean, for a coffee? Sometime?"

"But… but I just made your tea," I blurt out.

Holy shitcakes, is he asking me out? He's asking me out. Code red! Code red!

"Right," he says. "I meant some other time. This weekend, maybe? I just thought it might be fun to hang out. You know, outside of Kettle Black. We can talk about…" He picks up his novel, something with an old farmhouse on the cover. "…books! Or, you know, anything you like. What *do* you like? Other than tea, I mean. And rock climbing and biking—I know that much. Okay, I'm rambling. Save me, Stevie. Say something before I make an even bigger fool of myself."

"Kirin, I… I don't even know what to say."

"How about yes?"

My heart is going crazy again, and I'm trying to focus on his eyes, on his words, on what all of this means, but a big white blur outside the window captures my attention.

I chance a quick glance.

The sight makes me gasp.

A snowy owl hovers in front of the café, white with dark brown spots, his piercing golden eyes fixed on mine. The rain seems to part around him, as if he's encased in a protective bubble. He flaps his great wings, watching me. Studying me.

"Are you seeing this?" I turn back toward Kirin, but he's staring at something at the center of his table where his book used to be—something I'm certain wasn't there thirty seconds ago.

The Tower card.

My blood turns to ice.

"Tell me that's yours," I say, even though I know it isn't.

"You know I can't," he whispers.

Our gazes lock, intense in a way that has nothing to do with our innocent flirting. Suddenly, it feels as if we've known each other for decades. Lifetimes. Eons.

Something is about to break. The message hits me hard and fast, a shot of fear straight to the gut. Kirin feels it too. I know he does.

Outside, the owl takes flight, vanishing from view. A bolt of lightning splits the sky, the thunder immediate and fierce, so close it rattles the windows.

"Listen to me," Kirin says, his face pale, his voice a ghostly whisper. "Do you have a back door? You and Jessa need to—"

There's a commotion at the entrance, and three cops burst into the café, guns drawn.

"Starla Eve Milan?" the lead cop barks at me. He raises his weapon, aiming right for my head.

Kirin leaps from his chair, but a second cop approaches the table, holding up his left hand in warning, as if that's more convincing than the gun in his right.

"Sir, you need to remain seated," he says. "Hands on the table."

"What's this about?" Kirin steps in front of me, shielding me.

"You live at 129 Pinon Canyon Lane?" the first cop asks me, ignoring Kirin.

Petrified, I can only nod, stiff and dumb, my heart ready to explode.

"Sir, I asked you to sit down," cop two says, just as Jessa emerges from the kitchen with a plate of those cinnamon buns. When she sees the cops, she drops it, the ceramic shattering. Cop three turns a weapon on her.

"Yes, it's me!" I shout, desperate to keep them focused on me and not my innocent friends. "I'm Starla Eve. Stevie. I live on Pinon Canyon Lane."

Cop number one holsters his weapon, his pals keeping their guns raised. He removes the cuffs from his belt and slaps them over my wrists, ice-cold and bruising. "You're under arrest for public witchcraft and the murder of Lucas Hernandez."

SEVEN

STEVIE

Never before has the dawn been so cruel.

I crack open my eyes, squinting against the too-bright light slanting across my face. Everything aches, inside and out, and my first deep breath of the day unleashes a searing pain in my chest. My head is locked in a vise grip of pain.

For the first fifteen seconds of consciousness, I'm pretty sure I'm halfway to Death's door.

Then it all comes back.

The guards. The beatings. The fact that my body isn't healing as fast as usual—probably related to the meal plan; I've eaten nothing but cold broth, stale bread, and a few past-due vegetables since I've been here.

Don't even get me started on the caffeine withdrawal.

Welcome to hell, day three. Or maybe four? In the wake of my 24/7 headache, time is starting to blur.

I try to sit up, but my arms and legs are shackled to the bed.

One of the guards must've drawn the short straw last night, and crept in here while I was asleep to lock me in place. They don't like dealing with me one-on-one. Always afraid I'm going to fry them with my non-existent magick.

But in a group, armed with batons and tasers? Then it's party time, boys and girls, and I'm the piñata.

Could be worse. The fact that they believe witches are damaged goods is probably the only thing keeping me from getting something much more horrifying than a beating.

Nutless cowards. Once I figure out how to channel my magick again, I'm going to kill them first.

I wriggle my arms, but it's useless. The worst part? The restraints aren't even necessary—just a nice little touch to remind me who's in charge here.

I'm in a special cell reserved for witches and mages, with fancy "bars" made of some kind of deadly electricity— a complicated spell undoubtedly created by a crooked magick-user on the payroll. Upon arrival, I was given a demonstration of what would happen to me if I attempted to cross the glowing bars.

The poor mouse was vaporized on contact.

In addition to the bars, the cell itself sits inside a secure room that can only be opened via fingerprint scanner from the outside. The outer wall is made of a strange magickal glass, concentrating the sunlight on me until I feel like a bug under a magnifying glass.

It's impossible to break.

I blink the sleep from my eyes, try to swallow past the dryness in my throat. Outside, all I see is scrub brush and cacti for miles—a deadly, beautiful barrier that would likely kill any prisoner who dared attempt an escape—witch and human alike.

I don't even know what town we're in, whether we're still in Arizona or even in the states.

Tres Búhos feels so far away, I may as well be imprisoned on Mars.

"Wake up, heathen," a gruff voice barks over the intercom. The outer door beeps, then slides open, revealing my tormentor in chief—the Asshole in Charge Around Here. He's wearing his usual suit and tie, like maybe he's penciling in a few business meetings around his regularly scheduled beating of prisoners.

Two other guards file in behind him, meaty hands wrapped around their electrical prods.

"Bet you boys haven't gripped anything that big in a while, huh?" I ask. "Just remember—stroke, don't choke."

"Shut it, slut." Asshole in Charge taps a code into the keypad on the wall, and the electrical barrier vanishes. His face is even more dour than usual. "Your attorney's here."

I open my mouth to tell him I don't have an attorney, but think better of it. Sure, it's probably a trap. But whoever it is, they can't be worse than the guards. Maybe they can even help me escape this living hell.

Maybe it's Jessa…

The thought is as fragile as spun glass, and then, right before it turns into hope, I smash it.

If Jessa were allowed to visit me, she would've been here by now, even if she had to borrow a car and drive all night. She's probably going crazy, no idea where I am, no idea what's happening, no idea if I'm even alive. She tried to get answers from the cops the other day in Kettle Black, but once they had me cuffed, they hustled me out of there pretty quick.

My only comfort was Kirin. He stood by Jessa's side, gently holding her back from charging after me. He knew a losing battle when he saw one. His reassuring gaze—serious, sad, shockingly bare—was the last thing I saw as the cops dragged me away. In his deep, calming voice, he promised me that he and Jessa would find a way to help.

It was a lie—we both know there's nothing a mage can do for a witch ensnared in the human justice system.

He said it for Jessa's benefit.

I appreciated it more than he'll ever know.

Thinking of him now sends a little flutter to my heart, followed by a deep sadness.

We never got to go on that coffee date. Never got to talk about books or anything else.

All three guards crowd into my cell, the prods within zapping distance as Asshole in Charge unlocks my restraints. He hauls me to my feet, then cuffs my hands behind me and shoves me forward.

He doesn't issue any warnings or threats, doesn't rattle off the rules. He doesn't need to.

Outside my special room, the hallways are lined with regular cells packed with humans—women. Some of them don't look a day over eighteen. Others look like they've spent their entire adult lives behind bars.

None of them are friendly—not to the witch accused of murdering an innocent human. The witch who gets her own private room.

"Dead witch walking." They chant and whistle as I pass, throwing things at me from behind their cages. Balled up paper. Shoes. Books.

Halfway down the walk of shame, a soggy rag smacks me in the face, then slides unceremoniously to the ground.

It takes me less than one second to realize it's soaked in piss.

Asshole remains unfazed, tightening his grip on my arm as we continue down the filthy corridor.

Drops of urine roll down my cheek, but I don't complain. Just do my best to wipe my face on my shoulder, and keep on trucking. My visitor, whoever it is, represents a change in routine. And change? That's an opportunity—however dim—to find a way out.

It's the first flicker of real possibility I've felt since I got here. I won't risk it by starting trouble. Not now.

Cattle prods at the ready, they shove me down a few more corridors until we reach a large steel door at the ass end of the complex.

I don't know whether to be relieved or afraid.

Sure, there aren't any inmates around to torment me.

But there's no one around to hear me scream, either.

"Where are you taking—"

"Quiet, witch." Asshole digs his bruising fingers into my arm, then turns to the other two guards. "I got it from here."

He waits until they leave, then punches a code into the keypad. The door beeps, then unlatches, and he shoves me on through to yet another maze of hallways. Our adventure finally terminates in a windowless, Easy-Bake oven of a room, hot air looming in a dense, sour cloud as if the door hasn't been opened in years.

There's a table in the center, a chair on each side. He shoves me hard into the first chair, my teeth clacking together from the impact. Blood coats my tongue. My headache slides from a dull throb into borderline migraine territory.

"Comfortable?" He grins, then jerks at the cuffs behind my back, wrenching my arms up.

I press my lips together, taking the abuse. Waiting for the right moment. My eyes water.

A cockroach the size of a shoe skitters across the floor beneath my chair, probably sweating his little bug balls off. Asshole stomps on it, grinding it into the concrete.

"You're next, witch," he hisses in my ear. "So don't get any ideas."

He yanks hard on the cuffs, so hard I'm sure my bones are about to snap, but just before they do, I sense a presence in the doorway behind us.

"Restraints aren't necessary," a male voice says, smooth and commanding. "Remove them."

I can't see our new arrival, but the guard's energy shifts from disgust at me to aggression toward the new guy.

Whoever my so-called attorney is, he's no friend of the Asshole in Charge Around Here.

I like him immediately.

"You sure about that, *counselor*?" The guard jerks on my cuffs again—one-note-wonder, this fucker—forcing me to lean forward to relieve some of the pressure. "This one's dangerous. Mouthy bitch, too. My opinion? She deserves to be tied up."

"Nevertheless, restraints will only make the task more difficult."

After a long, uncomfortable pause, the guard finally releases his death grip and removes the cuffs. My arms fall to my sides like wet noodles, shoulders burning, but I don't dare turn my head. Something tells me to remain absolutely quiet and still, to wait until the guard is gone.

To conserve my strength.

"Anything else?" the guard asks.

"Leave," he orders. His voice carries so much authority, I find myself sitting up straighter. Wishing I were a bit more presentable. Hoping, truly, that he's on my side.

Asshole in Charge doesn't like it one bit. "Listen, fuck-stain. I'm in charge around here. You don't—"

"The longer you stand here wasting our time," he says, "the longer it will take me to do my job. The longer it takes me to do my job, the greater the risk for both of us."

Another heavy pause, then I feel the guard's aggression fade as he retreats toward the door.

"You got one hour," he barks. "Get it done." Without another word, he storms out, slamming the door behind him. It latches and beeps, sealing me inside with the man who—for the moment—holds my fate in his hands.

Firm steps thud against the cement floor as he walks to the other side of the table and sets down his briefcase, looming over me across the expanse of cheap wood and metal.

For a tense, silent moment, we assess each other.

I can only imagine how I must look to him—unwashed, bruised, reeking of piss. Shame heats my cheeks, but I hold his gaze.

He, on the other hand, immediately commands respect. Tall and broad-shouldered, clean-shaven, with wavy black hair that's just starting to gray at the temples and hard, flint-colored eyes that seem to take in every detail, every nuance. He's dressed in a black suit with thin blue pinstripes, a crisp white shirt beneath, and an understated gold tie tacked with a small silver pin in the shape of a shield.

My skin burns under his penetrating gaze. Like his authoritative voice, something about those eyes makes me feel like he can read every lie, see every flaw.

If he's truly a lawyer, he's probably a damned good one.

I try to get a read on his emotions, his intentions, but he's locked up like a vault, totally shielded.

I can sense his power, though, if not his feelings—he's definitely a mage. A well-practiced one at that; it's no easy feat to totally shield your emotions. Usually a bit leaks out around the edges.

He sits down across from me and inches closer to the table, giving me a better glimpse at the silver pin on his tie.

It's etched with four symbols—a cup, a sword, a wand, and a pentacle.

The suits of the Tarot.

He pops the latches on his briefcase and removes a fist-sized crystal, placing it in the center of the table. Holding his hand over the top, he whispers an incantation I can't hear.

"Hematite," he explains. "It's a shielding stone. It will ensure our conversation can't be recorded or overheard."

"Handy," I say.

"Trust no one, Miss Milan. That is your first lesson."

"Even you?"

A tiny smile tugs at his lips, but he locks it down, ignoring the question. From the briefcase, he pulls out a stack of papers and file folders, setting them up in an orderly row before selecting one and paging through its contents, taking a few notes on a legal pad as he does. The pen is silver and black. Expensive-looking, just like he is. His handwriting is small and neat.

I'm dying to ask questions—who are you? Who sent you? Who's paying the bill? What did the guard mean, 'get it done?'—but I don't dare interrupt.

The thing is… I *do* trust him. I can't get a read on him, but some part of me, some voice inside, tells me he's here to help. Circumstances being what they are, I've got no choice but to listen to that voice.

For now, anyway.

I shift in my chair. My traitorous stomach lets out an embarrassing grumble.

A dark eyebrow arches beneath his hairline, but he doesn't look up from his task. Just reaches into his briefcase and procures a bottle of lemon kombucha and a square glass container with a plastic lid, sliding them across the table to me.

My mouth waters at the sight of the rich, colorful bits of food visible through the glass.

"Eat, Miss Milan. We've got much to accomplish today, and we need you strong."

"Thanks, but I can't take your lunch. I'm—"

"No need to stand on ceremony."

My stomach growls again, begging me to dig in.

"I don't suppose you have a napkin or something?"

Still not looking at me, he retrieves a packet of hand sanitizer wipes from his briefcase and hands it over. I tear open the wrapper, the pungent smell of alcohol so clean and bright I could almost cry. I wipe my face—dry skin be damned—then scrub my hands, doing my best to cleanse away the prison grime.

I feel like a new person already.

Without wasting another moment on politeness, I pop the top off the glass dish and dig in, devouring the veggies and hummus inside, the boiled egg, the cubes of cheese. The kombucha tastes like nectar of the goddesses, fizzy lemon goodness exploding across my tongue, filling my body with much-needed hydration and nutrients.

Maybe it's my last meal, and this is all some crazy setup. Maybe it's poisoned. I don't care. Nothing has ever tasted so delicious, and with every bite, my body begins to heal again. I feel the bruises fading, my muscles strengthening, the kinks working themselves out of my back.

Miraculous.

After a few more minutes of non-conversation—me happily scarfing down the food, him scratching in his notepad, he finally sets down the pen and lifts his chin, meeting my gaze.

The air between us crackles. I grip the edge of the table, as if I need to steady myself for whatever comes next.

"My name is Dr. Cassius Devane," he announces. "I'm a professor of mental magicks at the Arcana Academy of the Arts, an extremely powerful mage, and your *only* chance at getting out of here alive."

EIGHT

STEVIE

The food that was so delicious minutes ago turns into a lead ball in my stomach.

The man—Dr. Devane—gives me about five seconds to absorb the shock of his drone strike, then says, "It's in your own best interests to set aside any preconceived notions you have about our institution. In case you haven't noticed, your options are *severely* limited, and you're not in a position to negotiate."

The initial shock fades fast, his tone like ice water to the face, and I'm out of my chair so abruptly it tips backward and slams against the floor.

The Academy?

"How did you find me? How did you know I was here?" There's no hiding the accusation in my tone. The malice.

"Miss Milan," he continues, "I realize this may be difficult to accept. But whatever your parents told you about us, there are other—"

"You knew my *parents*?"

A brief flicker of compassion softens his gaze, there and gone in a blink. "The tenure of Connor and Melissa at the Academy predates my arrival, though I'm aware of their reputation. I'm here on behalf of Headmistress Anna Trello, who did, in fact, know your parents."

My heart hammers, hundreds of new questions tumbling through my mind. Anna Trello? I've never heard the name. How well did she know them? Were they close? Was the headmistress a friend to my parents or... *No.*

Snippets of conversation filter through my memory— pieces of the past Mom and Dad used to argue about. They never mentioned names, but from what little I could put together back then, it wasn't fellow students who destroyed my mother's reputation and stripped my parents of all the protections normally afforded to coven members, ultimately forcing them to leave their magickal lives behind.

It was Academy officials.

And Anna Trello, headmistress? That's the most official witch on staff.

I glance around the room, looking for something else —*anything* else that might help me get out of here. But it's locked down tight; even if I could get through the door, they'd probably shoot me before I made it two steps down the hallway.

He truly is my only way out.

I meet his eyes again. A silent understanding passes between us.

I need him. And though he hasn't said it yet, I suspect he needs me too—or Anna does. Otherwise, he wouldn't be here.

"Why didn't the headmistress come herself?" I ask.

"Please sit, Miss Milan."

That voice again. The firm command of it. Every muscle in my body is screaming at me to obey, but I force myself to stand my ground, folding my arms across my chest and leaning against the wall.

He sighs, then continues. "Headmistress Trello is quite busy, so she sent me on her authority, with sincere apologies for our delay. Given the evidence against you, we had to get a bit more… creative."

"So you're, like, some kind of magickal superhero?" I press a hand to my chest, making my voice a little breathy. "Dr. Cassius Divine, swooping in to save all the little witches from wrongful damnation?"

He regards me with those piercing eyes, but if I'm getting under his skin, he doesn't show it. "Some witches deserve to be here, Miss Milan. Many people would say you're one of them. And it's Devane. Dr. Cassius Devane."

"Right."

"You said Divine."

Shit. "No, that's just what you heard."

"Miss Milan, this—"

"Anyway," I continue, "I don't care what anyone says or

what your so-called evidence shows, Dr. *Devane*. I'm *not* a killer. I'm barely even a witch."

His gaze snaps to the pentacle tattoo on my wrist, then back to his papers. "In the eyes of the law, you are *very* much a witch, just as dangerous as any other. More so, perhaps."

He holds out a folder.

Like a magnet, curiosity draws me close. I cross the room and snatch the folder from his hand, ignoring the little zing I feel when our fingers brush.

Wordlessly, I flip open the folder.

And immediately wish I hadn't.

Since my arrest, I've been so focused on surviving this hell, on trying to figure out an escape, on worrying about Jessa. But now, looking at the gruesome photos before me, the full impact of what happened that day on the Grande punches me in the gut.

Luke was my friend. And though I didn't kill him, he died *because* of me—because some sadistic mage set me in his sights and used Luke as the bait.

And he died horrifically.

I force myself to look at every picture, the gore a stark contrast to the gleaming metal exam table beneath Luke's body. His eyes are gone, no more than smoldering black holes. Under the swollen nose I'd already broken, his mouth is stretched in a perpetually silent scream. They cut out his tongue. They carved a pentacle into his forehead. They cut off his hands and feet. His torso is covered in blackened, burned flesh.

My stomach roils, and I reach for the bottle on the table, drinking down the last of the kombucha. It does nothing to erase the taste of bile from my mouth, to ease the endless pounding in my head.

In addition to the photos, there's a stack of articles from the Tres Búhos Daily and other regional newspapers. Through glazed eyes, I scan the headlines:

Local witch torches, kills former flame.

Killer witch spooks small desert town.

FBI's Magickal Enforcement Unit confirms illegal spellcraft used in wicked attack.

Security heightened across Arizona after local witch's brutal rampage.

Congress to consider new restrictions on magickal citizens in wake of September's deadly violence.

So that's how the Academy tracked me down. Headlines. Sensationalist, bullshit, dangerous headlines.

"Brutal rampage?" I snap. "September's deadly violence? Does anyone actually believe this crap? Do *you*?"

Devane shakes his head. "Of course not."

"Why are you showing me this?"

"I'm not doing it to be cruel," Devane says. "But I need you to understand what you're up against. The evidence is compelling. Even if you survive the next several months in here and this case goes to trial, you simply *cannot* win. They'll show the jury these photographs. They'll put the victim's mother on the stand and—"

"Rita," I gasp, my chest tightening. I can't even imagine what she's going through right now. Luke was her son. And

I was supposed to be one of his oldest friends. "Who did this? Do they have any idea? Any leads at all?"

"You *are* their lead, Miss Milan—case closed. They found traces of your magickal signature on the victim's body, along with your blood. GPS data from your phone places you at the scene at the time of death. A shirt recovered from the trash at Kettle Black contained large amounts of his blood."

"And mine." I drop the folder on the table. "He attacked me first, and I broke his nose in self-defense. Then he stabbed me. He was possessed. Luke—the real Luke—wouldn't hurt me. He's my—he was my friend."

I tell him the rest of the story, the crazy-ass storm, and—because I can't think of any other way to explain what happened—the magick.

His eyes widen at the part about the owl energy, but he doesn't question it.

"Before that day," I continue, "I've never done any real magick before. Just witchfire." I hold out my hand to show him, but in my still-healing state, I don't have the energy to conjure anything—not even a spark. "I left him alive in that cave. Possessed by a magickal psycho, but alive. I have no idea how they got to him, or how the police found him so quickly. This whole thing is a setup."

"I wouldn't be here if we thought otherwise." He glances at his watch, taps something into the screen, then puts the folder with the photos and articles back in the briefcase. "But the fact remains—unless another perpetrator drops out of the sky to confess to these crimes, they're going to let you rot in here. And at the very end, when your bones are brittle and your mind soft, they'll execute you. It won't be a quick death."

A shiver rattles my spine. Everything he says is true—I can feel it all the way down to my not-yet-brittle bones.

Still, some part of my mind rebels.

Execution?

"When was the last time they actually killed someone for practicing witchcraft in this country?" I ask.

"Does that matter? Whether you're the first or the fiftieth, the end result is the same." He sighs, then finally relents. "It happens more often than you think, Miss Milan. It's not typically publicized—the authorities know there are still plenty of non-magickal humans sympathetic to witches' rights, and they don't want to spark outrage. But yes, it happens. And we don't want it to happen to you."

"Dr. Devane, I don't understand why you're here. If you're so convinced I can't win a trial, why do I need a lawyer?"

"I'm not a lawyer."

"You know what I mean. A fake lawyer. Whatever you told them to let you in here today."

"I'm here to make you an offer, Miss Milan. On behalf of the Academy." He glances again at his watch. It's the same icy silver as the tie pin, emanating a faint glow that's definitely not man made. "I suggest you give it serious consideration, leaving emotion out of it. Your life literally depends on it."

His words, his tone, everything about the moment feels

charged. The hairs on my arms raise, my skin humming with something electric and unsaid.

I right my fallen chair, take up my seat across from him again.

After a weighty pause, he says, "We have reason to believe that the students and faculty—indeed, any magickal practitioners connected with Arcana Academy—are in grave danger. Your friend's murder bears a striking resemblance to others we've been tracking over the past decade. All of the victims were connected by one or two degrees of separation to former students or faculty. In the cases where arrests were made, the accused were all witches and mages with no prior criminal records."

"Were any of them ever acquitted?"

The briefest shake of his dark head confirms what I already know. Witches accused of capital crimes are never acquitted. That's not how it works.

"How many?" I ask.

"Prior to this month, for the ten years we've been keeping track, we've identified forty-seven murders connected, however loosely, to the Academy."

Goddess, that's a lot of people. Forty-seven innocent victims, possessed and carved and burned. Tortured. Stolen from their families, their friends, their communities.

And forty-seven *more* innocent victims, accused and imprisoned for crimes they didn't commit. Framed by our own kind. Executed. Not quickly.

"I'm afraid it gets worse," Devane continues. "In the last

three months alone, there have been an additional nineteen killings, including Luke Hernandez. We have no explanation for the sudden spike, but according to Anna, we can't say we weren't warned."

"Warned? I don't—"

"The Tarot prophecies."

The room spins, and my throat tightens, as though the words themselves have wrapped around my neck. I can't see straight, can't suck in enough air.

"Breathe, Miss Milan. Just breathe." He reaches across the table, grabs my hand with a firm grip. "It will pass."

His voice dims as the sound of rushing water fills my ears. The spinning room fades away, and all I see is my mother's face, her eyes beseeching me, her fingers outstretched as the water snatches her away…

Flame and blood and blade and bone… Flame and blood and blade and bone they will come…

"My mother," I breathe, my voice no more than a whisper. "That's what you're saying. My mother knew this would happen. She predicted it."

The room comes back into focus, the water receding into memory. I glance down at my hand, completely enveloped in his warm, strong grip. Heat crawls up my arm, and when I meet his eyes again, I find another flicker of compassion. He's closer now, leaning forward and searching my face, though I can't imagine what for. His scent carries on the air current, a warm sea breeze drifting tantalizingly past.

I've never seen the ocean, but suddenly I'm there, my

body lying in the sand, the midnight waves nipping at my bare skin as a hot, wet mouth devours mine, hands pinning my wrists, my body arching closer, welcoming, begging...

Across the table, I see the moonlight in his gaze, and I gasp as a shock of pleasure zings between my thighs.

Dr. Devane holds my hand a moment longer, his eyes widening as if he's witnessing the same vision...

He pulls away abruptly, and I gulp for air, shifting in my chair to relieve the aching pressure.

What the fuck was that?

"Not... not specifically," he says, bringing me back to the moment. Predictions. Prophecies. My mother. "But yes, we now believe she saw much of this unfolding. As well as the bigger purpose behind it—a purpose we *must* unravel if we want to prevent more senseless killings. Which brings me to—"

"No one believed her."

The cold, hard reminder douses the lingering heat from his touch.

"It's taken the Academy years to put the pieces together," he says. "Now that we're seeing the patterns, we have a broader understanding—and appreciation—of your mother's work."

"*Appreciation*? I don't know what Anna Trello told you, but that's not how..." I trail off and take a deep breath, trying to keep the anger at bay. "They basically ran my mother out of the Academy, Dr. Devane. Destroyed everything she ever worked for, destroyed the life she and my father had built. All their plans just... poof! They had to

SPELLS OF IRON AND BONE

move, to start over, to sever their connections to magick and everything it once meant to them. And that's just the stuff I overheard them arguing about—they never wanted to talk about it."

I hold his gaze, giving him the chance to deny it. To offer me some logical explanation for what his employer did to the people I loved most in this world. I'm practically begging for it—for an alternate take on the events that caused my parents to disavow their loyalty to the Academy.

Through her part in this treachery, Anna Trello is responsible for rerouting the entirety of my life around the one thing that's more ingrained in my DNA than my mother's eyes or my father's love of chocolate.

Magick.

Yet, sent here under her authority to bargain for my freedom, the doctor offers no further comment.

Instead, he glances at his watch.

I get back on my feet, fresh anger giving me the strength to stand. "If you've got somewhere else to be today, Dr. Devane, don't let me keep you."

"You will have the opportunity to make your judgments about me soon enough, Miss Milan," he says, seemingly unruffled. "But you *will* let me finish."

His eyes spark with new fire, and I sit back in my chair, waiting for the rest. The offer. My *only* chance—as he so eloquently put it—at getting out of here alive.

"According to Anna, your mother was the most gifted Tarot witch the Academy has ever known," he says, every word a revelation, a knife in my heart. "In the months before her departure from the Academy, she allegedly worked around the clock, researching esoteric occult knowledge, transcribing the visions and messages she channeled from her cards, desperately trying to correlate the two. Anna claims she was *obsessed* with her work. Utterly obsessed. Even your father didn't understand the innermost workings of her mind."

"That… sounds about right."

Of the two, Mom always seemed to have more innate power. I always got the sense Dad was happy to leave magick behind—that deep down, he believed he was meant for the so-called normal life. With my mother, it was different. Whatever compromises she and my father had made in order to live that mundane life, keeping her end of the bargain was clearly a struggle—one I only began to recognize after their deaths. I wasn't surprised to find her grimoire stashed in the attic; though there was no trace left of my father's magickal history, my mother's—however unspoken and unseen—practically permeated the house. The café. My childhood. My connection to her.

It still does.

"The research she left behind is thorough and impressive," Devane continues. "As a result, we've been able to piece together some of her prophecies and predictions, which is how we started—belatedly—connecting the dots on these murders. But while her notes are extensive, they're essentially written in code. Even with our most advanced witches and mages working on translations, we've hit an impasse."

An image of Mom's grimoire floats into my mind. Drawings and symbols, ancient words, rhymes, half-formed thoughts and incomplete sentences, footnotes and references to books upon books I've never read, authors I've never heard of, information that baffles even those great mages of Silicon Valley—a.k.a. Google.

If my mother's academic research is anything like her book of spells, it's no wonder they can't make sense of it.

"It's the Academy's belief," he says, tapping the table, "and our hope, that you might be able to crack that code."

"But… how? I don't know anything about magick, let alone my mother's secrets."

"Surely she told you something, even in passing. Some small thing that might help us find—"

"*No* small thing, Doctor Devane. Magick? The Academy? None of that was open for discussion in our house." The hope I felt when the guard first announced a visit from some mystery attorney dims, and I shake my head, knowing I can't give them what they want. "My parents died trying to keep me out of that life—away from all things magickal—all because of what your precious Academy did to them. Even if I *did* know something, I can't… I can't help you with this."

"Maybe not today, no. But with the proper training, we might tap into something… something you may only understand in retrospect. You have the potential to save hundreds of lives—maybe even thousands—from meeting the same gruesome fate as your friend Luke Hernandez."

I flinch at the mention of Luke, the images it stirs. Burned flesh. Blood. My old friend, throwing French fries at me under the Grande.

"Miss Milan. Starla…" Devane's eyes soften when he says my first name, and when he speaks again, his tone softens too. "We're just asking you to try. In exchange, you'll receive a top-notch magickal education that will not only assist you in this task, but will serve as the foundation for any private- or magickal-sector career you could want. You'll receive full room and board, research assistance from trusted advisors, and a personal stipend you'll find more than adequate. Best of all, you won't be here, awaiting your end. You'll be free."

I laugh, sour and bitter. "I'm on Death Row, Doc. So unless you've got a damn good escape plan—"

"Free, Starla. You'll be free." He glares at me, almost as if he's forcing the word through my mind.

Sighing, I fold my arms over my chest. "So this is your big offer, then. You'll get me out of here, but in exchange, you want me to… to…"

I can't even bring myself to say the words.

"I want you to enroll at Arcana Academy," Devane supplies for me, his eyes reclaiming their original fire. "To study your craft. To fully embody your Tarot magick, as you were meant to."

From the moment he introduced himself, some part of

me knew it would come to this—to the Academy. Why else would he be here?

Still, hearing it out loud makes it real.

Enroll at Arcana Academy… Embody your Tarot magick…

The idea sends a bolt straight to my gut—more guilt, mostly. Just being in the same room as a professor from my parents' traitorous alma mater feels like a betrayal. But there, flickering behind that white-hot tangle of guilt and shame, other things begin to surface, snapping at my heart like startled copperheads.

Excitement.

Anticipation.

A sense of inner rightness I can't deny, no matter how hot the rest of it burns.

They're not just offering me my freedom; they're offering me my dreams. Every last forbidden one of them.

A chance to learn magick. To unlock this power inside me. To uncover the mysterious past my parents tried so hard to outrun.

Forget magick, Stevie. It's a curse…

"You'll want for nothing at the Academy, Starla," he says, as if he has to convince me *not* to rot in jail. As if I really do have a choice here. "Absolutely nothing."

I lift a shoulder. "Nothing but my parents alive again. Nothing but my mother's reputation restored. Nothing but magick to be cherished and embraced in this world rather than feared and shamed." Then, pressing my fingers to my temples, "And maybe, if it's not too much to ask, a caffeinated beverage? Goddess, my head fucking *hurts*."

"Come with me and you've got a good chance at accomplishing three out of four."

"Yeah? Which three?"

He cracks a smile—real, dazzling, mysterious—but before he can answer, his watch blares an alarm, startling us both.

"Code black," a voice says from his wrist. Another male. Urgent. "Get her the fuck out of there, Cass. Plan B."

Devane's smile falls away. He glances at me, then at the watch, worry tightening his brow. "Time?"

"Thirty seconds," the other guys says.

Devane curses under his breath.

"What's going on?" I ask.

"Stay calm," he orders, getting to his feet. "Don't speak."

I press my lips together as he taps the watch face, then pulls something from his inside breast pocket and sets it on the table between us—The Moon card. I know its message isn't meant for me—not like the cards that randomly show up in my life—but I hear it anyway. Feel it.

A great deception is upon us.

Death is only the beginning.

The moon casts not its own light; in its glow, nothing is what it seems...

Beneath his touch, the card glows silver-white, then vanishes, casting the room in cool light, as if we've been bathed in real moonlight.

I'm so mesmerized by the effect, it takes me a second to meet his gaze again.

To notice the fierce determination in his stance.

To spot the gun in his hand, pointing right at me.

"Shit! *Shit!*" I bolt out of my chair. "What the hell are—"

"I'm sorry, Miss Milan," he says. "Truly."

Then Dr. Cassius Devane—professor of mental magicks at the Arcana Academy of the Arts, extremely powerful mage, and my *only* chance at getting out of here alive—shoots me point blank in the chest.

NINE

CASS

I toss the gun into the briefcase and scoop the woman into my arms just as the south wall collapses, an explosion of cinderblocks and steel chased by a burst of magelight that rivals the desert sun.

The mage responsible stands just beyond the wreckage, arms outstretched, sparks crackling from his fingertips.

"Subtle, Mr. Weber. As usual." Clambering over the rubble, I step out into the scorching desert heat. I haven't even taken my first breath of fresh air when the security alarms begin to wail.

Kirin, who doesn't do well with improvising when his precisely calculated plans run off the rails, glares at me. "Is she hurt?"

"She'll survive." I jerk my head toward the mess behind me. "Grab the briefcase and seal up that wall. We need to move."

"What happened in there?"

"Now, Kirin. I need to get her to Lala's. And you need to clean up that mess before the spell breaks down and the assholes inside figure out who we are."

Kirin's glare intensifies, but he nods, silently giving me his word.

Trusting the mage is on it, I whisper another incantation —a cloaking spell, this time—then run as fast as my burden will allow, crossing into the staff lot and the car I left there earlier. Glamoured, of course, like everything else about this jailbreak mission.

I get the woman situated and buckled into the front seat, then start the engine, rolling us out toward the exit. At the guard booth, I smile and flash a Tarot card.

Seeing only an employee ID badge, he raises the barricade and waves me through, wishing me a good afternoon. It doesn't even occur to him to notice the unconscious girl strapped in next to me, still dressed in her prison uniform.

Thanks to my spellwork, it doesn't occur to him to notice a lot of things.

I'm thirty minutes down the highway when Kirin's voice buzzes from my comms watch.

"All clear," he announces. "Straight from the internal communications system—one of the guards reported the bodies to the warden. Said the medical examiner already came to dispose of them, so it's out of their hands."

"Bodies? As in, more than one?"

"You had to off yourself in this story, Cass. Too many loose ends otherwise."

"Ah. Good point. Have I told you lately that you're brilliant?"

"You know, nothing says 'you're brilliant' like cold, hard cash."

"We'll discuss it later." I glance at my passenger, still unconscious, her head slumped forward against her chest. "And the death certificates?"

"I'm faxing them over now. Official cause of death— gunshot wound to the chest. The unofficial shit—well, the gossip is already making its way through the walls. Murder-suicide by a fanatic impersonating an attorney."

"The other prisoners must be loving it."

Kirin sighs. "It'll die down soon enough. A little luck, and everyone here will forget Starla Milan ever existed."

"That's the idea."

"Is she awake?" Kirin asks.

"Not yet. But she will be."

"You'd better be damn sure about that."

"Kirin? You may be brilliant. But try to remember who's in charge." I sign off, focusing my attention back on the road.

Another hour passes, and we're well off the beaten path now, traversing the old county roads long since abandoned for the faster, well-paved interstates. I haven't seen a single vehicle since I left the highway.

The road curves, and Starla tilts toward me, her long hair brushing the arm of my suit jacket. When the road bends again, she shifts back to the other side.

Wake up, Starla. Wake up.

My hands tighten on the wheel. I know she's unharmed —it was my spell. She'll come to in another hour or so, once the initial shock works its way through her body and the illusion magick fades.

That magick worked exactly as designed. It always does.

Doesn't make the hot rush of guilt in my chest any less painful. I'm pretty sure it's going to take more than a few non-magickal, very hard drinks to wipe my memory of that look in her eyes. The disbelief, the anger, the confusion. The raw terror when I pointed my weapon.

I glance over at the woman again, reaching out to tuck a lock of hair behind her ear. Her color is good, her skin warm and soft beneath all the prison grime.

I should take my hand away. Focus on the road.

But I can't stop thinking about what I saw back in that room.

When I touched her hand to calm her, I was pulled into some sort of vision, so strong I could've sworn it was real— a memory. I was walking through an ancient forest on a nearly moonless night, called forward by the peaceful sounds of night birds and running water. The trees thinned out, and I came upon a clearing—that's when I saw her. She was nude, kneeling at the edge of a moonlit pool, her long dark hair cascading over her shoulders. Behind her, a circle of standing stones rose toward the stars. She saw me watching her and got to her feet, approaching me with a soft smile. I returned it. Without words, she wrapped her arms around me, pressing her naked breasts to my chest, whispering my name as if we'd been lovers, finally reunited after far too long.

I kissed her with abandon, drinking in the taste of her mouth as my hands roamed her soft curves.

When I finally came back to reality, back to the wretched squalor of that room, I wanted to leap across the table, take her in my arms, and kiss her until she couldn't breathe.

And worse? There was a moment, no longer than a heartbeat, when she looked into my eyes and gasped, and I swore she'd seen the same thing.

That she'd *wanted* the same thing.

TEN

STEVIE

The harsh light on my face is all wrong, the angles shifting too fast, the crappy prison bed rumbling beneath me in a way that crappy prison beds typically don't.

It takes me half a second to realize I'm not in my prison bed. I'm in a BMW, with butter-soft leather seats and climate control.

Moving on up in the world!

Except... all indications are I've just been kidnapped.

I try to sit up, but my seat is reclined all the way back, restraints locking across my chest as I fight for freedom.

"Relax, Miss Milan," comes the stern voice beside me. The driver. He hits a button on his door, and my seat tilts upward, the restraints relaxing their grip. Seatbelt. Just a damn seatbelt. "You're all right. Unharmed, I assure you."

I unhook the belt and turn to glare at him, taking in the sight of his smug, handsome face as memories rush back in fuzzy fragments.

Dr. Devane, my so-called attorney.

Salad and eggs and lemon kombucha.

The Academy's offer.

The watch alarm and the Moon card and the pulsing light and the… the gun…

I gasp, clutching at my chest. "You shot me!"

He glances over casually, offering a raised eyebrow in lieu of a response.

My fingers search for the wound, for a tender spot, anything. But there's no pain, not even a dull ache from the beatings I took in jail. Peeking down the front of my construction-cone-orange jumpsuit, I see nothing but smooth skin. Dirty and slicked with sweat and more than a little ripe, but smooth.

And there's no blood on my clothing. No holes. If he had shot me, and I'd somehow healed myself, there would still be some kind of evidence.

I let out a breath. Apparently, he's telling the truth.

"There's water, if you'd like." He gestures to the cup holders beneath the radio, where two water bottles sweat it out.

"How do I know it's not poison?"

He lifts a shoulder, darts another quick glance my way, again with the stupid eyebrow raise. "Drink it. Fastest way to find out."

Oh, this one's a laugh-a-minute.

Taking my chances, I grab the water bottle and crack the cap, down half of it in a few gulps.

"Feeling better?" he asks as I relax back into the seat.

The superiority in his tone drips as thick as my boob sweat, and just as annoying.

"Other than the fact that you tried to kill me, I'm feeling awesome. Fit as a fucking filly." I blink the haziness from my eyes and look out the window, trying to get my bearings. It's afternoon, and we're still in Arizona, the rose-colored desert whizzing by as Dr. Devane cruises along a lonely stretch of roadway.

I wonder how fast we're going. How bad it would hurt to jump out and roll. I steal a quick glance at the speedometer—sixty-eight miles per hour. The scrub grass lining the roadway is a beige smudge out the window, but maybe…

"Don't even *think* it." Devane sighs, condescending as ever. "If you want out, just say so. I'll pull over."

I fold my arms across my chest. "Sure you will."

"You're not my prisoner, Miss Milan."

"You sure about that?"

He glances in the rearview and clicks on the hazard lights, despite the fact that there's no one else on this desolate road—rule-follower till the end—then navigates us to the shoulder. Killing the engine, he glances out the windshield and says, "We're a good fifty miles from civilization, and I haven't seen another car pass for two hours. But please—leave, if you must."

"So you can shoot me in the back? I may be a fugitive, Doc, but I'm not stupid."

No response from the good doctor now.

I sit there stewing, the engine ticking down like a bomb.

Without the air conditioning, the smothering desert heat is already creeping in through the vents, sending a fresh trickle of sweat down the valley between my boobs. Up ahead, the road looks like it's melting, the surrounding landscape wavering before my eyes.

I try to imagine the walk, how I'd look marching down the road. Devane's car, speeding away. Me, with the prison-issued slip-on shoes and fashionable orange jumpsuit. A neon target for the cops or the buzzards.

My shoulders drop. In the face of my piss-poor survival odds, most of my ire drains away.

"You tried to kill me," I remind him.

"I didn't try to kill you, Miss Milan. I only made you *believe* that I did."

"And I'm supposed to believe you *now*? After you've just admitted to messing with my head?"

"Oh for fuck's sake," he says irritably, like I'm a petulant child refusing to brush my teeth before bed. Then he grabs my hand and presses it firmly against his chest.

I try to pull away, but his grip is fierce, his heartbeat tapping a strong, steady rhythm against my palm.

It takes me a moment to realize what's happening.

He's letting me read him. Lowering his walls so I can feel his vibe.

I stop struggling, relax into his energy. It encircles me like a caress, like a cool night breeze drifting across the ocean, carrying with it the salt of distant lands and ancient secrets. In my mind, a picture forms, moonlight shimmering on black waves.

He's trying to help me. I know it like I know the feel of my own skin. Intentions can be obfuscated, but they can't be faked, no matter how skilled he is at mental magicks.

I blink hard, shattering the image behind my eyes. When I look at him again, he's staring at me intently across the small space between us, a wrinkle of confusion drawing his eyebrows together, like I'm a puzzle he needs to solve. The severity of his grip lessens, though he doesn't immediately release my hand. Beneath my touch, his heart beats a little faster now, just like mine.

Did he see it too, I wonder? The ocean, the moon?

"Miss Milan," he whispers, his eyes holding a thousand secrets but his lips refusing to betray a single one. "I'm sorry. I'm—"

"Not a killer." I jerk my hand away, buckle the seatbelt. "Just a sadist. Good to know. Can we get some A/C in here now?"

I feel his eyes linger on my face a moment longer, but then his energy recedes, walls going right back up. The silence is heavy and awkward as hell, but I don't care. Anything's better than facing the intimacy of his eyes, the hot touch of his body, the strange pull I'm starting to feel toward him.

"It was a tactical maneuver designed to outwit our opponents by making them believe I assassinated you," he finally says, turning away and starting the car. The blissful artificial chill blasts out from the vents. "And it worked. Exactly as intended, aside from a minor explosion that's since been remedied."

"Assassination? *Explosion*?"

He clicks off the hazard lights, hits the indicator, eases us back onto the lonely desert road as if his biggest concern is a traffic ticket and not the fact that he used impersonation and magick to literally bust a so-called killer witch out of jail and is now cruising across the state with her in tow.

"I was on death row," I say. "Why would you bother pretending to assassinate me?"

"As much as they love throwing you in lockup, witches actually pose a significant problem for the human authorities. Your execution may have been imminent, but they'd still have to guard you and keep you alive until then. It's costly, and as you probably gathered, makes the guards and the other prisoners uneasy. So, with a bit of help from an insider with flexible ideas about law and order, I offered to relieve them of that burden."

An insider?

Asshole in Charge, my tormentor in chief. No question about it.

You got one hour. Get it done.

"But it didn't go as planned," I say, remembering the alarm on the watch.

"Hence the last-minute improvisation."

"Hence the shooting me."

"Fear is our most primal, most powerful emotion. It leaves an imprint—almost like a ghost in the room. When I pulled the trigger, it didn't matter that the gun wasn't loaded. Your fear of death by gunshot was completely sincere and left an intense imprint that my spell was able to

amplify. That imprint, combined with the power of suggestion planted in the rich soil of a soft mind, was enough to
make the guard truly believe that I killed us."

"Us?"

"Murder-suicide. No loose ends."

"Won't they get suspicious when they don't find our
bodies?"

"They've already found them. Along with my associate,
posing as the medical examiner."

"Hmm. Sounds like more power of suggestion mojo
to me."

"And a couple of forged death certificates for the
archives, should anyone come sniffing around later."

"Who's the associate?"

No response.

"Whoever it is, you two went to a lot of trouble for one
witch," I say, which is about as close to a 'thanks' as my
exhausted brain can muster right now.

He turns and offers a quick smile, there and gone again.
"You're innocent, and a member of the magickal community. Trouble or not, the Academy has a duty to protect
you."

Now that's a stretch. Yes, the fact that the Academy
went to such extremes to get me out speaks volumes, but
probably not the volumes Devane is pedaling.

They *need* me. A lot more than he's letting on. Which
explains why they waited to make their so-called "offer"
until I was in such a compromised position I'd have no
choice but to take it.

I twist around and peek out the rear window. "You're sure this is going to work? No one's coming after me?"

"It's already worked, or we wouldn't be here. Understand, Miss Milan—the human authorities have jobs to do, but in the cases of magickal crimes, they'd rather not. Sure, the guard will receive a slap on the wrist for violating protocol in not logging my visit or confirming my identity, and we'll likely see some protests in the magickal community about your unfair treatment once news of the murder hits the papers. But in the end, it will all be forgotten." Devane sighs, adjusting his hands on the wheel. "It always is."

I take a deep breath, trying to make sense of this insane story. The fact that it was so easy for him to mess with the guards' minds, to make me believe I'd been shot, to cast that crazy spell with the Moon card...

"Mental magicks, huh?" I rub the chill from my arms, but the goosebumps remain in place. "You teach this stuff at the Academy?"

"Yes," he says, turning down the A/C. "As well as how to defend against it, which is the more important piece where you're concerned."

"I guess we're lucky the guards never took your class, or we'd both be capital-F screwed."

This gets another smile, then silence descends once again, tires humming along the road, the soft whoosh of the air conditioner lulling me into a comfortable daze. Ahead, the road stretches on like a thin gray ribbon, surrounded on all sides by the tall spires of red sandstone monuments rising from the earth like craggy fingers.

My own fingers itch to climb them, to feel their rough, warm grit against my skin. To feel part of the earth. Home.

I take another swig of water, washing away the tightness in my throat. "Where are we, anyway?"

"Still about sixty miles from our destination."

Our destination. The Academy.

I never knew the exact location—only that it was somewhere in my home state, which I always found strange. Fancy, all-important place like that? I figured it should be in Switzerland or Paris or New York City.

"How far from Tres Búhos?" I ask. "I'd like to see my friend Jessa and pack up some personal things if it's not too much trouble. I need to figure out what to do about my tea shop while I'm away, too. She can't manage it on her own."

There's a long pause—no smiles or raised eyebrows this time. Then he shakes his head and says simply, "I can't allow you to do that. It's much too risky."

Disappointment sinks in my stomach. "Can I use your phone? I need to call Jessa, let her know what's going on. She's my business partner. Best friend, too. She was there when the police came, and—"

"Again, we can't risk it. Not while you're still out in the open, outside the protective boundaries of the Academy."

"But you said your plan worked! The cops would've been after us by now if it hadn't."

"It's not the cops I'm worried about." He glances in his rearview, then hits the gas, pushing us a little faster—a whole five miles above the speed limit now. "No calls until you're safely settled on campus."

"What about my things? My shop?"

"Returning to Tres Búhos is no longer an option," he says, his tone much gentler than before. "I'm sorry."

"Wait. *Ever?*"

"You saw the headlines. The story has made national news. The reason we had to go to such elaborate lengths at the prison was so the guards have a plausible explanation for your disappearance."

"I thought you said all would be forgotten?"

"And it *will* be. But first, people need to believe you're dead and justice has been served."

Justice. What a fucking joke.

The images of Luke's desecrated body flash behind my eyes. He didn't get justice. His poor Mom didn't get justice.

"I'm going to find out who did this," I tell him, blinking quickly before the tears fall. "I'm going to bring the bastard to *true* justice. And after that I'm going home, putting on my bunny slippers, and fixing myself a cup of hibiscus ginger tea, and I really don't give a shit *what* the Academy has to say about that."

If Devane thinks I'm crazy or misguided, he wisely keeps his opinions to himself.

"You should probably get some rest. And I should probably just... think." He hits the button on the sound system, flooding the car with cello music and ending the conversation.

Just as well. I've got so many questions, my brain is on complete overload. For now, sleep is my only escape.

I snooze for another hour or so, waking only when I sense the ground beneath the car softening, our speed slowing to a crawl.

I open my eyes and take in the surroundings. We're still in the desert, though the paved roadway is long gone, the car winding up a long, dirt path toward the top of a rise. Late afternoon sunlight slants through the dust as we ascend, giving everything a smokey, magickal quality.

Slowly, like a plant blooming on a time-lapse video, a reddish-pink adobe house comes into view, nestled in among the saguaros.

There's no driveway or parking area. Devane simply pulls the car up in front and kills the engine.

We sit in silence for a moment, him still thinking, me not knowing quite what to do.

The house is tiny—just a single-story box, really, with a shabby wooden door and two windows near the top, eyes on a blank brown face. A row of potted plants lines the front, an explosion of bright pinks and greens providing the only color contrast.

"Strange," I say, unhooking my seatbelt. "I thought the Academy would be taller."

Ignoring my weak attempt at humor, Devane gets out, stretches. Waits for me to do the same. The moment I close the passenger door behind me, the car turns from a sleek black luxury sedan into a rusty Toyota Corolla, so old and decrepit it's impossible to tell what color it is.

"Um… what?"

"Glamour," he says. "We're safe here, Miss Milan."

Taking him at his word, I follow him to the front door, but I don't get too close. I'm still a little self-conscious in my prison garb and grime.

"Safe *where*, exactly? What is this place?"

"It's the home of Eulala Dominga Juarez," he says quietly, like he doesn't want to disturb her. "Lala for short. It's our way station—last stop before we cross over."

"Cross over?" At my words, a breeze stirs my hair, carrying with it the scents of warm earth and fresh tortillas, onions frying in a pan, and something else I can't quite put my finger on. It makes my nose itch, my heart beat a little faster.

"That would be the magick," he says, holding his hands out as if to grab hold of it. When he spreads his fingers, light dances across his skin.

I take another step toward the door, mirroring his motions. When the light touches my skin, it feels like a spray of warm water from a garden hose left baking in the sun, but less dense, and way more tingly.

"Lala is an old friend of the Academy and a formidable adversary to any who dare cross her, though you wouldn't guess it to look at her." Devane turns to face me, and here in the golden afternoon sun, he looks tired, weighted by some burden I can only guess at. His smile holds the ghost of a much younger man, but those flint-colored eyes are ancient.

Splitting the difference, I decide he's in his early forties.

Not quite old enough to be my father, but definitely too old to be... ahem... anything else.

Not that I'm thinking about ahem anything else.

...midnight waves nipping at my bare skin as a hot, wet mouth devours mine...

"Come," he says, snapping me out of the fantasy and stepping onto the unfinished concrete slab before the door. "She's expecting you."

I step up next to him, hoping my rank smell isn't too overpowering. He lifts his hand to the door, but before he can knock, I'm hit with another wave of magick, stronger than the last. This one is way more invasive. Assessing.

"Wait." I put my hand on his forearm as the magick dances over my skin like a hundred tiny fireflies. "The way station... Lala... Is this some kind of test?"

Isn't that how it works? The whole guardian-at-the-gate thing? Only the worthy shall enter the enchanted forest and search for the magickal elixir, save the princess, slay the dragon, etcetera, etcetera?

Why else would he drag me to a witch's cottage in the middle of the desert?

"A test?" Devane eyes me close, his gaze raking down my entire body before coming back up to rest on my eyes. Then, with a wink so fast I'm not even sure I catch it, he leans in and whispers, "Only for the soap."

ELEVEN

STEVIE

It's the little things, really. Fragrant lavender shampoo. Hot water and handmade oatmeal soap to scrub away the filth of desperation, the rough hands of the guards. Fluffy white towels still holding the faint scents of bleach and sunshine.

And lotion. So much luxurious vanilla lotion. I feel like I'm in a spa rather than a witchy hideaway in the desert, and if I could hit the pause button, I'd stay in this steam-filled bathroom oasis for the rest of the day.

Alas, the good doctor and my mysterious hostess await.

For a so-called "old" friend of the Academy, Lala doesn't look a day over twenty, with shimmering black hair, golden-bronze skin, and wide, expressive eyes the color of dark chocolate. She doesn't speak, either—at least not to me.

When she opened the front door, she looked right past me to Dr. Devane. He put a hand on my shoulder, and she nodded brusquely, as if the two of them had just shared a whole conversation about me in their minds. Entirely possible, given all the weird shit I'd already seen Dr. Devane pull today. I was about to ask them to let me in on the big secret when she gasped suddenly, grabbed my hands, and dragged me to the back of the tiny house.

Maybe the wind had changed and she got her first good whiff of the filthy beast formerly known as me, because suddenly I was being ushered into the bathroom and shown the towels and toiletries, along with a set of clean clothes folded neatly on the vanity.

I didn't even have time to get a read on her energy before she zipped out of there, but hell, she was offering a hot shower to a road-weary fugitive. Automatic friend in my book.

Now, clean and refreshed, I dress in the clothes Lala left —a pair of dark jeans, a sports bra, and a short-sleeved black V-neck. Her jeans are a little snug, and there's no underwear, but so what? I'll take a little chaffing and a muffin top over the orange jumpsuit any day.

Back in the main part of the house, there are no signs of life, but the place smells like the best Mexican restaurant ever.

"Doc?" I call out, my mouth already watering. *Please, please say we're staying for lunch.* "Lala?"

"Out here," he says.

I follow the direction of his voice to the back patio, where I find him sitting alone at a small outdoor table already set for lunch—yes, dreams really do come true—his eyes closed, face turned toward the sun. He's lost the jacket and tie, his white dress shirt unbuttoned, sleeves rolled up to reveal smooth and well-defined forearms.

Behind him, the property stretches out for miles, nothing but rolling red-dust hills dotted with scrub brush and the bent-arm silhouettes of the saguaros.

It's all so still and peaceful, and I take a moment to just breathe.

When I pull out a chair to join him, he startles and looks up. His eyes widen as he takes in the sight of me, and for a brief moment, his energy wall slips. His feelings wash over me, stirring something inside me—a strange connection, almost, like the one I felt in the prison. His own energy is a mix of surprise and heat—an attraction he's trying desperately to fight.

The combination of his sensual energy and the hungry way he's looking at me sends tendrils of heat spiraling through my insides, making my heart race.

Still gazing into his eyes, I bite my lower lip, afraid he might break our connection. Afraid of what I might do if he doesn't.

"Starla," he says softly, no more than a gentle sigh on the breeze.

"Were you expecting someone else?" I tease.

"I..." Dr. Devane closes his eyes, then shakes his head once, sighing through his nose. When he looks at me again, his eyes are clear, the wall firmly back in place. Connection cut. "Of course not. I just... You look really... rested."

"I think the word you're looking for is clean."

"Regardless, I'm glad you're doing better." There's an

awkward pause, him still staring at me, me still staring back, wondering what it would feel like to straddle him right here, to run my hands through his sexy dark hair, to feel the press of his palm against my breast.

But then he goes, "So, I hope you're hungry, because Lala and I made tacos," and I'm basically ready to marry him.

I laugh, because it's either that or kiss the man, and I'm not sure that's the best idea. I mean, it's not the *worst*, but...

No. I'm a student now, and he's a professor. *And* a mage. An old one at that. That's three strikes and... *Goddess*, I'm still staring at him.

Now it's *my* turn to close my eyes and shake some sense into my addled brain. When I look at him again, he's avoiding my gaze, pouring me a tall glass of iced tea from a pitcher on the table.

"Gotta hand it to you, Doc," I say as the ice cubes clink into the glass. "A hot shower *and* a hot lunch? You really know how to show a girl a good time."

Thankfully, he laughs, and I reach for the tea, grateful for something to cool the heat churning inside me.

"Lala's not joining us?" I ask.

"She's not big on company. Loves cooking, loves hosting, but the social aspects aren't really her thing."

"You said she was an old friend of the academy?"

"Eighty-four years old and a day," he says, dead serious. "Her birthday just passed."

"Wow. Glamour magick is a hell of a drug."

"Lala is one of the most powerful witches in the country.

In the world." He watches me a moment, the wheels turning behind his eyes, as if he's trying to decide whether to share a secret with me. Then, in a much softer voice, "She knew your parents, Miss Milan. I'm told she was one of the few who stood by them through the inquiry."

My eyes widen, but Devane only shakes his head, already anticipating my next question.

"Lala only speaks when she believes she has something vital to say. Asking her questions, pressing her about her memories... It will only overwhelm her. I'm sorry. I just thought you might want to know that your parents, for all the persecution they suffered, weren't entirely alone."

Tears fill my eyes, and I nod my thanks. It's all I can manage.

Dr. Devane has no idea how much it means to me. Not just to know that my parents had an ally during the darkest moments of their lives, but that he thought to tell me about it at all.

"I have no words for this." I take another huge bite of taco awesomeness, salsa roja and melted queso dribbling down my chin. "And to think just a few hours ago I wasn't sure I'd ever taste guacamole again."

Lala may have the presence of a ghost, but she and Doc sure cooked up a feast while I was showering, and now I'm shamelessly inhaling third helpings while the professor watches across the table, his eyes sparkling with laughter.

He pushes a covered dish of rice and beans closer, waiting for me to load up before he starts on another serving himself. He doesn't say anything for a moment, but just beneath our relaxed and easy mood, I sense something festering.

"You okay, Doc?" I ask. "You're being weird. Please tell me you're not one of those men who expect their lunch companions to daintily nibble on lettuce leaves while you go beast-mode on fifteen tacos."

He presses a hand to his chest, feigning offense. "Miss Milan, if you nibbled on lettuce in the presence of authentic homemade tacos, I'd drag you out to the middle of the desert and leave you for the coyotes."

"I'm glad we cleared that up." I wash down another bite with a swig of iced tea. "Now seriously, what's going on in that mental-magick mind of yours? I get nervous when you think too much."

"I suppose I am. Thinking too much, that is." He flashes a smile, but it fades fast. He pushes his rice around with the fork, waits another beat before speaking again. "In prison, did the guards... Did any of them... Were you..."

I shake my head, sparing him the awkwardness of filling in the blanks. "They knocked me around pretty good, talked a lot of shit about what they *could* do to me, but that was the worst of it. I think they were afraid of me. Afraid of my so-called murderous magick."

Devane exhales in obvious relief, but he's still gripping his fork so tightly his knuckles are white.

In that moment, in the light of a simple kindness from a near-stranger, the reality of my situation hits me.

I knew it was bad when the cops barged into Kettle Black. Hell, I knew it was bad up on the Grande, as soon as I figured out Luke wasn't Luke. But I guess some part of me still believed things would turn out okay. That I'd be acquitted. That someone—anyone—would put the pieces together and realize there was no way I could've committed that heinous crime.

But no one did. And if Dr. Devane hadn't shown up, I'd be one step closer to Death's door, slated for torment and execution, all because of the magick blood running through my veins, the damning pentacle inked on my skin.

He saved my life.

"Thank you," I blurt out, a rush of emotion bubbling into my throat. "Maybe I haven't said it yet, but I really... I just... Thanks. For breaking me out of jail. Literally."

And then I laugh, because I never, ever thought I'd utter a phrase like that, and sometimes laughing is the only thing that keeps the monsters from busting down your walls, grabbing you by the hair, and dragging you straight down to hell.

He's smiling again too, clearly glad for the levity. "I can't take all the credit, Miss Milan. We make a good getaway team."

"A regular Bonnie and Clyde." I drain the last of my iced tea, but when I go to set the glass down, the napkin I'd folded beneath it turns into a Tarot card.

A young man is at the center, dressed in a short tunic

and forest green wrap, a stick and bundle slung hobo-style over his shoulder. He carries a bouquet of mistletoe berries, and a black greyhound jumps up beside him.

Both are about to step gleefully off the edge of a cliff.

The Fool.

"Did that just... show up?" Dr. Devane asks as I pick up the card for a closer look.

An adventure awaits, Stevie. Leap with reckless abandon, a hopeful spirit, and all the optimism your youth affords. Yet you must remain ever watchful, eyes wide open, for danger lurks over every ledge...

"It's kind of a thing with me." I hand over the card for his inspection, but it vanishes at his touch. "It started happening a year after my parents died. I can't control it—just try to listen for the messages."

He rubs his thumb and forefinger together, as if he's trying to sense the magick that made the card disappear. "What does it mean?"

"It's always different. But right now?" I push out from the table and rise to gather up the dishes, our momentary peace at its end. "It means it's time to go."

TWELVE

STEVIE

Instead of climbing back into the Corolla-slash-BMW mystery machine, Dr. Devane leads us down a narrow dirt path behind the house to a rocky sandstone outcropping tucked in among the rolling hills. Down here, we're totally shielded from all directions, our only spies the black vultures circling overhead.

He's back in the suit jacket and tie again, proud and proper despite the heat and dust.

"What now?" I ask. "Is an Uber coming for us?"

Without responding, he removes the silver Academy crest from his tie and pricks the tip of his finger with the pin, squeezing until a drop of blood appears. Then, kneeling, he draws a complicated sigil with his finger in the red earth, whispering an incantation I don't understand. The sigil glows bright white, then sinks into the ground, swallowed by the desert.

Dr. Devane gets to his feet and reattaches his pin.

Seconds later, the earth vibrates beneath us. Blinking away the dust, I watch in awe as an ancient-looking stone staircase shimmers into view, framed at the top with an equally ancient archway. Peering into the portal, I can just make out the turrets of a large, gothic-looking building, four black flags waving from the facade.

"Sweet, sweaty balls of the devil," I breathe.

Dr. Devane's lips twitch, but he reins it in before an actual smile busts through. "Though it must be done with extreme caution to ensure complete secrecy, a portal to the Academy can be opened at any energy vortex by any witch or mage who's pure of intention. It's advanced blood and sigil magick—a skill you'll learn during your second year."

"What if I need it before then?"

"First-year students aren't permitted off-campus without an escort."

"I'm twenty-three years old, Dr. Devane. This isn't high school."

Surprise flickers through his gaze, and I wonder whether he thought I was older or younger. But before I can ask, he says, "And some of our first-year students are in their fifties. Age isn't the point. These are dangerous times for witches and mages. You needn't look farther than your own experiences to understand that. And in your case, you must be doubly careful. You're supposed to be dead. You can't risk someone outside recognizing you."

A chill creeps over my skin despite the oppressive heat, and I rub my arms. "What about on the inside? If I'm in the news, everyone on campus will know I faked my death."

"The Academy protects its own," he says, and then seems to realize his mistake. "It… it was a different time when your parents attended. The administration has learned much since those days."

"Right. Because all magickal people are such upstanding citizens."

"No. Because no magickal people want to draw attention to our Academy, risking their own safety."

"Self-preservation at its finest," I grumble. "*Goddess*, this feels like trading one prison for another."

"You're not a prisoner, but you *will* need an escort to bring you in and out." Devane dusts off his hands, his watchful gaze scanning the horizon beyond the portal. "Understand, Miss Milan. We are tolerated by the human authorities. When that stops being the case? When they decide—in an official capacity—that our presence is more than a nuisance, that our bribes aren't enough, that we pose a more serious threat? What do you think will happen then? It's already starting. It's what Anna believes your mother was trying to warn them about."

I rub the skin on my wrist, the pentacle tattoo glaring back at me like an unsightly birthmark. It sucks that he's right.

"You know what's really fucked up about all this?" I ask. "We're the ones with all the magick. Yet somehow, they have all the power."

"No. They have the *perception* of power."

"What's the difference?"

"The difference is, it doesn't have to be that way. If

witches and mages realized how much power we had collectively…" He trails off into his own thoughts. Pipe dreams, more like. Compared to the human population, there are so few of us, and outside of the Academy, there are few opportunities to join forces and storm the castle together.

"So what happens now?" I ask. Before us, the portal glows pink and orange and purple, like a brilliant desert sunset.

Devane clears his throat and straightens his tie, perspiration beading at his temples. "Now is the part where I tell you your life will be in grave danger. The moment you begin working on the prophecies, you'll be on the enemy's radar. And because we don't know exactly who that enemy is or when they'll strike next, it will be very difficult for us to protect you."

This isn't news, but it still sits heavy in my gut.

"My life was already in grave danger," I say. "Probably for a long time now. Something tells me that's just part of the gig."

He nods, a little sadly.

"Well, here goes nothing." I shrug and take a step toward the stone staircase.

"Not so fast." Devane places a warm hand on my shoulder, his eyes serious. "There's one more thing we need to discuss. Another option."

"What option? I've just faked my own death and escaped prison. I'm a fugitive. You said it yourself—it's not safe for me out here."

"No. But enrolling at the Academy isn't your only recourse."

"I'm listening."

"We can arrange for your relocation to another state, under a new and completely human identity. You'll be set up in an apartment and given a job, a bank account, non-magickal college classes if you'd like. Everything you need to start fresh. To move on."

"To move on from what? My life in Tres Búhos?"

"As well as your life as a witch."

"Hmm. Witchy witness protection?"

"If it helps to think of it in those terms, yes."

"No strings?"

"Not from us. But the offer isn't without its drawbacks. For starters, it will require a brief but extremely painful spell to remove your tattoo, and ongoing injections to mute your latent powers."

"Mute them?"

"As a natural-born witch, you'll never be able to fully disassociate from your magick, which means you'll live under constant threat of accidental exposure. Now, most witches can control their active powers, but the non-active ones, like your empathy skills and healing magick? Aspects of those powers work without your conscious direction. If anyone were to see something like that in action, you'd be identified as a non-registered witch and reported to the authorities. That's if the locals didn't decide to take matters into their own hands."

"So the injections basically kill the magick?"

"They block it, yes. To help with that, you'd also have to avoid anything that could trigger a magickal reaction, like crystals or Tarot cards, spellbooks, incantations, anything like that. And Miss Milan?"

I lean back against the red sandstone and cross my arms, waiting for the worst part, the part I know is coming next.

"You'll be completely cut off from anyone you've ever known," he says. "Permanently. You will never be able to speak to your friends again. Even now, with your so-called death undoubtedly reported to the media, you must be careful. But going into hiding at this level would be even more dangerous."

"So that's it, then? Enroll at the Academy or disappear off the map?"

I'm not sure why I was still hoping for a better option. Some last-minute escape route, complete with me getting my old life back and a perfectly happy ending.

"*Or* return to prison and explain your mysterious resurrection, though I wouldn't recommend it." He tries for a smile, but it misses the mark. "People are funny about witches returning from the dead. Damnedest thing, really."

When I don't say anything, his smile dims, his face turning somber once again. "The choice may be unpleasant, Miss Milan, but it *is* a choice, and it has to be yours. As much as I'd love to tell you what to do, I can't. Not in this matter."

He holds my gaze a moment, and I swear I see the spark of a challenge there. *Huh.* Makes me wonder if he thinks there are matters in which he *can* tell me what to do.

I close my eyes, my only relief from his penetrating gaze. Starting over in a new place doesn't sound so bad—maybe I could finally see the ocean, or New York City, or a snowstorm. And muting my magick? It's not like I've got much to lose on that front anyway.

What he's offering… Isn't that what my parents always wanted for me? A normal life? I could go to college—regular college. Meet a regular guy. Get a regular job.

Leave Jessa.

My heart aches at the thought.

But even if ghosting my best friend wasn't a prerequisite, it doesn't feel right. Maybe my parents wanted me to have a normal life, but if Mom were here now, facing this same dilemma, she'd *never* just turn her back—not with all those lives at stake. If she thought for a minute her predictions could help, she'd do everything in her power to make sure everyone understood them. That they could prepare for what was coming, and fight to protect their own.

Didn't she try to do just that?

Back then, no one believed her. But now, I have a chance to change that. To save lives and make the Academy elites understand how rare and special Mom's gift really was. How rare and special *she* was.

Enrolling might go against every principle I've been taught to uphold, every promise I've ever made.

But I know without a doubt what my answer will be. I knew it the moment he said the words back at the prison: *I want you to enroll at Arcana Academy. To study your craft. To fully embody your Tarot magick, as you were meant to…*

SPELLS OF IRON AND BONE

I open my eyes. Dr. Devane is watching me closely, his expression hopeful.

"If you enroll," he says, "I promise I will do everything in my power to keep you safe, to protect you, should the need arise."

Oh, the need is arising, Doc. Maybe not the need you're thinking of, but a need just the same...

Is it hot out here? It's hot out here. Anyway, moving on...

"*If* I enroll at the Academy—and right now, that's still an *if*—I would like my own room," I say, deciding to see how far I can push this. The man did shoot me, after all, even if it was just an illusion. I think I deserve a little pampering after an ordeal like that. "And I'll need more clothes, obviously."

"Hmm. You don't like Lala's jeans?" His eyes turn playful as he scans me head to toe.

"*Like* them? I've gotten more intimate with these jeans today than I have with a man in the last year."

Devane's jaw drops.

Oh, hell. I just said that out loud, didn't I?

"I mean..." I let out a nervous laugh and kick at the dirt, wondering if I can magickally convince it to open up and swallow me whole.

Alas, I'm still standing here.

And Devane is still watching me, that damn sexy eyebrow arched like an invitation.

But then he shakes his head, our flirty spark dying before it can even catch fire, and says, "Clothing won't be an issue. There are plenty of shops on campus, and your stipend will cover anything you need. As for the accommodations, most first-years share a room or suite with other students. It helps with socialization and studying, and—"

"Suites? You have suites? Ooh, I want one of those instead."

"Suites are designed to accommodate four to six students."

"Perfect. I'll have plenty of room to spread out." I lean back against the sun-warmed sandstone again and offer a shrug. "Since you refused to let me go back to Tres Búhos, I'll also need new rock-climbing gear. Shoes, harness, chalk bag, ropes—"

"Miss Milan, you can't possibly expect—"

"Cams, carabiners, hexes, guidebooks to the local routes, a crash pad for bouldering—"

"Don't you think you're being a bit... ridiculous?"

"It's an intense sport, Dr. Devane, and safety is a priority. The Academy has a duty to protect me. Isn't that what you said?"

Devane opens his mouth, then closes it, sighing loudly through his nose. He's caving, I can feel it. Supremely annoyed at me, but caving.

But just in case he needs a little more incentive to agree to my demands, I add, "That's *if* I decide to enroll. It's a lot of pressure, Doc. I've taken exactly three college classes, and none of them were magickal. I'm not sure I'm cut out for campus life."

"Really? Which classes?"

"Physics, business accounting, and art history."

"What was your major?"

"I… I didn't get that far. I was supposed to go to school at Arizona State, but after my parents passed away, I had to reprioritize the finances. So I ended up taking a few classes at Santa Clarita Community, but I couldn't make the payments. I had to stop after the first semester."

He watches a moment longer, but it's not pity I see in his eyes, thankfully. It's understanding. Sometimes there's a subtle difference, but right now, I'm glad Dr. Devane seems to know it.

"It's going to take some string-pulling," he says, exasperated, "but I'll arrange it with the headmistress. You'll have your suite and your clothes and your rock-climbing equipment." Then, with a brief smile I was beginning to fear I'd never see again, "Is there anything else you require, your highness?"

"Actually, yes." I take a deep breath, trying to find the words. After all my comparatively ridiculous demands, I don't know why this one makes me shy and uncomfortable, but I just can't bear the thought of him saying no.

Tea was always my parents' thing. With our shared connection to magick basically severed, our love of tea was the one thing that bonded us more than anything else.

Tucking my hair behind my ear, I say, "I'd appreciate a few supplies for making tea. A glass kettle, mesh strainers, a few herbs and spices, and just a couple of basic loose teas. Black, green… I can work with anything, really."

"Of course," he says without hesitation. "It's important to us that you feel at home on campus."

My sigh of relief quickly turns into a laugh. "See, you act all tough and rule-followy, but deep down, you're a big softy, Doc."

I stretch up on my toes, press a kiss to his cheek.

"Thank you," I whisper, placing my hand against his chest.

He wraps a hand around my wrist, his thumb stroking my skin. Warmth emanates through his shirt and tie, his heart hammering against my palm, his gray eyes so sultry and inviting it's all I can do not to stretch up and kiss him again. On the mouth...

"Miss Milan, about this..." He clears his throat, awkwardly taking a step back and breaking our connection. "Once we arrive on campus, we'll need to be more... appropriate."

"Appropriate?"

"You'll call me Dr. Devane, or professor if you'd like, but not Doc. And I'll call you Miss Milan, or whichever name you prefer. We can't..." He gestures between us, the space now feeling like a gulf. "We can't touch. We can't be overly friendly in *any* way."

"Okay, well, *ouch*." I lower my eyes, my cheeks burning with shame. He should've kicked me in the ribs. It would've hurt less. "But if that's the way you want it—"

"It's not the way I *want* it, Miss Milan." He slips a finger beneath my chin, tilting my face up toward his. "There's something... quite compelling..." But then he blinks and shakes his head, as if I've cast some ridiculous spell on him, and steps back once again. "It's the way it has to be. You'll be the subject of enough fascination and idle gossip, and I'll be one of your professors. I can't give the impression of preferential treatment. I must maintain clear boundaries, and I expect you to do the same."

I wave away his words as if it's all just fine and dandy, as if I totally understand. And I do, logically. But I can't say it doesn't suck.

For a minute there, Dr. Devane was almost starting to feel like a friend. Like a super-hot, older man friend who might want a little something more...

Shoring up my strength, I force a smile. "Well, no point standing around here talking all day. Let's get this prophecy party started."

"You're certain?"

"Absolutely certain. I want to help."

He can't hide the relief in his eyes.

Nodding, he gestures toward the stone steps. "Go ahead, then. I'm right behind you."

"Is there a password or anything?"

"Only your desire to enter the Academy grounds in peace. If you've got malicious intent, you'll be stopped at the barrier. Captured, to be precise."

"Good thing I have a jail-breaking, fear-spelling, mental magicks professor on my side." I offer him one last grin, mostly to show him there are no hard feelings about the boundaries thing, but also to show my gratitude. Not just for saving my life—for all of it.

Whether Dr. Devane realizes it or not, bringing me to Lala's was a gift. The shower, the delicious meal, the chance to breathe and laugh a little and soak up the sunshine after spending so many days in that dank, grimy hellhole...

Whatever's waiting for me at the Academy, however my life will change after I step through its magickal gates, I know I'll remember my last day on *this* side of the world as a good one, thanks to him.

"Miss Milan?"

"Stevie. You can call me Stevie."

Without waiting for a reply, I turn away from him and ascend the stairs. The magick intensifies as I get closer to the archway. It's similar to the magick surrounding Lala's house, but instead of gentle fireflies dancing across my skin, this magick is pure white light, enveloping me until I'm literally glowing.

I can feel it assessing me, like a sentient being. And then, just as I'm getting used to it, it releases its grip. The portal widens ahead, revealing a glowing pathway into the campus.

I close my eyes, take a deep breath. And then, carrying nothing but the clothes on my back, a belly full of tacos, and the fond memories of a life that no longer exists, I step through.

THIRTEEN

STEVIE

Now that I'm presumed dead, the population of Tres Búhos is down to 1,287 souls. We've got a library, one grocery store, and a credit union. There's an ice cream parlor that does buck-a-scoop nights, and down on Hidalgo Road, a drive-in movie theater that shows back-to-back 80s flicks on Fridays.

It's a small town, sure. The kind they write country songs about. But I never realized just how small it was until this very moment, standing at a fountain in the center of the Arcana Academy campus.

My entire hometown and everyone in it could fit on this one square. There are more people milling around the fountain than I've ever seen gathered in one place before, including the time at Sancho's Bar & Grill when Dave Staub won two grand on a lotto scratch-off and offered to pick up everyone's tab for the whole weekend.

Massive, gothic-style buildings dominate the landscape,

like something out of a black-and-white horror movie. You'd think the architecture would look out of place in the desert, but everything is built right into the surroundings, as if the campus was carved from the sandstone itself.

The fountain is a work of art—a giant marble sculpture representing all four suits of the Tarot. The chalice is in the center, with a wand and sword crossed behind it. A pentacle hovers above, slowly rotating as water overflows from the chalice.

I must look like a total tourist with my mouth hanging open, but I don't care. I can't even wrap my head around how amazing this place is.

"The campus was modeled after the original Arcana Academy in Great Britain," Dr. Devane says, appearing right behind me. If anyone noticed our sudden arrival at the fountain, no one seems to think it's odd.

Devane places his hand on the small of my back—in an appropriate, professorial sort of way, of course—and leads me around the fountain.

"The architects had to make modifications for the desert environment," he continues. "So what we're left with is an old-world-meets-old-west motif. An odd mix, perhaps, but it works."

"It's breathtaking."

"You were right at Lala's," he says. "The Academy *is* taller in person."

I laugh, slowly turning in place to take everything in. It's impossibly large and sprawling, buildings and rock formations and saguaros and sculptures intermingling like one big natural landscape. There are so many nooks and crannies to explore.

"Is the Great Britain campus still there?" I ask, jogging to catch up as Devane leads us away from the fountain. "I thought this was the only Arcana Academy."

"Oh, no. There are six campuses throughout the world, though ours is the largest, and one of only three still actively teaching students, along with Paris and Copenhagen. Buenos Aires and Tokyo are used as magickal research facilities only, and the original campus in London now serves as headquarters for APOA—the Association for the Preservation of the Occult Arts."

"What's that?"

"They work as both archivists and public relations managers, essentially. It's APOA's job to ensure that our traditions, history, culture, and important artifacts are preserved for future generations, as well as to interface with the non-magickal public to try to help people better understand us."

"Sounds like they could use some more help in that department."

"They're chronically understaffed. Many of our graduates do go on to work for APOA, but it's not as hands-on as some of the other magickal careers out there, and infinitely less exciting. Here, this way."

I follow him down a wide stone pathway lined with blooming zinnia and hedgehog cactus flowers in bright pinks, oranges, and reds. Students and teachers pass us by, many of them nodding or smiling at Dr. Devane, most offering me the same greeting. We're all moving too fast for me to home in on any individual energy signatures, but the overall vibe I'm getting is one of excitement and happiness, the eager anticipation that comes with the start of a new school year.

A gentle breeze caresses my skin, the normally blazing afternoon sun muted to a pleasant glow. At this time of day, the heat should be oppressive, but it feels balmy and relaxing, much lighter than it did in the desert at Lala's.

"How am I not melting right now?" I ask.

"We have our air- and water-blessed students to thank for the temperature control," Dr. Devane explains. "Though we do try to keep our interference with the natural environment to a minimum. It's important that we have access to the elements in their purest form, since the natural world is such a core component of our magick."

"Are we even in Arizona anymore?" Looking around at the vast campus, I can't figure out where this place would fit on a map. There are saguaros, which only grow in the southwestern part of the state and into Mexico. But other than that, I have no reference points.

"We are, though it's not the Arizona most people know. The Academy, just like our counterparts overseas, exists in a sort of middle space between the earthly realm and the astral. That's why we use the portals—we literally *can't* walk or drive off the campus."

"I guess Uber's out of the question then."

"Actually, there is an astral version that can travel through the portals, but you don't need to worry about that just yet. Escorts at all times moving to and from campus—remember that, Miss Milan."

"Stevie."

Dr. Devane smiles. "Stevie. Right. And I meant what I said earlier." He lowers his voice, leaning in just a little closer. "You're in danger out there. It's best if you stay put for the time being—keep your off-campus wanderings to an absolute minimum."

"No problem. Especially now that I see how much crazy stuff there is to explore here. I'll keep myself busy for at least a month."

He laughs, a breathtaking sound that makes me wish we didn't have to have those pesky professional boundaries.

"You'll receive a full tour of the campus shortly," he says. "First, we need to head to the administration building to get you officially checked in. Our semester begins on October first, so you'll have a couple of days to settle in, shop for your supplies, maybe make a few friends. Sound good?"

I nod, because—much to my own surprise—it does sound good.

"Here we are," he says, stopping in front of a huge building that dominates the landscape—the looming spires I saw through the portal.

I crane my neck to look up at the four black flags waving atop the entrance, each emblazoned in silver with one of the symbols of the Tarot suits.

The flags snap in the breeze, the silver catching the light and sparkling like diamonds. As the metal grommets clank against the flagpoles, a sensation slips over my skin like soap bubbles in a hot bath, luxurious and inviting and utterly perfect.

It's the magick, I realize.

The magick of the Tarot, and the Academy itself, wrapping its arms around me. A Tarot card appears—not in my pocket or my shoe, not on the pavement at my feet, but in my mind. A couple stands on a grassy spring meadow, he in a bright green tartan, she in a long blue dress. They gaze into each other's eyes, sharing wine from two chalices.

The Two of Cups.

You belong here, Stevie Milan. We are your family, and you are ours. Welcome home.

It's one of those messages I can't quite explain, but my heart trusts it fully, despite all of my reservations, despite all of my fears, despite all of my shame at breaking my promise to Mom and Dad.

Whatever happened back then was all part of the path that eventually led me here. I know it, right down to my bones. A spiral within a spiral within a spiral.

I am meant for this.

And maybe now, by being here, I can finally find some answers to the questions that have haunted my family for decades.

Maybe now I can finally let them go.

Tears blur the flags, and I shield my eyes from the sun, as if that's what's causing the waterworks.

"We follow the house system here," Dr. Devane explains. "Each house corresponds with a Tarot suit and its element, and each student is assigned to a house based on their strongest elemental gift."

"How do we know which one is our strongest?"

"There's a test. You'll take it inside. Nothing to worry about—it's really just a guided meditation to reveal your affinity." He stretches his fingers toward the flags, pointing at each one in turn. "House of Flame and Fury is wands—fire. House of Blood and Sorrow is cups—water. House of Breath and Blade—that would be swords, or air. And pentacles—the earth element—that's the House of Iron and Bone. Lucky for you, you *won't* be tested on all the names. Not today, anyway."

"Flame and blood and blade and bone," I breathe.

"What was that?" He leans in closer to catch my fading words.

"Flame and blood and blade and bone." But it's still just a whisper, my mind spinning, my heart hammering in my chest as the pieces click into place.

They'll come for you, Stevie. After the sky falls and the scorpion stings, after the star takes flight and the lightning burns... Flame and blood and blade and bone...

The sky falls—that was the hailstorm that nailed me on the Grande, and it certainly felt like the sky was falling. The scorpion sting? That has to be Luke, the scorpion king himself, seemingly betraying me, stabbing me in the gut. And the star takes flight—I'm the star. Starla. Mom used to call me Starlight. And what else could I call that great leap from the rock face—the spread of the owl's magickal wings —but taking flight? The "lightning burns" part fits, too. The minute I was on the ground, lightning blasted the smaller rock behind me.

Holy. Shitcakes.

"Stevie, what is it?" Devane asks.

"My mother." I grab his arm—fuck propriety. "She knew you would come for me."

He considers me a moment, but doesn't press for an explanation. Thank Goddess; his eyes are full of so much compassion, I'm pretty sure I'd spill everything if only he'd ask.

Instead, he says simply, "Your mother was a talented seer. It seems she knew a great many things."

"What things? What else do you know about her? Does anyone ever talk about her? Or my father? What about—"

"Stevie, all of your questions will be answered in time. You'll just… you'll have to trust us right now. Trust *me* right now." He puts his hands on my shoulders, looking deep into my eyes. "Can you do that for me?"

I want to. Goddess knows I want to. But despite everything Dr. Devane has done for me, how well do I really know him?

At the end of the day, he still works for the enemies of my parents. I let my guard down, let his kindness and good looks and taco-making skills lull me into a false sense of security.

But trust is earned, not presumed. I'd be smart to remember that.

"Not yet," I answer honestly, stepping away from the warmth of his touch. It's too confusing, too easy to believe.

A sly smile breaks across his face. "Good. You're learning already."

"Trust no one?" I repeat, recalling his earlier advice.

"Precisely."

"Noted." I pull my hair back into a loose knot and square my shoulders. "But I *am* here, Dr. Devane. And I'm willing to give this a chance."

"Fair enough." He glances up at the flags once more, then back to me, a passing group of students making the air swirl around us. "Let's get this over with. Rip off the old Band-Aid, so to speak."

"Wait, what? You said the test would be easy!"

"The house test, yes. Meeting the headmistress? I'm afraid that's another story entirely."

FOURTEEN

CASS

Power.

It emanates from her in subtle but distinct ways, if one knows where to look. The fire in her eyes, the spunky edge in her words, the sharp turns of an analytical mind. Even the way she carries herself across the landscape of this strange new place speaks to her fierce determination.

Not even half a day after being liberated from her own personal hell, Stevie moves through the hallowed marble halls of the Academy's oldest building like she owns it. Like it's her birthright.

She's a witch, through and through. Despite her parents' best efforts, once she begins her studies in earnest, there will be no steering her from this magickal path.

I'm not surprised that after spending so many months in Tres Búhos, Kirin has grown so attached to her.

I tried to warn him when Anna dragged us into this.

He tried to ignore me.

And now, I understand why.

Something about the woman draws me in, too. It isn't just that inexplicable vision at the moonlit pool. There's a spark in her, a flicker of something that a deep, ancient part of me recognizes. I feel like our paths have crossed long before—it's the only explanation. Perhaps before she was even born—at least, in her current incarnation of a fiery, beautiful young woman.

Emphasis on young…

Christ, Devane. Where are your damn priorities?

Not only are student-professor relationships forbidden, unprofessional, and highly unethical, but I can't afford to be distracted—not by Starla Milan or any other woman, for that matter. Kirin and the others need me. Our mission is the absolute priority now. Too many lives are at stake, including our own.

Including that of our newest enrollee.

A wave of fierce protectiveness rises. The thought of her coming to harm—more than she's already endured—sends me into a dark fury.

But I can't let those thoughts take hold.

My only interest in Starla—Stevie—is the prophecies. That's how it has to be. For me, for Kirin, and for anyone else who may find himself inappropriately fantasizing about peeling her out of those delectably tight jeans and pressing his mouth between her thighs…

"Should we knock?" Stevie asks, startling me from my musings.

Somehow, we've already reached the office at the end of

the hallway inside the main administration building. The wide oak door rises up before us, its brass name-plate polished to a shine.

ANNA TRELLO — HEADMISTRESS

"Ah, yes. Here we are," I say awkwardly.

"You'll back me up in there, right Doc? Sorry—I mean, Dr. Devane?"

Ignoring her question, I turn toward the door and knock, hoping she hasn't noticed the bulge in my pants.

Boundaries, Devane. Take your own damn advice for once.

"Come in," Anna calls, rather unceremoniously in my opinion, considering the importance of this meeting. I texted her from Lala's; she knew we were en route, that Stevie had accepted our offer.

Still, cold stoicism has always been Anna's way. Maybe things were different before the incident with Stevie's parents, but in the time I've known Anna, she's always played her cards close to the vest.

I push open the door to her office, then stand aside so Stevie can enter.

"Guess it's trial by fire," she mumbles. "Thanks a lot." But, undeterred as ever, Stevie simply rolls her eyes and marches in ahead of me, straight to the center of the room.

Anna is seated at her desk, flanked by Professor Phaines, the Academy librarian and archivist who'll be assisting Stevie with the research, just as he assisted her mother. At our entrance, the pair looks up from their busy-work. Phaines offers his grandfatherly smile, but Anna shows no emotion, no curiosity. No warmth.

The air is charged, tension sparking between the two women like an electrical field that intensifies with every passing second.

When it's obvious no one else is going to make the introduction, I clear my throat and say, "Starla Milan, meet Anna Trello, our headmistress, and Professor Phaines, our esteemed librarian. Colleagues, meet Starla Milan."

To her credit, the girl—woman, rather—raises her chin, her eyes resolute as the others extend their hands to shake.

Stevie obliges, but there's a definite chill in her demeanor, her movements stiff and reserved.

Understandable. She's standing before the very woman responsible for ousting her parents. Despite the complexities of that particular tale—most of which I don't even know myself—the terrible outcome is clearly all Stevie knows of it.

"I'm so pleased you've decided to join us, Miss Milan," Anna finally says, motioning for Stevie to take an empty chair in front of the desk. "I trust Dr. Devane filled you in on the requirements of your enrollment?"

Stevie remains on her feet. "My understanding is that I'll be taking classes to gain a foundational knowledge of magick, and working via independent study on my mother's Tarot research."

"You make it sound as if it's all work and no play at the Academy." Anna laughs, a tight, strangled sound that's nothing like the woman's genuine expression. "But I assure you, there will be plenty of opportunities for you to enjoy yourself. You'll be meeting lots of other witches and mages, mingling, learning new things. We've got shops and restaurants, arcades, pools. If you enjoy the outdoors, there are many natural areas to explore—all protected, of course."

Stevie offers a nod, but says nothing.

Smart girl. Anna is shrewd and discerning, ferreting out information like a vulture scenting carrion. Ingratiating herself is only the first step. Thankfully, Stevie seems immune to it.

"We want you to be happy here, Starla," Anna continues. "Or at the very least, comfortable. This is not a prison."

"So I've been told," Stevie says.

"One thing I'd like to address immediately," Anna says, "is the classified nature of your work. I cannot overstate the need for discretion. If word were to get out, it could cause a lot of unnecessary panic. We're not even sure what we're dealing with, and until we are, we must take precautions to ensure secrecy at all times."

"I understand," Stevie says.

"The people in this room, along with one other graduate research assistant you'll meet later—are the *only* ones you can rely on in this delicate matter. Whether you've made a discovery or hit a wall, you can count on us to help you— but only us. As far as the other students and professors are concerned, you are an Academy student working on a special research assignment for Professor Phaines. Is that clear?"

"Of course, Miss Trello."

"I'm looking forward to working with you on the

prophecies," Phaines says. "The library is simply magnificent—wait until you see it."

Stevie offers another polite nod. There's a flicker of a smile at the mention of the library, but then it's gone, the office descending into awkward silence once again.

There's an elephant in the room—one that undoubtedly matches the size and shape of the hole in Stevie's heart.

Stevie's pain is almost palpable. When she speaks, I can hear the animosity simmering beneath the polite veneer.

Can Anna truly not feel it?

I narrow my eyes at the older woman, silently begging her to do the right thing. In this moment, she has one shot to set the tone for Stevie's entire academic career. With her next words, she can either build a bridge... or burn it down.

"Miss Milan," Anna says, and I know from the sudden sap dripping from her voice she's going to burn it, likely taking us all down with her. "We are so glad you're here. Magick is your legacy, regardless of what happened in the past. I know your mother would—"

"Stop." Stevie holds up a hand, immediately halting Anna's words. "I'm going to stop you right there, because I don't believe for a *minute* you knew my mother. Not enough to speak for her."

Anna bristles. "Begging your pardon, but your mother was a friend and mentee of mine for many years, both as an undergraduate and a graduate student. I actually knew her quite well."

"Really? Hmm." Stevie shrugs. "It's a shame you

couldn't make it to the memorial service—you know, since you guys were so tight and all."

Anna lowers her gaze, absently fidgeting with a stack of papers on her desk. "Miss Milan, I only meant—"

"Here's something I bet you didn't know. My mother loved yellow roses. And Dad—you haven't mentioned him, though you must've known him too, right? He had a thing for Mexican chocolate—the kind with chili peppers ground up inside—even though he had high blood sugar and the doctor was always nagging him to cut back on sweets."

Anna sets down her papers, but still doesn't meet Stevie's eyes.

Fucking coward.

Every instinct is telling me to go stand by Stevie's side, to put an arm around her, to let her and everyone else in this room know that I *do* have her back, rules and propriety be damned. But she's so focused, so intent on getting the words out, I don't dare interrupt.

"After they died," Stevie continues, stepping closer to Anna's desk until the woman has no choice but to look up and meet her gaze, "I'd pop into Sienna's Gifts a few blocks from Kettle Black—that's our tea shop. Every Friday, without fail, I'd buy a big bouquet of roses I couldn't really afford and a box of Mexican chocolates to go with them. Sometimes, if Sienna's daughter was working, she'd take pity and cut me a deal. Then I'd hop on my bike and ride out to Los Piñones Cemetery, flowers sticking out of my backpack, sweat stinging my eyes. I couldn't afford a car, since I was supporting myself by then, but it didn't matter.

I'd pedal hard up the hill that led to their gravesite, park the bike, then kneel at the headstone with my meager offerings. Of course, the flowers would be dry and the chocolates melted by sunset—I knew that. But I did it anyway. I did it because my mother loved flowers and my father loved chocolates, and I wanted them to know I still remembered, even if no one else did."

"Miss Milan," Anna says, attempting a gentle tone. "I understand. You don't have to relive this. You—"

"Here's something *else* you probably don't know about my parents. By the time their bodies were recovered, the floodwater had all but evaporated from the canyon, but not from their flesh. They were so bloated and blue, the medical examiner wouldn't even let me view them up close. Wouldn't let me say goodbye. If it wasn't for dental records and the government-issued serial numbers tattooed on their skin, they wouldn't have been able to ID them."

My stomach churns, my heart breaking for her. How she managed to get out of bed again after this tragedy, I can only imagine.

Anna shakes her head, eyes full of sympathy, cheeks dark with shame. Genuine, for once. "I am so sorry for—"

"The day I buried them," Stevie continues, her voice quavering now but her chin still held high, "it was a hundred and ten degrees in the desert. I stood there in a black dress that was much too heavy for the day, melting in the heat, the whole thing like a hazy mirage as they lowered the little box into the hole. Yeah, just a little box— we had to cremate them, so there wasn't much point in having anything bigger. That worked out okay, because after the other expenses, caskets weren't in the budget. So I stood there, hot outside and dead inside, my best friend Jessa the only thing keeping me upright. There were a handful of neighbors too—Kettle Black customers, Mom's book club. Rita Hernandez. Not a big crowd by any means, but enough to remind me that my parents meant something to the people in our community. That someone other than me and Jessa would miss them, remember them. There weren't any other witches or mages there, funny enough. No one from the Academy, from their coven. *You* weren't there, Miss Trello—I would've remembered if you had been, or if you'd called to offer your condolences for the deaths of your so-called friends. But it didn't matter. My parents were loved, and if they were watching over us that day, they knew it. The rest of us made sure of that."

A few tears glitter on her cheeks, but she doesn't stop.

"The funeral was on a Friday. So I started going back to the cemetery, same day each week, with the flowers and chocolates. Sometimes I brought a to-go pot of their favorite tea, too. Vanilla mint—they both liked that one. Silly, right? It's not like they could drink it. Or smell the flowers or eat the chocolates. I don't know why I kept going. After a while, it just became my ritual. I never missed a visit."

Anna doesn't speak. Doesn't move. Everyone in this room knows what's coming next.

"What day is it today?" Stevie asks casually.

"It's…" Anna tries to speak, but it gets stuck. She clears her throat. Tries again. "It's Saturday."

"Do you know where I was yesterday, Miss Trello?"

My own heart feels sticky and sluggish, and it's an effort not to go to her. To comfort her.

"Yes," Anna replies. "I know you were in prison."

"Yep. I missed my visit to the cemetery for the first time in five years. First time since I buried them, because even in the months after, when I was basically catatonic, I still found the strength to go. But I missed yesterday, and now I'm here, a dead murderer for all anyone in Tres Búhos believes, so I guess future visits are out of the question, too. I didn't even get to say goodbye, to tell them what I had to do by coming here, to beg forgiveness for breaking the one promise they'd ever really asked of me—no magick. I didn't get to leave one more bouquet and box of chocolates, or to remind them how much I love them. All because some crazy-ass mage decided to light up my friend and frame me for murder—a murder that my mother probably saw in the cards, which means you probably could've interceded."

Stevie leans forward, her hands flat on Anna's desk as she peers into the woman's steely eyes.

"My parents died heretics, Miss Trello. Betrayed by you and your Academy. Afraid of magick—theirs and mine. Convinced that the only way I could live a long and happy life was to avoid that magick at all costs, despite the fact that this power has been churning inside me since birth. I was born on a fault line between two worlds, between loyalty and destiny, torn between them every day of my life. That pain, that confusion, that uncertainty? *That's* my legacy. Not the one left by my parents, but the one left by the Arcana Academy of the Arts."

There's absolutely nothing Anna can say to that.

"But," Stevie says, brightening as she stands up straight again, "I have no interest in rotting in jail or being executed. The Academy gave me an out, and I'll always be grateful for that. But you're also boxing me in, and that's just a shitty thing to do. I need you to know that."

Phaines and I exchange a tense glance, and I hold my breath, waiting for Anna's response.

"I suppose I deserve that," Anna says, back to straightening her papers. Her voice, gentle and almost chagrined moments ago, is cool and collected once again. "Though it's my hope that we might get to know each other, Starla. Perhaps come to an understanding, or even a friendship." Anna's smile is as false as they come. "In time, of course."

Stevie sighs, then shakes her head. "I'm here willingly, under no coercion. Dr. Devane gave me a choice, and I chose to enroll at the Academy. In exchange for my freedom, my education, and my living expenses, I'll do everything in my power to decipher my mother's work. I'll attend classes, commit myself to my magickal studies, and work harder than I've worked on anything in my life, including running my business. We have a deal, and I'll uphold my end for as long as I'm able—that's a promise. And I'll show you the utmost respect as headmistress, despite the Academy's history with my family. But we *aren't* friends, Miss Trello. We won't *become* friends. That's not why you invited me here and it's not why I accepted. So

I think it'd be best if we agree to a policy of honesty rather than pleasantries and avoid wasting each other's time."

The words settle over Anna's shoulders like a heavy winter coat. She looks almost—shockingly—wounded.

I glance again at Phaines, but he's not meeting my eyes. Stevie may not realize it yet—and I doubt he plans to elaborate on the matter—but he, too, is complicit in the crimes against her parents.

Did Anna really think they could have any kind of personal relationship after everything that happened?

"Hindsight is…" Anna shifts uncomfortably in her chair, licks her lips. Strands of gray hair have sprung loose from her usually sleek bun, now framing her face in a frizzy white halo. More than aging her, it simply undermines her, cracking her ever-present shell of authority and composure.

For the first time in the years that I've known her, Anna looks weak. And in that moment, I know without a doubt, it's all an act.

Anna Trello *never* looks weak. Not unless she means to.

"Understand, Starla," she says, her eyes shiny with fake compassion. "Academia is fraught with politics—magickal academia, especially. The situation with your parents was… Well, it was a confusing time. If I could do anything to change things, to bring them back—"

"But—spoiler alert—you can't." Stevie unleashes a deep sigh, dashing away the last of her tears. Then, with a shrug and a smile that makes me wonder if the last several minutes even happened, she turns to Phaines and says, "So, what's this about a magick test?"

FIFTEEN

STEVIE

Professor Phaines ushers me to a small mahogany confer-
ence table on the other side of the office and invites me to
sit, take a few deep breaths, and relax.

Gladly. It may not show on the outside—Goddess, I
hope it doesn't—but my knees are still quaking from my
confrontation with Trello. Definitely not how I planned to
make a first impression, but once the words started, I just
couldn't stop.

Better it's out in the open, though. Better we all know
where we stand.

"Okay?" Phaines asks, smiling as he takes the seat kitty-
corner to me. He's got kind eyes, I decide, and a warm
smile to match.

I never knew my grandparents, but Jessa used to tell me
stories about her grandfather in Jalisco, showing her how to
grow tomatoes and peppers in the garden, sneaking butter-
scotch candies to her when her grandmother wasn't watch-

ing. The professor—with his thinning white hair, bulbous nose, and sparkling green eyes—reminds me of someone like that.

Of course, I'm pretty sure Jessa's Abeulo Marco isn't rocking a long green robe piped in silver and a ring that looks like it might *possibly* have been forged in the fires of Mount Doom, but the post-modern wizard aesthetic seems to work for the Academy's esteemed librarian.

Returning his smile, I take some deep breaths, inhaling the faint scents of ink and candle wax that linger in the office. Relaxing isn't all that easy with Anna and Dr. Devane peering over at me every five seconds like I'm some kind of lab experiment, a chimp learning how to play Monopoly—*look! So human, so expressive!*—but I don't sense any danger.

Granted, I don't trust them any farther than I can cast my witchfire—Trello least of all—but I *do* trust that they truly want me here, and they want to keep me safe. As for whether it's for my personal well-being or their own selfish reasons? Doesn't matter. I'm out of that hellhole prison, safe from the guards' filthy hands and electrical prods, safe from angry women throwing piss-soaked rags at my face, safe from the psycho mage who murdered my old friend.

For now, I'm counting it as a win.

"The ritual is relatively simple," Professor Phaines says, his voice taking on a mystical quality that feels more sincere than showy. He retrieves a deck of Tarot cards from a pocket in his robe and sets it on the table. "We start, as in so many magickal rituals, with the cards."

With brick-red backs etched in gold with a simple Celtic knot design, the cards are much larger than the decks I've seen at The Rock Shop, the metaphysical store in Tres Búhos that caters to the new agers. Their size isn't the only difference, either; unlike those Rock Shop decks, this one emanates a faint vibration, a buzz that tickles my palm as I pass my hand over the stack.

"What do you know about magick and Tarot?" he asks, then laughs, undoubtedly realizing the immensity of his question. "A large can of worms, perhaps, but we have to start somewhere. Do you understand the basics?"

"Honestly? I don't know what I understand." I look into those kind eyes and smile, my nerves untangling a bit more. "I know our magick is connected to the Tarot, and that unlike regular humans, witches and mages are born with open channels to receive that magick. And I know my Mom could divine things from the cards, obviously. Aside from that, I'm not really sure how it all works. My witchfire was just something that started happening when I was a kid—like, I'd think about fire, and *pop*." I hold up my palm and conjure up a small silver flame, relieved that it's working again.

After everything that happened in the prison, I wasn't sure it would.

"So yeah, I'm basically a noob." I shrug. There's no point in being embarrassed. After all, it's the Academy's fault my magickal childhood was stripped from me in the first place.

"Bah." Phaines waves a hand, his eyes sparkling with

mirth. "You know a good deal more than some of our first-years from the most prominent magickal families, not naming names, of course." He gives me a wink, then says, "Magick is the natural energy that flows through all things, living and inanimate, whether we see and feel those things or not. The Tarot is a physical, pictorial channel through which mages and witches can harness, repel, amplify, diminish, and alter that energy—to do magick, essentially. There are lots of legends depicting how the cards came to be, and how we came to use them, but you'll learn about all of that in your classes."

I nod, excitement bubbling in my stomach. Sitting here with the professor, feeling the magick of the cards... It's becoming more real by the minute. This is it—I'm enrolling in the Academy. I'm going to study magick.

"Before we begin," he says, "do you have any feelings or instincts about what your gifts might be? The witchfire would suggest a fire affinity, of course, but there may be more dominant gifts inside you."

I consider the question. My knack for tea blending is likely connected to the earth element, as is the rock climbing. The fact that I can sense people's emotions and intentions has qualities of both water and air. And after my experience with the magickal owl energy... Well, I'm not even sure where that fits. Air? Fire? Was it an earth spirit connected to El Búho Grande? Or something not of this earth at all?

Leaving out the owl bit for now, I tell Professor Phaines my thoughts on the rest.

"It sounds like you may have multiple gifts," he says. "We do have some other students this year with two dominant affinities, and one with three, actually. The test will confirm yours, and then we'll take it from there."

He gestures for me to pick up the Tarot deck, then continues.

"I will lead you through a meditation to connect with your inner guide or guides, which may appear to you in human or animal form. They will be emanations of the Tarot—sometimes the court cards, but other Minor Arcana are known to appear as well. Depending on which Tarot energies you see, that will give us a clue to your dominant elemental gifts."

"So if I run into the King of Wands, I'm fire-blessed?"

"Precisely—the wands represent fire. Although the King would be an indication that you're quite advanced in your magickal practice, so it's unlikely you'll see him just yet." Professor Phaines pats my arm. "A more likely example would be the Eight of Pentacles. That would tell us that earth magick is your dominant gift, and would suggest that you're a dedicated and conscientious worker. You see?"

I nod—it all makes sense. After the Tarot cards started appearing to me a few years ago, I researched everything I could about them. So I know about the elemental correspondences and the areas of life they rule over.

Wands correspond with fire and rule things like passion, inspiration, creativity, and spirituality.

Pentacles, the earth suit, connect to the material realm—

money and resources, career, home, physical health, sensual pleasures.

Emotions and relationships belong to the suit of cups, the water element.

And air, the element connected with swords, has to do with both conflict and mental energy. Thoughts, communication, words, ideas, things like that.

I share all of this with Professor Phaines, who beams at me like a proud gramps.

"I think you're farther along on this path than you give yourself credit for, Miss Milan." Then, with an excited gleam in his eyes that probably mirrors my own, he says, "Now, are you ready to reveal your gifts?"

SIXTEEN

STEVIE

The old professor's voice is soothing and serene, guiding me into the meditation like the wise yogi grandpa I never knew I needed. I follow the cadence until the scents and sounds of the office fade away, replaced with the pleasant touch of cool, humid air on my skin and a symphony of crickets.

I open my eyes and find myself standing on a rocky rise, a narrow dirt path winding downward toward an end I can't yet see. It's a moonless night, the stars glittering across an inky, endless sky.

Huge boulders line the path on either side, blocking my view of the surrounding landscape. With no other clear options, I follow the path, the air cooling as I descend, my footfalls softly padding against the dirt. The rhythm of my steps lulls me so completely, I don't see the lake until I'm practically walking into it.

I stop short, then look across the expanse of dark water.

It's as still as a mirror, reflecting the black sky and the blanket of bright stars. It's surrounded by a lush forest, and just beyond the far horizon, a grove of standing stones bloom from the earth like a copse of ancient stone trees.

I feel like I'm in a painting, and I'm not sure I want to leave.

But then the wind shifts, blowing my hair back and sending ripples across the lake.

The water sparkles, then smoothes out again, and from its dark depths, four women emerge—fierce and beautiful, awe-inspiring, like goddesses from another world. Despite the water, their hair and clothing are dry, fluttering in the breeze. Each woman holds something in her hand, and though I'm not close enough to identify the objects, I know instinctively that they're magickal.

I watch in mute admiration as they approach. As if commanded by some invisible general, they stop at once, standing shoulder-to-shoulder at the edge of the lake.

Silently, they watch me. Assess.

It feels like hours, days, months, and none of us moves.

The seasons change before my eyes, the lush green forests of summer turning the fiery red-orange of autumn. Moments later, the leaves fall, the lake freezing pure white. My teeth have just started to chatter when winter releases its icy grip, and the first green buds of spring decorate the earth.

As the spring gives way once again to summer, returning the scene to where it began, the woman on the far left steps forward.

Her face is gentle and untroubled, framed by long, red-gold hair that reminds me of the autumn leaves that fell just moments before. A bright red dress covers her from head to toe, her shoulders wrapped in a wine-dark cloak that flutters out behind her. A simple crescent moon circlet adorns her head.

I see now that her object is an old-fashioned chalice, much like the one in the fountain on campus. She closes her eyes and drinks deeply, then extends the cup toward me.

I wrap my hands around it, and when our fingers touch, I feel her energy, warm and compassionate, deeply sensitive. *Sister,* I think, and she smiles, as if to answer my thought.

She guides the chalice to my lips, and I drink, surprised by the warm sweetness flooding my mouth. It tastes like mulled wine, and fills me with a deep sense of comfort and belonging.

When I open my eyes again, I find her watching me intently, still wearing that serene smile. She offers a gentle bow, then returns to her place beside the others.

The next woman approaches. Where the first was calm and soft, this woman is bold and commanding, with long dark hair and a circlet of pale blue flowers. She, too, wears a dress, but hers is woven in shades of blue like the sky, her cape tattered at the edges as if she's endured a great many storms. A raven perches silently on her shoulder, ever watchful.

As she smiles at me, a sword flashes in her hand, but I know she means no harm. She presses the flat of the blade to her lips, then extends it toward me, touching me on each shoulder like a knight.

As with the first woman and the chalice, I know instinctively what she wants me to do. Obeying, I hold out my hands, allowing her to press the tip of the sword into the center of each palm. As soon as the blade draws blood, a rush of power courses through my veins, straight to my heart. I watch as the blood beading on my palms glows bright, then vanishes.

In its place, a sword appears, slim and sharp, glowing with magick. I close my fingers around the grip, that same rush of power surging anew. The feeling is so intense, so incredible, I laugh with giddy pleasure.

The woman mirrors my smile and bows, then returns to her place. My sword vanishes, but the sense of power it inspired remains.

The third woman is dressed in a bright orange strapless dress printed with dark green salamanders and trimmed with the same Celtic knotwork featured on Professor Phaines' cards. An olive green cape hangs elegantly over one bare shoulder. Her hair flows down past her waist, dark auburn shot through with golden highlights. When the breeze catches it, she shimmers like living fire.

She carries a long staff and holds it out to me now. The moment I touch it, witchfire engulfs the wood, hot and bright, but neither of us pulls away. At first I think the magick is entirely hers, but then I feel my own, our two fires merging, growing stronger together. Just like with the others, I feel nothing but welcoming kindness. She's fierce, but compassionate, her power destructive and creative in equal measure.

The fire fades away, and she steps back with a smile, allowing the last woman to approach.

She's the youngest of the group, no more than fourteen or fifteen, with thick dark hair and eyebrows and a round face still clinging to the last vestiges of childhood. She wears a simple long-sleeved gown in a checkerboard pattern of alternating greens and a luxurious velvet cape, deep red trimmed in golden Celtic knots.

When she looks at me, I can't help but feel like I'm under the microscope. She doesn't smile, but finally nods her approval, holding out her small hands to show me a pentacle made of gold. When I touch it, I feel her energy surround me like a protective cloak, merging with my own energy, our magick twining and sinking into the earth like the gnarled roots of a tree.

Eventually, she returns to the others, all four watching me intently, the breeze catching their hair and gowns.

"I will not disappoint you," I say, though I don't know why those words come to mind. I sense the rightness of them, though, and press my hands to my heart, silently thanking them for their gifts.

These women feel like sisters, like allies, but there's an expectation among them, too—one I hope I can meet.

In perfect unison, they bow to me, then turn their backs and return to the lake, vanishing beneath the water once again. Sensing the ritual is at its end, I'm about to turn back

SPELLS OF IRON AND BONE

up the dirt path, but something else stirs in the water, beckoning me closer.

I approach the shoreline, and suddenly it explodes from
the depths, a blinding silver-white light bleaching the
surrounding landscape to a pale gray.

I know before the light fades that it's my owl, the
magickal spirit that saved me on the rocks the day Luke
was murdered. He glides toward me, and I hold up my
arm, inviting him to perch.

He lands with grace, his talons strong and fierce, his
weight almost more than I can bear. Bright golden eyes
gaze into mine, and up close like this, I can see all the
shades of his beautiful plumage—whites and creams, spots
of dark brown and even gray. He's a fierce predator, but I
know I have nothing to fear from this magnificent creature.
We're connected in ways I can't even begin to understand.

We gaze into each other's eyes a long moment before the
bird finally turns his head, breaking our connection. Then,
with a breathless span of wings, he takes flight, launching
from my arm and darting into the sky.

I jog around the edge of the lake, hoping to track his
flight, but I've already lost him.

"Wait!" I cry out, but at the sound of my call, the landscape vanishes around me.

I'm back in Trello's office, seated at the mahogany table.
Professor Phaines watches me closely, the other two
standing behind him. All eyes are wide with surprise.

I glance down at the Tarot deck in front of me and notice

four cards spread beneath it, facing upright—the Princesses of the Tarot, one from each suit.

I reach out to touch the cards, and the backs of my hands glow with bright silver symbols—a sword, a wand, a cup, and a pentacle. They burn brightly for a moment, and then fade away, their power sinking deep into my skin.

When I look up at Trello, her eyes are wide, glittering with something that looks an awful lot like reverence.

"All four," she whispers. Then, composing herself, "Tell us what you saw, Miss Milan."

I tell them about the vision, about each of the women who approached me and the gifts they shared.

"What does it mean?" I ask. "I'm not very strong on the court cards."

"In some traditions," Devane says, "the Princesses are known as Pages. They are closely aligned with young people, particularly students. They're quite powerful in their own right, representing the intense transition between adolescence and adulthood, between the apprentice and master of magick." He smiles at me, broad and genuine. "To have their blessing is quite a gift indeed."

Professor Phaines puts a gentle hand over mine. "You're not the first student to be blessed by a Princess, nor the first to be blessed with multiple elemental affinities. But it's been many, many years since we've seen a student with all four affinities, and none that have ever been blessed by all of the Princesses in the Tarot court."

"I still don't understand what it means," I say.

"It means that the Princesses are watching over you,"

Trello says, "and that your studies—your dedication to magick, your understanding of each of the elements and suits, your work on the prophecies—are going to be very intense, and of a far greater importance than any of us could've predicted."

She and Professor Phaines exchange a look I can't quite read, and Dr. Devane just keeps staring at me, as if he's trying to figure something out.

The tension in the air is so thick I'm practically choking on it, and a nervous laugh bubbles up inside me. "You don't have to give me the hard sell, guys. I'm here, right? I'm not backing out of our deal."

None of them joins in on the laughing.

"This is not just about your own education, Starla," Professor Phaines says. "Your work here, your arrival... It was destined, and that cannot be taken lightly."

A shiver rolls over my skin at the rightness of his words.

"Is there anything else?" he asks. "Any other details about the vision you'd like to share?"

I nod, but as soon as I open my mouth to tell them about the owl, something stops me. I hear the rush of air and the flap of great wings, but somehow I know it's only in my mind. It feels like a warning.

I look up and catch Devane's eye, see the same warning in his gaze.

Don't tell them, his voice practically echoes in my mind.

I swallow hard. I'm not sure whether I should be more concerned that I can sense his intentions without him

SARAH PIPER

speaking the words... or that he's asking me to keep this part of my vision a secret.

I thought I was supposed to be able to count on everyone in this room. So why doesn't *he*?

"What is it?" Trello prods, snapping me back to the moment.

"Just... the seasons," I say quickly. "While I was standing at the lake, the scenery around me moved through all the seasons."

"That's a lovely thing to see, Starla," Trello says. "Each of the Princesses is connected to her own season. They were simply introducing themselves."

The three exchange more veiled glances. Then Professor Phaines touches my shoulder and says, "I think we've kept the poor girl long enough. Starla, my research assistant will meet you out front. He'll give you a tour of the campus and show you to your suite."

"That's it?" I ask. "No homework or anything?"

"There will be plenty of time for that," he says with a laugh. "And once your computer system is set up later, you'll need to sign in to the student portal and review your registration documents, school policies, holiday calendar, things like that. You'll also find your class schedule. But for now, you've got a couple of days to find your footing—I suggest you make the most of them before the semester gets hectic."

"Thank you," I say. "I will."

"I'll walk you out," Dr. Devane says, and I rise to follow him to the door, wishing the others a good day.

"What does it mean?" I whisper when we're out in the hallway. "Did I pass the test? What's my house?"

"It means you possess all four elemental affinities in equally powerful measure. You are what we call spirit-blessed, Stevie. Very powerful, very rare, and—if some of the old stories are to be believed—very dangerous."

His words stir something inside me, a dormant creature yearning to yawn and stretch and step out into the light.

"What about my house? Is there a special dorm for spirit-blessed students?"

"No, as you are currently the only one." He smiles, shaking his head as if he still can't quite believe it. "You'll spend one year studying with each house. That way, you'll be able to connect with all four of the elements, and the other students who work with those elements can help you on your path."

"But what about—"

"I'm sorry, Stevie. I need to get back inside—we have a meeting that doesn't concern you. In the meantime, follow Professor Phaines' advice and take a few days to get to know the campus, do a little exploring. I'll see you in class very soon."

"You think so, huh?" I tease. "I don't know, Dr. Devane. You're kind of a cranky old bastard. Maybe I won't sign up for your class after all."

"It's a requirement." He winks, and then, without another word, disappears back into Trello's office, shutting the door behind him.

And I scoot my ass right back over there and press my

ear to the gap.

"What is your initial assessment?" I hear Professor Phaines ask, his grandfatherly tone taking on a sharper edge, even as it's muted through the door.

"The woman is unsettling, to say the least." This, from Dr. Devane.

Unsettling? Really. Says the man whose idea of a first date—yes, I'm calling it a date, sue me—is a fake murder-suicide followed by tacos?

"She reminds me so much of her mother," Trello says, and I can't tell from her tone whether she thinks this is a good thing or not.

"I was afraid you'd say that," Professor Phaines says.

There's a prolonged silence, then Trello speaks again.

"Keep a close watch on her at all costs," she orders. "I want to be kept informed in all matters, including her coursework and social activities. Now, we need to discuss the fire alarm upgrades scheduled for next month..."

Certain I'm no longer the hot topic of the day, I leave them to their meeting, heading back outside to meet this research assistant. The sun is just starting to dip toward the horizon, bathing everything in a rose-gold glow that reminds me of the sunsets behind our trailer on Pinon Canyon Lane.

How many nights did Jessa and I sit out there with a bottle of wine and a mellow jazz playlist, talking about life and death and everything in between?

Goddess, it's only been a week, and I already miss her like I haven't seen her in years. When I think about her now, about all the things I love about home, my heart breaks a little more.

Everything I love about Tres Búhos is now a memory.

The way the sun sets fire to the rock towers, making them look like candles burning in some great birthday cake.

The stately saguaros keeping watch over the Santa Clarita.

Two-for-one margaritas at Sancho's Bar & Grill.

The way Jessa's face lights up as she pours her heart into everything she bakes at Kettle Black.

Our quiet moments before the day's opening, our only company the soft tick of the ovens.

The sweet, comforting scents of her cinnamon and chocolate confections mingling with the fragrance of my favorite teas—a heady mix I can only describe as home.

As gone.

The force of it hits me all at once, and I sway on my feet, then sit down on the admin building steps to keep from face-planting. I rest my head in my hands, trying to breathe, trying to relax, trying to rearrange my mind to accommodate this new place. This new life.

"Stevie, you okay?"

A familiar voice floats to my ears, a warm hand touching my shoulder.

And when I look up, the eyes looking back at me are full of concern, glittering behind black-framed glasses in a beautiful kaleidoscope of pale greens and golds I never thought I'd see again.

"Kirin?"

SEVENTEEN

STEVIE

I almost don't recognize him outside the context of Kettle Black. He's traded his usual form-fitting T-shirt and jeans for a pair of equally form-fitting gray slacks and a mint green dress shirt that brings out his eyes. Instead of a paperback, he's carrying a cardboard to-go tray in one hand, balancing two cups with black lids.

The warm, creamy scents of cinnamon, espresso, and honey drift to my nose.

He remembered...

But then I see the silver academy pin on his collar, and I remember, too.

He's an Academy student—probably a graduate. He's... Oh, hell. He was waiting for me out here. He's the research assistant tasked with giving me the tour. With helping me decipher Mom's work.

And he knew—for *months*—who I was. That I'd end up right here.

SPELLS OF IRON AND BONE

Stevie, you clueless, heartsick idiot.

It takes a full minute for the anger to bust through the shock, and when it does, I'm rocketing to my feet, fire in my veins, ready to explode.

"You're one of them? You've been *spying* on me?"

"It's not like that," he says. "I swear. Stevie, let me explain."

"Talk fast, Kirin. You've got one minute. And the only reason you're even getting that much is that I don't know another soul on this campus other than two professors and the headmistress, and that's not saying much."

"Okay, okay. Can we just…" He nods toward an alcove on the side of the building. "Please?"

Reluctantly, I follow him into the shadows, out of sight from the other passersby.

"Thirty seconds." I fold my arms across my chest and lean back against the rough stone wall.

"Stevie, I just…" He sighs, frustrated, his brow creasing above the black frames. "Okay. I don't know all the details, because the headmistress has been extremely tight-lipped about the whole thing. But yes, I've been spying on you. Keeping a protective watch, more accurately."

"Fifteen seconds."

"From the few details she shared, I know she had it on good authority that you'd be arrested and jailed some time this summer or fall for crimes of public witchcraft, and the outcome would be devastating. She didn't know the exact date, or what would precede it—only that you'd be arrested at Kettle Black, and it would happen in the morning between ten and eleven. So I was sent to just... just be there, I guess. Every day. We had no idea if I'd be able to see it coming, or to help, or to stop it, or just... Well, in the end, I guess all I could really do was phone it in after the fact."

I close my eyes, trying to process all this. The fact that he phoned it in is probably the only reason I'm standing here rather than rotting in that prison.

Right now, even being supremely pissed off feels like a privilege.

"You just bought yourself another two minutes," I say, some of my anger receding. "Who's this so-called 'good authority' that told Trello I'd get pinched?"

He shifts uncomfortably, his glasses sliding down his nose. I see now that his eyes are rimmed in red, as though he hasn't been sleeping much.

It reminds me of all the times I read his energy at Kettle Black, made him the perfect cup of tea to brighten his day, put a little pep in his step.

"From your mother, Stevie." Kirin's voice is gentle now, which tells me he knows a lot more about the situation with my mom and the Academy than he's letting on. "Apparently, one of her predictions was about this. Again, not specific enough that we could totally prevent it, but we managed to piece together enough details to know you'd be in trouble, and that you'd need our help."

"How do I know this entire thing isn't a setup? That the Academy didn't orchestrate the thing with Luke so I'd end up in jail, with the Academy being my only shot at freedom? Devane and Trello both said it—you guys need me. No one else has been able to figure out the prophecies."

"That's not how we operate. It just isn't."

"So I happened to get framed for magickal murder exactly when the Academy most needs something from me? That's a hell of a coincidence."

"No, it isn't." He points to the sky and steps closer, his summer-storm scent lingering. "That's the universe nudging you onto a path you've been ignoring for far too long."

I take a step back. "You don't know anything about me, Kirin, so do me a favor and stop acting like a font of fucking wisdom on all things Stevie Milan."

Hurt flashes through his eyes, and instantly, I regret my harsh tone.

Maybe patronizing Kettle Black was part of his job, but still... Hadn't we become friends? Friends on the verge of something more?

That date... it could've led somewhere. Even with my reluctance toward romantic entanglements in general and mages specifically, one day, I might've made an exception for Kirin Weber.

But we never got the chance. And now, we never will. Everything just got *way* too complicated for that.

"No, I don't know you, Stevie," he says sadly. "Not well. But I do know *some* things." He steps closer, closing the gap between us once again. "I know that you make the most perfect, amazing cup of tea on the planet. I know you love rock climbing and biking, so much that not even a crazy storm can deter you when you're on a mission. I know you're sweet and kind and funny, and sometimes you get nervous when we talk, which always makes me feel a little better about the fact that *I'm* nervous just standing next to you. And I know that for the last few months, the hours I spent with you in Kettle Black every morning were the absolute best part of my day."

My heart thaws, melts, falls right out of my chest.

Did I say complicated? I meant impossible. Why does he have to be so sweet? Why does he have to be a mage?

Why did any of this have to happen at all?

Softening my tone, I say, "My parents never wanted to talk about this place, Kirin. They just wanted to forget about their time here. They didn't want me to enroll or study my magick at all."

"How do you know that if they never talked about it?"

"I used to ask them about it, you know? Like any kid who wants to know the story of how her parents met, where they fell in love, how I came to be. They never lied about me being a witch, so when I learned they'd attended a magickal academy, I told them I couldn't wait to come here. I mean, I just figured that was the way things worked for witches and mages. But then they'd get all quiet or change the subject. Eventually, when I got old enough to notice how weird this was, they admitted they left here under duress soon after I was born. But whenever I tried to ask about their classes, or the teachers, or any of the things they'd studied, they flat-out refused to tell me. 'It's a curse,' my mother said. That summed up her entire view on magick."

"I don't know what to say, Stevie."

"Well, I'm here now, right?" I sigh, my shoulders slumping. "No use dwelling on that. It's just… It's a lot right now, okay? When I woke up last Saturday and strapped on my gear, I had no idea it would be the last time I'd climb the Grande. Or make tea at Kettle Black. Or hug—Oh my Goddess, Jessa!" I blurt out suddenly, the shock of Kirin's presence finally clearing from my mind. "You were there that day. What happened after the police took me? Is she okay?"

"Jessa's okay," he says. "I stayed with her that day, assured her I would find a way to help you. I couldn't give her all the details, but she knows about me—my work here. She also knows that you're safe—we didn't want her to hear about your so-called death and freak out."

A sigh of relief rushes out. "I was so worried about her."

"The feeling was mutual, trust me. But you don't have to worry anymore. She's got a secured cell now, spelled with encryption and warded from any outside interference or tracking. You'll have the same setup. We can't risk anyone else in Tres Búhos finding out you're alive."

I nod, though the whole thing weighs heavy on my shoulders. "When can I talk to her?"

"As soon as they get your phone set up."

"When?"

"An hour or two at most."

"Thank you," I manage, my anger evaporating. "For phoning it in, and for looking out for Jessa."

He smiles, the familiar sight of it twisting my heart. Was it only a week ago that he asked me out for coffee?

Did he mean it, or was it just part of his job?

"So, should we maybe… walk?" Tentatively, he holds out his coffee tray. "I brought treats."

The inviting scents curl around me like a hug, drawing me closer despite my best efforts to keep a distance.

"Just so you know," I tell him, plucking one of the cups from the tray, "I haven't decided whether to forgive you or not."

"Understandable. Unfortunately for you, I'm the best tour guide on campus, as well as the only one available at the moment. So unless you want to wander the grounds aimlessly and end up somewhere you shouldn't…"

"I'm pretty good at finding my own way around."

"I know." He smiles, his energy gliding over my skin like a tender caress, warm and sincere. Then, holding out his arm for me to take, he says, "But you don't *have* to find your own way. Not anymore."

I look at his arm, knowing he's offering me much more than an escort and a tour.

He's offering friendship.

And despite the deception—and the fact that there's probably a lot more to the story he's not sharing—deep inside, he still feels like a friend. Maybe the only one I have here.

I take a sip of the latte, sweet and delicious, even better than the ones at Froth.

"Perfect," I say with a sigh.

"Yeah?" Kirin's smile breaks through the last of the tension between us like the dawn. "Does that mean I'm forgiven?"

"I meant the *latte's* perfect." Then, rolling my eyes and offering a smile of my own, I finally take his arm. "This little tour of yours better be good, or I'm totally getting my money back."

EIGHTEEN

STEVIE

"Okay, the House of Iron and Bone," I say, following Kirin down yet another red stone path. The entire campus is connected by them, a vast web lined with the same flowers I saw with Dr. Devane earlier. There are bike trails, too, running around the perimeter of the campus and through the desert behind the dorms, and free bike stations at most of the buildings so students can just hop on and ride anytime. "How did they get Iron and Bone from pentacles?"

"I'm so glad you asked." Kirin's eyes light up, just like they have at every single one of my questions. He really is in his element, and I suspect he knows even more about the campus and its history than the architects and founders themselves. "In the legends about the First Fool—basically, the guy who sacrificed himself to the elemental deities so humans could access magick—the first pentacle was crafted from iron of the earth and—are you ready for this? The dude's *actual* bones."

"Of course! Because *that's* not creepy at all."

"It gets creepier. The chalice of blood and sorrow was fashioned from the top of his skull and filled with his blood and tears, which his friends and ancestors then drank to unlock their own channels to the magick."

I wrinkle my nose. "Eww."

"The first sword was said to be forged from flames stoked by his final breaths—hence the breath and blade bit."

"What about the wands? Did they just set him on fire after that? I mean, what else, right?"

"Actually..." Kirin cringes. "They performed a prolonged sexual rite, capturing and infusing the wand with the essence of his final moments of ecstasy—flame and fury. Then they cut off his head—that's when they made the chalice."

"Wow, the first mages were kind of extra, huh?"

"You don't know the half of it. But you will. You'll be expected to memorize all the old legends and write so many essays on it that by the time you graduate, you'll never be able to look at a Tarot deck the same way again." Kirin laughs, but it's not the shocking stories that linger in my mind.

It's his *other* words.

By the time you graduate...

Graduate. From magick school. Me. The idea still feels so foreign, so forbidden. When I told Trello that my legacy was to be caught between two worlds, I meant it. Now, I wonder if that feeling will ever pass. If I'll ever feel totally comfortable on this strange new path.

"What do you think of my tour so far?" Kirin asks, still grinning. "I told you I was a good guide."

I drain the last of my latte, toss the cup into a nearby trash container. It vaporizes in a cloud of pink smoke before it even hits the rim—magickal recycling at its finest.

"I think you're quite possibly the *creepiest* guide in existence," I say.

"What? I haven't even shown you the Chapel of Severed Heads yet!"

"You can't be serious."

He wriggles his eyebrows, making his glasses jump. "The clergy wears rosaries made of baby teeth."

At my horrified gasp, Kirin unleashes a laugh so big and bright, a few students ahead of us on the path turn to look, then start laughing too, infected with his charm.

"It's all just legends, Stevie," he says. "The first written records we have about it are from the fifteenth century, and those are just translations of the originals, which likely date back thousands of years before that. Who knows how much was changed or mistranslated, or misheard from back when the stories were all passed down orally? For a long time, nothing was written down at all, for fear the non-magickal humans would find out about our world."

A breeze drifts along the path, and I fight off a shiver, wishing I had more latte to warm me up. "The ancients were smarter than us. Maybe the stories should've stayed secret."

We wander a little farther, and Kirin points out the shopping center on the western edge of the campus—a small outdoor mall called the Promenade with at least two dozen different stores, a good mix of regular shops that sell clothes and shoes, office supplies, games, and sporting goods, along with stores catering specifically to witches and mages. Glancing at some of the signs, I spot ads for everything from Tarot decks and crystals to magickal herbs and potions, enchanted jewelry, wands, occult books, and—

"Broomsticks? Are you serious?"

Kirin laughs again. "They're mostly used in rituals. Though for the students who have the power of levitation, they make a fun prop at parties. You want to stop in and get something?"

I'm not ready to shop till I drop just yet, so we continue on toward the dormitories—one for each house. Set on a huge semi-circle connected by another arcing pathway, four impressive gothic buildings that look like a cross between cathedrals and castles stand tall, carved from the same color stone as the surrounding landscape. They're smaller than the administration building, but more ornate, with towering spires, stained glass windows, and gargoyles perched along the eaves.

Each dormitory has five floors of student housing, plus the main level, which includes a massive common room and kitchen area, art and photo installations depicting the history and magickal legends of each house, and multiple cafés featuring different international and regional cuisines.

"House of Blood and Sorrow has a bar called Pour Your Heart Out," Kirin says. "They do karaoke nights on Fridays. Pretty fun, if you're into that sort of thing."

"Karaoke? I love karaoke! Jessa and I used to bring the house down at Sancho's with our rousing rendition of Beyonce's *All the Single Ladies*."

"Now *that* I'd pay money to see." Kirin grins. "All the cafés are open 24/7, and you can eat in any one you choose, no matter your house affinity."

"Good to know, since I've got all four."

"You... what? Hold on." Kirin turns to face me, stopping me in my tracks. "You're spirit-blessed, and you're just mentioning this to me *now*?"

"I'm a little overwhelmed and distracted at the moment," I explain. "But yeah, that's what they told me. Spirit-blessed."

"Which cards did you see?"

"The Princesses." I tell him about the vision, once again leaving out the part about the owl.

Kirin watches me with an eager glint in his eyes, the gears of his researcher mind turning so loudly I can practically hear them squeaking.

"Fascinating," he says.

I flash him a sexy smirk. "Well, thank you."

"You know I'm going to bug you about this, like, every day. Especially as your magick starts to develop."

"I would expect nothing less. What's your affinity, anyway?"

He's still nursing his coffee, and now he holds the cup in front of him, then releases it. It floats before us, not spilling a drop.

"Air," he says. "I can move it and manipulate it, among other things."

"I might be bugging you, too," I say, eager to know more. "I'd really love to learn how to do that."

"It's a deal." Kirin grabs his cup, swigs back the last of his coffee. "In the meantime, let me show you the house grounds. We'll need bikes for this part."

He tosses his cup into one of the magickal bins, and we head over to the nearest bike station, selecting two sleek white mountain bikes.

We ride along another path that winds behind the dorms. I've barely broken a sweat when the landscape suddenly cracks open before us, revealing a vast, beautiful space that looks as huge and pristine as a national park.

"I see now why we needed the bikes," I shout, pedaling to catch up to his long strides. "This is just... wow. I live here. I actually live here."

When Trello mentioned that there were plenty of outdoor areas to explore, she was seriously underselling that fact.

The dorms fade behind us as we ride deeper into the backcountry, and Kirin points out the natural features associated with each house, each one more impossible and stunning than the last, making me giddy—and super glad I pushed Devane for the rock-climbing gear. I've already spotted at least a dozen potential spots to try.

Behind the House of Breath and Blade, tall sandstone spires called the Towers of Breath and Blade rise out of the earth, their craggy fingers stretching so high into the sky, the jagged peaks are obscured by the clouds. They look too fragile to climb, though; in fact, their very existence seems to defy the laws of nature, as if the weight of a single feather could send them toppling to the earth.

Riding past the spires, we weave through desert mounds of red and lavender and gray until we reach the boundary to the House of Iron and Bone lands, a petrified forest bearing the same name, its crystalized tree remnants sparkling like diamonds in the setting sun.

Next is the Cauldron of Flame and Fury, a huge bowl canyon that Kirin says glows like fire at sunrise, situated behind the House of Flame and Fury.

Behind the House of Blood and Sorrow, the last stop on our dorm tour, a red river called—wait for it—the River of Blood and Sorrow winds through the landscape, richly colored by the iron in the soil.

It's so perfect and amazing my head's about to explode.

"How is it that the landscape is so well-suited to each house name?" I ask when we stop the bikes to catch our breath. "And what about the Academies in other countries? Do they have the same features?"

"The architects always build the academies around the existing natural landscape, taking great care to situate each house in the most suitable place—whatever is most compatible with its element. So the House of Blood and Sorrow will always be near water, though it won't always be a red river like we have here."

"It's just… It's breathtaking. It all feels so… so…"

"Magickal?" Kirin smiles, the warmth in it reminding me of all our mornings together at Kettle Black. "That's the idea. In magick, everything is symbolic, taking power from the words we name it, the physical features, the scents and textures… everything. We're elemental magicians, Stevie. To wield that magick, we need to connect with the natural world as deeply as possible."

I take a moment to soak it all in, looking out across the vast landscape. The sun is sinking low, the air cooling slightly, the crickets just starting to sing. My eyes track the bend of the river, roaming out to an area we haven't explored yet. From here, it looks like there are more sandstone spires, but it's hard to tell. Everything out that way is covered in a thick, white mist.

"What's over there?" I ask, jutting my chin in that direction.

"That's… not a place you want to go. Ever."

I roll my eyes and laugh. "Well, now you *have* to take me."

"I can't, Stevie. I'm serious. It's forbidden to students and staff alike."

"Forbidden? Sounds like code for the best party spot on campus. Let's go." I hop back on my bike, but Kirin doesn't move.

"Kirin. Come on. What's over there?"

His face turns contemplative, and it's a long beat before he speaks again. When he does, an ominous weight hangs over him, a shadow sliding into his normally bright eyes. "Have you ever heard of *L'Appel du Vide*?"

Holy red-hot cinnamon buns, he's speaking in French. This is not a drill, people. Kirin Weber is speaking in French, and my thighs are clenching at the sound.

"Say again?" I ask. Beg.

"*L'Appel du Vide*," he repeats, his accent as rich and buttery as a croissant. "It literally means 'the call of the void.' It's said that there are places in this world so deep, so dark, so... compelling... when you peer down into them, they literally beckon you to jump."

An icy finger traces a path down my spine.

"That place..." He thumbs at it over his shoulder, as if he's afraid to even turn and look at it. "It's like that. We call it the Void. A sheer cliff that descends hundreds of feet— maybe thousands—into abject nothingness. Before they finally warded and fenced it off in the 1930s, dozens of students and teachers committed suicide there—people that were otherwise completely content."

"The Void," I repeat, the words themselves seeming to echo on the breeze. "It's not on any map of Arizona I've ever seen."

"Nor is the Academy, or Lala's place..." Kirin shrugs. "Some places just aren't meant for the rest of the world to know."

"Only us?"

"Only us."

The breeze stirs again, the mist roiling in the distance, and I swear I hear it calling me. *Starla Eve... Starla Eve... Starla...*

A shiver grips me in a tight fist, shaking me head to toe. Suddenly, I want to be as far away from the Void as possible.

Kirin must sense my sudden need to escape, because his brow creases again, and he hops on his bike without another word, beckoning for me to follow him back to the dorms.

I've never pedaled so hard in my life.

Safely back in front of the buildings, we stash the bikes and stop in the shade of a huge saguaro so Kirin can check his phone.

"Okay, your suite should be all set up now," he says. "They've got you in..." His eyebrows jump, the muscle on his jaw ticking. When he speaks again, his tone is tinged with disappointment—and maybe a little annoyance. "House of Iron and Bone."

"Is that a bad thing? I mean, it would've been cool to be in the House of Breath and Blade with you, but I guess they figured with the tea and rock stuff, I'm pretty earthy, so..."

"It's not a bad thing. It's just—"

"Weber," a guy calls out from several paces ahead of us on the path. "Who's your new friend?" He laughs and waves at Kirin, but takes his sweet time sauntering over here. Sauntering is the only word for it, too—gray henley pushed up to his elbows, hands in the pockets of his faded black jeans, shoulders slightly hunched, his lean but well-muscled frame moving through space-time as if he hasn't a care in the world.

Kirin closes his eyes and says, "Baz. It's Baz."

"*What's* Baz?" I ask. "The reason you're being weird about my house, or the guy heading our way?"

"Both."

There's a playful spark in Kirin's eyes, but I can't tell if he's joking or not. I'm about to ask, but then the guy in question is standing right before us, looming like a dark shadow.

Oh, damn.

NINETEEN

STEVIE

We lock eyes immediately, his slow-burn smile sexy and wolfish behind a few days' worth of stubble. Messy, chocolate-brown hair falls lazily into his eyes, which are a deep auburn-brown that looks almost reddish in the light.

Devil's eyes, I decide. More red than brown, and too intoxicating for his own good.

Bastard knows it, too. When I reach out for his energy, I find a smug aloofness. A cockiness trying hard to hide something else festering beneath.

He still hasn't removed his hands from his pockets, and I can't help but stare at his sculpted arms flexing in the fading sun.

The forearm porn is strong with this one…

"You must be the little jailbird Trello's got her panties in a bunch over," he says by way of introduction, and Kirin rolls his eyes, letting out a groan.

I lift my gaze to Baz's face, my eyebrows shooting

skyward. Forearm porn or not, that was a jackass thing to say.

"And *you* must be the guy who cops attitude to compensate for a small dick," I retort. "You don't have to do that, you know. I'm sure there are plenty of fine women out there who like a guy just for his personality. I mean, I don't know any of them personally, but if you believe it hard enough, dreams really can come true!" Then I flash him the double thumbs-up and a wide, cheesy grin. "Think good thoughts!"

His eyes flare with fire.

Kirin puts a hand on my shoulder and clears his throat, glaring at Baz in what feels like a show of dominance. It's a protective gesture that I appreciate, but then, out of nowhere, Baz just laughs.

"Oh, I like this one." He leans in close, throwing his arm around me in a congenial side-hug. "Can we keep her?"

"Keep yourself, jerk." I slide out from under his arm, but I'm basically full of shit. At least *half* full, anyway. Because this guy, as epically assholian as he may be, is a specimen of male perfection, and there's something intriguing about him I can't quite put my finger on. His sense of humor may be a little rough around the edges, but it's there, a genuine good nature he's trying hard to hide.

"If you change your mind, Kirin has my number." He's still standing way too close, his scent invading my space—like woodsmoke and black pepper and freshly turned earth—and the longer he looks at me, those devil eyes flashing with mischief, promising all sorts of naughty trouble, the closer I am to taking him up on that offer…

Get a hold of yourself, you horny slut!

I force myself to take a step back and breathe in some normal air, recapturing a few brain cells I've clearly lost along the way.

Goddess, what is my deal? Kirin is one thing—I've been crushing on him for months. I could even give myself a pass on my brief attraction to Dr. Devane, considering the extreme circumstances under which we met, and how he saved my life and fed me tacos, a combo that's nearly impossible to resist.

But this dickhead? He's a… well, a dickhead. Obviously.

Must be these damn jeans Lala gave me. They're creeping up too close, rubbing me in all the wrong ways, activating areas of my anatomy that have no business coming out of hibernation.

Go back to sleep, my pretties! Your services will not be needed at this time, thank you!

"I assume you have a name?" Baz asks me.

"Don't tell him, Stevie," Kirin says, laughing. "It's like the ancient tales—he'll only use it against you later."

"Kirin! Remind me not to trust you with any *real* secrets." I give Kirin a playful punch on the arm. "It's Stevie. And there will be no using *anything* against me later, or I shall be forced to use my most devastating form of torture on you—singing karaoke."

"You told me you love karaoke," Kirin says.

"Yes, but as you might well learn, there's often a wide,

wide world of difference between loving a thing and being good at it."

"That sounds like a dare," Baz says. "Kirin, don't you think that sounds like a dare?"

"Now that you mention it..." Kirin taps his lips. "We might have to make a mental note of this for future reference."

I crack up. "Fine by me. But don't say I didn't warn you."

"Which house are you in?" Baz asks.

"Iron and Bone. You?"

"It must be fate." Baz spreads his arms slowly, grinning like he's showing off his personal domain. "Welcome home, Little Bird."

I glance over at Kirin, who offers another apologetic frown.

"Baz," he says, "you know we have a strict anti-harass-ment policy, right? Perhaps you should re-familiarize your-self with it before Stevie moves into the house."

Baz flashes an exaggerated frown, then turns to me and whispers conspiratorially, "He's always trying to ruin our fun."

At the sound of our laughter, a trio of women ahead on the path looks up, simultaneously narrowing their eyes. One of them—a tall, willowy beauty with waist-length raven hair—whispers to the cute redhead standing next to her, both of them giggling. Then Raven shakes out her hair and marches toward us like a woman on a mission, the other two trotting along behind her.

"Hey," she says when she reaches us, her eyes on Baz and Baz alone. Wrapping his hand in a possessive grip and turning her back on me in a way that tells me pretty much everything I need to know about *her*, she says, "You're supposed to take me to Brew Burger for dinner."

Baz, who seconds ago was cracking up and standing around like he owned the place, is suddenly tense and ornery, his energy taking on a prickly edge. "That's tomorrow night, Carly."

"It is? Oh, right! Sorry! Guess I just couldn't wait to hang out." She tries to lean her head on his shoulder, but he turns away, a movement that leaves her bobbing her head like a chicken.

"Carly," he says, "this is Stevie. She's new here, so, you know. Maybe be... less you?"

"Who?" she asks, still not looking at me, even though Kirin and I are standing right here. Behind her, the two groupies titter and bounce without speaking, and I can't help but think of those bobblehead hood ornaments.

Baz glares at Carly. "What did I just say, Car?"

She makes a show of rolling her eyes, then turns to me as if she's doing me the world's biggest favor. I'm already trying to think of a way to shut this whole thing down when her eyes go wide, her jaw dropping to her chest.

"Oh my Goddess," she breathes. For the last few minutes, she couldn't spare me a single glance, but suddenly she's staring at me like I'm the last Louis Vuitton bag at a half-price sale. "You're... you're spirit-blessed!"

Baz raises an eyebrow at that, but doesn't say anything.

"Sure am," I say with a shrug, as if it's no biggie. As if I have any idea what it *really* means. Everyone else seems to be either impressed, astonished, or both. "How did you know?"

"I have my ways," she coos. "We should totally hang out sometime. Get my number from Baz, okay?"

Her minions frown. I'm beginning to wonder whether they need her permission to speak. Maybe they do—maybe her Tarot affinity is a Queen.

I don't respond, but Carly offers me a blindingly insincere smile anyway, then turns to Baz, pushing out her perfectly pouty lips. "Can you help me with something in my dorm?"

He blows out an annoyed breath. "Yeah, sure. Whatever."

I didn't think it was possible to be jealous over a guy I've known all of seven minutes, but when he turns to follow her, there's a nasty little ping in my chest.

Why, little ping? Why are you doing this to me?

Carly collects her friends and moves on, and Baz turns to look at me over his shoulder, his smile bright once again. "See you around, Little Bird."

"Sure thing." Then, waiting until they're several yards down the path, I call out again. "Hey Baz!"

He turns around, grinning.

"Remember what I said about women!" I give him the thumbs-up. "Think good thoughts!"

He cracks up again, shaking his head before turning back to the bobbleheads and vanishing down the path.

"So that was Carly Kirkpatrick," Kirin says. "Of the Boston Kirkpatricks, also known as the Academy's biggest donors."

"Great. Something tells me she's going to be trouble."

"Good instincts." Kirin removes a small white cloth from his pocket and polishes his glasses, then pops them back on with a fresh smile to match. "So yeah, your suite is in Iron and Bone—you've got the top floor, northwest corner, which means lots of stairs to climb, but you've also got a huge space and a killer view of the Petrified Forest and the Towers of Breath and Blade."

My smile stretches wide.

"Your basics should be in there already—stocked fridge, tablet, laptop, phone. They probably told you to sign in to the student portal—you'll find instructions on how to do that when you boot up the laptop. Oh, there's a credit card, too—it's prepaid every month with your stipend, so you can pick up whatever personal things you need at the stores around campus."

"That's amazing."

"You're telling me. You must know somebody in high places," he teases. "Or you *are* somebody in high places."

"Either way, you're officially in my squad now, so you're good."

"I've never been in a squad before." Kirin laughs, then jumps, his phone buzzing in his pocket. "That's probably about your move." He pulls it out and glances at the screen. "Yeah, it's Cass—Dr. Devane. He says to tell you—well, here."

He flips the phone to show me the message: *Her suite is ready. Please tell Stevie I will deliver the tea order and climbing gear tomorrow afternoon. If she's planning to be away, I'll need temporary access.*

"I assume you know what he's talking about?" he asks.

"I do." My smile is getting wider by the second. Of all my crazy demands, the tea was the most important, the gear a close second. Devane came through for me.

Maybe the good doctor isn't such a cranky old bastard after all.

"You can set a temp access code for him on your external security pad—you'll see it outside the door. It's easy to figure out, but let me know if you need help. I asked them to program my number into your phone. There's a student directory app too, but I wanted you to have me on speed-dial just in case."

"Thank you, Kirin. For the tour, and the latte, and everything back home… If you hadn't been there…"

He steps closer, putting his strong hands on my shoulders, peering at me over the tops of his glasses. "But I *was* there. And now *you're* here. That's what matters. Whatever happens next? We'll deal with it."

I nod, barely keeping the tears in check. It's been a long day—a long week—and I'm starting to crash. "Don't take this as a reflection on your tour-giving skills, but I think I'd like to head upstairs and settle in, maybe take a nap."

"No problem. You want company?"

"Um…" I raise an eyebrow, my face going hot as Jessa's words from that last day float through my mind.

I'm warming up his buns... Maybe one day you'll get to do the same. In bed. Naked.

Kirin shoves a hand through his hair, the tips of his ears turning the color of the river. His embarrassed smile is the most endearing thing I've seen all day. "I meant... shit. I meant company to walk you to your room."

I shake my head and laugh. "I think I can manage. But I'll keep the offer in mind next time I'm up for some naptime company."

Now *Kirin* raises an eyebrow.

Oh, lips. Why are you always moving in such stupidly mortifying ways?

In the end, Kirin walks me partway, just to the entrance of Iron and Bone. Overhead, the black flag bearing the house insignia hangs proudly, flanked by two stately gargoyles.

"You good?" Kirin asks.

"Not completely," I answer honestly, reaching for the door to my new home-away-from-home. "But I have a feeling I *will* be."

I just have to figure out how to learn magick after living twenty-three years in the mundane darkness, decipher Mom's cryptic prophecies before everyone freaking *dies*, steer clear of the bobbleheads, and—most importantly—convince my libido to run for the hills, batten down the hatches, and take cover, shoving Kirin, Baz, and Dr. Devane so far into the friend zone they'll need to take a fucking bus just to say good morning to me.

Yeah, I got this... Said no one, ever.

TWENTY

STEVIE

Dr. Devane totally lied to me.

This isn't a college dorm suite. It's a Goddess-damned luxury apartment straight out of Architectural Digest, with red Spanish tile flooring and thick, hand-woven rugs, walls the color of freshly churned butter, and furniture as gorgeous as it is cozy. Tarot-themed paintings hang on every wall, and there's a bright, oversized novelty deck on the coffee table next to a stack of board games. Throw pillows in reds, turquoises, and oranges accent the couch and chairs in the living room, which opens into an island kitchen with granite countertops, stainless-steel appliances, and blonde oak cabinets. Huge, floor-to-ceiling windows dominate the north and west walls, giving me a million-dollar view across the Petrified Forest and the Towers of Breath and Blade, just like Kirin said.

Standing in the middle of the living room, I feel like a peasant who accidentally wandered into the palace, and though the suite unlocked for me when I placed my hand on the security scanner outside, I keep looking back at the door, half-expecting Trello to show up and tell me they've made a terrible mistake.

After a good ten minutes, when it seems no one's coming to kick me out after all, I finally allow myself to venture as far as the bedroom.

Make that bed*rooms*. Two of them, fully furnished, connected by a huge white-and-turquoise bathroom complete with jetted soaking tub, separate shower, and dual sinks.

At the edge of the tub, there's a tray with a few candles, a jar of bath salts, and a book with a post-it stuck to the front. I recognize it from that day in Kettle Black—the paperback Kirin was reading, with the old farmhouse on the cover. He must've asked Dr. Devane to leave it for me.

The invitation still stands, the note says, and my heart does a little flip, remembering all the good things about that day, those sweet moments before the cops showed up and hauled me out of my life.

I just thought it might be fun to hang out. You know, outside of Kettle Black. We can talk about...books! Or, you know, anything you like. What do you like? Other than tea, I mean. Okay, I'm rambling. Save me, Stevie. Say something before I make an even bigger fool of myself...

I leave the book on the tray for now, but grab the note, bringing it into the bedroom and sticking it on the dresser mirror, my cheeks aching from the dopey smile on my face.

Reflected in the mirror, set up on a white wooden desk

in the corner, I spot some computer equipment and—thank Goddess—a phone.

Jessa!

I power on the device, letting out a little victory yelp when it actually blinks to life with my name on the screen. Just as Kirin promised, his number is already programmed in, along with the office numbers for Dr. Devane, Anna Trello, and Professor Phaines. They've included a few of the campus restaurants too, and there—between Hopscotch Brewery and Jumpin' Jack's Java—is a name that brings tears to my eyes.

Jessamine Velasquez.

I hit the button for video chat, holding my breath as I wait for it to connect.

"You're alive!" Jessa's smile takes up the whole screen, tears running down her cheeks, her perfect eyeliner wings melting before my eyes. "Blazing fucking *balls,* Starla Eve Milan, I'm going to kill you! I would've killed you a lot harder if you were dead, but I'm still—"

"Yeah, I miss you too, Jessa."

"Less missing," she says with a laugh, sniffing and swiping her hand across her eyes, "more talking. Kirin told me you were safe, but I didn't let myself believe it until now. I need to know everything."

I curl up on one of the soft chairs in the living room—holy shitcakes, I have an actual living room!—and pull a fleece throw over my shoulders, settling in for the tale.

In a breathless rush, I tell her everything—prison, Dr. Devane, Mom's prophecies, Lala, the Academy. My vision and the spirit-blessed thing, all the people I've met so far, this insane apartment. By the time I stop blathering on, the evening sun is no more than a memory, a pale purple mist creeping across the Towers and forest beyond my windows.

"Your turn," I tell her, stretching and heading into the kitchen for a snack. The fridge and pantry are well-stocked, but I grab the first thing I see—a box of crackers and a jar of natural peanut butter. "How are you holding up? What happened after I left? How's... how's Rita?"

Jessa's face falls, her eyes watering once again. "It's not great here, Stevie. Rita's a mess, to be expected—the town is really rallying behind her, doing fundraisers and stuff. But you should know... She doesn't believe for a minute it was you. She said she knows you always loved Luke like a brother. She wanted me to know that. When she heard the news tonight about your so-called suicide, she was devastated."

My throat tightens. *Poor Rita.*

"I wish I could talk to her," I say, "but that's impossible now. I'm not sure when—or if—I'll ever be able to come back."

Jessa nods, tucking a lock of black hair behind her ear. She looks exhausted; I can only imagine what it's been like for her.

"Stevie, I'm sorry to say this, but since the arrest and the uproar about witchcraft..." She closes her eyes, shakes her head as if she can't believe what she's about to tell me.

I know what's coming next, and I do what I can to brace myself.

"No one's been in Kettle Black aside from Rita," she continues. "The landlord said they have to re-let the space. He was nice enough to give me till the fifteenth to get everything cleared out, but there was nothing I could say to change his mind. To change *anyone's* mind."

I've got no words for it, nothing but a sad resignation.

Kettle Black—my parents' dream, the place Jessa and I basically grew up in, the place where we spent more of our time than any other place in Tres Búhos—is gone.

I look around the apartment, taking in the award-winning decor, the stunning views, the beautiful artwork. I think about Dr. Devane and Anna Trello, the professor, Kirin, Baz, the other students. I think about the campus shops and the cafés and the karaoke.

I think about that day up on the Grande, lighting my palo santo, paging through Mom's grimoire, still trying to convince myself that I could live a normal, mundane existence.

What a difference a week makes.

"I'm so sorry, Stevie. I hate that it's come to this. I hate that you're all the way over there and I'm here and I can't even hug you."

"Good thing you're so extra I can feel the love all the way over here." I smile, drying my own tears. "Thank you for trying."

"I've got all the T-shirts and stuff, the memorabilia. I'm going to hang on to it for you, okay? With all your other things from home."

"What are you going to do for work? For a roommate?"

Jessa blows a breath into her bangs, looking up at the ceiling to keep the fresh tears at bay. "I've decided to go back home. To Mexico."

The news is shocking, in the way that sudden change always is. But it's not surprising—not really. She always talked about going back. If it wasn't for my parents' death, I think she would've returned soon after high school, gone to college there, built a life close to her big, boisterous *familia*. But then the accident happened and I was such a mess and she just… she simply refused to leave my side. Even after I was able to function again, to work, to go places other than our "estate" and the cemetery, she still refused to leave me.

"You're my wifey, *loca*," she used to say. "Stop trying to get rid of me."

"I'm happy for you," I say now. "I feel like this was meant to happen. Maybe not exactly this way, but… I don't know. Sometimes things have to blow up in your face in order for you to find the good shit underneath."

"If you say so, Confucius." Jessa laughs, and I can't help but crack up, too.

"I think… I think this is going to be good for both of us," I tell her. "Not that I love the idea of you being in a totally different country from me, but still."

"Different country? Girl, you're basically in another dimension!"

"We're just going to have to figure out a schedule for vacation visits. Because you have *got* to see this place."

With the serious stuff behind us, I grab my box of crackers and take her on a full video tour, walking her through each room, posing in the soaking tub, showing her the views and the dishes and the little cactus- and star-shaped soaps in the soap dish. I show her the bedroom I'm reserving for her, and the paintings of the four Tarot aces that hang over my bed, reminding me to treat each new day like the blessing that it is.

And then, when I've covered every square inch and flicked every switch and played with the cards and games in the living room, Jessa says, "I want to see what's in your dresser."

"Nothing. I haven't gone shopping yet."

"I think you should check anyway. Top drawer, maybe?"

"Jessamine Marie... What are you up to?"

"Who, *me*?"

Laughing, I head into the bedroom and pull open the top drawer.

"Looks like T-shirts and leggings, some underwear... I guess they got me a few things to hold me over until I can get to the shops."

"Okay, try the second drawer, then."

I do as she asks, sliding open the next drawer.

And there, nestled in tissue paper, is my mother's grimoire.

I gasp, my hand flying to my mouth. "But... How did... *What*?"

"After they took you away that day," she says, "I hid it. I didn't know what the hell was happening, but something told me to keep that book safe. When more cops showed up later to search for evidence of your so-called crimes, I was glad I'd listened to that little voice inside. Anyway, when Kirin told me they were going to basically smuggle you into the Academy, I asked him to give it to you."

"That was sweet of him. And you. And just... Wow. I don't know what to say."

Jessa's smile goes from touching to conspiracy theory in five seconds flat. "So yeah, speaking of Kirin... I think it's safe to say the boy likes you."

"He's not a boy, he's a man."

"Even better."

"And he's just a friend. A man-friend."

"Mmm-hmm. I think we're well past the denial stage here, Stevie. Besides, I've got a feeling about you and Mr. Cinnamon Buns—I always have. And you know I'm never wrong about these things."

"Okay, okay, you've made your point." I roll my eyes, but I can't help the stupid grin on my face.

I close the drawer, saving Mom's book for later, and let out a sigh.

"So here I am," I say, more to myself than to Jessa. "Magick school."

"So there you are," she says. "Magick school."

"I have no idea what I'm doing. For eighteen years, I followed the map my parents set out for me—Tres Búhos, you, Kettle Black. After they died, I just... I just kept following it, you know? Even though I knew something was missing. I guess I thought it was the only way to keep them with me."

"You'll always carry them in your heart. But it's like you said earlier, about stuff blowing up and being good for us even if it sucks in the moment. This whole thing with Luke and prison and the Academy... Well, maybe it's time for you to ditch that old map and start blazing your own trail."

At her words, a heaviness slides off my shoulders, and something inside me sparks up. It's a feeling of hope, of newness, of opportunity.

Everything I knew before is gone.

And now, for the first time in twenty-three years, I have a chance to find out what else is out there for me.

"Hey, I want you to promise me something," Jessa says. "Promise me you'll make the most of your time there, okay? I'm not talking about learning magick—that goes without saying. I'm talking about people."

"What do you mean?"

"No one knows you at the Academy—not even Kirin. You get to start all over. So do that. Jump in, and don't hold yourself back anymore. You're in a magickal place, surrounded by witches and mages, by people who *get* you —but only if you let them in."

"Hmm. I think all this Oprah talk is just code for you telling me to hook up with Kirin so I can recount all the dirty details later."

"Well, *obviously*. Wait, *are* there dirty details? Already? You holding out on me, Milan?"

"Never," I say with a wink.

"Seriously, though," she says. "I want you to find love. Friendship kind of love. Connection. Even if it's with just one other person. You deserve that, Stevie. So I'm asking you to promise me you'll put yourself out there. Take risks. Open your heart and give people a chance to know how fucking awesome you are."

Goddess, the whole idea of it is terrifying. Opening my heart, trusting people...

Looking out across the Towers, now just dark purple fingers stretching into the night, I can't help but think of the Void. The inescapable compulsion to jump, the disastrous ending.

The idea of love and friendship feels a lot like that.

"Hey," she says at my silence. "You've got this, *loca*. You know that, right?"

My stomach ties itself into a pretzel. "Maybe you shouldn't have so much faith in me."

"Maybe *you* shouldn't have so little. Look, making friends is going to be so easy for you. You're amazing at reading people, you make a mean-ass cup of tea, and you're hilarious and fun, to name a few. Oh, and let's not forget your best selling point."

I try for an epic sigh, but my best friend is the reigning queen of pep talks, and a smile is already breaking through my scowl.

"Hmm." I hold the phone out and show her my backside. "You *must* be talking about my great ass."

"I'm *talking*," she says, rolling her eyes, "about the fact that you're so damn brilliant and lovable you could charm the pants off pants, let alone a bunch of college kids and stuffy old professors. Now stop freaking out, trust in your awesomeness, and show me some of that Stevie Milan sparkle, because for the first time in your life, you're in a place where you don't legally have to hide it. Flaunt that shit, girl!"

Caught up in her endless cheer, I slap a high-five and a fist bump against the phone, then I snap my fingers, calling up a burst of silver fire. The flames dance in my palm for just a moment before I purse my lips and blow, scattering sparks like dandelion seeds.

"*That's* what I'm talking about," she says. "Now promise me."

"Okay, *chica*. For you, I promise to try."

"No. Not for me. For *you*."

"Right. For me. I promise for me. I fucking love you, Jess. You know that?"

"And I love you. More than the mooooon," she says dramatically. "More than double-dark chocolate scones with peanut butter icing."

"I miss your baking already." I laugh, then the water-works start up again. "What am I going to do without you?"

"Stevie, I'll tell you what." Squaring her shoulders, staring straight into the camera, she says firmly, "You're gonna walk straight out onto that campus—every single day for the next four years—and learn your magick like a fucking boss bitch. And you're gonna own your power, be ruthlessly unapologetic about it, and rock that shit like the Goddess-damned, sparkly-ass, witch queen of the desert you are. *That's* what you're gonna do. Deal?"

"Deal," I say emphatically.

Outside my floor-to-ceiling windows, far beyond the Petrified Forest of Iron and Bone, lightning flickers across the purple sky, and I press my hand to the glass and smile, claiming that lightning for myself. A confirmation that I'm on the right path. A gift from the universe.

And a warning to anyone who dares to stand in my way.

TWENTY-ONE

KIRIN

The lightning flickers once, twice, three times. That's the signal.

I pull the black hood low over my eyes, whisper a cloaking spell, and head out into the night, slipping unseen into the Petrified Forest of Iron and Bone.

I find two of the others already assembled at the Fool's Grave, a sacred cave hidden deep in the forest and almost entirely surrounded by steep, rocky outcroppings. This far north, the only way through the maze of rock is a single narrow passageway, invisible to all but the four, guarded by the magick and blood of the Brotherhood.

The wall sconces have already been lit, the fire throwing long shadows on the cave walls.

"How did the tour go?" Cass asks, the concern in his eyes a dead giveaway, despite his attempts at playing it cool. "I trust she's settling in all right?"

"She's a little overwhelmed," I reply, "which is to be

SPELLS OF IRON AND BONE

expected. She wanted some time alone. But she was in good spirits when I left her at the dorms."

"She'd better be in good spirits," Baz says with a graceless snort. "She's living pretty large for a first-year. Better than any of us ever got. Hell, I've been here for years and I still haven't achieved sixth floor, corner room status."

"Yeah, but you're an asshole," I remind him.

Baz grins. "The Academy has a non-discrimination policy."

"Not against assholes."

"I'm here, I'm here!" Ansel's voice echoes down the winding narrow canyon, the rest of him tumbling in soon after.

"You'd think after all these years he'd figure out how to be on time," Cass says. Then, to our latecomer, "Thank you for joining us, Mr. McCauley. I hope we're not pulling you away from anything important."

His cheeks are red with exertion, clashing with his ginger hair, which is now sticking up in every direction. "That last mile's a bitch. I kept getting turned around."

"Christ, Ani." Baz grabs the back of Ansel's neck, gives him a playful shake. "You need a GPS chip embedded in your skull."

"Now that we're all assembled..." Cass clears his throat, the warning glint in his eye letting us know there's no more time for jokes.

As the oldest and most experienced of the Brotherhood —at least in our current incarnations—he's taken point on the matter, and we've gladly let him. Cass is a good man. A hardass at times, but he's led us this far, and I trust him to see it through. We all do.

Pulling our black hoods low over our brows, we gather around the altar, a chest-high pillar of petrified wood, the top polished smooth from years of ritual use, carved with a large pentacle. In that moment, a sacred hush falls over the space, and all other thoughts and concerns evaporate.

Cass pulls a silver athame from his robe, whispers the incantation against the blade, then draws it quickly across his palm.

Each of us follows suit with our own blades, then, as one, we clench our fists over the top of the altar. Blood fills the channels, the grooved pentacle glowing red for a moment, then clearing, our blood absorbed by the earth, leaving the surface smooth and clean once again.

"Who gathers here as bonded brothers?" Cass asks, his voice clear and commanding.

The rest of us respond in unison: "We, the Keepers of the Grave."

"Who spills his blood as a symbol of our commitment to one another and in the service and protection of the First?"

"We, the Keepers of the Grave."

"Who vows, by his life or his death, by his silence or his words, in this and all incarnations henceforth, to protect the one true source?"

"We, the Keepers of the Grave."

"We, the Keepers of the Grave," Cass echoes. He then turns away from the altar and presses his bloody palm against a rock that juts out from the wall. Beneath it, a small alcove illuminates, revealing the large black book tucked inside.

We call it the Book of Reckoning, though officially it has no name.

Officially, it doesn't exist. Not this copy, nor the others of its kind used in rituals such as this at the other Academies, in other times.

But now he retrieves it and opens it on the altar, and each of us signs our name with the tips of our blood-soaked athames. After the signing, Cass places a Tarot card in the center of the page—The King of Swords—and speaks another spell.

> Let our thoughts be true, our messages clear
> Both words and intent are recorded here
> Leave nothing unwritten, no secrets to bear
> Among brothers in blood, all things are shared.

The card glows faintly, and when we speak again, our words will appear on the parchment, then vanish, recorded for posterity, hidden to all but members of our sacred order.

The robes, the blood magick, the King of Swords... It's the same ritual we've done since the beginning.

Old-fashioned, maybe, but we do it anyway. We do it because we must. Because it's the only way to ensure the secrecy of our mission.

Even at Arcana Academy, warded against outside intrusion, spelled to keep our secrets close, the rocks still listen with eager ears, the skies still whisper with treacherous mouths.

"Kirin," Cass says, "please update us on your research."

"I've reviewed the library's remaining historical records on the Academy itself, including personal correspondences between the founders and the architects, as well as to and from family members during the initial build and dedication. I loaded everything relevant into the database, cross-referencing all dates against previous documentation mentioning the Book of Shadow and Mists, including fictionalized accounts written around the time we believe it disappeared. I also wrote some new macros, trying to find patterns or anything I may have missed from my manual review."

"Wow," Baz says. "Kirin, I had no idea you were so dedicated to the mission... of never, ever getting laid again."

"Hey. Witches dig smart mages," I retort, then continue with my update. "I've got several more volumes of the architectural plans to review, but if the builders knew about the book or planned some secret cache, they don't mention it to anyone else, or to each other. Those guys were fucking vaults."

"Maybe not." Baz leans against the rock wall, folding his robed arms in front of him. "Maybe they don't talk about it because they truly didn't know about it. Guys, if the book were here—anywhere *near* here—we would've found it by now. Someone would have. Things like that don't stay hidden, and they sure as hell don't stay secret."

SPELLS OF IRON AND BONE

"It's here," Cass says. "Somewhere on this campus. I just… I can feel it. The key to finding it *must* be hidden in the prophecies. Now that Starla Milan is here, things will be set in motion."

"Why is Anna so sure the little jailbird can crack the code on Melissa's research?" Baz asks.

"Blind hope, perhaps. A hope we share." Cass pushes his hood back, revealing a grim face, the lines around his eyes made deeper by the torchlight. "She's Melissa's daughter. If she can't do it, there's no witch alive who can, and we're back to the drawing board."

"And more databases," I say. Which, under normal circumstances, I'd get a little hard-on about. But in this case, time is ticking.

Ani shakes his head, his normally cheerful demeanor fading. "More witches and mages are getting caught up in this net every day. We have to find that book."

"I'm well aware," Cass says. "All the more reason to be sure Starla has everything she needs to do the translations."

"Do you think she already knows about the book?" Ani asks. "The artifacts? Any of it?"

"No way," I say. "I took her through the whole campus today. We talked about the names of the houses, of course, and she was curious about the legends. But her questions and reactions weren't out of the ordinary. Certainly not the behavior of a woman keeping secrets of this magnitude."

"And the whole time you were with her in Tres Búhos," Baz says, "you never saw anything freaky? No spellcraft, no strange customers, no secret meetings in the back room?"

"I wasn't spying on her, Baz," I say. "I wasn't with her 24/7. But the time I spent in her café, or the few times I saw her around town, no, there wasn't anything strange or magickal going on. As far as I know, the woman hadn't even touched serious magick until she was attacked by a mage possessing her friend, and we all know how that ended."

The group falls silent, all of us pondering the seriousness of the situation. Stevie's story is tragic, but she's not the first witch to be targeted by dark magick in recent years. Unless we can protect the Book of Shadow and Mists and the arcane artifacts, she won't be the last.

But how do we protect something we can't even find?

Something most witches and mages believe is no more than a legend?

"I don't think she knows about any of this," Cass agrees. "Beyond the immediate threats of the attacks on the magickal community at large—something she's only just beginning to see, thanks to her personal experience—she's as new to our world as a child raised by wolves."

"The attacks are a symptom," I say. "She knows nothing of the deeper meanings of the prophecies, or her importance here."

"So, here's a thought." Baz steps away from the wall, joining us at the altar again. "Which, feel free to ignore, but... Is anyone planning to, you know, clue the little bird in? Or are we just going to let her stumble blindly through, hoping she doesn't unleash hell along the way?"

"She'll be informed if and when the need arises," Cass

says. "The less she knows right now, the safer she is. The safer we all are. Agreed?"

"Agreed," Ani and I say.

Baz sighs. "Yeah, okay. I agree. But for the record, I don't like it. Feels like we're leading her to the slaughter."

"Nothing could be further from the truth," Cass says.

"I'll do what I can to guide her research," I say. "Keep her away from anything that could endanger her or the mission, beyond the prophecies and whatever resources she needs to understand them."

"Excellent." Cass looks to Ansel. "Ani, I'd like you to reach out to her as well, student to student. Offer her some support, a shoulder to lean on. She could use a friend here, too."

"I've got it covered," I say. "She already knows me."

"As a spy and traitor," Baz points out. "No offense."

The accusation stings, but that's only because it's true.

"Yes," I say, "things were a little rocky after she found out about my involvement with the Academy, but we've talked it out. I think she'll come to trust me."

"It's not about trust," Cass says. "It's about proximity. You're a graduate student, Kirin. She's a first-year. Aside from your work together at the library, you won't have an opportunity to keep a close eye on her."

"She's a first-year," I repeat. "Exactly. So Baz and Ani won't be in any of her classes, either."

"We'll make sure they are," Cass says. Then, to the duo in question, "You boys up for a little do-over on your core curriculum? I'll have Trello work something out with the other professors, head off any questions."

"No problem," Ani says.

Baz flashes a thumbs-up and a big, goofy grin. "Education is my middle name."

"Dickhead is your middle name," I grumble, but ultimately, Cass is right. This isn't about my pointless little crush anymore—feelings that can only lead to more trouble. It's about keeping Stevie safe. It's about honoring our oath.

"Operation Friend Zone starts now," Ani says with a mock salute.

"Friend Zone?" Baz looks mortally wounded. "Why rule out the possibilities before we've even—"

"Mr. Redgrave." Cass levels him with a deadly glare. "Behave yourself. We can't risk this mission on account of your insatiable appetites. Particularly where Miss Milan is concerned."

His tone is harsher than usual, a hot, protective ire swirling in the wake of his words that makes me wonder just how close he and Stevie got on their post-prison road trip.

Before I can let my imagination run too far down that path, Cass shakes his head and says, "There's more. It seems she's already bonded with a familiar. A snowy owl."

"Shit. I've seen it," I tell them. "A snowy owl appeared outside her tea shop seconds before the police arrived that day. It felt like a warning. I knew it was magickal, but didn't think to associate it with a familiar. Stevie can barely conjure witchfire."

"That's... concerning." Baz glances at Cass. "I thought you said she was totally uninitiated?"

"She is," Cass confirms. "A familiar is unexpected at this early stage, but it's not unheard of for a spirit-blessed. I don't believe she can conjure it at will, though, and the bond isn't yet strong enough for it to tune into her instincts with any reliability."

"She's a ticking time bomb," Baz says. "That much power, no idea how to wield it, how to rein it in?"

"We'll do our best to guide her," Cass says. "Until then, we can't reveal too much. She's overwhelmed enough as it is."

I rub my forehead, tension throbbing behind my eyes. Stevie thought her arrest turned her life upside down, that being forced to leave Tres Búhos was the worst thing to happen since her parents' deaths.

But the poor woman has no idea how much darker and deadlier things are about to get.

"You should've relocated her when you had the chance," I snap. "At least then she might've had a fighting chance."

Cass doesn't take the bait, just places a reassuring hand on my shoulder. "We need her here, Kirin," he says gently, and when I look into his eyes, I see the same concern that I'm feeling. The same fears. "You've known that from the start."

"Doesn't make it any easier to swallow," I say.

"At least we can protect her here."

"Can we? We don't even know where the danger will

ultimately come from. Only that it *will* come. And we're no closer to figuring this out than we were a month ago. A year. Five years."

"But we *are* closer," Ani says. "She's here, right? And Trello seems to think she can unlock the prophecies. So for now, we hold on to that. Deal?"

We all agree, the tension falling away once again.

Ani's got a gift—the man's like living sunshine. Hard to stay wound up when he's around, spreading that perpetual optimism.

"We need to exercise extreme caution," Cass says. "I don't want anything provoking her familiar-response magick. If she feels threatened or backed into a corner, if her life is endangered in any way... Hell, even if she's upset or anxious about something, the magick could surface and attempt to protect her. That's fine in situations where her life is truly at stake, but right now, she has no control over it whatsoever."

"Good point," Baz says. "Last thing we need is her blowing up the dorms because she finds one of Chef Milbey's cat hairs in her meatloaf."

"It's just seasoning," Ani and I say with a laugh, repeating one of Chef's oft-quoted responses.

"But it *is* a good point," I say. "We need to keep her relaxed, focused on her work, and safe."

"Right," Cass says. "I don't want anyone to know how powerful our witch truly is. Including the witch herself."

"A familiar. Fuck me." Baz shoves a hand into his hair,

scratching his head. "How can she be so powerful, and so… so fucking ignorant?"

It's all I can do not to deck the guy. A common feeling where Baz is concerned, but one I'm in no mood to indulge in tonight. We've got bigger concerns.

"She was kept in the dark her entire life," I say, a bit defensively. But what the hell does Baz know? He's spent all of five minutes with Stevie, most of that time staring at her breasts. "Her parents told her just enough to whet her curiosity, then forbade her from ever practicing her magick or even so much as cracking a book on the subject. And then they died. I get the feeling she's spent every day since then trying to resist the temptation. And now she's got no choice. She *has* to learn magick. To open up all the old Pandora's Boxes her parents tried to nail shut. So ease up on her, okay?"

Baz raises a curious eyebrow, his eyes dancing with some new light.

"Interesting," he says.

"If you took the time to talk to her instead of just hitting on her, you might learn something interesting about her, too."

Baz rolls his eyes. "So Weber's got a thing for the jail-bird, and we're supposed to just trust—"

"I don't have a *thing* for her. I'm just saying we shouldn't make assumptions about her past or judge her for something she had no control over. She's smart as hell and she's eager to learn. And from what I've seen, she's going to make one hell of a witch. One we're all going to be thanking one day for saving our asses."

Baz opens his mouth, thinks twice, shuts it. After a beat, he shakes his head and says, "I don't get it, man. Her parents were basically Academy royalty. Her mother…" He glances at the Book of Reckoning, but whatever he's thinking about Stevie's mother, he keeps it to himself. "What the fuck happened? And why did they hide all this from her? They had to know it would come out eventually. She's a spirit-blessed witch, for fuck's sake. It doesn't just go dormant."

"I'm sure they believed they had no choice," Cass says. "I don't know the details of the situation here, what drove them to leave. Trello refuses to give more than the barest of sketches. But her parents… I'm sure they were looking out for her."

"Looking out for her?" Baz laughs, but there's nothing teasing or lighthearted about his tone now. His eyes, red and menacing in the torchlight, spark with a smoldering danger I feel all the way down to my bones. "Then they should've done everything in their power to keep her away from here."

With that ominous end, Cass packs up the book in silence, and we file out of the Fool's Grave and into the darkness, our minds echoing with the part Baz *didn't* say.

Stevie's parents should've done everything in their power to keep her away from *us*.

TWENTY-TWO

STEVIE

Wow. Declaring oneself a badass witch-queen is a surefire way to work up an appetite. After saying goodbye to Jessa, and—okay, fine, practicing a few Wonder Woman poses in the bathroom mirror—I abandon my crackers-and-peanut-butter dinner plans and head down to Smash, one of the Iron and Bone cafés.

It's a mashed potato bar. Seriously. With a dozen kinds of potatoes and at least a hundred different stir-ins and toppings. And, the pièce de résistance, a big-ass golden chalice overflowing with five streams of melted gourmet cheeses.

Let that settle in.

Five. Streams. Of melted. Gourmet. Cheeses.

No wonder non-magickal humans want us dead. Clearly, witches and mages are fucking next-level geniuses poised to take over the world.

I load up a plate, starting small with just three of the

twelve potato options—brown sugar sweet potatoes, scallion-and-walnut white potatoes, and red potatoes whipped with dill. For toppings I've got sour cream, bacon, buttered corn, buttered peas, and some sunflower seeds for good health, along with a smattering of things I can't even identify but holy *balls*, do they smell amazing.

I'm all about the adventure tonight.

I've just gone two rounds with the fountain, cheese dripping over the sides of my plate, when I nearly run smack into two women who've just loaded up at the toppings bar.

"I'm so sorry!" I swivel my plate around just in time to avoid a collision. "I guess I'm just distracted by all the cheese."

"Yes," one of the women says with a big, friendly smile, her braids practically bouncing with cheer. She's wearing a pendant in the shape of a teardrop, and when she laughs, it winks against her dark brown skin. "We heard you moaning all the way across the café and had to come say hi. Clearly, you're our people."

"I should probably feel embarrassed about the moaning," I say, "but I don't. Not one bit."

She and her friend both crack up.

"I'm Isla," she says. "This is Nat. We're first-years, too."

"Hey," Nat says, balancing a plate piled with sweet potatoes and toasted marshmallows. She's got shoulder-length hair, dyed silver and shot through with streaks of bright purple, blue, and teal—the kind of haircut that just screams, "I'm way more fun at parties than you are."

I immediately like them both.

"Is my utter newbie-ness that obvious?" I ask.

"They say the moaning subsides by year two," Nat says.

"We'll see about that." I laugh, even as cheese drips all over my hands. "I'm Stevie."

"Come sit with us," Isla says, and—with my promise to Jessa fresh on my mind—that's all the invitation I need.

We settle into a corner booth beneath a huge framed painting of two foil-dressed potato people kissing, and I reach out for the women's energies, confirming my earlier assessment. Warmth and kindness, a genuine desire to meet new friends. If they'd just come into Kettle Black, I'd offer them a cup of chocolate lavender tea dusted with crushed vanilla bean, the brew rich and calming, perfect for sipping over long conversations with friends.

"Is today your first day on campus?" Nat asks me. "We haven't seen you around."

"Yeah, it was a last-minute decision," I tell them. "It's… it's kind of a crazy story, actually."

So crazy, I don't even know where to start.

"Ooh, cliffhanger," Isla says.

"It's my way of keeping you coming back for more." I give them a playful wink. "I'll have to dole out the details sparingly—a little more each day until I've totally reeled you in."

I pop a spoonful of gouda-drenched sweet potatoes into my mouth, trying to buy myself some more time. These are the first friends I've made here outside Kirin and Doc, and truthfully, the jury's still out on whether Doc is actually friend material. I don't want to scare Isla and Nat off before we've even exchanged numbers with tales of murder charges and prison breaks.

"Right now," I tell them, going for the diversion, "my plan is to basically make out with these potatoes, then figure out my shopping list. I've got jack in the way of clothing and school supplies, and classes start on Monday."

"We're planning to hit the Promenade tomorrow after breakfast," Nat says. "You should come with us."

"Yeah?"

"Come for breakfast, too," Isla says, sweeping her braids behind her shoulders to keep them out of her potatoes. "Meet us at Broken Yolks at nine—it's the diner over at the Breath and Blade dorms. Gotta start strong if you want to keep up with Nat on a shopping excursion."

Jessa would totally laugh at me if she could see this. I *hate* shopping—truly. Back home, my wardrobe consisted mostly of jeans and Kettle Black T-shirts, and I got all my groceries delivered from the café suppliers.

But then I think of the sleek black credit card sitting on top of my dresser upstairs, and suddenly the idea doesn't sound so bad. I've got a feeling shopping is a lot more fun when you're doing it with someone else's money.

"All right," I say. "I'm in."

"Stevie! Hey, girl!" Across the café, Carly Kirkpatrick waves at me from the entrance, flanked again by her minions—the cute redhead, who's now wearing a rather un-cute scowl, and the other woman I saw on the path earlier—a pretty Latina who looks like she could be Jessa's taller, snobbier sister. There's a fourth woman with them now, too, with pierced eyebrows and pale pink hair twisted into a messy bun.

"Oh no," Nat whispers, rolling her eyes as the quad saunters our way. "It's the Claires."

"Claires? I thought her name was Carly?"

"It is," Nat says, "but they're all—"

She cuts off as the group descends upon us in a cloud of expensive perfume and a collective mojo that can only be described as peak superbitch.

"Stevie, I'm so glad I ran into you here!" Carly slides her ass onto the edge of our table, forcing Isla to move her plate out of the way or risk a butt-cheek imprint in her guacamole-infused mashed potatoes. "I think we may have gotten off on the wrong foot before. I was *super* PMS-y, and Baz has a way of pushing *all* my buttons, if you know what I mean."

She laughs and tosses her glossy black hair over her shoulder, the ends of it dragging through Isla's dinner.

"Carly, do you know Isla and Nat?" I ask with a pointed glare, hoping she'll take the hint and get her perky little butt off the table.

Carly glances down at Isla and nods, but doesn't move or say hello or even crack a smile.

Turning her gaze back on me, she says, "The girls and I were wondering if you'd thought about pledging a coven this semester?"

"There's no pledging here," Nat says, grabbing Isla's plate and moving it away.

"There is now," Carly says. "We can't let just *anyone* into the coven, *Matt*."

"It's *Nat*," Nat and I say at the same time.

"So anyway," Carly says, "our coven has certain *standards*, magickal and otherwise." The way she says standards makes it clear she thinks this table is lacking in that department. "We expect each member to bring her own natural gifts to the sisterhood, and pledge complete loyalty."

"Oh, yeah?" I ask, feigning interest. Call me cynical, but something tells me the more I can find out about these women, the better I can defend myself. "What are your natural gifts?"

Carly lights up as if I've just offered her her own reality show. "I'm clairsentient, so I basically know things before they happen. I've been that way since I was born. Literally—I predicted my own birthday in the womb."

"Isn't that something?" I ask Nat.

"It's something, all right," Nat grumbles. "Not sure what, but something."

Plowing on, Carly nods at the redhead standing beside her and says, "Amelia is clairvoyant, so she sees things, like movies in her mind. Emory hears things."

"I don't *hear* things, Carly," the one who reminds me of Jessa says, clearly annoyed. "It's called clairaudience. Aural premonitions."

"Right," Carly says, then thumbs at the pink-haired woman with all the eyebrow rings—at least six on each side, as far as I can count. "And Blue here—"

"Your name is Blue?" I ask, blinking up at her pink hair.

"Is that a problem?" she replies, the challenge obvious. She's definitely gunning for a fight, even though she looks like she weighs about a hundred pounds at most, twenty of which is the hardware in her eyebrows.

I'm pretty sure I could crack her between my thighs like a walnut, but I'm not much for fighting. Besides, I'm not about to ruin my cheesy potatoes over this middle-school bullshit.

"It's a cool name," I say with a smile. "That's all."

"Anyway," Carly says, "Blue can taste things. Clair—"

"Clairgustance," I say, familiar with the term. I'm pretty sure my mother had a bit of that power. She used to wake up sometimes, dreaming of her late grandmother, tasting the woman's lemon meringue pie. "Sounds like you've collected the whole set."

Nat chokes back a laugh, but Carly and her aptly named Claires don't seem to appreciate my sense of humor.

Eh, no accounting for taste.

I pop a spoonful of brown sugar sweet potatoes into my mouth, wondering just how much more bizarre this conversation is going to get, and also, whether I should just get a stent put in my arteries now, or wait until the cheese completely blocks off blood flow to my heart.

"Anyway," Carly says, "I was talking with the girls, and we decided you should totally join."

"But... I don't have a clair," I reply, though I suppose that's not strictly true. I'm pretty sure my empathic skills rank somewhere on that list, but I'm not about to divulge that to Carly.

"Everyone has special abilities, or they wouldn't be at the Academy." Carly rolls her eyes, then smiles, a bright grin that doesn't reach her cold blue gaze. "It's just that some people aren't as developed. In my household, we were expected to take our magick seriously, so I started private lessons at age two. But I understand not everyone has the financial means for something like that."

I glance at Isla and Nat. Isla's glaring hotly at our visitor, but Nat's got her eyes downcast, her cheeks dark with shame. Something tells me this isn't their first run-in with the Queen of the Claires.

I want to tell Carly to fuck her merry little way all the way off to someone else's dorm, but her energy holds me back. As much as I don't want to feel it, I can't help it; for all Carly's bluster and bullshit, there's a deep sadness in her, a longing for connection that she's apparently not getting from her minions.

So, in an effort toward diplomacy—and not making enemies on my first day—I offer a smile and say, "Why don't you guys pull up some chairs and join us here? We can all get to know each other a little better, start the new year off strong. Strength in numbers, you know?"

There's a spark of hope—I can feel the shift in Carly's energy. But then Emory clears her throat and bumps her shoulder against Carly's, and Carly tosses her dark waves and laughs. She actually laughs, as if the suggestion that we all get to know each other is the most ridiculous idea she's ever heard.

"We're a coven," Blue pipes in, twisting one of her eyebrow rings. "We've already got the numbers."

"Suit yourselves, then," I say, then turn back to Isla and Nat. "But if you wouldn't mind un-planting your ass from our table, we'd like to finish our meal."

"Did you just... Did you seriously just say that to me?" Carly fumes.

"As someone who quote-unquote simply *knows* things," I say, "you can probably figure that out yourself."

A chill ripples through the room.

And just like that, it seems I've chosen sides, planted my flag, and flipped a giant middle finger to the most powerful self-appointed coven at Arcana Academy.

Carly's nostrils flare, and suddenly I feel like I'm on the big screen, trapped in every mean-girl movie ever made. This is the part where she tells me I've just made the worst mistake of my life, or I'll regret this one day, or the clincher —do I have any idea who I'm dealing with here?

But instead, she flicks one last icy glare my way and says, "See you around, Stevie. Oh, and one more thing? Keep your slutty little eyes off Baz. He's *not* available."

She slides her ass off the table—*hallelujah*—and saunters away with her posse. But before they reach their table on the other side of the café, I catch Blue flicking a hand in our direction.

All three of our soda glasses tip over.

Before a single drop of liquid hits the table, the glasses upright themselves, the soda sliding back inside.

I look up to see Isla holding her hands out, faint sparks fading from her fingertips.

"Water's kind of my thing," she says, touching the teardrop pendant at her throat. "Three of Cups, specifically."

It made sense, then, why she was so welcoming. The Three of Cups card always reminds me of girlfriends, of people joining together to celebrate something or support each other. There's just something comforting about that card, and now I'm even more glad that I ran into her and Nat.

"You okay?" Nat asks, reaching across the table and grabbing my hand. "I know Carly can be a bit much."

"I'm okay." I let out a breath. "But guys, tell me something. Honestly."

"Girl, what's wrong?" Isla asks.

"Do I..." I peer up at them, my lashes fluttering dramatically. "Do I have slutty little eyes?"

"Well, I didn't want to say anything," Nat says, "but yeah, your eyes are basically begging for it."

"Dial it down, eye-whore," Isla says, and in that moment, I'm pretty sure her original assessment was right: she and Nat are definitely my people.

"I know it's easier said than done," Nat says, "but try not to let Carly get to you. The Claires are all from super-rich, super-witchy families whose bloodlines go back generations. They're under the mistaken impression that money, power, and status means they're better than everyone else."

"Unfortunately, it kind of does mean that. In our world,

anyway." Then, tightening the leash on my cynicism, I ask, "How do you guys know so much about them already? Have you all been here that long?"

"We met them at orientation weekend last month," Isla says. "Suffice it to say, we figured out Carly's M.O. pretty fast. The others just kind of glommed on to her, and they've been inseparable ever since."

"I don't think they actually like each other very much," Nat says. "That's the sad part. But, you know, birds of a feather and all."

"Mostly we try to stay off their radar," Isla says. "But considering you're the new girl—well, the newest new girl, anyway—it's going to be harder for you."

"But also," I say, pointing at her with my spoon, "we're not in middle school. So we've got that going for us."

Isla shrugs, pushing away her plate. Poor woman never even got to eat before Carly spread her DNA all over the table. "Some people never outgrow it, even at a university for highly gifted magick-users."

"Hopefully she'll get bored of me and move on to some other drama," I say.

Nat and Isla exchange a loaded glance.

"What does that look mean?" I set my spoon back on the plate. "I don't know you guys well enough yet to decode your looks on command."

"Well, it just means…" Nat cringes, then offers an apologetic frown. "Before you showed up, Carly was the most advanced first-year on campus, blessed with three affinities."

"Everything but earth," Isla says, imitating Carly's fake plastic voice. "She went on about it for two days straight at orientation. Apparently she was so gifted in high school, her teachers had her tested early."

"So then *you* come along, and…" Nat shrugs, leaving me to fill in the blanks.

Perfect. No wonder I'm already on her hit list. As a spirit-blessed witch, I've got one more elemental affinity than Carly does, *and* I've got the complete package—something she's obviously coveting.

"So is it tattooed on my forehead?" I ask, wondering how Isla and Nat already know about my gifts. "Super-special snowflake, coming in hot?"

They both laugh.

"Welcome to Arcana Academy of the Arts," Nat says. "I'm afraid there aren't many secrets here."

Across from the cheese fountain at the other side of the restaurant, the Claires rise from their table en masse, apparently changing their mind about their dinner plans. On their way out, they stalk past us, glaring at me in warning as they do. Their energy washes over me like hot lava—a twisted mix of competitiveness, jealousy, anger, and fear.

I think of what Nat said about secrets. About the Claires, and their game-playing. About the Void, and Anna Trello's history with Mom and Dad, and Dr. Devane, who warned me not to trust anyone.

Not many secrets at Arcana Academy?

Sorry, Nat, but I'm pretty sure nothing could be farther from the truth.

TWENTY-THREE

STEVIE

No one told me the limit on my Academy-issued credit card, but even after eight hours of back-to-school shopping and restaurant-hopping with Isla and Nat, the thing hasn't melted yet.

I wish I could say the same for myself, but by the time I get back to my suite on Sunday night, my whole body feels like wet goo. All I want is to make some tea, slip into a hot bath, and lose myself in Kirin's book.

Lucky for me, Dr. Devane—patron saint of ridiculous demands—is proving to be a man of his word. Not only did he come through with some A-plus climbing gear, he also stocked my pantry with a collection that rivals my shelves at Kettle Black.

I stand in the kitchen now, staring at the overflowing shelves, not even sure where to start. There are glass jars, metal canisters, bottles, and paper sacks in every shape and size. I find more loose teas than I can count—greens and whites, three kinds of rooibos, black teas from a dozen different countries. There are bottles of floral essences and oils, herbs, spices, dried fruits and nuts, even chocolate shavings in white, milk, and dark. He got me tea strainers and scoops in multiple sizes, a tea press, and two glass kettles—one for a single brew, and a big one for company. There's also a cute selection of cups and mugs—some fancy ones, a couple of stainless-steel to-go mugs, and a few novelties, including one decorated with Bugs Bunny, with a carrot for the handle and lettering on the inside that reads, *What's up, Doc?*

I laugh, my heart already warming. I hope this means he's planning to stop by for a cup one day.

He really has thought of everything.

I'm not a fan of the phrase *lady boner*—I think we deserve our own expressive terminology that has nothing to do with a dude's cock—but right now, there's nothing else that better encapsulates the feeling.

I snap a picture on my phone, then text it to Jessa.

Doc Devane has just given me a huge LADY BONER.

There, I said it.

Jessa sends back a string of laughing emojis, and for the first time since the cops hauled me out of Kettle Black, I'm starting to feel—well, not exactly at home. But if I were the weather, my forecast would be mostly content with an eighty percent chance of happiness in the near future.

It's the end of a long but good day, and the moment calls for decadence—my famous White Chocolate Raspberry Bliss. I grab a canister of rooibos tea, a package of white chocolate shavings, some dried orange peel, raspberry essence, and honey, then I fill the single-use kettle with filtered water.

While I wait for it to boil, I get the bathtub started, then head into the bedroom to slip into my new robe, already anticipating the luxurious bath that awaits me. But it seems the surprises aren't over yet—on the end of my bed, there's a black shoebox painted with silver stars and moons, a cream-colored envelope resting on top.

Inside, I find a notecard embossed with the Academy logo and Trello's name and title.

Starla —

These items belonged to your mother. Now they belong to you. I hope you're finding the suite to your liking. Dr. Devane has left some things for you, but please let me know if you require anything else, or if there's anything we can do to make your stay more comfortable.

— A. Trello

My hands are trembling. Other than the grimoire and the climbing gear I had to leave behind on the Grande, I never really had any of my mother's personal belongings. She always said she was too practical for things like jewelry, or for buying books she could borrow from the library. She thought knick-knacks were useless dust collectors and too many photos were a sure way of staying stuck in the past.

So I'm struck dumb when I open the box and find just that: a treasure trove of photos and tchotchkes, some mundane, some magickal, all of it precious.

I start with the pictures—a pile of old-fashioned Polaroids with pinholes at the top, probably once stuck in a bulletin board. There are lots of Mom and various witches and mages—friends of hers, I'm guessing—posing on hikes and camping trips, at school dances and parties. My father comes onto the scene eventually, with all the cute duck-face selfies and stolen kisses you'd expect. There's even a picture of them dressed for some kind of formal event, Dad in a tux and Mom in a silver gown that slides over her body like liquid mercury. They're both glowing and happy, so young, their entire future stretched out ahead of them.

But at some point, something changed, and the happy glow started to fade. When I put the photos in a rough timeline, the transformation is a lot easier to see. Her bright eyes become haunted, her smile tight, the lines deepening in her forehead. She's losing weight, then gaining, then losing again. My father seems beside himself, and in every photo, they get further and further away, as if some invisible force is slowly wedging them apart. There's a manic energy to the later photos, and then they just end. No graduation ceremony, no silver Academy pins.

Who are you, I wonder, tracing my fingers over their faces. *What happened here?*

I keep waiting for an answer, but no matter how hard I wish it, photographs just can't speak.

I set them aside and take the other objects out of the box,

handling each one like the treasure that it is. There's a silk pouch of small, brightly colored crystals that look like jelly-beans and give off a slight magickal buzz when I touch them. I find old sage bundles tied with lavender ribbon, a collection of raven feathers, and a carabiner that says *Get Hung Up in Yosemite National Park!* in bright pink script. There's a chocolate-brown ceramic pig the size of a golf ball, with three legs and a chipped ear, and a half-melted white candle. And lastly, a necklace—an Egyptian Eye of Horus pendant set with a dark silver stone. Hematite, I believe. The same stone Dr. Devane used to shield us at the prison.

I fasten the necklace around my neck, its magick pulsing over my skin in soft, warm waves. The protective energy feels almost parental, and I touch my fingers to it, tears slip-ping down my cheeks.

I used to think Mom and Dad were just always Mom and Dad, you know? Like they were born that way. Adults. Parents. People Who Knew The Way Things Worked. Even after they died, sorting through their things didn't really give me much more insight, because everything they owned was just practical stuff from our life in Tres Búhos—clothes and shoes, dishes, basic things like that. There were no childhood photos, no old yearbooks or favorite toys or mysterious objects with even more mysterious origins.

Until now.

This little stars-and-moon shoebox contains more of my parents' history than our entire house once held.

Looking at the photos once more, I can't help but wonder what their friends saw. Wonder who tried to help them, whether any of those smiling faces ever noticed something was unraveling.

So often, darkness lurks in the brightest places, a smile hiding an ugly secret, a fancy dress covering the pain that the heart bears in silence.

Bailing on the bath, I brew my tea, drain the cup, and fall asleep on top of the covers, surrounded by my mother's history and a thousand questions floating into the night.

* * *

I'm not surprised when she comes to me tonight, here in the space between asleep and awake, the mist where all things are possible.

I'm standing at the lake again, my owl spirit soaring high above, the moon glinting off the soft ripples. My toes dip into the water on the shoreline, and from the center of the lake, something emerges.

Four women, just as before. The Tarot Princesses who blessed me with their protection.

But this time, the gift they're offering isn't magick.

It's my mother.

Her hair is pulled into a high ponytail, dark brown waves with a streak of gray on the left side. She's wearing a pink T-shirt coated in flour and an apron bearing her favorite saying: *There's no problem a proper cup of tea can't fix.*

She smiles when she sees me and opens her arms to welcome me into an embrace. But she doesn't move from the center of the lake.

"Mom!" I gasp.

"My sweet Starlight."

Tears fill my eyes, and I try to run to her, to reach out for her, but my feet aren't cooperating. I look down to discover my lower half has turned into a tree, my roots twisting deep into the earth.

"The worst has happened, hasn't it?" my mother asks, her smile fading. Surrounding her, the Princesses watch us in silence.

"What do you mean?" I ask. "What's happened?"

"You're there now, aren't you?" Mom shakes her head, her eyes full of regret. "I knew it would come to pass. I have always known. We never meant to leave you, Starlight. Not like this."

"I know. You didn't—it wasn't your fault."

"Nor yours." She smiles again, tears glittering on her cheeks.

I try to reach for her, but my arms turn into tree limbs, my hands covered with bright green oak leaves that shake and quiver in the breeze.

"Now you find yourself back in the very place we tried so hard to leave behind," Mom says, and I know she means the Academy. "Well, I suppose there was no outrunning that path, was there? Leaving was our failsafe, the escape hatch for the worst-case scenario."

"What do you mean?" I cry out, frustration mounting. "What escape hatch? What's the worst-case scenario? Where's Dad—is he with you?"

I have so many questions, but everything's getting

tangled up in my head, twisting inside like the roots of this tree. The more I talk, the less I understand, my words no more than a soft rustling on the breeze.

"We tried to give you a normal life," Mom says. "To prevent this. Yet, as always, things unfold exactly as they are meant to. You could no more avoid your fate than we could avoid ours."

She smiles, but it's full of sorrow, nothing like the smile I hold on to in my memory. Now, it looks more like the smile in her photographs, the one she plastered on to hide the pain inside.

Her gaze shifts to a point beyond me, far away from here, and I can't turn to follow it.

"I'm sorry we couldn't prepare you better for this," she says. "You're in grave danger at the Academy. Ironically, it's also the place where you are the safest. I wish I could have told you more, Starla, but I do not see in specifics, and to reveal much more than this would be to place you in even graver danger. Already, we risk everything by meeting here."

I shake my arms, shedding some of my leaves. I want to ask her about the prophecies, about what Trello wants me to translate, but I can't form the words.

"The dark book," my mother says suddenly, and I wonder if she heard me, if that's her answer. Then her face turns shockingly pale, her eyes wide with fear. She tears at her hair, pulling out handfuls, the lake around her starting to roil.

The Princesses step closer, then cast me a look that warns me that our time is coming to an end.

"What dark book?" I try.

Mom shakes her head, tears streaming down her cheeks, sizzling when they hit the lake.

"Book of darkness," she says. "Book of shadow. Book of mists…" She's rambling now, and when she meets my gaze again, her eyes are milky white, her voice a ghostly echo that reverberates through my skull.

Book of shadow, book of mists
What magick draws, you won't resist
Death to those who shun its call
Where one shall rise, the others fall
Book of shadow, book of mists
The truth emerges from the myths
Flame and blood and blade and bone
What starts with zero ends with one.

She repeats the verse, again and again and again, and with each new beginning, my leaves change, shifting through the seasons—the bright green summer to red-orange autumn, the bare branches of winter to the new buds of spring. When I'm finally lush and green again, the Princesses nod at me in unison, then vanish.

I glance down, relieved to find myself a woman once again.

My mother, alone in the water, repeats her mindless chant.

"What book?" I ask, finally able to run toward her. But as soon as I step into the water, she begins to flicker and fade. "Mom, wait! Don't go!"

She sinks into the center of the lake, and I trudge in up to my knees, fear paralyzing me, holding me back. Suddenly the water rises, and I can't move my legs. It sucks me under, and I hold my breath until my lungs burn and my vision turns black…

I wake with a gasp, shocked to find myself lying in the bathtub, cold water already up to my chin. The faucet is still running, but it's not water that's filling the tub now.

It's Tarot cards. Hundreds of them. Thousands. The same two images, repeated over and over, covering my body and overflowing onto the white marble floor.

One features a frail old woman dressed in a hooded green cape, a sickle tied to her waist. She holds a skull in her hand and stands before a steaming cauldron. A snake slithers along the wall behind her.

On the other card, a young boy emerges from a tomb, a ritual horn summoning him from his eternal slumber.

Death and Judgment—definitely not a pair you'd invite to your next party.

I clamber out of the tub, my clothes and hair dripping all over the floor. The cards vanish, leaving their eerie message behind, a warning that echoes as clearly as if my dead mother were bent over me now, whispering in my ear.

The darkness is already rising. Judgment will come for us all.

TWENTY-FOUR

STEVIE

October has always been my favorite month of the year. Pumpkin carving, caramel apple cider, relief from summer's oppressive heat, Halloween tricks-and-treats. Something about it always speaks to me of new beginnings.

And now, it ushers in the first day of magick school, too.

Not sure I'll ever get used to saying that, but man, does it put a smile on my face.

I've got on Mom's Eye of Horus necklace, and thanks to my shopping spree, I'm decked out in a pair of dark stretchy jeans that actually fit, a lavender v-neck sweater that highlights my best assets, and black leather boots that make me feel like my very best, bad-bitch self.

Complete with flat-ironed hair and a glossy red lip, I'd say it's a pretty stellar first-day look.

But when I head out into the bright fall morning in search of my first of three classes, I still haven't shaken off my dream's icy grip, my mother's cryptic chant and the warning in the Death and Judgment cards tempering my first-day excitement. After I got out of the tub last night, I wrote down every possible detail I could remember from the dream, staring at the words until the sun came up. Even by the light of day, I still couldn't make much sense of them.

Riddles and rhymes, my mother's native tongue. I'm no closer to understanding her in death than I was during her life.

Pushing those thoughts aside, I take a breath of crisp autumn air, thankful for the air- and water-blessed students for adding to the ambiance of the season. With fresh starts on my mind and a pep in my step, I walk my cute self over to the main lecture hall, another towering gothic building behind the admin building where most of the classes are held.

My first class is an intro-level lecture—Foundations of Tarot and Magick. When I finally locate the classroom—a large, auditorium-style hall already packed with about a hundred students—I'm relieved to see Nat inside, waving brightly and pointing to an empty seat next to her.

I look up across a sea of faces, most of them complete strangers. Thankfully, it seems I'm not the oldest first-year in the room—far from it. There are a handful of people my age and maybe a year or two younger, but a lot of them look to be in their thirties and even forties. I spot at least three women with gray hair, and a man who has more

SPELLS OF IRON AND BONE

wrinkles than a raisin. I guess Dr. Devane wasn't lying about the mix of ages.

As I'm making my way toward the seat, I see Baz and another guy sitting a few rows behind Nat, bookended by Carly and her pink-haired companion, Blue. The four of them look pretty chummy together, joking and laughing. Well, Baz is a little on the broody side—complete opposite of the cheerful-looking guy next to him—but broody seems to be part of Baz's signature style.

I'm not surprised to see the two Claires here—we're all first-years, after all—but what the hell is Baz doing in an intro-level class? I could've sworn Kirin told me he's been at the Academy a few years.

Either way, I'm not complaining. Getting a side of his drool-worthy forearm porn with my Monday morning Tarot Foundations isn't a bad way to start the week.

I wave at the whole group, and then smile extra bright at Baz, fluttering my lashes in the sluttiest way I can manage.

Carly glares at me, and I'm pretty sure Blue's whispering some kind of curse on my perky boobs, her ringed eyebrows drawn tight. I hit the pause button on my shameless flirting long enough to scrape the bottom of my *fucks to give* bucket, but sadly, I come up empty.

All out, ladies! Sorry!

There may come a day when I look back on my petty behavior and cringe, but today is definitely not that day, so I smile once more at the guys, giving Baz a nice eyeful of my enhanced cleavage before settling into my seat.

Thank you, Isla, for convincing me to buy this push-up bra!

"That was amazing," Nat whispers. "You are such a stone-cold bitch. I think I kind of love you."

I slide the tablet out of my bag and power it up, hoping I don't have to take too many notes on this thing. "I swear I'm not usually like this. But women like that need to be given a dose of their own medicine sometimes, and I'm still pissed that Carly ruined Isla's potatoes."

"Remind me never to get on your bad side."

"Or mess with my food."

Our laughter fades as the clock chimes nine and Professor Maddox stalks into the room, her stern, no-nonsense vibe immediately commanding our attention.

"Where does magick come from?" she begins without introduction. "And what, if anything, does it have to do with Tarot? Some say Tarot was invented as a game in the fifteenth century. Others believe it's a much older divinatory system, passed along from an ancient Egyptian source —the Book of Thoth, specifically. Possible? Fanciful? Maybe a bit of both, yes?"

She looks over each of us in turn, her gaze calculating and shrewd, but her smile full of passion. When she sees me, she pauses, her eyes widening just a fraction. A tendril of her energy reaches out, rising above the din of energies in the room—a mix of familiarity and surprise, followed by kindness.

She seems to recognize me, or at least know who I am. Did Trello give everyone advanced notice about my arrival?

Or was Professor Maddox one of Mom's professors, and now she's noticing the resemblance in my eyes?

No, she doesn't look old enough for that—in fact, she looks about the same age as Mom would've been now.

Maybe they were friends.

I'm not sure if that's a good thing or not.

When she finally moves on to Nat, I let out a sigh of relief, wondering if it's going to be like this every time I meet a new professor—them wondering if they've seen me before, me wondering if they knew my parents. If they were supporters... or something else entirely.

"Very good," she says with a sharp and sudden nod, as if she just had an entire conversation in her mind and figured out the answer to the most pressing question in the universe. "While the pop-cultural, human-centric mythology of the Tarot is a fascinating subject, witches and mages have a fundamentally different understanding of this most sacred tool. It wasn't invented as a fortune-telling device or a card game for wealthy aristocrats. In fact, it wasn't *invented* at all, but recorded—a pictorial accounting of our magickal energy source. The very thing that makes us tick."

Her eyes dance with excitement as she launches into an explanation of the Tarot suits and elemental correspondences, most of which I'm already familiar with. I relax a bit, glad that I'm not totally lost on the first day of class.

"All of us exhibit specific powers and talents connected to—and mirrored in—the Minor Arcana of the Tarot,"

Professor Maddox says. "Your affinities can play a huge role in many aspects of your life, influencing not just your magickal abilities, but your interests and hobbies, your favorite foods, your friend groups, and even your romantic partners."

At these words, a sudden tingling sweeps across the space between my shoulder blades, quickly racing up the back of my neck. I squirm in my seat, waiting for it to pass, but the feeling only intensifies.

Blue better not be putting an actual curse on me.

I turn around to glare at her, but she's not paying me a lick of attention. Even Carly seems riveted by Professor Maddox's trip through the Minor Arcana, and their other guy friend is doing something on his phone.

There's only one person staring at me.

Baz Redgrave.

He's slouched halfway out of his chair, legs stretched out casually, pen tapping absently against his knee. He's making a *supreme* effort to appear bored, but it's clearly just that—an effort at appearances.

Bored? Hell no. This man's energy is so singularly focused, it's like he's trying to set something on fire.

Or someone.

Baz is still staring at me. Hard. Normally, a person who gets busted ogling you in the middle of class has the grace to look away. Not this guy. When I meet his eyes, he winks at me, his lips twitching as if he's trying to hold back a smile.

Sometimes I wish I *couldn't* sense people's emotional

torment. It would be a whole lot easier if I could just take people at face value and write him off as a sexy but egotistical ass who just assumes women will melt at one glance from his pretty, red-brown eyes... or fight with each other for his fleeting attention.

Granted, I might've brought that on myself with my cleavage shot earlier, but still. This isn't about my flirty little games.

Whatever Baz wants everyone else to think? Deep down, he's drowning in darkness.

My heart clenches. They say the bad boys are the most alluring. That we just can't help but be drawn in, because we always want to fix them.

I get it, really. I nursed Jessa through a pretty rough bad-boy phase last year that damn near shattered her heart *and* her savings account.

But in my case? It's a hundred times worse.

Whatever the source of my empathic gifts, it's in my very *nature* to want to fix Baz—some innate part of me that I can't control or dim. Just like it's in my nature to make people their perfect cup of tea and to invite Carly and the Claires to sit with us at dinner last night despite their obvious attitudes. Even now, I feel the tiniest bit guilty about trying to needle Carly a few minutes ago, because I know that her raging bitchface is mostly for show.

The difference is—I've never been attracted to my Kettle Black customers (other than Kirin, who's definitely a special case). And Carly and the Claires aren't my type either.

But Baz?

That boy is hard to ignore, and he fucking knows it, too.

He holds my gaze, his smoldering intensity cutting right to the bone. And to other parts. Suddenly I want to kiss that stupid half-smirk right off his face, to make him ache for me, to hear him moan my name as I ride him into the sunset...

As if he can read my thoughts, he lifts his eyebrows, then smiles.

A trickle of sweat runs down between my boobs, and I turn back around and shift uncomfortably in my chair, trying to pretend like I dropped something.

"And how about you, Miss Milan?"

I startle at the sound of my name and whip my head up, my cheeks already flaming under the weight of my classmates' collective stare.

"I… I'm sorry," I stammer. "Could you repeat the question?"

"We're discussing our elemental gifts, which you would know if you were paying attention to the lecture rather than to Mr. Redgrave. As handsome as it may be, that face of his will not help you understand your magick or—more importantly—pass my class."

A snicker rolls through the room, along with a few whoops and catcalls, and I'm just sitting here like a total chump, trying to melt away into my chair.

"Don't keep us in suspense, Miss Milan," Professor Maddox pushes.

"I… I'm blessed with all four," I say, then rush to add, "as far as Miss Trello and Professor Phaines told me."

"Did you not complete the test?" she asks.

"I did. It could be wrong, though, right?"

"What could be wrong?"

"The test? The vision… thing?"

"I suppose in magick, anything is possible. But no, Miss Milan. In the hundreds of years the Academy has been fostering witches and mages, the test-vision-*thing*, as you've so eloquently called it, has never been wrong." She shakes her head as if to admonish me, but her energy tells a different story. She's amused, and more than a little curious about me.

She turns back to the rest of the class. "What Miss Milan is too modest to say is that she's one of our rarest magickal students—a spirit-blessed witch. This means she possesses all four elemental affinities and will eventually learn to wield the full spectrum of elemental magick. Definitely someone you want in your corner, even if she *is* easily distracted by charming mages."

Another collective laugh, and I'm just about ready to set witchfire to my own ass.

Lucky for me, she stays on point with the rest of her lecture, talking about the Minors and the elements until the clock finally strikes ten. At the telltale chime, the class abruptly stows their notebooks and tablets, spilling out of the rows toward the exit.

"All of you should be signed up for one of the companion labs!" Maddox shouts above the rush. "Tarot Divination and Spellcraft with Professor Eames or Professor Nakata! Happy Tarot-ing!"

As Nat and I pass by the podium at the front of the room, I'm half-expecting Professor Maddox to pull me aside and scold me for my lack of attention. But she only raises her eyebrows, her lips curved in a sly smile as if she's having another one of those conversations in her head.

I offer her an apologetic smile in return, then scoot out of there as fast as I can.

Out in the hall, Nat and I make plans to meet up with Isla for a late lunch, then part ways.

I've just made it outside when someone calls my name from behind. I turn around to see the cheerful-looking guy that was sitting with Baz and the others.

"It *is* Stevie, right?" he asks. When I nod, he says, "I'm Ani. I'm a friend of Kirin and Baz."

He's got red-gold hair and eyes the color of melted caramels. When he smiles, two dimples wink from beneath a thin beard, and I can't help but return it.

"Annie?" I ask. "Because of the red hair?"

"No, *Ani*. Short for Ansel." He's still grinning, his bright, happy energy like a warm hug. "Anyway, don't let Professor Maddox get to you. She's kind of a stickler sometimes, but she's not so bad. Really knows her stuff."

"I could've done without the mortification, but it was my fault. I should've been paying attention."

"Yeah, well… Don't be too hard on yourself. Baz has that effect on most women." Ani laughs. "Half the guys, too."

"Are you a first-year?"

"Third, actually."

"Why are you in an intro class?"

"It's a core class. I tested out of it at first, but then Trello decided I needed a little more foundational work, so here I am."

"Baz too?"

Ansel flashes a knowing smirk.

"I'm just curious!" I say defensively. "We met the other day, and I thought he was a few years ahead. I was surprised to see him here, that's all."

"Baz repeats a lot of classes. Personally, I think he's a little slow, but don't tell him I said that. He's sensitive about—"

"Personally, I think you're an asshole, and you shouldn't be filling the jailbird's easily distractible mind with lies." The class-repeater himself appears behind us, tossing an arm around each of us as he wedges into our conversation. Turning to me, he says, "Miss, is this gingersnap bothering you?"

"No, but *you* are."

Baz winks at me again, his smile maddening. "You'll get used to it."

"Anyway," Ani says, "Kirin mentioned you're pretty new to all this, so if you need help with anything, just ask us. Well, not Baz." He shoves Baz in the shoulder, but both are laughing, their affection for each other obvious. "But Kirin and I have your back."

"And I've got your front," Baz says, "so you're covered all the way around."

"Seriously?" Now I give him a shove, too. "Do you *ever* let an innuendo pass by unsaid?"

"Is that like the whole tree-falling-in-the-forest thing?" Baz strokes his chin, pretending to be deep in thought. "If an innuendo passes by unsaid, does anyone ever really get laid? I think not, Little Bird. I think not."

"Yeah, I'm beginning to sense that about you," I say. "The whole not-thinking part."

Ani cracks up. "What's your next class, Stevie?"

"I'm meeting Kirin, actually. He's supposed to show me —" I cut myself off abruptly, remembering what Trello told me about the delicate nature of our work. Ani is so open and easy-going, I almost can't help but trust him. I'll have to be on guard for that, lest I start spilling state secrets about my mother's research and whip the whole place into a panic.

"He wants to show me around the library," I say, leaving it at that.

"Cool," Ani says. "I've got a fire potions class in that direction. I'll walk with you."

"And I'll just be over here," Baz says, "playing with myself."

"Have fun with that," I say with a smile, deciding Baz isn't such a bad guy. He's certainly amusing, anyway.

"Always do, Little Bird."

After waving goodbye to our hot third wheel, Ani and I fall into an easy conversation, chatting a bit more about classes and campus life. He's fire-blessed, originally from northern California, but he lives at the Academy year-round. Before I get the chance to ask him more about that, we've arrived at the library building.

"So listen," he says, leading me to a side door that goes to Kirin's office. "What are you doing tonight?"

"Right now, my big plans consist of making a pot of lemon ginger hibiscus tea and reading a few dozen books."

Ani's brow creases, as if I've just made a major faux pas. "Seriously? It's only the first day."

"I have a lot of catching up to do."

"Plenty of time for that later. Tonight's the annual Back-to-School Blood and Sorrow Soirée."

I laugh. "Well, as fun as *that* sounds, it's a school night. I need to be up early tomorrow."

"It's tradition. Every year, the water-blessed throw a big bash to welcome everyone back and show the new recruits how it's done. We took a vote, and it was unanimously decided that your attendance is mandatory."

"Hmm. Who's *we*?"

"Me and Baz." Ani knocks once on the door, then pushes it open. Kirin's sitting at a massive, L-shaped oak desk scattered with books and papers and various computer monitors. "But if Kirin ever left the library, he'd vote yes, too."

"Vote yes on what?" Kirin glances up from his keyboard, his dark hair disheveled, glasses crooked on his nose.

Alert! Alert! Quintessential hot nerd on the premises!

A smile spreads across my face. I've never seen Kirin in his element before. It suits him.

"So?" Ani asks. "Is that a yes?"

"I'll think about it," I say.

"Awesome. I'll bug you about it at least eight more times throughout the day."

I laugh. "Sounds good, Ani."

"What was that all about?" Kirin asks as Ani heads off to his next class.

"I think he just asked me out."

"He… what?" Kirin blinks rapidly, the muscles in his jaw ticking.

I was half-kidding about the date, but the force of Kirin's emotions hits hard and fast anyway.

He's jealous. And a little bit pissed.

"Just a party," I say. "I'm probably not going, anyway. I've got so much reading to do."

"Good. I mean, not that you shouldn't have fun, but… Well… Okay, then!" He hops up from behind the desk and gestures toward a second door on the interior side of the room. "This way to the library."

There's a stained-glass window at the top of the door, and through it, I can just make out a few pillars and bookshelves. My heart flutters, knowing that what lies beyond the door is so much more than a collection of magickal books and manuscripts.

Beyond that door lies my mother's life's work—as much as she was able to accomplish before she left the Academy.

Beyond that door lies the reason I'm here.

And—if Dr. Devane, Anna Trello, and whoever else is involved in this is right—beyond that door lies the key to stopping unspeakable horrors against the magickal community…

If I can crack the code.

I look up into Kirin's pale green eyes, my hands trembling as I reach for the doorknob. "Now or never, right?"

TWENTY-FIVE

STEVIE

When I was a freshman in high school, my parents and I took a road trip to the Grand Canyon. I didn't want to go— why did I need to see some stupid hole in the ground when I could be staying home, climbing up to the top of the world with Luke and Jessa in the Santa Clarita?

But they dragged me anyway, as parents often do. We got out of the car at the visitor center, and while my parents went to use the restroom, I plodded over to the railing where people were crowded around with cameras and selfie sticks, eager to see what all the fuss was about and prove my point that we'd wasted our time.

But when the crowd parted and I got my first glimpse of the Canyon, I was instantly overcome. The people faded away, the sounds drifted into nothingness, and suddenly I was standing on the edge of the world, gazing into the most beautiful, breathtaking, awesome wonder I'd ever seen. A condor soared overhead, and as I looked down at the red and purple layers of rock and mud and bone, I felt as though I could see the entire history of Earth, of life, of existence.

By the time my parents found me, I was shaking; tears streamed down my cheeks.

"It's just so beautiful," I whispered, and Mom kissed my face and said, "I know, baby. I know."

Now, walking into the library with Kirin, I'm overcome with that exact same feeling. Awe and wonder, a sense of absolute timelessness, utter amazement that something so beautiful even exists in my world. I blink away the tears, trying to take in the splendor that seems to stretch out in all directions, all the way up to the heavens.

The library is built in a spiral around a circular marble floor in deep shades of blue, with four massive pillars—two stationed at each side of the space, almost like gateways. Shelves upon shelves climb so high along the spiral I lose sight of them, even as I tip my head all the way back. The ceiling is domed, but there are no wooden beams or angelic paintings. Only the sky itself, bright blue in the autumn afternoon, sun gleaming through the glass.

"The pillars are reminiscent of those in the High Priestess and Hierophant cards," Kirin says, "symbolizing gateways to inner and outer knowledge. The sky was left visible, representing the clarity and insight we strive to attain through learning, questioning, reasoning, and wonder. The floor mimics the ocean—the depths of our souls and deepest intuitive selves."

Looking down at the floor, I see now that the marble

isn't just blue, but shot through with swirls of violet and green and black, everything changing in the light.

Kirin leads me through the pillars on the north side of the space onto what I now realize is a wide wooden staircase that spirals all the way up to the top.

"Stairs or elevator?" he asks.

"You're talking to a climber."

"First day on the job, and you're already giving me a workout."

"You'll thank me one day. Stamina's a good quality in a man." *Oh, Stevie. You continue to amaze us with your verbal prowess.*

My cheeks flame with heat, my stupid mouth getting ahead of my brain once again.

But unlike Baz, Kirin is a gentleman, and lets the innuendo pass with no more than a raised eyebrow.

We ascend together, my eyes growing wider with every step as we pass by towering shelves of books. There are sections on amulets and charms, plants and herbcraft, animal familiars, conjuring benevolent as well as evil spirits, communicating with the dead, crystals, elemental magicks, Tarot history, Tarot theory, Tarot spellcraft... Wow. The "T" section is the largest by far.

I read every sign out loud, excited laughter bubbling out of me. "I want to learn all of it!"

Kirin laughs. "You've got at least four years to accomplish that goal, six or eight if you stay on to do graduate work."

"That feels too far away."

"In the meantime, if there are any books you'd like, you can put in a request on your phone. They'll be delivered to your door within an hour."

"Seriously? How is that even possible?"

"Magickal library, remember?" Kirin winks, then says, "Here we are. This way."

Halfway up the endlessly winding stairs, Kirin puts a hand on the small of my back and leads me into an open space with gleaming hardwood floors. Several students are working at tables in the center, every flat surface stacked with books and scrolls and laptops, the only sounds the clack of keyboards and the swish of pages turning. Along with the unmistakable scent of old books, a faint hint of lemon oil hangs in the air, probably from whatever they use to polish the wooden shelves and floors.

On the back wall is an ornately carved oak door with a plaque that reads, ARCHIVES—AUTHORIZED ACCESS ONLY.

"We'll be working in here," Kirin says, pressing his hand to the scanner outside the door. It looks a lot like the one in my suite. Once we're inside, he shuts the door behind us and presses his hand to another scanner just like the first. The door beeps, then latches, locking us in.

We're standing in a nondescript room the size of my bathroom, with a tall, phone-booth-looking machine at the other end in front of another door.

"What's that?" I ask.

"You know the scanners at airport security?"

"I've never flown."

"Really? Wow. Okay, well, this machine scans your

magickal signature and matches it to your Academy records, making sure you're authorized to enter. Only one person at a time can enter. If the scanner picks up anyone else's signature along with yours, it won't grant access. It's to ensure no one is coerced to let someone inside, or tries to smuggle them in. You have your phone on you, right?"

I pat my back pocket and nod.

"Good. Go on ahead."

I step inside the booth and stand on the footprints helpfully painted on the platform, holding my breath. After a brief moment, the machine beeps and the lights inside turn green, a disembodied voice telling me to step forward.

Inside my back pocket, my phone buzzes with a text.

"That's your security code," he says. "Enter it on the touchscreen outside the door."

I pull out my phone and tap in the ten-digit number.

"Is that it?" I ask. "No blood samples, social security number, signing away my firstborn, stuff like that?"

Still on the other side of the booth, Kirin laughs. "Your magickal signature is all we really need to identify you. The rest is just another layer of security. Go on in—I'm right behind you."

I open what I hope is the last door on this little adventure and step inside. Seconds later, Kirin follows me in.

Rather than the dark, dusty room I associate with a word like *archives*, we're standing in a large, bright white room that looks like a high-tech science lab, with gleaming metal tables, lightboxes, microscopes, and other equipment I can't even begin to identify. Two of the four walls are lined with glass-walled chambers full of file cabinets in all shapes and sizes.

"The documents kept in the archives are extremely rare, extremely valuable, and most importantly, extremely dangerous. Everything is stored in environmentally controlled file cabinets behind the glass, taken out only for an hour or two at a time. The documents stored in the red cabinets can only be handled while wearing a mask and gloves, which can be found in the supply closet over there. We won't need those today, though."

He invites me to take a seat at one of the tables, then heads into one of the glass rooms and retrieves a stack of thin, leather-bound notebooks.

"All our work must be completed here," he says. "We won't be able to remove anything from the archives—not even your mother's notes and sketchbooks. You'll also need to lock up any translations you've made in the black cabinets over there. You'll see the drawers with your name on them—you'll be asked to set a password on the touch screen the first time you use it."

"More security?"

"The archives house some of the rarest magickal documents in existence. We get visiting professors from all over the world, along with our own graduate students and professors. A lot of witches and mages come through here, Stevie. We can never be too careful."

"I can understand keeping the antiquities safe, but my mom's stuff? My own translations?"

"Think about it," he says, keeping his voice low even

though we're alone. "If the prophecies are true, anything you translate will put you on the map of whoever's behind the attacks. They'll know you're onto them—or at least working on it. Even if the prophecies *aren't* true, your mother believed something terrible was coming. If her work or your notes fall into the wrong hands, it could either put you in danger or cause a mass panic, and we're not going to risk either of those things. Not when witches are being targeted all across the country right now—and that's not even taking into consideration what's happening overseas."

Kirin sets the stack of notebooks on the table and turns away from me, blowing out a sigh. The muscles beneath his shirt bunch with tension.

I rise from the table, place a hand between his shoulder blades. "Kirin, is something wrong?"

He turns to face me again, his eyes full of concern. "There was another attack last night. In New York, a small town just a few hours north of Manhattan."

"What happened?"

"A house fire—four people dead. From the few details available online, I'd say it was caused by magelight. But they arrested the witch who lives next door—she's claiming she and the family were close friends, that she's devastated about the news. Down in the city, they've already started protesting—some of them for her freedom, but a good majority for stricter penalties and additional sanctions against witchcraft."

"How can you get any stricter than execution?"

Kirin holds my gaze, all the unspoken fears hanging in the air between us.

Sometimes, there are a lot worse fates than death.

"I need to get to work," I say.

Kirin nods solemnly, but a faint smile touches his lips. "Just remember, Stevie. You're not alone in this. We're a team, okay?"

We get situated at the table, Kirin taking the chair across from me. He slides the stack of notebooks toward me and says, "This is some of your mother's earliest research, dating back to her second-year studies. Professor Phaines and I feel you should start here. The more recent writing is a lot more... convoluted."

"How so?"

"Witches and mages gifted with foresight typically develop their own symbolic language and metaphor families. Sometimes it's clear-cut and closely follows the known symbology of the Tarot—things like pillars representing gateways, animals for intuition and guidance, white lilies for purity, along with basic astrological and numerological correspondences. But as a witch advances in her practice, she often delves deeper into her own internal meanings and symbols, relying on this much more personalized language system to communicate with the universe. Now, many divinatory witches will attempt to provide more generalized translations after recording their initial interpretations of a reading—this way, others can better understand and take action on any important prophecies. But Headmistress Trello said that toward the end of her time here, your mother was so engrossed in her work, so frenetic about the prophecies, she didn't stop to process it or translate it. She simply channeled the messages straight from the cards through her personal symbology and onto the page."

"Her grimoire is like that too," I say. "You probably saw it—a lot of it reads like the rantings of a madwoman."

Kirin shakes his head. "I didn't read it, Stevie. I wouldn't—not unless you wanted to share it."

I smile, grateful for his thoughtfulness. "So her initial work is a little less crazypants?"

Kirin laughs. "If that's what you want to call it, yes. Plus, looking at the earlier stuff might help you develop an eye and ear for her symbology—the more personalized language that comes through later. Our scholars—myself and Professor Phaines included—haven't been able to do that yet. I also developed a computer program that models spoken and written language development across all known human languages and cross-referenced that against your mother's work, but so far, that's been a dead end too."

"Um, what?" I gape at Kirin, my head already spinning. "And you think *I'm* going to be able to figure this out, genius-boy? I hope you're not placing any bets on me."

Kirin taps the notebooks between us and shrugs. "You're her daughter, Stevie. There's a deep connection there—a bond we can't simulate, not even with the most advanced magick and technology available."

Goosebumps tighten across my arms, my eyes filling with tears. Kirin's right. And now I'm sitting in this room, my mother's work at my fingertips, the dream-visit still lingering in my mind. I feel closer to her in this moment than I have at any time since the day she spoke her final, ominous words.

The day I watched her die.

I slide a notebook from the top of the stack and open it to a random page in the center, just trying to acquaint myself with it for now. Her handwriting leaps out from the page, tiny and neat, with occasional messy scribbles, as if she got so caught up in something she just couldn't take the time for precision.

I run my fingertips across the page, reading the passage aloud:

> *Between the space where black meets white*
> *Betwixt the woods of dark and light*
> *A mirror flat reveals the sky*
> *But turn it 'round to know the why*
> *Zero begets the next, the One*
> *Innocence lost, magick undone*
> *Beware the rise when darkness falls*
> *For magick corrupts, and blood trumps all.*

"Wow, that's a little intense. I thought you said this was her early work?" I look up from the page to see Kirin staring at me, his mouth open.

"What was that?" he asks. "Did you just… make that up?"

"It's my mother's. It's right here."

"I've read through these books a hundred times. I promise you, it isn't."

"Look." I spin the book around to show him.

Kirin scans the page, then flips to the one before it and the one after, shaking his head. "This is just a list of Tarot cards and positions. Current situation, The High Priestess. Crossing, Magician reversed. Past influences, The Fool. Future influences, Judgment reversed."

I come around to his side of the table and peer down over his shoulder, ready to smack him for the practical joke.

But Kirin's absolutely right.

"How is this possible?" I ask. "I know what I saw. I wouldn't screw around about this. Also, I suck at rhymes."

"Wait, you were touching it before," he says. "Touch it again."

I run my fingers along the lettering, and once again, the chant appears. He can't see it, but I can.

"Holy shitcakes," I whisper.

"It's her magick." Kirin looks up at me with wide eyes full of astonishment. "Try another one."

I grab the next notebook from the pile and go through the motions. The same thing happens, this time with another verse.

"You're picking up on her magick," he says, getting to his feet. "She must've known you would come back here… She left this for you and…" He's pacing the room now, a broad smile stretched across his lips. "Of course! Why didn't we think of it? This is amazing!"

I get to my feet, his energy contagious. "Kirin, what are you talking about?"

He stops pacing and grabs my shoulders, his eyes dancing with excitement. "The key to cracking the prophecies isn't in the actual words, it's in the magick itself. Your mother put some sort of locking spell on it—a spell only you can access. Maybe it's tuned to you specifically, if she did it after she found out about her pregnancy. Or maybe it's just keyed to her blood, to any of her descendants."

"Do you understand the chants? Because they still sound pretty cryptic to me."

"Not off the top of my head, but if we pair the verses with the card positions she recorded, it may start to unlock some of her symbology, thereby unlocking some of the more complex language from the later research." He pulls me into an unexpected hug, his heart banging wildly, his strong arms holding me close. "Stevie, we've been at it for less than fifteen minutes and we've already had a major breakthrough."

I lean into his embrace, my own heartbeat mimicking his, my body buzzing.

When he finally pulls back, his eyes are glazed, his hair disheveled. His hands slide to my upper arms, warm and solid, and for a moment it looks like he just might—

"Wait, the dream!" I blurt out, unintentionally breaking the trance.

Disappointment flashes in Kirin's eyes as we break apart, but it's probably for the best. Kissing him is definitely a terrible idea, especially now that we're colleagues.

Ugh, priorities.

"My mother came to me in a dream last night," I continue. "She said something that sounded like a similar chant."

I close my eyes, repeating it word for word.

> *Book of shadow, book of mists*
> *What magick draws, you won't resist*
> *Death to those who shun its call*
> *Where one shall rise, the others fall*
> *Book of shadow, book of mists*
> *The truth emerges from the myths*
> *Flame and blood and blade and bone*
> *What starts with zero ends with one.*

When I finish, I open my eyes and ask him what he thinks.

Kirin looks a little shellshocked. After a beat, he blinks at me and says, "Can you write it down for me?"

"Sure. There's got to be something with the zero and the one, right? And maybe the blood?"

"Yeah," he says, but I can tell he's distracted, his mind already racing again.

"Kirin, do you know what she might've meant by 'book of shadow, book of mists?' Does it sound like a real book to you? Before she started chanting, she said something about a dark book."

Kirin's skin turns the color of old milk, but he presses his lips together and gazes skyward, as if he's thinking.

"Those are pretty generic terms. Back in the days before magick was widely known, a lot of witches and mages called their spellbooks and journals names like book of shadows or book of mirrors. It was all part of the necessary secrecy, I suppose."

"Right, but this feels different. Book of shadow, book of mists… She mentioned it twice. And she repeated the chant several times, too." I tell him about the rest of the dream. "I just wonder if it was an actual book or scroll or something."

"Doesn't sound like it," he says dismissively, then scoops up Mom's notebooks. "You should go. You've got Devane's class next—you don't want to be late for that, trust me."

Kirin laughs, but it's forced and tight.

I narrow my eyes, watching as he locks the notebooks back in the file cabinets.

He's lying to me. His energy went from open and excited to dark and evasive in about five seconds flat, and I have no idea why.

What is it about this shadow and mists business?

When he turns around again, his smile is brighter, but his energy is totally anxious, and he's having a hard time meeting my eyes.

Damn it.

Kirin is keeping secrets—secrets that have nothing to do with wanting to kiss me.

And something tells me if I'm going to figure out the *real* truth behind Mom's prophecies, I'll need to start keeping them, too.

TWENTY-SIX

STEVIE

If I thought our vigilante road trip had bonded us in some deep, unbreakable way, or that Dr. Devane's excellent selection of rock-climbing gear and tea-blending supplies was indicative of his fondness for me, he's quick to squash all those childish fantasies.

"You're late," he announces as I try to sneak into class unnoticed. His eyes flick over my body so subtly I doubt anyone else sees it, but I do.

So much for the unnoticed part.

"I know, I know. I'm sorry. I got hung up at the library." I offer a quick smile—one I hope is at least a *little* bit disarming, considering what they charge for this lipstick— then scan the room for an empty seat near a friendly face.

As far as friendly faces go, looks like I'm out of luck there—Baz is closest to fitting the bill, but he's already boxed in by Carly and Emory.

Unlike the big lecture hall from my intro Tarot class, this

room is tiny, the desks arranged close together. Twenty pairs of eyes track me as I squeeze between rows to the lone available seat in the middle of the room, wishing Dr. Devane would just carry on with whatever lecture I interrupted.

But he waits in silence until I'm firmly in my seat, my tablet powered on, my tapping finger poised and ready to tap out whatever wisdom he's here to impart.

"Are you comfortable?" he asks, his hospitable tone dripping with mockery.

I glare at him. "I'm great, thanks."

"Ready to be, I don't know, *educated*? This is, after all, an institute of higher learning, correct?"

"Sure thing." I give him a mock salute. "Learning mode —engaged."

His nostrils flare, his icy energy like a warning shot blasting right over my head. "In my class, we respect one another's time, Starla Milan."

"Stevie," I remind him, but it's too late. Snickering starts up in the back, catching on like kindling.

"Twinkle, twinkle," someone sings, and I don't have to look to know it's Emory. Carly may be the face of the brand, but out of all the Claires, Emory and Blue seem to be the worst actors.

"Carry on, Doc," I say, shooting him a pleading glare.

"It's Dr. Devane, Miss Milan. Professor Devane is also tolerable. Not Divine, not Doc, not any other nickname or insult you might be considering."

I press my lips together. Wow, Doc has a *serious* hard-on

for authority. He's kind of cute when he gets all riled up, too.

Holding back a smirk, I decide to honor his wishes—for now. This is his classroom, after all, and he has the power to pass or fail me. I probably shouldn't piss him off just yet.

"Sorry, Dr. Devane," I say. "It won't happen again. The lateness or the nicknaming."

He holds my gaze a moment longer. "Good. See that it doesn't."

Though a hint of his scent still lingers in my suite from the day he delivered my stuff, this is the first time I've actually seen him since our prison break and subsequent meeting in Trello's office. He's dressed similarly—dark gray dress pants, white button-down and pale yellow tie, jacket. But here in his classroom, far away from the desolate desert highway and tacos and portal magick, he looks almost... sad.

I try to get a read on his energy again, but he's got his walls firmly back in place.

"Mental magicks," he says, finally breaking our gaze and pacing the room before us. "A subject as fascinating as it is dangerous, and one you'll need to master if you have any hope of succeeding—not just in my class, but in the world that exists beyond these hallowed walls."

He continues pacing, all of us riveted. He may be cranky, but the man sure knows how to command a room.

"If I tell you *not* to imagine a unicorn," he says, "what are you now imagining?"

"A unicorn," comes the unanimous reply.

"Precisely. My words easily and immediately influenced your thoughts." Devane grins, holding up a hand in question. "Is it magick? Is it manipulation? Something else entirely? Miss Kirkpatrick, what do you think?"

"I think it's a little of both," Carly says. "I mean, anything can be considered mental magick if you think about it. Dressing a certain way to attract male attention, for example."

I feel her eyes on the back of my head. It's all I can do not to turn around and flip her off.

"Okay," Dr. Devane says, "that's a fair point. I suppose you could argue that's similar to glamour magick, something that absolutely affects the mind. But what I want you to consider this semester is that a true mastery of mental magick is not just a matter of tricking your opponent, or simply implanting your thoughts into the mind of another person with words, as I did with the unicorn example. The skilled mental magick-user wields his or her mind like a sword, knowing when to block..." Devane holds up his arms, blocking as if he's wielding an imaginary sword.

Then he looks at me and charges forward, stabbing me through the chest with his invisible blade. "When to *thrust*..."

I look down at my tablet, pretending to take copious notes, but oh *Goddess* I do *not* need to be thinking about words like *thrust* around my hot, wound-up professor...

"And when to walk away. Miss Milan," he announces, so abruptly I jump in my seat. "What is your opinion on the use of mental magicks to gain an advantage in a situation?"

"I don't know." I glance up from my tablet. "I guess it depends on the situation."

"Does it?"

"Of course. There's a big difference between fending off an attacker and, say, sabotaging a competitor for a job you both want."

"Is there a difference, though?" He smiles, his eyes casting a wicked gleam. "In both scenarios, two parties are fighting over a single outcome, yet only one can win. Who's to say which person is more deserving?"

"Nine times out of ten, you're talking about a complete violation. It's a slippery slope, and no offense, but I personally don't plan on using mental magicks unless my life is in danger. Maybe not even then."

I cross my arms, shooting him a meaningful look. Maybe it's not a big deal to him, but I won't soon forget the fear of being shot in the chest by someone claiming to be an ally. Granted, he saved my life, but still—there could've been another way. I don't want to put someone else in that position—not ever.

Dr. Devane watches me a moment, then claps once and says quickly, "Debate. Use all available resources and persuasive techniques to make your case. Mr. Redgrave, you'll be arguing against the use of mental magics. Miss Milan, you'll be arguing for."

"You know I can't do that, Dr. Devane. I've just told you I don't support it on principle."

"You can," he says calmly, "and you will, unless you prefer to fail my class on principle."

An F on my first day. Perfect.

I close my eyes, forcing my hands to unclench. He's just trying to get under my skin, and I'm playing right into his trap.

Mental magicks indeed.

The good doctor thinks he can break me? Fine. Two can play at that game.

"Mr. Redgrave," he says. "Make your opening statement."

"Mental magicks is wrong," Baz says flatly from the back of the room. "It's a violation. Do unto others and all that."

Give me a break. Baz doesn't believe anyone should be spared this mental torment any more than I believe it's justifiable.

Goddess, I'm going to kill Devane. Maybe not right now, with all these witnesses around and no good place to hide the body, but one day he'll pop in for that cup of tea, and I'll see his Bugs Bunny mug sitting there, and... Oops? Was that hemlock that just accidentally fell in there unnoticed?

"Miss Milan," he says with a grin. "Any time you're ready, please make your opening statement."

Eager to prove myself, I head to the front of the room and face the class, take a deep breath, and square my shoulders. "It's my belief that... Well, when a person finds herself in a situation in which there are no options... That person may... It's challenging, of course, but..."

"Miss Milan, your assignment is to convince the class that the use of mental magicks is justifiable, not to convince them that you're a waffling politician devoid of opinions. We both know nothing could be further from the truth."

The Claires are snickering in the back, half the class yawning and tapping messages into their phones. It's Tres Búhos Middle School all over again, and I'm the weird witch-girl trying to give an oral report about the mating habits of kangaroos while all the kids spit at me and make signs against the evil eye.

I glare at Devane. He's sitting behind a large desk with his arms folded across his chest, smug and superior, as usual.

That's it, buddy. Gloves are off. You're fucking with the wrong witch today.

"Let's say you're faced with a formidable... *opponent*," I say, finding my voice and shooting a pointed glare at the good doctor. "He's backed you into a corner, left you vulnerable and defenseless. He's taking great pleasure in asserting his presumed power over you. Maybe you've got combat training. Perhaps you're packing weapons. Maybe you're an ace spell-caster, and with a few simple words, you can blast your opponent to oblivion.

"But it doesn't always go down like that, does it?" I ask, making eye contact with each person in the room. "Sometimes your opponent catches you unaware and unprepared. Sometimes he's a person you know, a person you might be starting to trust. You've got no weapons, no spells, nothing at all with which to defend yourself. After all, why would you need weapons against a so-called ally?

"I'm here to tell you—buck up, girlfriend. You're not

down for the count yet. You've got a weapon no one can match."

"Pussy power!" someone calls out. Pretty sure it was Emory, and okay, *fine*, that one's kind of funny.

"All right, two weapons," I say with a smile. Then, tapping my temple, "I'm talking about this one. Your brilliant, beautiful mind. One whose potential we've only just begun to tap."

I pace before the class, adopting the same techniques I witnessed Devane using moments ago. I wait until they're hanging on, desperate for my next statement, then I whirl around and lock eyes with our illustrious professor.

"Dr. Devane."

"Yes, Miss Milan," he says, clearly amused.

"I want you to imagine a moonlit beach." I approach the desk, my boots clicking against the floor. "Waves lapping seductively against the shore, a gentle breeze ruffling through your hair like a soft caress."

He cocks his head, his eyes flashing a warning. I keep waiting for him to throw up his mental shields or call off the exercise, but he doesn't. It's like he's testing me, wondering just how far I'll push this.

If he thinks I'm going to back down easily after all his attempts to humiliate me in front of the class, he doesn't know me at all.

I gaze into his eyes, daring him to look away.

He doesn't.

In my mind, I let my thoughts roam into dangerous

territory, the kind of superheated, inappropriate thoughts that could get me into *serious* trouble.

But there's no going back now.

"You see a woman sitting on the shoreline in the distance," I say, "gazing out over the glittering sea. Everything about this night, this moment, is pure serenity…"

My words fade away, and suddenly my thoughts no longer feel like mine. The classroom vanishes, leaving only the good doctor and me standing on that moonlit beach.

Wordlessly we join hands, the waves lapping our toes. In the distance, a wolf howls into the night, and Dr. Devane pulls me into a passionate embrace, his lips on my jaw, my neck, my collarbone. Our clothes fall away, and we kneel in the sand, our kiss unbroken as we tumble backward…

The class bell chimes, and the vision falls away instantly.

I'm back in the classroom, breathless, completely disoriented.

Dr. Devane is still sitting behind the desk, and still staring at me, just like in the vision. But instead of the desirous gaze of a man devouring his woman with kisses, Devane's eyes are full of red-hot fury.

That's my cue, thanks for playing along, bye for now!

I rush back to my desk and grab my bag and tablet, then scoot toward the exit to file out with the rest of the class.

But I'm not fast enough. In a low whisper that slides across my skin, he says, "Miss Milan, a word, please."

I wait until the rest of the students leave before finally turning to face him.

"Explain," he demands, his eyes fiery once again. "Now."

"I was hoping *you* could explain."

No response.

"You're the one who wanted a word with me," I say defensively. "So what's up?"

"You're playing a dangerous game here, Miss Milan. A *very* dangerous game."

"I was doing what you asked. Defending my position."

"That little charade you just put on?" He barks out a laugh. "I hardly call that defending your position."

"I completed the assignment, did I not?" I shrug, hoping he doesn't spot the tremble in my body. Maybe things didn't go exactly as I intended—honestly, I was just going to ramble on with a little sexy paint-by-number story for the class, see if I could make Devane uncomfortable or embarrassed. He's such a freaking rule-follower, I expected him to shut me down and move on to the next lesson before my story even got *close* to the naughty parts.

But then the words no longer felt like my own, and suddenly I was tumbling headlong into the same vision I had with him back at the prison, each second evolving into something much more intense.

"When I met you—mere days ago—you claimed to have no active powers outside of witchfire," he says. "How and when did you learn to dreamcast?"

"Dreamcast? I've never even heard of it."

"Well, you just did it." He rakes a hand through his hair, revealing that sexy hint of gray at his temples. "Dreamcasting is when you conjure a dream or vision for yourself, then pull your target into it by casting it into his mind. Hold him there long enough, and eventually, the target will have no idea that the vision is coming from another person. It's powerful, complex magick, highly unethical, and advanced beyond even our graduate teachings."

I stare at him, mouth open, just as shocked by all this as he seems to be.

"You wove a spell," he continues, "verbally and mentally, that essentially cast the vision from your mind into mine. A person could literally go insane from magick like that."

"But I thought the ocean on the beach was *your* vision. From that day in the prison? Well, the wolf was new today, but all the other details were similar."

"Ocean and wolf?" He shakes his head, his brows knitting together in confusion. "I'm not talking about your words, Miss Milan. I'm talking about the dreamcast. There was a lake, not an ocean. Today, and yes, that day in the prison too. I saw a lake before a circle of standing stones, and you were there... You were... you were bathing, taking off your clothes. You wanted me to..." He clears his throat and tugs at his tie. "To join you."

My heart skips, and I force out a laugh to hide my nerves. "So you're daydreaming about me taking off my clothes, and *I'm* the one getting a lecture?"

No one speaks. The air feels impossibly heavy between us, crackling with an electrical heat. My mouth fills with a strange taste.

Saltwater.

"I should fail you right now," he finally says, shaking his head. "Boot you right out of this class and forbid you from re-enrolling until you can learn to take your studies seriously."

"You don't think I'm taking this seriously?" I take another step toward him and lean forward on the desk, closing the space between us. "You failed to establish any boundaries for this assignment, Dr. Devane. Then you pushed me into a corner and told me to fight my way out. To use all available resources and persuasive techniques to make my case."

He grabs a stack of papers on his desk and shuffles through them, clearly flustered. "Regardless. Flirting with your professors is hardly a tool for—"

"Oh, I wasn't flirting. I was making a point." I grab the stack of papers from his hand, wait until he meets my gaze again. "So whether my words inspired your own vivid imagination, or I actually did that dreamcasting thing, the end result was the same."

For the briefest instant, I let my gaze drop to his crotch, where the evidence of my persuasive techniques still stands at attention.

"Now, if you'll excuse me, *Doctor* Devane." I return his papers, then heft my bag over my shoulder. "I need to get to my next class. As you've so cleverly ascertained, failing is *not* something I care to do on principle."

TWENTY-SEVEN

STEVIE

My heart is still jack-hammering when I reach the third floor for my Potions and Charms class, and it's *not* from running up the stairs.

You're playing a dangerous game here, Miss Milan. A very dangerous game…

His voice echoes in my mind, and it's only by sheer force of will that I can even move my legs.

I still can't believe I stood up to him like that. That I pushed things so far and ended up in that insane dreamcast vision, or whatever the hell that was.

And if it was *my* vision, why did Doc and I see something entirely different?

And more importantly, why am I still trying to go back there, imagining both of our visions playing out to their natural endpoints, with Dr. Devane and I naked and kissing and—

"Stevie, hey! You're in this class too?"

It's Isla, coming to my rescue with her bright smile and kind eyes, saving me from going down a path that—however fun it may seem in the moment—almost certainly ends in misery.

We head inside and find seats together, my heart rate slowly returning to normal.

Fortunately, Potions and Charms is a breeze—best class of the day by far. Under the guidance of a perpetually happy, highly over-caffeinated woman named Professor Broome, we spend the entire hour playing with herbs and spices, identifying them by taste, texture, color, and scent. I'm totally in my element, and even better, free from the Claires, distractingly hot mages, and anyone else trying to mess with my vibe today.

After class, we hook up with Nat for our lunch date at Tamayo, a Mexican fusion place in the Breath and Blade dorms, and after that, my first official day of magick school is blissfully done.

And so far, it seems I've lived to tell the tale.

Back at my suite, I nearly squeal with delight when I see the stack of books piled neatly outside my door. Kirin wasn't kidding when he said the library was magickal—I only just requested these while the girls and I were at lunch.

Inside, I change into yoga pants and a big red Arcana Academy sweatshirt (go, school spirit!), put on some music, light a few pumpkin spice candles, and brew myself the perfect cup of salted caramel chocolate tea.

I've just snuggled into the most comfortable spot on the big squishy chair by the window, teacup and saucer balanced on my knee, a book open on my lap, everything about this peaceful moment pretty much the best thing ever… when my door chimes with a visitor.

"I'm not home!" I shout, but I'm already getting out of the chair, my promise to Jessa always echoing in the back of my mind.

I check the security monitor, then open the door to my visitor, my annoyance instantly vanishing.

"Hey, Ani." I smile, stepping aside to let him in. "You want some tea? I just made some—one of my specialties. It's called Sex with a Caramel, because it's *that* good."

"Sounds… sticky. I'm in." He follows me inside and takes a seat on the couch while I prepare a cup for him.

"Dark Magick: A Brief History," he says, checking out the stack of books on the coffee table. "The Fool's Journey and You. Dancing with the Cards: Ten Techniques for Incorporating Music into Your Tarot Studies." Ani shakes his head, his eyes filling with concern. "Oh, Stevie. Looks like I got here just in time."

"For what?"

"You're about one bad book away from falling headfirst into a lonely life of isolation and boredom. Sure, it starts with a few library books. Maybe a few more after that. A magazine subscription or two. A cat. Two cats. Seven cats. Next thing you know, you stop showering, you're talking to your thirty-seven cats in a language only you understand, and the only reason anyone knows you're still alive is that you're still mailing in your Publisher's Clearinghouse sweepstakes entry each week."

"First of all, I'm pretty sure that's not a thing anymore. And what do you have against cats?" I hand him his tea, then resume my position in the chair by the window, finishing my own tea before it gets cold.

"I'm worried about you, Stevie," he says with mock seriousness.

"Well, don't be. I haven't had enough alone time to be lonely, and I'm definitely not bored. Or in the market for any cats just yet." I nod at the stack of books. "I'm trying to get ahead. Or catch up, actually. There's so much to learn. Kirin took me through the library today, and I basically wanted to adopt every single book in the place."

"Even..." He picks up another one, wincing at the title. "Thirty Days to Becoming a Badass Blood Witch?"

"That one came by accident," I lie.

"Look, I'm not criticizing your reading selection. Well, maybe a little bit. But your timing is terrible." He sips his tea, his eyes widening. "Holy shit, that *is* sexy."

"Glad you approve. Now don't take this the wrong way, but... Why are you here, exactly?"

"Seriously?" He holds out his hand like I'm the most impossible creature he's ever encountered. "The party?"

I squeeze my forehead. "Shit. I totally forgot."

"I sent you at least eighteen texts. Maybe more."

"I think my phone was off."

"If you miss this party, you'll set the tone for the whole year."

He picks up one of the giant Tarot cards from the novelty deck on the table—Three of Cups, featuring three women dancing in celebration, drinks held high.

"Dear Universe, my name is Stevie, and I hereby declare that I don't want to have *any* fun this year." He turns the card upside down and frowns, indicating a reversal of the normally celebratory meaning.

When I laugh, he pulls out another card—Seven of Swords, featuring an older man who reminds me of Professor Phaines holed up in a castle and poring over old manuscripts, seven swords on the table in front of him. "I want to spend all my time locked away in the library reading dusty old books and discussing unpronounceable theories with Kirin Weber, who looks so cute in his hipster glasses and artfully mussed, slightly-mad-scientist hair it's hard to believe that on the inside, he really is an absolute snore."

Now I'm totally cracking up, but Ani's just getting started.

His next card is the Four of Swords, a dead knight entombed in eternal repose beneath a wall of swords.

"After all my hard work," Ani says, "I'm going straight home to bed, to sleep in a stone coffin for the next eighty years, hoping one day my prince will start to miss me and show up to entertain me with a magickal wake-up kiss."

I snort. "Like I need a prince to entertain me. Hello? That's what vibrators are for."

Ani lets out a whoop, then holds up the Ace of Wands, which is probably the most phallic card in the deck, with a huge wand shooting up from a chasm between two rocky cliffs.

"Well, damn," he says, tossing the card onto the table and holding up his teacup in salutation. "Gotta admire a witch who can entertain herself."

"I wish." I reach over and turn the Ace of Wands upside down, making the sad-trombone sound. "There's one store your fancy Promenade is definitely missing. Someone should write a letter to whoever's in charge."

Of the few possessions I left behind in Tres Búhos, I'll probably miss my vibrator the most. I keep thinking I should text Jessa a warning before she starts packing up our trailer for her move, but letting her discover Mr. Winky under my bed in all his bright purple, multiple-attachment glory sounds so much more fun.

"Okay, Stevie. Point taken. And I'm all for equal rights —I swear. But in this case, you definitely need saving."

I pick up the Knight of Swords from the pile. "And you're just the prince in shining armor for the job?"

"The party is tradition," he says. "You don't want to mess with that."

"What you call tradition, every college movie for the past fifty years calls hazing the clueless new girl."

"We don't haze here. Cuts into prime drinking time. It's the mundane humans that haven't figured that part out yet."

"Good. Because if I agree to this ridiculousness and you

end up hazing me, I'll... Well, I don't know yet. But I promise you it'll be super painful and/or embarrassing."

Ani wriggles his eyebrows. "Will it involve a vibrator, though? That's the question on *everyone's* mind."

"Haze me and find out, Gingersnap."

Ani laughs, then finishes the last of his tea. "No hazing, I promise. Only a little fresh air and a few beers to ring in the new school year. You might actually have fun."

"Who else is going?" I ask, stalling for time. I was really looking forward to a quiet night with my books, but Ani's making a compelling argument.

"It's open to anyone," he says. "You can invite people if you want."

I think about calling Isla and Nat, but they've got some kind of magickal moonlight dance class tonight out behind Breath and Blade.

Sorry, party girl. You're on your own.

I let out a put-upon sigh, but Ani just keeps grinning at me, his golden-caramel eyes glittering, his dimples flashing. It's hard not to get swept up in his perpetual optimism.

"*Ugh!* Fine." I get up from my chair and grab the empty teacups. "Give me twenty minutes to get changed."

"Take your time." Ani grabs one of my books—Magick Rituals for Connecting with Your Inner Goddess—and opens to a random page. "I'm pretty good at entertaining myself, too. With *or* without batteries."

TWENTY-EIGHT

STEVIE

I've always hated parties.

Probably has something to do with Luke's whole scorpion-down-the-pants thing, but I just never saw the appeal after that. Bunch of people standing around outside, freezing their asses off, sucking down booze and doing stupid dares so they don't have to really talk to each other.

As Ani and I make our way to the red river behind the Blood and Sorrow dorms, and I spot the unmistakable glow of a bonfire, I'm starting to worry this party will be no different, and that I've made a terrible mistake.

I slide my hands into my back pockets, finding a Tarot card there—not one of the big cards Ani and I were playing with before we left, but one of my mysteriously appearing messages.

It's the Eight of Swords. At the center of the card, a woman stands barefoot in a circle of swords, the blades stuck into the ground like a cage. She's blindfolded, her hands and body bound with ropes.

Watch your back, Stevie. Don't give away your power.

Great. Not ominous at all.

"You want a drink?" Ani asks me, and I nod, hating myself for defaulting so quickly. It's not that I don't like drinking, it's just that I prefer doing it in smaller groups, with people I actually know and trust. Out here, standing around in a magickal desert with a bunch of strangers, I feel like I'm just looking for some liquid courage. Or better yet, a wall to keep people away.

As Ani goes on the hunt for beer, I work my way through the crowd, looking for someone I know. Baz, maybe. Or Kirin, unless Ani was serious about him never leaving the library.

I recognize a few people from my classes—mostly the younger crowd—and everyone is all smiles and laughter. A few people are sitting near the fire strumming guitars and playing bongos, and another group is engaged in what sounds like a deeply philosophical discussion about the pros and cons of using mind-altering substances during rituals. I'm just starting to relax, to think maybe I was a little too quick to judge the scene before really getting a read, when a commotion next to the river catches my attention.

My stomach sinks like a rock when I spot the source, and I know without a doubt that my assessment of parties won't be changing anytime soon.

The Claires are holding court by the water, regaling a

few other party-goers with displays of their magickal prowess. Carly is juggling multiple streams of water, while Blue does the same with balls of fire, which actually looks pretty cool. Emory is straight-up levitating. Amelia is standing off to the side, staring at her phone, looking like she'd rather be anywhere but here.

Across the crowd, Carly catches my eye.

Shit. So much for pretty cool.

"Hey, Carly," I say, approaching them and trying my best to smile. "Blue. That whole water-and-fire thing you guys have going on is kind of awesome."

Carly almost smiles. Well, either that or she's about to sneeze, but I'm pretty sure that's a budding grin making her lips twitch.

But then Blue rolls her eyes and says, "Look, girls. It's Starla I'm-too-good-for-the-coven Milan."

"Twinkle, twinkle," Emory says, gazing down at us from her floating perch five feet off the ground.

Carly casts aside the water and immediately resets to her default factory setting of uber-bitch. "I didn't know *you* were invited."

"Really?" I feign concern. "For a self-proclaimed clairsentient, it's weird that you're always the last to know things. Maybe you should, like, have your aura cleansed?"

A few people snicker, but inside, my gut turns hot and prickly. I'm not about to let anyone walk on me, but I really, really hate this petty, pissing-contest bullshit. We have a hard enough time making our way through life as it is.

Shouldn't we be supporting each other? Lifting each other up instead of tearing each other down?

"Professor Phaines doesn't seem to think there's anything wrong with my gift," Carly says, raising her voice to ensure maximum distribution and attention, though by this point most of the crowd is dissipating, moving on to some new entertainment. "And Phaines would know. He's a powerful seer, and a personal friend of our family."

"How nice for you all."

"You're not the only special little snowflake he's taken an interest in, either. The girls and I are doing a group independent study with him. He's helping us enhance our natural psychic abilities. He says our gifts are among the strongest he's ever seen, especially among first-years."

As Carly continues to blather on about her most wonderful qualities, I turn away from her, desperately seeking Ani and our drinks.

I don't see him, but it looks like there's a line and a crowd milling over by a big boulder across the way. That's probably the beer spot.

Tuning Carly out, I'm about to make my way over there when I feel a hand clamp around my arm.

"I *said*," Carly says, spinning me back around, "what kind of tricks can *you* do?"

I snatch my arm back. "Excuse me?"

"We showed you ours, Twink. Let's see yours."

"See my *what*, exactly?"

The river is just a few feet behind us, and now Carly lifts

an elegant hand, making a jet of water jump and swirl into a graceful arch over the crowd.

The few remaining revelers paying her any mind cheer and clap, shouting slurred praises.

Emory's still levitating, and now she bends herself into a yoga pose midair, a few students laughing and trying unsuccessfully to knock her off balance.

Blue goes for her fire magick again, this time forming a ball of it between her palms, then throwing it up in the air. It explodes in a starburst, raining down around her in a show of beautiful sparks.

"Sorry to disappoint," I say, because there's no point in lying in a situation like this. "But I can't compete with any of that. I'm still figuring out where my on-button is."

A few people laugh, and for a minute, I actually believe Carly and her band of bobbleheads will drop it and go back to their own magickal mutual circle jerk.

But then a shadow falls over my face, and Emory—still levitating—casts a mean glare from above. "Maybe we can help you find it."

"Hard pass," I say. "But if I ever need help, I'll know just who to call."

She floats down and lands on her feet before me, an elegant dark-haired swan, and the rest of the Claires close ranks around me, including Amelia.

The Eight of Swords drifts into my mind, and fear prickles across my skin, settling in my belly like ice.

My eyes dart around for an escape, but before I can make a move or even call for help, Carly and Blue grab me by the arms and drag me over to the river. Somebody—Emory? Amelia?—kicks the backs of my knees, and I go down hard.

Everything after that happens in a blur.

I can hear the water rushing behind my head, the air cooler down here, even as the fire crackles and pops in front of us. The music is still going, and a few people gather at my feet, some laughing, some taking photos, most everyone drunk and babbling. They don't know this is real. That I'm in danger.

Someone's pushing against my shoulders, tipping me backward...

Someone's sitting on my legs, telling me not to squirm...

"Don't touch me!" I shout. "Let me go! Don't fucking touch me!"

They're laughing and I can't kick out, can't move my arms, and now the water's sucking at my hair...

"Let's see if we can activate your water magick, you spirit-blessed bitch," Blue says. Here in the darkness, the fire raging behind her, she looks like a demon. "If that doesn't work, next we'll try fire."

"Let go!" I shout again.

Where is everyone? Why is no one helping?

"Guys," someone says, her voice small and weak. A flash of curly red hair before my eyes, and I know it must be Amelia. "Maybe we should stop."

"Quit fucking around," Carly says, but she's yelling at Amelia, not Blue, and Blue's got malice in her eyes, violence on her breath.

"Amelia, help me! Please!" I sputter and gasp, the panic taking hold in earnest, but Amelia looks behind her, then back to Carly, as if she's waiting for permission to do the right thing.

The water soaks my hair, my shoulders, and Blue pushes harder, impossibly strong. Soon the water's slipping across my chest, icy cold, sucking me down, and suddenly I'm back in that canyon five years ago...

Don't leave me! Don't go!

My whole body trembles, and I cough and spit out water, struggling against Blue's terrible hold, but there are too many hands now, too many angry faces swirling before me, too much laughter, too many camera flashes and the water's coming and I can't breathe and I can't move and I can't—

White flame explodes from my chest, and the witches holding me down scatter like mice. There's a scream, and suddenly I'm on my feet, my arms spread wide, my hair on fire with magick. It sings through my blood, through my very soul. My owl's wings stretch across the span, and when I raise my arms, I call forth the wind and smolder the fire.

I let out a howl, a yell, a primal scream from the depths of my darkness.

The party falls silent.

Then, as quickly as it appeared, my owl energy dissipates, and a real snowy owl floats to the sky, soaring higher and higher, leaving me a woman once again, wet and shivering on the banks of the river, all the faces staring back at me in drunk, shocked confusion.

I level an icy glare at Blue.

"Next time someone tells you not to touch them," I mutter through chattering teeth, "maybe you should listen."

I try to storm off, but the moment I take a step, I lose all coordination. My legs go numb, my body heavy, and I sway on my feet, the whole scene darkening around the edges.

"What the fuck is going on?" A man shouts from somewhere I can't see, pushing his way through the tangle of drunk bodies. His voice is familiar—and angry. Ani?

No. Baz.

Baz, help me! I try to reach for him, but I can't move my arms. My heart is beating fast—too fast—and my breathing is much too shallow.

"We're just messing with her," Carly says. "She totally overreacted and freaked out."

"Let's go home," another says. "This party sucks." Blue, it sounds like. There's a smudge of pink hair in my peripheral vision, but everything is fuzzy around the edges.

"I'll deal with you later," Baz says, and then he's walking toward me. His eyes go from concerned to terrified in an instant, and he starts to run. Sprint. But he's too far away...

"Stevie!" he shouts. "Watch it! Somebody grab her!"

The world tips backward again and spills me into the river, the cold water reaching up to claim me once and for all.

TWENTY-NINE

STEVIE

I'm naked.

Soft, green grass tickles my bare flesh, sunlight sparkling on my eyelids through a lush canopy of leaves overhead. Slowly, I open my eyes, inhaling a breath of sweet summer air and the fragrant scent of lilies from the floral crown on my head.

My nude body aches, but it's the best possible pain, abs and leg muscles burning from some unknown exertion. Between my thighs, heat still pulses. A haze of pure pleasure hangs over me like a soft cloud.

There's a rustling in the grass, and I turn to see the source. A man sleeps soundly beside me, his head encircled in a crown of leaves, arms painted with tattoos that swirl in beautiful black patterns across his skin.

At the sight of his bare flesh, a shock of new, red-hot desire floods my core, the sudden intensity of it making me dizzy. I crawl to him, desperate to caress his skin, to feel his warmth beneath my fingertips.

He stirs at my touch, his eyes opening to look at me, full of fire and light, much more red than brown in the shifting sun.

A slow smile spreads across his face, and wordlessly he pulls me on top of him, his hands sliding down to caress my backside, his hard length ready for me once again.

He grips his cock, and I rise up onto my knees, letting him tease my entrance with slow, tempting strokes. When I can't take another moment, I finally claim what's mine, sliding down over his shaft, taking him in deep, one sinfully delicious inch at a time.

He moans in pleasure, his eyes fluttering closed, hands gripping my thighs.

I want to ask him his name, to tell him mine, but I don't want to break this spell. Instead, I sink into the pleasure of his thrusts, rolling my hips, finding our perfect synchronicity.

He slides his palms up my rib cage, fingers teasing and tugging my nipples as I ride him harder, faster, deeper.

I feel like I should recognize him. I know him, know his touch, the sounds of his breathy moans. But when I tried to reach for the memory of his name, it eludes me, chased away by the mounting pleasure between my thighs.

He slides his thumb between my lips and I lick the tip, tasting the salt of his skin as my body clenches around him, demanding more with every thrust. I lean forward, the crown of lilies falling from my head as I steal a breathless kiss.

Beneath me, my lover arches his hips, both of us wanting more, needing more, the fire building between us, pushing us farther toward that edge…

He grips my hips and drives into me, his body shuddering, and I cry out in ecstasy, the birds scattering from the trees, bright green leaves falling like rain in their wake.

I collapse on top of him, waiting for my breath to return. It's in that blissful, hazy moment that I know we're not alone.

I peer through the mossy trees behind us. There, watching from the shadows, a dark figure looms. He's twice the size of a man, with massive horned antlers and a long, mossy beard filthy with leaves and sticks. Beneath thick eyebrows, his eyes glow green.

"Cernunnos," I whisper. The beast behind us doesn't move.

I look down at my lover, fear squeezing my chest, but he only smiles, his eyes glinting with mischief.

"Cernunnos," I whisper again, but he only pulls me closer, pressing his mouth to mine and rolling on top of me, pinning me beneath him.

He's hard for me again, and my core throbs with a fresh ache of desire, but the beast behind us is still watching. Warning.

My lover breaks our kiss, and I gasp for breath, my heart hammering wildly as the lush, green world around us begins to dim. I try to focus on his face, his lips, the thin sheen of stubble on his jaw, those devilish eyes, but it's all fading... fading... gone.

The lush, sun-dappled meadow is a field of boulders in the moonlight, the tittering birdsong a rushing river.

"Cernunnos," I whisper again, but the eyes looking back at me now are no longer the eyes of my mysterious lover from the meadow.

The eyes looking back at me now belong to Baz Redgrave.

THIRTY

BAZ

Cernunnos.

The witch shouldn't know that name.

She shouldn't be looking at me like that either, eyes full of desire, lips parted, cheeks darkening.

But she *definitely* shouldn't know that name.

Hell, my heart's slamming into my rib cage so hard I can barely think straight, but I gotta ask.

"What did you say?" I whisper.

"Cernunnos," she mutters, delirious, still struggling to break into consciousness. "Don't. Please don't."

I lean in close, my ear brushing against her soft mouth. "Don't what, Stevie?"

"Don't stop… Don't stop touching me. Don't ever stop touching me."

Fuck, this woman's about to give me a heart attack. And on any other night, I might just let her do it, too. But not now. Not like this.

Where the hell is Ani? I turn around and peer into the darkness, but he's nowhere to be seen. I sent someone to go find him, but half these drunk fucks don't know their dicks from their magick wands right now.

The girls, of course, are gone. High-tailed it right out of here as soon as I pulled Stevie out of the water. *Fucking Carly.*

I shake off the anger, turn my attention back to Stevie. Behind us, the river rushes past, the bonfire nothing but ashes. She can't stay out here like this—she'll freeze.

"Wake up, baby. You need to wake up." Using my sleeve, I wipe the river water from her chin. "Come on, Stevie. Come back."

She coughs again, then blinks rapidly. When she looks up at me now, recognition finally dawns in her eyes. "Baz?"

"The one and only."

"I thought I was… What happened?" She tries to sit up, and I slide a hand behind her back to steady her.

"Careful, Stevie. You swallowed a lot of water."

She clears her throat, then presses her fingers to her lips and closes her eyes. "You… you kissed me."

At this, I grin. *Ah, if only the explanation were that simple, Little Bird.*

She looks at me again, some of the old spark finally returning to her eyes. "Did you seriously try to make out with a half-drowned woman at a party?"

"Well, when you put it like that… No," I finally admit. "But I *did* put my lips on you."

The sparks in her eyes turn to a blaze, hot enough to warm us both.

I raise my hands in mock surrender. "You were turning blue. I didn't know what else to do."

She's quiet a long moment after that, and I leave her to it, the din of the party carrying on behind us, like someone falling into the river and nearly drowning is no big deal. Honestly, I don't even think many people saw what was going on. Carly and her cronies are always gunning for attention—just another day in the life for those psychos. Hell, Carly's been like that since we were kids—nothing new to see here.

After a few solid minutes of Stevie's silent brooding, I can't take it.

"See, I get that you're new at all this," I say, "but the whole idea of skinny dipping is that you leave the clothes behind."

"Super helpful, Baz. Thanks." She strips off her sopping wet sweater, leaving only a thin tank top beneath, her nipples poking against the fabric. She wrings her sweater out into the dirt. Water runs in muddy rivulets behind her. Her arms are covered in goosebumps.

I shrug out of my hoodie, wrap it around her shivering body. She sighs in relief, the chattering teeth finally subsiding.

I try to rub some more warmth into her arms, but she tenses up.

"You're shivering your ass off," I point out. "Don't be stubborn."

Slowly, she relaxes under my touch.

"Don't try to sneak a feel," she says.

"Sneaking's not my style, Little Bird. When I touch a woman, I make *damn* sure she knows about it."

She shivers again.

It's not working.

"All right," I tell her. "This is useless. We need to get you inside."

She nods, and I get to my feet, helping her up and keeping an arm around her waist. She leans against me, swaying, our faces close.

"I had a strange dream before," she says softly, nuzzling into my warmth, and there goes my damn heart again.

Boom-boom-boom-boom-boom-boom...

"I was in a meadow, with... with a man. And we were... you know. And there were these mossy trees and ferns and this... this half-man, half-animal, megabeast with huge antlers. He was watching us." She looks into my eyes, a thousand thoughts swimming behind her gaze. "His name was Cernunnos. I don't know how I knew that, but I did."

"The horned god of Celtic mythology," I say. "You must've come across it in a book or something."

"The devil," she breathes. "I thought he was the devil."

Now my heart's thundering so hard, she can probably hear it too.

"It was just a dream, Stevie. You were in bad shape."

"It felt so real, though. Everything about it." Her voice is low, her eyes glistening with an emotion I can't read. She reaches toward my face, and when she speaks again, her soft breath whispers across my lips. "And you... your eyes..."

I grab her hand, give her a reassuring squeeze. "Just a dream, baby. Come on. Let's go."

She nods and tries to walk, my arm tight around her waist, but after just a few steps, she sways again.

"Shit," she says. "Guess I'm not feeling so hot right now."

"Don't worry about it. I got you." I scoop her off her feet, hold her close to my chest.

Stevie doesn't fight me on it. Just puts her arms around my neck, finally allowing herself to relax. "Where are we going?"

"Common room back at Iron and Bone. You need to be someplace warm, and you should probably eat something, too."

"Come on. You're not *seriously* going to carry me a whole mile."

"You're right." I take her a few steps away from the party, the last of the revelry fading behind us. Two jagged boulders jut up beside the river, forming a sort of gateway. Before we step through, I smile and give her a quick wink. "Hold tight."

Stevie opens her mouth to speak, but before she can even get the first question out, there's a blaze of purple magick, and then we're standing in the middle of the Iron and Bone common room.

"How the hell did you do that?" she asks now, her eyes wide.

"Earth-blessed. Me and rocks? We go way back." I laugh, then set her in the big chair by the fireplace. It's down to embers now, so I throw on a few more logs, get it roaring again. "Just a little teleportation spell I whipped up my first year here. Maybe I'll show you sometime."

"I'd love that. I'm still trying to perfect my witchfire." She holds out her palm, calls up a bright silver flame.

"Looks pretty damn perfect to me."

Stevie smiles—almost back to her old self.

Once the fire's good and hot, I find a blanket for her. "Probably best to get out of those wet pants and boots. You can use this."

She shoots me a glare, her lips pulling into a cute smirk that's doing nothing for the semi-hard-on I've been rocking since she told me about that damn dream.

"Slick, Baz," she says with a laugh. "If you think it's going to be that easy to get me out of my pants…"

I cock an eyebrow, returning that flirty little smirk of hers. "I'm just trying to spare you some hypothermia. But clearly, your mind is somewhere else. Anything you want to tell me, Little Bird?"

"Oh, there are a few things I'd *love* to tell you," she says. "But I think I'll quit while I'm ahead. Now turn around so I can disrobe in private like the proper, modest lady I am."

I laugh, then head into the common kitchen to see if I can find her something hot to eat. Pickings are pretty slim—most students eat in the cafés these days—but I manage to find some instant vegetable noodle soup. I boil some water, mix it all up in an oversized mug.

By the time I get back to the fireplace, she's all wrapped up like a mummy, her face small inside the hood of my sweatshirt, firelight glowing on her cheeks.

"It's not the best meal I've ever cooked," I tell her, handing over the mug, "but it's hot."

She takes a sip, a soft moan escaping her lips.

"Better?" I ask.

"Amazing." She smiles again, big and bright, and I try not to sigh in relief. She's still a little on the pale side, but overall, I think she's okay. Physically, anyway.

I pull up another chair across from her, hold my hands out toward the fire. She's awful quiet over there, knees pulled up to her chest, her face half-buried in the big soup mug.

"So, you ah… wanna talk about it?" I ask.

No response, and for a minute I worry she's sinking back into that damn dream again. But then she shifts in her chair and says, "I don't like rivers. Well, rushing water in general."

"Yeah, I don't blame you."

"No, I mean…" She looks down at her soup, stirring it around in the mug. When she speaks again, her voice is so soft, I have to lean closer to hear it above the crackling flames. "A few years back, my parents drowned in a flash flood."

"Oh, fuck." I knew they'd died awhile back—Devane told us as much. But he left out the details, and now I feel completely out of my element. I don't even know what the fuck to say. "Stevie, that's shit. I'm sorry. I mean…

Fuck, I'm making it worse. It's shit. That's all there is to it."

"Thanks. It *is* shit." She offers a sad smile. "We were hiking in the slot canyons and it just... it came out of nowhere. I got caught up in it too, but there was an opening in the canyon wall just above the waterline—looked like a cave. My dad basically shoved me into it. He and my mom tried to climb in after me, and I tried to reach for them, but the current was too strong and it just... it swept them away. It happened so fast, Baz. I kept watching the water, screaming their names, waiting for them to pop up on the other side. They never did."

The fire snaps, a log tumbling against the grate. I grab the poker and push it back in, trying to figure out what the hell to say.

But I can't, and eventually, Stevie sighs and says, "The water didn't stop. It just kept rising, and I had to go deeper into the cave. A day passed. Another. All I had with me was a daypack with a couple of soggy granola bars and two bottled waters, and I knew things were getting dire. The water had reached the cave, and it was getting higher by the hour. I thought I was going to die. I thought I *wanted* to die."

She sips her soup, and I'm still holding the fire poker, afraid to move. Finally, I work up the nerve to speak.

"You didn't die," I say, eloquent as fuck. "How? I mean, how did you finally get out?"

"Search and Rescue found me on day three. They had to send in divers. I'd climbed up higher inside the cave to escape the water, and the rest of it got flooded, basically cutting me off. I had to wear scuba gear to get out."

Holy shit. I can see why she has a thing about rushing water. In fact, she's holding it together pretty damn well, considering.

"You know, the last conversation I had with my parents that day was about this place. I'd just graduated high school, and I wanted to come here—more than anything, even though I didn't know much more about it than the name. Mom and Dad were adamantly against it, and they refused to tell me why—just the same old lines about how it's a dangerous place, how the administration can't be trusted, how magick is a curse."

Stevie looks around the common room, taking in the dark teal walls, the rich wooden beams, the huge windows.

"Anyway, when Blue held me down like that tonight, the water rushing over me, Carly laughing... I don't know. I guess some part of me knew they were just screwing around—that they weren't really going to drown me. But all that old shit came back and I just... I snapped. I don't know what that owl magick is all about, but it seems to happen lately whenever I'm threatened. It's like a defense mechanism or something. I wish I knew how to control it."

"I didn't see the whole thing—got there right at the end. I saw the owl take flight, though. That part was actually pretty badass."

She smiles, shaking her head like she still can't believe it. "Crazy, right?"

Not as crazy as she thinks, but Devane wants us to keep

it all on lockdown for now, so I just shrug and say, "Keep studying, Stevie. The more you learn about your magick, the more you'll understand it. It's not going to happen overnight."

"No, I suppose not." She drains the last of her soup, and silence drifts between us again. After several uncomfortable minutes, she nudges me with her foot and says, "Hey. Don't do that."

"What did I do?" I hate the thought that I somehow made it worse for her. "I'm sorry. Whatever it is, I'm sorry."

"I just mean... Don't clam up like that and get all weird on me now. I'm fine—seriously. I didn't even mean to get into that whole story—it's all in the past now. I just... Can we talk? About anything? Something random, I mean."

"Random?"

"No rivers or caves or people dying. Anything else is fair game."

"Yeah, all right. I can do random. Let's see... Oh, *I* know!"

She glances up at me, a mix of fear and humor touching her face.

I lean forward, elbows on my knees, hands rubbing together, and in this moment she looks like a mouse who just wandered into a snare.

"Let's talk about that insane shit you pulled with Cass today," I say, "because watching *that* little movie has given me all sorts of random thoughts."

She laughs. Thank Goddess and the devil too, the woman laughs.

SPELLS OF IRON AND BONE

"Cass?" she asks. "If you're talking about Dr. Devane, that so-called *shit* I pulled... Well, it wasn't what it looked like."

"Good to know. 'Cause for a minute there, it *looked* like you were eye-fucking each other in front of the whole class, which is totally against protocol, and also, totally hot."

Her eyes flare for a second, then cool, a smirk sliding across her smart mouth. Whatever this girl feels, she isn't about to let anyone get a solid read on it.

"Eh." Stevie shrugs. "Angry, tight-ass academics aren't exactly my type. Especially ones as ancient as Devane. He's gotta be, what, pushing fifty?"

I laughed, wishing Cass was here for this. Sonofabitch could stand to be knocked down off his high horse once in a while.

"Don't let him hear you say that. He'll fail your ass for sure."

"Seriously. How old is he, anyway?" she presses.

I narrow my eyes. Does she actually *like* that motherfucker?

"Seventy-five," I say quickly. "Actually, closer to eighty, but we all round down to be nice."

"Come *on*."

"He's got a really intense self-care regiment. Bubble baths, face creams, green smoothies."

She cracks up, and suddenly I feel powerful and alive, like I just invented fire or something.

"So if angry, tight-ass academics aren't your type," I say, "what is?"

"Hmm. Maybe you should ask your girlfriend that question."

"I don't have a girlfriend."

"Pretty sure Carly would put your balls in a jar if she heard that."

"Shh!" I press a finger to my lips, trying to hold back the laugh. "Don't say that. She's a Claire—she'll know we're talking about her."

"I'm not the one with balls in danger of removal."

"Nah. Carly and I grew up together, that's all. And for the record? I'm supremely pissed at her about the shit she pulled with you tonight. Soon as I see her again, we're gonna have a nice long chat."

"Um, Baz? Hate to break it to you, but the woman is totally in love with you."

I wave away her words. "Irrelevant."

"For you, maybe."

"Look. Carly and I go round and round about this every year. Yeah, she's in love with me. She knows I don't feel the same way. The only reason we even hang out at all is that her family…" I run a hand through my hair, shake my head. "You know what? Forget it. Seriously, Stevie. I'm sitting by a roaring fire with a hot, pants-less woman, and you want to bring Carly into it?"

She smiles at me, her lips soft and seductive, damp hair curling around her face, the fire crackling beside us, and for a single red-hot heartbeat, it looks like my night's about to head in a *very* good direction. But just before I get too far into the fantasy of tasting those sweet lips, some dick-for-brains barges into the common room, scaring the shit out of us both.

"Stevie, I've been looking everywhere for you!" Ani rushes over, bringing the cold with him. He drops to his knees in front of her chair. "I just heard what happened. Are you all right?"

"They nearly drowned her, Ani," I say. "The fuck you think?"

How the hell did he lose sight of her in the first place?

He shrinks under my glare, knowing he's in deep shit later. Not as deep as Carly, but still.

"Fuck," he says. "I'm so sorry. I'm so fucking sorry." His eyes are rimmed in red, his hands trembling. I don't think I've ever seen the guy so bent out of shape. "I went to get the beers, and the line was crazy long, and then I heard a commotion but just thought it was some drunk people... Stevie, shit. I can't believe... I'm so sorry."

"Ani, chill." I put a hand on his shoulder, my anger fading. Seeing him wound up like this isn't good for anyone, least of all Ani himself. "It's all right now. She's safe."

"It's not your fault, Ani," Stevie says. "Carly and Blue and I just... Well, we're not exactly a love match."

"So you're okay?" he asks.

"Thanks to Baz."

"Can you forgive me for losing you?"

"Already forgiven." Stevie laughs. "But I swear I'm never, ever going to another party with you again."

Ani smiles, blowing out a relieved breath. "I won't ask. I

promise. Next time we're staying in and reading horrible books and drinking sex tea. Deal?"

"It's a date."

"Um, what?" I glare at them both. "What the fuck is sex tea, and why wasn't I told about this?"

No response.

"You guys are seriously not going to share?"

"Nope," they say in unison, then Ani goes, "Sorry, Baz. You had to be there."

"All right, you two troublemakers. That's enough excitement for one night." Stevie disentangles herself from the blanket and stands up, her bare legs peeking out beneath the hem of my sweatshirt.

Fuck, she looks good in that thing.

Now I'm imagining her in my room, climbing out of my bed in the morning with sheet marks on her face and crazy sex-hair, pulling my hoodie over her bare curves...

"Night, guys," she says, picking up her wet clothes and boots. She touches Ani's shoulder, then leans down and presses a kiss to my cheek, less than a hair's breadth from my mouth.

"Thanks for fishing me out back there," she says. Then, with a devious smile that makes me instantly hard, she whispers, "But next time you put your lips on me, let's make sure I'm conscious for it."

THIRTY-ONE

STEVIE

The sky is a deep shade of violet when I'm called urgently from a restless sleep.

I wander into the living room, not entirely sure if I'm dreaming or awake, and stand before the big windows.

It's still hours before the sunrise, and the entire dorm is silent, save for the figures moving through the Forest of Iron and Bone. They're dressed in black, but their bodies are limned in a faint light. I press my face to the window, but they're too far away. I can't make out their faces from here.

I wish I'd picked up some binoculars.

The instant the thought enters my mind, an explosion of white feathers streaks across my window, and suddenly I'm outside the glass, soaring high into the sky, wind rushing through my feathers, my keen eyes easily tracking the figures through the shadows below.

I'm flying. I'm fucking *flying*! The entire campus sprawls out below—the buildings no bigger than models at this height. Soaring over the Petrified Forest, I can see the towers reaching up toward the moon, the thin red ribbon of the river, the swoop of the Cauldron of Flame and Fury, shadows crawling across the bowl. I can even make out the white cloud of mist near the Void.

I fly higher, so close to the stars I swear I can pluck them from the sky and drop them into the Cauldron below.

Somehow, I've become the owl. Or he's become me. I still don't know if this is a dream, but I spread my wings and ride the night air, swooping and swirling, never losing sight of the glowing orbs below. They twist through dark paths in the barren, rocky forest, one right after the other, and I track every turn, flying high enough to ensure they don't see me.

Eventually, they vanish, entering a deep cave along the northern edge of the forest.

I perch on the top of a jagged rock and peer into a crack in the cave roof, just wide enough to see the space below. It's a small cave with some sort of stone altar at the center, a pentacle carved into the top. Torches along the walls cast an inviting orange glow, but everything else about the moment feels dark and sinister.

The men gather around the altar, their faces finally illuminated.

Kirin, Baz, Ani, and Dr. Devane.

They tug their black hoods low, throwing their faces in shadow once again.

I watch as they slice their palms with ritual blades, then

squeeze blood onto their altar. The pentacle on the surface glows bright red, then dims.

"Who gathers here as bonded brothers?" Dr. Devane calls out. It's his voice, but different somehow—deeper and more commanding. Older, if that's possible.

"We," the others respond together. "The Keepers of the Grave."

Keepers of the Grave? What kind of fucked-up secret society game are they playing here?

"Who spills his blood as a symbol of our commitment to one another and in the service and protection of the First?" Devane asks in that same authoritative voice.

"We, the Keepers of the Grave," they say.

"Who vows, by his life or his death, by his silence or his words, in this and all incarnations henceforth, to protect the one true source?"

"We, the Keepers of the Grave."

"We, the Keepers of the Grave," Dr. Devane repeats on his own.

With all that done, he presses his palm to the wall, and a soft red light glows beneath the spot he touched. It's some sort of secret alcove—there's a book inside, which he now retrieves. It's old, with a cracked leather cover and pages as thin as onion skin.

The moment he opens it on the altar, my stomach clenches, a wave of nausea rolling through my gut. My mouth fills with the taste of blood, my ears ringing painfully. The book smells like fire and ash, and when I look at it for too long, I feel it sucking at me like a deep, black hole.

It's evil. Pure, unadulterated evil.

"She asked about the book," Kirin says, as he and the others sign it in blood with the tips of their athames. "Claims her mother mentioned it in a dream."

Holy shit. He's talking about the Book of Shadow and Mists. That must be it.

That fucking liar.

What does that evil thing have to do with my mother's prophecies? Was she warning me against it? Telling me to find and destroy it?

"If Melissa knew about the book," Ani says, "there may be something about it in the prophecies."

"Then we must do everything in our power to find out, and to keep that knowledge from Stevie," Dr. Devane says, placing a Tarot card on top of one of the pages. I can't tell which card, but immediately, he begins another chant.

> *Let our thoughts be true, our messages clear*
> *Both words and intent are recorded here*
> *Leave nothing unwritten, no secrets to bear*
> *Among brothers in blood, all things are shared.*

"The book is the least of our worries right now," Baz says. He pinches the bridge of his nose and sighs into his hand. "When I pulled her out of the river, she wasn't breathing. I had to give her mouth-to-mouth. When our lips

SPELLS OF IRON AND BONE

touched, I saw… Guys, this whole thing is fucking bizarre as hell."

"What happened?" Kirin demands, arms crossed over his chest.

"I had a vision," Baz says. "Well, *had* isn't the right word. More like, I was sucked into it."

"What did you see?" Devane asks. His voice is tight with concern, though I can't tell whether it's for me, for Baz, or for himself.

"It was Stevie, but not," Baz says. "I felt her calling to me. I followed the pull down a path through the forest. It was nighttime, and the moon was just a sliver. The stars were so bright, and I was staring up at them for a long time. By the time I looked down again, there was a lake, and Stevie was there. Totally naked in the shallow part of the water." Baz takes a breath, shakes his head as if he still can't believe what he saw. "She was kneeling on a rock, her other foot in the water. She had two urns, and she poured water from both of them—one onto the rocks, the other back into the lake."

"Was there a circle of standing stones behind her?" Devane asks.

Baz nods, and for a moment, no one speaks.

It sounds eerily similar to the vision Dr. Devane told me about in his class—the one I supposedly pulled him into.

"After she came to," Baz continues, "she said some real weird shit. Seems she had a vision, too."

He tells them about my dream with Cernunnos.

"Holy shit," Ani whispers.

Kirin shoves back his hood, revealing a shocked face. "How is this possible?"

"I *knew* it," Ani says, and now he's grinning. "I didn't have a vision, but I felt the connection from the first time I met her. I knew it!"

What the fuck is going on?

"I don't buy it," Kirin says. "She's uninitiated, spent her entire life in isolation from magick... You might be able to explain away the spirit-blessed thing, but this? This kind of power wouldn't just lie dormant all those years. No. No way."

"I've seen it too, Kirin." Dr. Devane puts his hand on Kirin's shoulder, as if to offer comfort. "The first day I met her. We had an intense moment in the prison—not physical, the way Baz describes—but a connection nevertheless. I saw the same vision at the lake. I tried to convince myself it was coincidence, but it happened again in my class yesterday."

"Dreamcasting," Baz says.

"Yes, that was my first thought," Dr. Devane says. "But now I don't believe it's as simple as all that. How can it be? If what you're telling me is accurate, then she's seen our true forms, Baz. My wolf spirit. Your horned god."

True forms? Wolf spirit? Horned god?

There was a wolf in that ocean vision I had in Devane's class. And after my dream at the river, Baz told me Cernunnos was the horned god of Celtic myth.

But what does that have to do with them?

True forms? Are they saying Devane is a freaking wolf,

and Baz is a god?

Baz is pacing now, his energy anxious. "That means the things we're seeing… The lake, and the standing stones… She's giving us a glimpse of her true spirit as well."

So he's a Celtic god, the good doctor's a wolf, and I'm a *lake*? Okay, I may experiment with a lot of herbs in my tea blends, but even *I'm* not perpetually high enough to buy that.

"No way," Ani says, still smiling. "No fucking way. Guys, this is awesome."

"You say that about everything," Baz says.

Ani's practically bouncing. Kirin looks like he's about to throw up. Baz looks dazed, and—if I'm being honest—a little turned on. And Devane? He looks like he just figured out I'm the bringer of the Goddess-damned apocalypse.

"Cass," Baz says, and Devane just goes, "I know, Baz. I fucking know."

My heart is beating wildly—I don't know whether it's mine or the owl's, or some strange interlocked spirit we both share.

What do you know? I want to shout.

As if he can read my thoughts, Devane sighs and says, "Starla Milan isn't just the witch who can translate her mother's prophecies. She's the—"

The owl takes flight, and the vision vanishes.

I awaken in my bed with a start, bolting upright, my heart still hammering.

On the pillow next to me, glowing in the moonlight filtering in through the window, is an owl feather.

THIRTY-TWO

STEVIE

Armed with a giant travel mug of black tea blended with crushed vanilla bean, fresh mint leaves, and a dash of black pepper—yes girl, my tea game is on point—I head out the next morning for the library.

After the crazy owl incident, I didn't sleep at all, too afraid that if I closed my eyes, my feather would disappear and I'd have to accept it was all a dream.

But when the sun finally rose, the feather was still there, soft and beautiful and as real as the pillow it rested upon.

As for everything else that happened last night?

My head is still spinning. Baz saved my life, and there was a moment there in the common room when I could've sworn he wanted to kiss me. Not just in that flirty, constantly-sexualizing-every-word kind of way I've come to expect from him, either. There's some kind of connection between us, and every time I think of him, I can't help but recall that strange dream in the meadow. The man with the beautiful tattoos, with the same color eyes as Baz. His sensual kisses, his moans, the way his every touch set my body on fire…

Cernunnos…

Goddess, my core aches just to think of it again. But those are dangerous thoughts—totally forbidden from this moment on. Because now I know the cold, hard truth: For whatever reason, four Academy mages—including the illustrious Dr. Devane—are hiding something from me.

Something *about* me.

It's enough to set my blood boiling, and I'm *this* close to blowing the lid off the whole thing, demanding a full explanation, and refusing to do a single line of translation on the prophecies until I have my answers.

But when Kirin opens the door to his office, his smile and energy wrapping me in a warm welcome, my anger turns into something much worse.

Pain.

Looking into his green-gold eyes—eyes whose mesmerizing beauty captured my heart months ago—I try unsuccessfully to keep the sting of betrayal from eating away at my heart.

We're supposed to be a team—Kirin said as much.

So how come I feel like I've just signed a deal with the devil and missed most of the fine print?

"Good morning," he says brightly, stepping aside to welcome me in. "You ready to hit the books?"

I'm ready to hit *something*, but I rein it in. Going ballistic isn't going to bring me any closer to the truth—not to the ones in Mom's prophecies *or* the ones hiding behind Kirin's sexy smile.

"How was the party?" he asks as we climb the stairs to the archives.

"You didn't hear?"

The way Baz was talking about it in the cave last night, it was clear he and Ani had already told Kirin and Doc what happened at the river.

"Hear what? I was in the archives until about three or four in the morning, totally secluded. Crashed in my office after that. In fact, I just woke up about ten minutes before you got here—hence the bedhead. Well, to be more accurate, office-chair-head."

"Nice." I force a laugh. "Anyway, the party was okay. Nothing to write home about."

I watch for a reaction. A raised eyebrow, a twitch, but there's nothing but fake morning pleasantries in his eyes.

"Kirin," I say, fighting to keep the irritation from my tone, "Last night... Did you guys go out? After the party, I mean?"

Something finally flashes behind Kirin's gaze, and his energy shifts. Suddenly, it seems like an effort for him to hold that smile in place, and I know right then and there that his next breath is going to be a lie.

"Me? No. Baz and Ani didn't mention anything either. They're probably still sleeping—they were pretty wrecked after the party."

"What about Dr. Devane?"

"I'm not really up on his social calendar, but I'm pretty

sure he doesn't have one. Why are you asking about this?"

My heart sinks into my stomach.

It's one thing to tell myself I don't know them all that well, and I'm misunderstanding things. Or that there are so many people on campus, maybe I'm getting their energies mixed up.

But Kirin is flat out lying to me, and I don't know why.

I *do* know that what I saw last night wasn't a dream. Not because I have so much faith in my visions, or even because of the feather.

But because Kirin, graduate mage and Keeper of the Grave, whatever the hell that means, just made a stupidly human mistake.

Kirin told me he hadn't heard anything about the party last night—that he'd been sequestered in the library.

Yet now he's telling me the guys were pretty wrecked after.

How many lies and half-truths is that now? I'm quickly losing count. The spying at Kettle Black. The dodginess when I asked about the Book of Shadow and Mists. The party.

I hate lies. Hate liars. And this Academy is filled with both.

It's all I can do not to lay it out right here, to demand he tell me about the Keepers of the Grave and the dark book and those dreamcasting visions.

Demand he explain what Dr. Devane meant when he said that I'm not just the witch who can translate her mother's prophecies.

But I can't figure out how to do it without telling him about my crazy owl trip across the sky, and I *definitely* don't want to share that right now.

For now, my best course of action is to stick with the plan. Work on Mom's research, make the most of my classes, try to get a handle on my magick, avoid the hell out of Carly and her merry band of psychotics, and most importantly?

Stick to these conniving, secret-society scoundrels like a wart on a witch's tit, hoping they fuck up and spill their secrets before they figure out all of mine.

Inside the archives, Kirin retrieves the notebooks we started with yesterday, and also hands me a thick manila folder full of computer printouts. News articles, I see when I peek inside.

"I wanted you to take a look at all this, see what you make of it. It's part of what we've been tracking—what we believe are the wrongful arrests of witches and mages since magick first became public knowledge. It doesn't account for all of them, of course—some locales don't even bother reporting when a magickal citizen is taken into custody. But it gives you some perspective on why our work here is so important."

I take a deep breath and page through the printouts, skimming the headlines. Explosions, fires, murders. Dastardly plots to steal, maim, torture. Sensationalist commentary on the dangers of unregulated witchcraft. Calls for more restrictions. More executions.

The articles date back decades, starting right around the

time magick was publicly revealed. There seems to be a slowdown in the early 1990s, but then it spikes again—right around the time my parents left the Academy.

The last batch of articles are all about me—the same articles Devane showed me in prison.

I snap the folder shut, not wanting to see one more gruesome headline.

"So in all these so-called crimes and attacks," I say, the pieces sliding into place in my mind, "the victims themselves are witches and mages—just like the accused parties. Witch-owned businesses are being destroyed. Mage family members killed. The homes of witches torched, supposedly by their own hands. You'd think that if whoever was behind the attacks wanted to freak out the public, get more restrictions put on us, they'd go after non-magickal humans."

"That's the crazy part," Kirin says. "It's almost ridiculous. Why would witches destroy their own businesses? And hurt their own friends and families? It just seems so… so random."

"That's just it," I tell him, making the connection. "The attacks are being staged to *look* random."

"But why? What's the endgame here? If they wanted to thin out the magickal population, there are probably more effective ways."

"Throughout history—even before people knew about real magick—the number one tactic used to isolate witches was dehumanization. It happened during the Salem witch trials, and in Europe, and long before that, too. And the fastest way to dehumanize us is to make sure everyone else fears us."

"Exactly. So why not attack human-owned businesses and keep fanning those flames?"

"Because it's more effective this way," I say. "The message our enemies want to send is that magick is so powerful, so corruptible, that even witches and mages themselves can't be trusted to control it. That we can just erupt at any time, causing chaos and death without warning. They want everyone to believe that we're so unbalanced, we can turn on our own kind in a heartbeat. Turn on our own families."

Kirin nods, his brow furrowed as he follows this to its logical conclusion. "And if we can do this to our own kind, imagine what we might do to them?"

"Brilliant strategy, really." I rub my thumb over my wrist, over the slightly raised edges of the pentacle tattoo. "And they know exactly where to find us. How to target us."

The registration is part of a national database. It's supposed to be confidential, accessible only at the highest levels of law enforcement, but everyone knows how that goes.

"Something tells me it's not just a bunch of human fanatics working with a few crooked magick-users to stoke the flames," Kirin says. "There are witches and mages working on this from the inside. Possibly at the highest levels of the magickal community."

"You said you wanted to give me perspective?" I ask. "Consider it gotten."

Shoving aside the folder, I grab one of Mom's notebooks from the stack, opening it to a random page. Just like yesterday, new passages appear at my touch.

"It's still happening," I confirm. "Same as yesterday."

Kirin's eyes light up behind his glasses, and I read the latest verse to appear:

> *Hexed and cursed, bruised and broken*
> *What comes first, the dark words spoken*
> *The veil is torn, the spells diminished*
> *Mage firstborn, the final finish.*

"Wow," he says, his eyes filling with the same excitement I saw yesterday. He taps on the table, glancing around the archive lab. "Okay, here's what we'll do. You transcribe the new phrases you're seeing, I'll compare them with the original texts detailing all the Tarot card placements, and we'll see what kind of sense we can make of it."

"Sounds good," I say, and just like that, we snap into work mode, both of us diving headfirst into our tasks.

It's painstaking work. My mother's passages don't always appear clearly, and sometimes the words rearrange themselves, scrambling into nonsense before I can even finish transcribing them. I end up having to do a lot of re-work, and even after two hours, I only manage to transcribe a few pages.

Kirin's got the original texts on a laptop, doing his best

to match up my notes and make sense of it all, but I'm not sure he's making much progress either.

"You holding up okay?" he asks when he catches me watching him.

I close Mom's notebook and set down my pen. "I think I've hit my wall."

"You did great, Stevie. I know it's slow going, but we'll get there. I can feel it." He smiles that go-team smile again. It makes my heart hurt.

We lock eyes, neither of us speaking for several long, uncomfortable seconds.

"Kirin," I begin, finally breaking the silence, "what do you know about my mother? About her time at the Academy?"

Kirin removes his glasses and rubs his eyes, letting out a long, slow breath.

This time, when I feel the pulse of his energy, I know he's going to tell me the truth.

"According to Headmistress Trello," he says, "your parents were among the most powerful magickal students the Academy has ever seen. First as undergrads, and then as graduate students. Your father was studying potions—he was earth-blessed. Your mother had three affinities—all but fire. Her gift, as you know, was prophecy.

"But as the years went on, they became more and more isolated, your mother spending almost all of her time in the library, poring over old tomes, drawing cards, writing everything in these notebooks. I don't know when things went bad, or how everything unraveled after that. All I know is that she and Anna had a major falling out that essentially divided the staff and graduate body into two camps—those that supported your parents and wanted to know more about the things your mother's prophecies foretold, and those that... Well, to be blunt—those that thought she'd gone mad.

"She was pregnant with you by that time, and your father finally convinced her to leave—that the stress of staying would do irreparable damage to her *and* to you."

A long, heavy sigh escapes my lips. It's more than anyone else has ever told me, but still not anywhere close to enough. Not anywhere close to the full truth.

"I understand why Trello wants me here," I say. "Witches being targeted like this, the attacks still happening—it affects us all, and my mother knew it would. But I can't help but sense there's a lot more to the story about my parents than anyone is telling me. Professor Phaines seems kind of above the gossip, but Trello's definitely keeping secrets—you should've seen her clam up when I met her the other day. She tried to act sympathetic, but it's so obvious she's just protecting herself. Dr. Devane is... Well, I'm still trying to figure him out. And you're..."

I trail off, not sure where to go with that.

"I'm *what*, Stevie?"

"I don't know," I say softly, lowering my eyes. "That's kind of my point. For all the time we saw each other at Kettle Black, I really know nothing about you, Kirin Weber."

SARAH PIPER

"Not true. I was there every day for nearly three months. That has to count for something."

"But it was just a couple of hours a day. And of that, I spent maybe fifteen minutes at your table. Add all that up, and we've probably spent less than a day or two together."

He glances at the ceiling, literally doing the math.

Goddess, he's such a nerdy genius.

"Okay, fair point," he says, then reaches across the table and takes my hand. It's a friendly gesture more than a romantic one, but a spark races up my arm just the same. "But now we have the opportunity to change that, Stevie."

I want to believe him. So, so badly. And he's right, we do have the opportunity. I'll be sitting here in this lab with him for hours, multiple times a week, probably on the weekends too. And that's not counting going out for coffee —didn't he say the invitation still stands?

I almost smile, but force myself to hold back.

It sounds lovely, but spending time with someone doesn't mean getting to know him if all you're getting to know are more lies and omissions.

I wish I could convince myself otherwise, to tell him what I know he wants to hear. But I can't find any more words to fill the awkward spaces creeping in between us, and eventually, he seems to run out of them, too.

So when he rises to put Mom's research back in the cabinet and lock up his laptop, I lock up my notes, gather the rest of my stuff, and slip out of there before he even knows I'm gone.

THIRTY-THREE

STEVIE

"A witch's mind is her sharpest tool, but a Tarot deck is her closest companion. Her confidante, her trusted advisor." Standing at the front of our Tarot Divination and Spellwork lab, Professor Nakata beams at us, her brown eyes sparkling. "A Tarot deck is, for all intents and purposes, your squad."

There are only fifteen of us in the lab, our desks set up in a U-formation, and we all laugh. It's hard not to; Professor Nakata looks about Dr. Devane's age, but where he's cranky and controlling, she's got a bouncy, youthful energy that immediately makes me feel light and happy.

It's almost enough to help me forget those infuriating mages.

I say *almost*, because one of them is in my lab.

As if he can sense me thinking about him, Baz looks at me across the U and grins.

It's so hard to reconcile that devastating smile and the

tenderness he showed me last night with the men I saw in the cave, slicing their hands, chanting about brotherhood and service and the one true source and that book—that black, evil, soul-sucking book...

"The stronger and more intimate your bond with your Tarot cards," Professor Nakata continues, shuffling her own deck as she does, "the more you'll come to rely on them in your magickal practice. Practically speaking, the Tarot can be used for all manner of spellwork and divination."

She draws a card from her deck, holding it out for us to see.

"The Moon," she says. "Often associated with the realm of dreams and fantasies. Tuck this card under your pillow at night to inspire lucid dreaming and clear dream interpretation."

She shuffles it back into the deck, then selects another one. This time, it's a Minor Arcana from the suit of Pentacles—the Page, as it's called in her deck. The Princess, as I saw in my vision.

"Cards can be used for manifesting certain outcomes," Professor Nakata says, "or charging up food and drinks with specific magickal intentions. For example, if you need help passing your classes, you might slip the Page of Pentacles under your morning coffee mug. This card promises an infusion of positive energy for learning new material."

I make a mental note of that, wondering if there's a specific card to help me pass Devane's class. Mental Magicks is probably the one I'm most in danger of failing.

Then again, it's only day two. Plenty of time to piss off more professors. Hey, shoot for the stars, right?

"Similarly, cards can be used to charge ingredients for magickal workings and potions, to enhance love spells or banishing spells, and..." She draws one more card—the Lovers—then smiles. "To encourage a healthy sex life."

We all snicker at that one, and I'm pretty sure Baz is staring right at me, but I refuse to look at him.

"Good," Professor Nakata says with a nod. "Just making sure you're all paying attention. You'll have only one assignment for this class, but that assignment is something you'll do each and every day—multiple times, if you feel called to do so. Can anyone guess what it is?"

Baz raises his hand. "Does it have anything to do with the hot sex spell?"

Professor Nakata laughs. "It might, Mr. Redgrave. That's up to you."

He gives her a wide smile and puts his hands behind his head. "I'm all ears, Professor."

"For the remainder of the semester—indeed, for the remainder of your lives, if I do my job right—you'll be keeping Tarot journals. Handwritten, of course, to encourage a stronger connection from hand to heart. You'll draw at least one card to reflect on each day, either first thing in the morning or at the end of the evening, in addition to any other spreads you may do. I want you to pay particular attention when your elemental affinities show up in a reading—they'll always have the strongest messages for you. Now, who's ready for the fun part?"

Baz raises his hand again. "Does *this* have anything to do with the hot sex spell?"

The class chuckles, and Professor Nakata shoots him a faux-warning glare, but it's clear she finds him as amusing and charming as the rest of us do.

She sets her cards on her desk and pulls out a rolling set of shelves from the back wall, steering it to the center of the classroom. There are five shelves, each holding dozens of rectangular packages, all of them wrapped in black silk cloth and tied with silver ribbons.

"Meet your future besties," she says, and we all lean forward for a better look. "Each one of these very special packages holds a deck of Tarot cards, cleansed and consecrated by the elder witches and mages of the Academy. Tarot decks give off energetic vibrations like everything else, and you'll want to find the one that feels like a good energetic match for you. They're wrapped, so you won't be able to pick based on visual cues. You'll need to open up your senses and really feel into the deck energies."

She calls us up one at a time, and I watch as my fellow classmates run their hands along the shelves, selecting their decks.

"Don't worry about someone else choosing a deck meant for you," she says. "That won't happen. There are plenty of cards here for everyone, and you'll know your unique energetic match when you find it."

When it's finally my turn, my stomach is so fizzy I can barely contain myself. Not counting the big novelty deck in my living room, I've never had my own deck before—just the magick cards that show up at random, and vanish just as quickly.

As I run my hands over the shelves, a mix of different energies touches my fingertips. Some are warm and welcoming, others slick and cool, one or two cold and prickly enough to make me pull back. I take my time, following the gentle pull of a deck on the bottom shelf, all the way toward the back. When I pick it up, my hands immediately tingle, my heart beating a little faster. It's almost as if the deck is whispering in my ear, "I'm yours! Take me home!"

Back at my desk, I carefully untie the ribbon and unwrap the silk covering. The cards are face down, their backs a deep purple that's so dark and inviting it's almost black, edged in silvery ink with crescent moons at the center.

When everyone has selected their cards, Professor Nakata invites us to shuffle while she draws three card-shaped rectangles on the whiteboard at the front of the room, then writes a question beneath each one.

"Once you're ready, I'd like you to start with a simple three-card deck interview spread to help you bond with your new cards. Simply ask the deck the question, then draw a card and see what comes up for you."

I shuffle my deck one last time, then ask the first question.

"What are you here to teach me?" I draw The Hermit, an old man with a long white beard, standing on top of a rocky outcropping that overlooks the valley and river below. He's holding a lantern, illuminating the path ahead.

My sense from this card is that the deck is going to teach me to know and trust myself, to be my own guiding light.

"How can I best honor our connection?" I ask, then turn over the Three of Cups. In this version, there are three men gathered at a table, sharing a meal and holding up their cups in salutation. I've always associated the Three of Cups card with friendship, particularly Jessa's, and seeing it here now makes me smile. The message coming through is that the deck wants me to treat it like a friend, to ask it for advice and include it in important decision-making conversations as well as fun and frivolous chats, just like I would a real friend.

"Now," I ask, taking a deep breath for the final question, "is there anything else you'd like to share with me at this time?"

In response, I draw The Star.

And my heart nearly leaps out of my chest.

There's a nude woman kneeling in a lake, an urn in each hand, a circle of standing stones behind her...

It looks almost exactly like the vision Dr. Devane and Baz described last night. The dreamcast I supposedly sucked them into.

Dr. Devane said something about my true form. Does it have something to do with this card? The Star?

Is that what the deck wants me to know?

My hands are trembling, my thoughts racing. I can't even process this message, whatever the hell it's trying to tell me. Hastily I assemble the cards back together again, but before I can wrap the deck in its silk cloth, two cards slip out, landing face up on the desk.

The King of Wands, a stern-looking man with long auburn hair and bright red robes, sitting on an ornately carved throne, a huge wand in his hand. The other card is…

Shit.

Trump Fifteen—a card that most decks have labeled The Devil. But in my deck, the card has a different name altogether.

Cernunnos.

The imagery on the card is an exact replica of my vision.

Suddenly, the room around me fades, and I'm back in the meadow of the beast. But instead of the gentle green ferns I saw last night, now I'm standing on scorched earth. All around me, a fire burns, consuming everything in sight. Through trees engulfed in flame, I spot a battle raging in the distance, soldiers firing magelight, bodies falling, rivers of blood washing over the land.

The fire continues to rage with all the sound and fury of a runaway train, and when I turn around in search of an escape, I see him.

Not the beast.

The man.

My lover.

His crown of leaves is engulfed in flames, his body burning.

"No!" I launch myself at him and knock him to the ground, swatting at the flames with my bare hands until

I'm certain not a single ember remains. His eyes glow through the smoke, red-brown and full of fire, just like the burning trees…

When the smoke clears, I realize I'm no longer in the burning meadow. That I was never in that place.

It's just Professor Nakata's classroom.

And I'm on the floor.

Straddling… Baz.

"Not that I'm complaining," he says quietly, his ever-maddening smirk stretching wide, "but maybe we should take this somewhere private?"

Suddenly I'm aware of the laughter, the phones snapping pics, the whispers.

Gritting my teeth, I say to Baz, "Are you that desperate for action that you have to spell unsuspecting girls into climbing on top of you?"

Baz is still grinning at me, clearly enjoying this. "To be fair, *you* knocked *me* down."

"To be fair, I thought you were on fire."

"To be fair, you're still sitting on top of me." He shifts beneath me, letting me feel the hard press of his cock. And it's… very hard.

And very big.

"To be fair, I…" Oh, fuck. I'm still straddling him, and I'm quickly losing brain cells as his arousal threatens to ignite my own.

I get to my feet as gracefully as I can, and Baz follows suit, but the damage is done. I wonder how long it will take for this to get back to Carly.

"Don't panic," Professor Nakata says, her eyes bright as she joins us in the center of the room. "The Tarot can be a very powerful tool, and clearly it had something important to show you, Stevie. Would you like to share your vision with the class?"

"Not... not right now," I say, trying my best to save face. "I'd like a little time to process it first, if that's okay."

"Of course! You know, I think this experience will make an excellent first entry into your journal. Perhaps you and Baz can write something together?"

"Great idea," Baz says, sliding an arm over my shoulders like we're the best of pals.

"Excellent," Professor Nakata says, then reminds us about our daily draws and journaling. I'm so flustered and tangled up about that damn fire-vision and that damn Baz-mounting that I barely register what she's saying. When the bell finally chimes, it's all I can do to grab my new Tarot deck and my bag and get the hell out of there.

Out in the hall, the exit blazing a beautiful white light ahead, I'm just steps away from blissful freedom when I hear the call I've been dreading.

"Stevie, wait up!" Baz says.

Keep walking, just keep walking…

I hear his footfalls as he jogs to catch up. "Come on, it *was* kind of hilarious. Admit it."

"If by hilarious, you mean humiliating, yep, I admit it."

"Hey. Stevie, stop. Please."

Closing my eyes and letting out a deep sigh, I finally stop walking and turn to face him.

"What do you want, Baz?"

"Lunch, actually."

"Great. Don't let me stop you."

His brow creases, a flicker of hurt flashing through his eyes.

"I'm sorry," I say. "I'm just... I'm not very good company today."

"Well, that blows, because I was really hoping you'd join me."

"For lunch?"

Baz flashes his killer smile. "Since we've already moved on to the dry humping stage of our relationship, I thought we should at least grab a meal together. I'm not sure we even know each other's last names."

"Mine is leave me the hell alone, and yours is jerkoff."

"So if we got married, and you decided to hyphenate, you'd be—"

"What do you *want*, Baz?"

Married? Is he serious right now?

"I told you. Lunch. I thought you might want to check out the Thai place at Flame and Fury. Their Pad Thai is insane. You don't have a peanut allergy, do you?"

My stomach grumbles, my mouth watering on command, which of course reminds me of Dr. Devane and his stupid mental magicks tricks.

I love Thai food, but I don't love the good doctor right now, or Kirin or Baz or any other guy for that matter.

As far as I'm concerned, the more distance I can put between me and anyone with a penis, the better.

Especially a huge, hard penis like the one that was pressed between my thighs minutes ago…

"I can't," I say, shaking off the memory and hoping that's the end of it. "I have plans."

"With Kirin?"

"No," I snap. "With a wall of solid rock. Because it turns out talking to *them* is a lot easier than talking to men."

THIRTY-FOUR

STEVIE

I refuse to go down. I refuse to go down. I refuse to go—

My grip slips, the rock scraping my fingertips raw as I plummet to the ground.

Again.

Thank Goddess Dr. Devane didn't cheap out on the gear, because this crash pad is getting a workout today.

I get back to my feet and give it another go. This time, I manage to hold on a little longer, my feet scrambling for purchase, the next handhold just one good stretch away...

"Best view of the rocks I've seen in years," comes the voice from below.

I crash down in a blaze of humiliating glory, landing hard on my ass, glaring up into the face of the very man I came out here to forget.

One of them, anyway.

"Climber, huh?" Baz holds out a hand to help. "That's pretty hardcore."

"More like a crasher today," I grumble, taking his hand and hauling myself up.

"Didn't mean to distract you." He smirks, but then it fades into a smile that's slightly more chagrined. "I probably should've kept my mouth shut this time, huh?"

"Hmm. Which of the many, *many* possible times are you referring to?"

He gestures toward the rock overhead.

"Yes, probably." I give him a playful shove. "But it's not all your fault. I'm off my game today. I haven't been on the rocks since… Well, it's been a while."

I dust my hands off and take a step back to gaze up at my nemesis. The rock wall, not the man, though I'm still on the fence about the man's allegiances, especially after that shady-ass brotherhood meeting I witnessed last night.

Part of me wants to ask him about it, just like I wanted to ask Kirin. But that was definitely some next-level secret society shit, and the whole point of secret societies is to keep them—wait for it—secret. Asking him now will only alert him to the fact that I'm onto them, and then I'll have zero chance at figuring out what's going on.

Best to play it cool, see what I can suss out for myself.

Besides, despite all the sneaking around and half-truths, I still don't get bad vibes from any of them. Their intentions, their energy, even their eyes when they look at me—it's all genuine. Protective, even.

I don't know what to make of it, but I do trust that I'm not in any immediate danger. Not from the guys, anyway.

"Look, Stevie," he finally says, kicking at the dirt with

his toe. "I came out here to apologize. Not about distracting you. About mouthing off, making everything a joke... I know you've seen some shit in your life, okay? And it can't be easy for you right now, being here with all of us... I just wanted to say sorry if I've done anything to make it harder on you."

"Make it harder on me?" I press my lips together to keep from smiling.

"Right."

"Shit, Baz, if you don't jump on this innuendo, I will."

"Hey!" He cracks up. "Don't encourage me!"

"From the way things felt before, I don't think you need much encouragement."

"Not where you're concerned, apparently." His gaze sweeps down to take in my outfit—sports bra, leggings, climbing shoes. That about sums it up.

Heat rises inside me, my body still clinging to the memory of straddling him in class. To the vision in the meadow last night, when the only fire we had to contend with was the one between us.

Us. Me and Baz. I know now that it was him, my mysterious lover. That we connected somehow, probably when our lips touched after he pulled me from the river. For me, it was through the Devil card. For him, through the Star.

I don't know what it means. Whether I can control it. Whether it's the same thing that's happening with Dr. Devane and the vision at the ocean.

But I can't pretend I don't feel something. Some deep, primal attraction, especially where Baz is concerned.

"Apology accepted." I jab a finger into his chest, anything to break the tension roiling between us. "But don't think that's carte blanche for future indiscretions. And also... I'm sorry, too. I shouldn't have snapped at you after Divination."

"I like you snappy." He wraps his hand around mine, presses it against his chest. His heart is beating wildly, and for a minute I feel myself drifting back to our meadow...

"So why the fuck does this asshole rock keep throwing you down?" he asks, breaking the vision before it can take hold. "You need me to kick its ass?"

"If only it were that easy." I point to the overhang about fifteen feet up. "See that lip up there?"

He steps closer to take a look, crowding right into my space, still holding my hand.

"I can't seem to make it over the top," I say. "And I don't want to go higher without a belay. This rock isn't bolted, and I'm not familiar enough with it to go too far up on my own."

"You want some help?"

He's totally serious. But he's also still holding my hand, and when he looks down at me with those devilish eyes, the very last of my self-control marches away.

Okay, straight talk. I have a personal rule, enacted soon after I came out of the post-tragedy haze and started going out on occasional dates again.

No sex with anyone I actually like, or can see myself liking in the future. Nothing that could possibly lead to romantic entanglements, falling in love, heartbreak. I can't deal with a major loss—not again.

It's the one thing that always made me keep a little distance from Kirin back in Tres Búhos, as much as Jessa liked to tease me about hooking up with him.

I like Kirin—I have for a long time now. That automatically makes him a bad candidate, because if circumstances were different, I could put myself right on the path to heartbreak.

But Baz?

He's impossibly sexy, strong, mysterious... and he should totally come with a warning label. I've only known him a few days, but already he drives me crazy at the best of times. If we were in a relationship, I'm 99% sure one of us would end up looking for an alibi and a place to hide the body, probably sooner rather than later.

So that makes Baz a pretty safe bet for a little fun.

No chance of a relationship. No chance of getting hurt when that relationship comes to its inevitable end.

So maybe that's why I squeeze his hand now, close the last of the space between us, and look at him with a smile that can only be interpreted in one way.

"Um, Stevie?" he asks. "I don't want to make assumptions, but—"

"But in this case you're totally right, and if you don't kiss me right now, I swear I'm going to—"

Baz grabs the back of my head, claiming my mouth in a fiercely possessive kiss I feel all the way down in the bones of my bones. He backs me up until my shoulders hit the rock, staking his claim with every delicious stroke of his tongue, every soft moan he unleashes from my lips. His scent invades my senses—smokey and earthy, a hint of black pepper, sexy and masculine.

Just when I'm certain I'm about to pass out from lack of oxygen, he breaks our kiss and spins me around, pinning me against the rock from behind, pressing his body against mine as he devours my neck with kisses, trailing his lips down to my shoulder and back again, his hand sliding across the front of my waist, slipping down behind my waistband.

"We good?" he whispers in my ear, his breath hot.

"*So* good."

Baz groans in response, his fingers sliding deeper, seeking my wet heat. He teases my clit, making slow circles, then dipping lower, his teeth grazing my earlobe, his fingers slipping inside me, then pulling out, teasing over my clit again, and holy hell my legs are already starting to tremble…

I want him. All of him. No more teasing and touching. I need to feel him inside me. Now.

"Wait!" I cry out.

He stops immediately, and I turn around to face him, panting from his touch.

"You okay?" he asks.

I nod emphatically. "But if we're going to do this, we need some ground rules."

He blinks at me, a little shellshocked, then smiles.

"So you're not just a pain in the ass, but a high maintenance pain in the ass?" His tone is light and teasing, even as his cock presses urgently against his jeans. "Why am I not surprised?"

"I just mean this has to be a onetime thing. One and done." I put a hand on his chest, still trying to catch my breath. His heart is thudding as hard and fast as mine. "And we never speak of it again—not to each other, and absolutely not to anyone else."

He lifts a shoulder in a casual shrug, but I can feel his energy—he doesn't like the idea. Which part of it specifically, I'm not sure. But he doesn't like it.

"Fine by me," he says anyway.

"That's all you have to say about it? Fine by me?"

"Nothing else to say."

"Okay, well, you're definitely not the most romantic man I've ever met."

"No." The smile is back, brighter than ever, his eyes glinting with mischief. "But I can pretty much guarantee you'll be screaming my name soon."

I return his devilish grin. "Because you're going to torture me?"

"Oh, you can bet on it." He puts his hands against the rock, caging me inside his arms. He's so close I can see the facets of the rock reflected in his eyes, as hard and wild as he is.

When I don't respond, he tilts his head, sizing me up. The cockiness fades from his gaze for just a moment, and he lowers his voice, as if the rocks are listening in and he doesn't want to be overheard. "You like playing with fire,

Little Bird."

I want to tell him no, I don't. Not with guys. Not *ever*. Dangerous boys and me don't mix. Mages especially. But something about this place, about my visions, about him… *Goddess*, there's a wildness that calls to something deep inside me, an animal begging to be let out of her cage after years of captivity.

And no one brings out the wild girl in me like Baz.

"I'm not the gentle, cuddle-for-hours-afterward type," he says. "You should probably know that going in."

"You make it sound like you're a—"

"Yes." His eyes go fiery hot, and he wraps a hand around my throat, squeezing just enough to get my attention. There's no more teasing now, only heat. Only passion. Only a promise my core is begging him to keep. Brushing a thumb across my lips, he whispers, "That's *exactly* what I am, and you'd do well to remember it."

Holy shit, I'm so wet for him, my clit is already throbbing with every heartbeat, my nipples straining uncomfortably against the fabric of my sports bra, my whole body on fire for his hands, his mouth, his cock.

I force out a laugh, but instead of the cool nonchalance I'm going for, it comes out wobbly and faint. "Um… Am I going to need a safe word for this?"

Baz, unfazed as ever, slides his hand down my backside and grips my thigh, hitching my leg up around his hip. The thick length of his cock presses against my center, and I let out an involuntary gasp.

Back in the classroom, I thought I'd gotten his… *ahem*… full attention.

Clearly, he was holding back before.

The bastard is *seriously* packing, and now he wants me to know it.

I hate that my body wants him so badly. *Needs* him so badly.

"Safe word?" His molten gaze sweeps down to my mouth, and he leans in close, the rasp of his breath teasing my lips with a gentle caress that belies his bruising grip on my thigh. "It's cute you think you'll still be able to *form* words while I'm fucking you."

Something escapes my mouth—a squeak? A protest? A prayer? I'll never know, because in that instant, Baz claims me with another kiss even more possessive than the first, plumbing my depths, demanding access I'm all too eager to grant him.

He's all darkness and shadow, rage and pain, each emotion hitting me with a wave that threatens to pull me under.

But it seems he's also a man of his word, because as much as I want to put an end to this—as much as I know I'm making a terrible mistake—I can't force my lips to form a single word. Instead, I find myself breaking away just long enough to tear off my sports bra.

Baz moans and palms my naked breasts, then lowers his mouth to my nipple, grazing it with his teeth as he sucks and teases…

"Last chance, Little Bird," he says, then moves to the

other nipple, flicking it with his tongue as his hand slides down the front of my leggings, seeking my wet heat once again. "You want to change your mind? Now's the time."

"No," I say, fisting his hair and arching my hips to get closer, to take his fingers in deeper. "I want you to touch me. To—"

"And here's a wildlife mating ritual you don't see every day, kids!"

Baz and I break apart in a heartbeat, whipping around to see Emory standing before us, straddling a bike. She's smirking at us, holding out her phone like she's the paparazzi and we're the celeb snap of the century.

"For fuck's sake, Emory." Baz jumps in front of me to block her view. "Don't be a dickhead."

"I'm not the one whoring around the whole Academy," she says.

"It's none of your business how I spend my lunch hour, who I spend it with, or what I spend it doing. Now hop back on that bike and fuck off somewhere else, preferably far, far away from me."

She flashes a glittery smile, then turns it on me. "I wasn't talking about *you*, Baz."

Seriously?

Why is it that the girls who refuse to move on from middle school only keep the *worst* parts of middle school? Why can't they ditch the backstabbing, name-calling, mind-game-playing bullshit and just, like, draw doodle-hearts in their notebooks and have crushes on boy bands and argue over the best-scented body lotion?

Emory holds up her phone again, snaps another shot. "Carly's going to *love* this. Maybe Trello will put it on the student website, too. Right on the home page."

Shirtlessness be damned. I'm about to launch myself at her, give her a *real* photo opp, but by the time I work up my nerve, she's already pedaling away, zooming back down the path the way she came.

"Fuck." Baz drags a hand through his hair. "I should probably go run interference. I need to get that phone."

"Do you really think she'll send stuff to Trello?"

"Trello? No. But she's got photos of you, Stevie. Of us. And as beautiful and spectacular as you are…" Baz grins. As if to prove his point, he lowers his mouth, blazing a trail of kisses across the top of each breast, thumbs stroking my nipples, making me ache for him once again.

But then he sighs and says, "You said you didn't want anyone to know about this. And even if you did, I can't imagine you'd want them finding out from Emory and her damn homemade porno."

I lean back against the rock and sigh, crossing my arms over my chest. "No, I wouldn't."

Baz crouches down and grabs my sports bra, hands it back to me. "Look, I don't want to leave you. Are you fucking insane? But if I don't go, not only are those pictures fair game, but she's gonna ride back here with Carly and the rest of them in tow, and make a big fucking scene, and I really don't want you caught up in all that bullshit."

"You sure about that?" I yank the bra over my head, get

the girls situated again. "Maybe it's *you* you don't want caught up in it."

His eyes flare, his energy smacking me hard. I hurt him with that comment.

"Sorry. Shit, I'm sorry." I blow out a breath and lower my eyes. "I know you're looking out for me. I just don't think there's much point. She's probably halfway to the dorms by now."

Baz smiles. "Good thing your boy knows how to teleport."

Despite the disappointment that our happy little afternoon delight got shat upon by one of Carly's bobbleheads, I can't help but agree.

"Hey." He leans in close, cradles the back of my head, and brushes his lips across my mouth in a kiss so tender, I can't believe it's from Baz. Then, with one more flash of that deadly smirk, "To be continued, Little Bird."

I return his devious smile.

On behalf of myself, my aching nipples, and my throbbing core…

You can fucking bet on it, Baz Redgrave.

THIRTY-FIVE

STEVIE

I keep telling myself it's for the best. That Emory actually did me a huge favor by interrupting us before things got totally out of control.

But I'm completely full of shit.

I wanted him. I still want him.

See, this is why I have rules in the first place.

Shaking off the funk, I grab my daypack and head to a nearby boulder—one that isn't so keen on showing me who's boss—and haul myself up to the top, finding a nice flat spot to plunk my ass down and enjoy a chocolate-covered granola bar. Not as good as sex with Baz would've been, perhaps, but it satisfies a need in its own right.

After the snack, I take out my phone, snap a selfie for Jessa.

Getting my rocks off in the Forest of Iron & Bone, I text. *Wish u were here.*

Bitch, why are you so hot? she replies. *BTW, your boyfriend says... Hey girl! Miss your fine ass... literally!*

I'm about to ask her who she thinks my boyfriend is when her pic comes through.

I laugh like a damn machine gun, so obnoxiously loud I'm pretty sure I scare all the rattlers out of their hidey-holes.

It's Mr. Winky, propped up next to a potted cactus on the windowsill of my old bedroom.

Goddess, I miss that place.

I miss Jessa. Her balls-out sense of humor, her smile, her hugs. All of it.

Still laughing, I reply, *OMG, you found him!*

Yeah, and you're lucky I love you, or else that could've ended badly for both of us.

Love you too, I text. *BTW, he's single now if you want your shot!*

She sends me the pondering emoji, then a string of laughing-crying emojis. *Girl, don't tempt me.*

I send back the eggplant emoji, followed by the cactus. *Just don't mix them up, b/c good luck explaining THAT at the ER!*

You are terrible and beautiful and I love you the mostest. Gotta finish packing, and no, that's not a euphemism. Call me soon!

I send her a kissy-face, then put my phone away, lying back against the sun-warmed rock to watch the clouds drift by. I guess I pass out at some point, because when I open my eyes again, the light has changed, the air a few degrees cooler.

I blink the sleep from my eyes and rub my bare arms, trying to rally. I should probably head back to my suite and take a shower, get some sleep in an actual bed.

As soon as I sit up, the air around me wavers, the sky flickering ominously.

It doesn't feel like a storm, though.

It feels like a glitch in the matrix.

The breeze stills. The Petrified Forest, normally alive with the rustling of sagebrush and the chittering of birds and insects and reptiles, goes completely, eerily, impossibly silent.

No animals or birds. No students on bikes along the pathways. No shouts or laughter in the distance.

I can't even hear my own breath.

I get to my feet on top of the boulder and peer down the path, past the rock I was climbing earlier, back in the direction toward the dorms. Suddenly my vision sharpens, zooming in close.

The dorms loom in the background, the pathways packed with panicked students and faculty, everyone fleeing some unknown nemesis.

"What the fuck?" I gasp. Then, behind the running masses, the source of their fear emerges from the chaos.

Mages and witches with yellow glowing eyes, their skin gray and lifeless, blood dripping from their teeth. They pour in over the rocks and pathways like scampering beetles, devouring anyone in their way, leaving only bones and blood in their wake.

Bringing up the rear, a chariot roars through, mowing down some of its own soldiers. It's drawn by two horses, a white and a black, urged on by a fierce woman with flowing auburn hair, dressed in a blue tunic and green cape, a huge staff in one hand, the reins in the other.

Behind her, an old man sits in the back, but I know in an instant he's not some feeble, wounded passenger.

He's the general.

Dressed in a long gray tunic and a cape made of raven feathers, he holds a single wand in his right hand, his lips uttering some terrible spell that gives the dead their strength. His blue eyes are wild with madness and purpose in equal measure.

He raises his wand higher, and the charioteer pushes her steeds harder, through crowds of the living as well as the dead. Students I recognize from my classes, Professor Nakata, Professor Maddox—all of them try to flee, and all are mangled in the wake of this deadly, gruesome army.

I try to cry out, to move, but I'm only a witness to the carnage, frozen in place, forced to watch helplessly as terror and death consume the Academy. Smoke rises, the stench of blood turning my stomach.

Finally, from out of the smoke, an ally emerges. She runs to me, leaping onto the boulder. Her blue gown is tattered, her crown of flowers smashed and tangled in her wild dark hair.

The Princess of Swords stands before me, blood soaking

her dress, a blade gripped in each hand. Her face is grim, her eyes flashing in warning.

"Help me!" I shout, finally finding my voice. "I don't understand! Show me what to do!"

She whirls her swords in the air, those fierce eyes blazing. For a moment I wonder if my own sword will appear—the magickal blade I held when I first met the Princesses in my vision.

Instead, she jabs her vicious blades into my calf.

It's only when the images of the gruesome army fade and the pain burns hot through my veins that my Princess of Swords vanishes, and I realize she wasn't a vision at all.

She was a rattlesnake. As real as the rock beneath my feet.

Back here on planet Fuck My Life, I may not have an undead army to contend with, but my leg is already swelling from the bite, the pain like lava chewing through my skin.

I try to scramble off the boulder, but I stumble and land on my ass. The puncture wounds are already closing, but the venom is working its way into my bloodstream—pretty sure I can't heal that on my own.

Fuckrabbits. I can't stay here. I need to find help. I reach for my pack with the phone, but my fingers graze the strap, and it slides down over the side of the bolder, wedging itself into a crack I can't reach.

Seconds later, my leg goes numb, my lips tingly.

I try to remember everything they ever taught us in Tres

Búhos elementary school about rattlesnake bites, but it's no use.

My stomach lurches—pretty sure I just puked up that granola bar.

My vision is swimming, darkening.

The last conscious thought I have is one of pure fear. Not that I'm going to be destroyed by an undead army, but that I'm going to die on this rock, and someone is going to find my phone, and instead of being remembered as the spirit-blessed witch who mastered her magick and translated her mother's prophecies and saved countless lives, I'll be forever immortalized as the girl who felt compelled to issue unsolicited warnings about the dangers of masturbating with a cactus, and then got herself killed by a poisonous snake.

Son of a hairy-ass bitch, I always knew Mother Nature would be the one to take me out.

I've got just enough energy left to laugh and flip a middle finger up to the sky.

And then the world simply fades away, taking me right with it.

THIRTY-SIX

CASS

Her fever still hasn't broken, her words coming fast and furious now.

"Flame and blood and blade and bone, what starts with zero ends with one. One, five, seven, twenty. Arcana devours, all and plenty."

"Easy, Stevie. You're all right. You're home safe, resting in your bed." I dip a clean cloth into the ice water, then press it to her forehead.

Twice in as many days, the woman has fallen victim to this landscape. First the river, rising up as if to claim her, well after the other women had already backed off. And now the snake.

It's too much to be a coincidence.

She's a target. We knew it was a risk, but I didn't expect it to start so soon. Unlike her home in Tres Búhos, the Academy is warded against dark magick.

Which only proves how powerful our adversaries truly are.

"I saw his army," she says. "Death and rot and blood and ruin. Zero begets the next, the One. Innocence lost, magick undone."

Her voice is high-pitched, frantic, her words mixing her own visions with translations Kirin shared from her mother's work. It's all interwoven, but so far, none of us has been able to connect those dots.

"Shh," I murmur, stroking her face. "Try to rest."

She slips into a light sleep, but her dreams are perilous, her body twitching, soft whimpers escaping her lips. I lower the lights, ignite candles instead. Place the Four of Swords card on her bedside table in an effort to calm her.

I don't dare leave her side. Though her body heals external wounds quickly, the venom is largely immune to her magick. In fact, it seems to feed off it, sending her into a fevered state even after the Academy healer administered the antivenin.

For now, all I can do is keep watch.

There's a soft knock at the door, and Baz enters.

"How is she?" he asks. Here in the candlelight, his features are thrown into sharp, exaggerated relief, his eyes glinting with a wicked tint. But I know he's already grown to care for her. We all share the same worry.

"Not out of the woods yet," I tell him, "but getting better. She'll be okay—her fever is just starting to break."

Sweat beads on her brow, and I blot it gently with the cool cloth, relieved.

He kneels beside the bed, taking her hand and pressing a kiss to her palm. "I didn't... I thought..."

"It's not your fault, Baz. It could've happened to anyone."

"But it happened to her. I shouldn't have left her alone."

"She's a skilled climber and outdoors-woman. She's perfectly capable of handling herself out there. This was an accident, plain and simple."

"Or a targeted mage attack."

"Either way, it was out of your control."

He nods, but I can tell he's not buying it.

"Baz, if anyone deserves the blame in this, it's me. I'm the one who brought her to the Academy."

"And Anna's the one who wanted her here, and her mother's the one who left the prophecies that no one else could translate, and we could go all the way back to the dawn of time looking for someone to blame, but what's the point?"

I offer a smile. "I believe you just made it."

His stern face cracks into a small grin, and he finally releases the breath I'm fairly certain he's been holding since we found her hours ago.

He kisses her hand once more, then gets to his feet. "I'll give the guys the update."

"Everyone still here?"

"We're not leaving until we know she's in the clear."

"Good."

Alone with her again, I pace her bedroom, trying to focus on something other than my worry for her. The Tarot

Aces hang above her bed, the Academy-issued furniture and window treatments decorating the space, and I wonder if she'll ever feel at home here. The room is full of her scent, like honeysuckles after a gentle rain, but other than some lotions and perfumes she must've purchased at the Promenade and a few photographs and other items Anna left for her, the space feels strangely impersonal.

The thought opens a hole in my chest. I wish it could've been different for her. For all of us.

But that's not our lot, in this life or the next.

"What... what happened?" a small voice emanates from the bed, and I'm back at her side in an instant, taking her hand in mine.

"Stevie?"

Her eyes open slowly, and she lifts a hand to my face. Exhaustion weighs heavy in her movements, but her fever has broken, and her gaze is clear once again.

"You completely mortified me in front of the whole class yesterday," she says, her words still slurred.

I hold back a laugh. I should've guessed she'd choose her first lucid moments to give me hell.

But then she pats my cheek and smiles, and my heart melts. "I thought we were friends, Doc."

"You know you're not supposed to call me that," I say gently, damn near mesmerized by the candlelight glittering in her eyes. Here in the privacy of her bedroom, in the intimacy of the moment, I allow myself to break my own rules and press a kiss to her palm, just like Baz did.

"How do you feel?" I ask.

"Like someone who got bit by a fucking rattlesnake."

I let out a soft chuckle. "At least you're coherent enough to remember what happened."

"Did they have to amputate?" She tugs the blanket aside to inspect her leg. Other than the last bit of swelling, it's almost impossible to tell she was bitten.

"You seem to be healing quite well on your own," I say.

"I remember a sharp pain, and a few minutes later, I got really queasy. My lips were tingling... I guess I blacked out. There was... Well, the Princess of Swords visited me, and I thought she'd give me my own sword, but..." She closes her eyes, her brow furrowing.

I brush my knuckles across her soft cheek. "You told me about the vision, Stevie. No need to relive it now."

"What does it mean?"

"I don't know, but we'll figure it out. Right now, let's just focus on getting your strength back."

"I left the gear," she confesses. "It was really good gear, too."

"Not to worry. Baz retrieved everything, including your pack and phone."

"You found me," she whispers. "How? How long was I out there?"

"Long enough." I press my lips together, suppressing a shudder. To think what would've happened if things had gone a different way...

"I couldn't reach my phone," she says. "Rookie mistake."

"You didn't need your phone." I look to the window, the

moonlight illuminating the Forest of Iron and Bone beyond. We'd all hoped to introduce her more slowly to the full scope of our world, to have time to properly train her.

But that was before we knew the extent of her powers.

Knew what she was.

"The owl appeared in my office while I was preparing tomorrow's lesson," I say. "You can imagine my surprise when he landed on my desk."

"*My* owl?"

"He led us to you, and without a moment to spare. When Kirin and I found you, you were unconscious on the ground beside the boulder, your leg badly swollen. You'd cut your head, too—probably in the fall."

She touches her fingers to her forehead, the once-deep gash no more than a faint pink line.

"I wish I could call him up at will," she says. "I'd like to thank him for his most excellent timing. Although, maybe next time he could show up *before* the rattlesnake. Don't owls eat those things?"

"Eventually, you'll be able to communicate with him."

"How?"

"The snowy owl is your familiar, Stevie. An animal soul connected to yours, bound to travel together for eternity. He has always been with you, but most witches don't connect with their familiars until they're much farther along on their magickal path."

"My familiar," she says, her voice reverent. "Do you have one?"

"Sadly, no. Mages can adopt animal companions much

in the same way that humans do. But we don't bond with familiars—that honor belongs solely to witches."

She closes her eyes, processing this. I can only hope she's too tired for more questions.

There's so much more she has to learn. So much I wish I could tell her, but to do so now would overwhelm her. The Brotherhood is walking a thin line as it is, all of us growing far more attached to her than any of us could've predicted.

Which only lends credence to our theory. Well, I'm certain it's not a theory now. Not after the visions she's shared.

"I need to ask you something, Doc," she says, all traces of reverence gone. When she meets my eyes again, I see only determination.

I swallow through the tightness in my throat. "What is it?"

"I need you to be straight with me."

"I'll do my best."

"Yesterday in class, you said something about a lake and standing stones."

"It was your dreamcast."

"It's not a dream," she says. "It's the Star. Trump Seventeen. What does it mean?"

"It means you're connected to its energy," I say, which is the truth, though not all of it.

"I thought my affinities were with the Princesses of the Tarot?"

"They are. This is… different. Not an affinity, but…" I let

out a breath, searching for the words to explain this, wondering if now is the right time. If I should call the others in. If we're all making a grievous mistake. But before I can utter another word, her eyes turn glassy, her features twisting into a deformed sneer that looks so out of place on her beautiful face, it's like she's just donned the mask of an ugly, terrible monster.

"Why do you have the dark book?" she asks, her voice high and childlike, her sneer turning into manic laughter. "It's a very, very, very bad book, and you are a very, very, very bad mage, Cassius Harding Devane."

She giggles, and a chill slithers down my spine.

This isn't Stevie. It's something else—some dark force twisting her face, her voice, her words.

"Which dark book do you mean, Stevie?" I ask, playing along. Whatever this thing is that's taken hold, I don't want to alert it just yet.

"Book of Shadow and Mists," she says triumphantly, as if she's proud to be in on the secret. "It's a very bad book, and you have it. I saw it when you wrote on it with your blood."

How could she have seen that?

"Legend," I say automatically. "Just a legend."

"What does the legend say? Will you tell me the story? *Please*?" Now she pouts, her eyes suddenly big and round, making her look about ten years old.

My mouth has gone so dry, I have to take a drink of her water before I can continue.

"I don't know, Stevie. It's an old tale, a long one, and

you really need to rest now. Perhaps I will tell you another time."

"Myths and legends come to pass," she says, her voice taking on the lilting, sing-song quality of a child taunting a rival. "When all are dead and first comes last. He wants his book, Cassius Harding Devane. He really really really wants it."

She laughs, a nervous giggle quickly boiling over into hysterics.

My heart bangs a tympani drumbeat against my chest, and I school my features, praying she—it—doesn't see right through me. "Who wants it?"

For a minute she says nothing, her eyes rolling back, her head lolling against her pillow. I try to convince myself it's the delirium of the venom, still working its way through her bloodstream. That she's hallucinating, repurposing images and stories from her library books.

But then she shoots bolt upright and grips my arms so tightly I'm sure her nails draw blood. A low rumble vibrates in her chest, quickly turning into a growl.

"The Dark Magician is rising," she says, the voice no longer high and child-like, but deep and raspy, older, darker. Ancient. Terrifying.

And it's not simply recounting her visions or mixing up old legends.

It's warning us.

"Tell the Arcana that the son of the Fool has come to reclaim his birthright. And this time, he's bringing an army. None will survive."

THIRTY-SEVEN

ANSEL

"Once again," Kirin says to Baz, "we're running damage control on account of your complete inability to keep your dick in your pants."

"Shut it, asshole."

"Oh, I would love nothing more than to shut the book on this topic. To be fair, your dick has been the subject of more conversations than I care to count."

"Guys, please," I say. "Keep your voices down."

We're all standing around Stevie's place, Kirin pacing, Baz leaning against the kitchen island, me shuffling the novelty cards on the table, none of us knowing what else to do. Stevie's hurt and I'm going out of my mind with worry. The only thing I *do* know right now is that arguing isn't going to help.

"Stevie would kick your asses if she caught you acting like dickheads in her living room," I say. "And don't think she can't. Have you *seen* those biceps?"

Kirin glares at Baz. "You know how I feel about her."

Baz lets out a bitter laugh. "Does *she*?"

"Irrelevant."

"Oh, I'd say it's totally relevant. Maybe you're not the only one who feels a connection."

"You hardly know the woman," Kirin says.

"And you do?"

They've been bickering like this all night, neither of them willing to address the big fat magickal elephant in the room—the fact that Stevie is connected to all of us, and we're connected to her. No, not necessarily in a romantic way, but still. Kirin could no more talk Baz out of his feelings—whatever they may be—than I could pretend I haven't felt the tug of that bond, too.

Not that I need to bring *that* up right now. There's enough dick-measuring going on in here as it is.

But at some point? We're going to have to deal with this.

"Hug it out," I say. "You know you want to."

Kirin snorts, but Baz is already smiling. Despite his macho bullshit, he doesn't like fighting any more than I do.

He stalks over to Kirin, puts him in a headlock until Kirin has no choice but to relent.

"Fuck off, Redgrave," Kirin grumbles, but I catch the relieved smile on his face.

The two are still screwing around when Cass finally emerges from the back bedroom, his face as pale as the moon.

All of us snap to attention.

"Is she okay?" I ask.

"She's better. Fever broke, and she was awake for a bit. She remembers everything that happened. That's the good news." Cass settles in on the couch, and we take seats around him, the air heavy and ominous with the question no one seems to want to ask.

Finally, I break the silence. "What's the bad news?"

"The rattlesnake wasn't just a random accident. It was an omen. A warning."

He tells us about Stevie's visions, the gruesome battle, details so horrifying she couldn't have possibly invented them.

"For whatever reason, she's been given a glimpse of what's to come," Cass says. "She's... she's seen it."

And though his foreboding tone leaves little doubt as to what he means—as to what *any* of this means—Kirin asks anyway.

"Seen what, exactly?"

"The rise of the Dark Arcana." Cass pales, his eyes aging a hundred years in a single heartbeat. "She's seen our end."

THIRTY-EIGHT

STEVIE

"Is that what I think it is?"

Standing in my bedroom doorway, Kirin holds up the coffee tray and offers his sweet, captivating smile. "I thought you might be ready for a pick-me-up."

"You *must* be psychic." I wave him in, grateful for the latte as well as the company. Isla just left—in fact, she must've let Kirin in—but Kirin's basically my oldest friend here, and I was starting to miss him.

I haven't seen him in three days—at least, not while I was coherent. Not since that day in the lab when I left without saying goodbye.

But seeing him now, standing there in a Dark Crystal T-shirt, his glasses askew, holding those lattes, I hardly remember why I was upset with him in the first place.

I take a deep breath. If all the crazy visions I've experienced over the last few days have taught me anything, it's that here at Arcana Academy, nothing is what it seems, everything is a fucking mystery, and I don't know jack shit.

So until I know at least a little *more* shit, I'm willing to give the mages the benefit of the doubt—for now.

Beaming up at him from my bed, I return his smile, thankful that Isla made me take a shower this morning and helped me braid my hair.

He sits down in the chair next to my bed and hands me a latte, which I greedily sip, practically moaning into my cup.

"This is the first time I've felt human in days," I tell him.

"You look good," he says. "I mean, not that you ever look bad, but… You know. Your color is back now."

He sips his own coffee, dodging my gaze, his cheeks darkening. When he meets my eyes again, I feel a little jolt, straight to the heart.

Ridiculous.

"So I'm supposed to tell you that Baz sends his regards," he says.

"Um… okay? Send mine back?" I'm not sure if Baz was here during my three-day, snake-bite acid trip, but I haven't had an actual conversation with the man since we made out at the rocks.

Since we almost…

I close my eyes, sigh through my nose. Whatever Baz said about things being continued? Pointless. I'm sure he's come to the same conclusion I have: it was a bad idea to begin with, probably best left buried.

A new thought enters my mind, making my heart skip.

Did Baz tell Kirin what happened between us?

"Stevie? You okay?"

I open my eyes, force a smile. "Right as a rockslide."

"I'm not sure what that means, but as long as you're not slipping into a coma…"

"No, nothing like that." I take another sip of latte, watching him over the top of the cup. When our eyes meet again, hot pinpricks of guilt race up my spine.

Which is ridiculous, because it's not like I betrayed him. He may be my oldest friend here, but we aren't together—not like that. We still hardly know each other.

Why am I so tangled up about this? Do I have actual feelings for him? For Baz?

For *both* of them?

All I know is that when Baz kissed me, my heart felt like it was going to explode. And now, when Kirin looks at me with the sunset-behind-the-saguaros eyes I've loved for so long, I feel that same rapid-fire burst in my chest.

Sipping the drink, I let the honey-cinnamon sweetness wash over my tongue. I'm being crazy. There's no way I could have feelings for both of them—not serious ones. It's just this place. The stress of all the new experiences, the expectations with translating Mom's prophecies, the insane shit that's been happening.

Hell of a first week.

"I'm glad you're okay," Kirin says, picking at the rim of his cup. "We were all really worried. When Cass and I found you on the ground like that, I just…" He closes his eyes for so long I start to worry *he's* falling into a coma.

I reach out and squeeze his hand. "But you guys got there in time, and now I'm all good. Crazy trip, but I think the worst of it is over."

"Let's hope so."

"I assume Dr. Devane filled you in?"

"On all the fire and brimstone?" Kirin tries to laugh, but it sputters out halfway. "Yeah, he told me."

"Any idea what the hell's happening in this crazy mind of mine?"

His eyes darken, his jaw tightening. "We think it might be connected to one of the old legends. The rise of the Dark Arcana."

"Dark Arcana? That sounds… dark."

Kirin gazes out the window, his eyes going far away. When he finally comes back to me, he stands up and says, "You up for a trek to the library? There are some things I'd like to show you."

"Are you kidding me?" My heart leaps at the idea. "I've been cooped up in this suite for three days. I'm *more* than ready for some hot action between the stacks."

"Well, I don't know that I'd call paging through dusty old manuscripts 'hot action,' but…"

"*I* would. That sounds like the best date ever."

Kirin presses a hand to his heart. "Marry me."

I hold out my left hand, wriggling my fingers. "Put a ring on it and we'll talk."

"Hey! I brought you a honey cinnamon latte!"

"Point taken. Let me think about it." I laugh again, but

then my smile fades. "Dr. Devane said I need to be on bedrest until Monday. Think we'll run into him?"

Kirin flashes a conspiratorial wink. "You leave that old codger to me."

"Done and done!" I jump out of bed so fast, I forget I'm not wearing pants. Just a T-shirt that barely skims the tops of my thighs.

Kirin's eyes go wide, his cheeks blushing once again. He clears his throat and stares down into his coffee cup so intently it's like he's divining the future in his espresso grounds.

Putting the poor man out of his misery, I grab my jeans and say, "Give me twenty minutes to get dressed, then we're busting out of this place."

THIRTY-NINE

STEVIE

When we get to the library, we spot Professor Phaines outside, walking Carly and Blue down the main steps. Both women look like they've been crying, and for about three seconds, I feel bad for them. But then their energy hits me, a tangled mess of anger and deceit, self-preservation, betrayal.

The usual.

Professor Phaines nods when he sees us, then holds up his hand, indicating we should wait for him.

He wraps it up with the Claires, then jogs over to us.

I bite back a smile. Pretty spry for an old mage in wizard robes.

"Stevie! How are you feeling?" He puts a hand on my shoulder, his concerned energy wrapping around me like a grandfatherly hug. "Dr. Devane tells me you've had quite an eventful week."

I almost laugh.

Eventful? Oh, not really. Unless you mean the part where I basically tried to seduce my mental magicks professor in front of the whole class, nearly drowned in the River of Blood and Sorrow, discovered I have a familiar that can fly me around campus and spy on secret society meetings, almost fucked one of my super-hot classmates, and got bitten by a rattlesnake who may or may not have been the Princess of Swords warning me about the end times...

"Nothing I can't handle," I say.

Behind him, Kirin winks at me.

"Good, good," Professor Phaines says. "Listen, I'm glad I ran into you both." He gazes out across the pathway in the direction Carly and Blue headed. "I want to share this news with you before it becomes fodder for the rumor mill. A witch was detained last night on charges of murder in Taos, New Mexico. They're saying she butchered her three children in a blood offering to the devil. Terrible business." He shakes his head, his shoulders slumping. "Her name is Danika Lewis. She's Amelia Weatherby's aunt, the poor girl."

"Oh my Goddess," I say, remembering the redhead in Carly's clique. Of all of them, she seems to be the least horrible, and now this? "Is Amelia okay?"

"She's taking the rest of the month off to be with her family. I don't suspect this will be an easy time for any of them, or for her friends, for that matter. Carly and her group seem to be close knit." He looks down the path again, then shakes his head. "Always good to lean on friends at a time like this, but I do worry about the morale of the group as a whole. Anyway, I just wanted to share that with you in case you see the girls in your classes. Might be a good time to reach out."

"I'll keep that in mind," I say, not making any promises. "Thanks for letting us know."

We part ways, and Kirin and I head straight up to the archives lab, where he's already left a stack of books on the legends he was talking about.

"I've been reading up while you were resting," he says. "I was able to find some books on the legend of the Dark Arcana. Specifically, the Dark Magician. The books can explain it better than I can."

"You're already familiar with the legends?"

"Somewhat. They're difficult to study because there are so many different interpretations, and so much of our real history has either been hidden, lost, or destroyed. What some historians call facts, others call legends, others call lies, and on and on it goes."

"Well, most legends have a grain of truth. I guess that's what we need to find."

We take chairs side by side, and Kirin opens a book to a passage he's marked with a Post-It.

"Okay, listen to this," he says, reading aloud. "The true source of magick has been debated since the earliest recorded times, and magickal occult historians have never agreed on a single accounting. But in the broader magickal community, it's generally accepted that magick was gifted to humans by the source elemental beings many eons ago—salamanders, presiding over fire magick; undines presiding over water magick; sylphs presiding over air; gnomes presiding over earth. It is unknown whether these beings operated in a hierarchical structure, but historians have postulated that emissaries from each elemental group were elected and sent to interface with humans, particularly as mankind began to encroach on natural lands in greater numbers, posing a threat not only to the elemental beings, but to the natural world at large, despite the fact that mankind was and continues to be part of that natural world."

"I feel like we're the only species stupid enough to shit where we eat," I say.

"Yes, and we've been doing so for millennia."

"Keep reading."

Kirin flips the page. "The more the humans interacted with the elemental beings, the more they began to desire their own power, their own elemental magick. Eventually, some sort of bargain was struck between the humans and the elemental beings, though we do not know all the details. This is where most of the legends diverge, the most popular and widely accepted version being thus:

"One of the larger factions of humans sent a tribal elder to negotiate. The elemental beings warned him that magick would come at a great cost, but he was prepared to sacrifice his life so that his people could come to power, and he accepted the terms without question, diving into this new journey with childlike wonder and innocence.

"As part of the sacrifice, he gave his bones to create the first pentacle, representing earth magick; his skull for the

SPELLS OF IRON AND BONE

first chalice, and his blood and tears to fill it, both representing water; his last breath to stoke the flames that forged the first sword, representing air; and the energy of his final ecstasy through forced ceremonial orgasm, representing fire."

"Like what you told me about on the tour," I say.

"Exactly." Kirin continues reading. "From there, these ancient artifacts were said to channel all elemental magick, and the man's spirit became the ultimate essence of that magick, known thereafter as the First Fool from which all magick flows. Most magickal practitioners honor this legendary sacrifice every year on April 1st—First Fool's Day."

"So at what point does Tarot come into play?" I ask, struggling to make sense of it all. No wonder the historians couldn't agree on a single accounting—after just a few pages, I'm already totally overwhelmed. "Other than the Fool reference, I can't see how the elemental magicks connect in with the Arcana."

"Ahh, but the story continues." With an adorably nerdy gleam in his eyes, Kirin closes his book and grabs another one, flipping to another marked page. He adjusts his glasses, then reads: "The system of Tarot—through which modern practitioners channel their own magick, create a wide range of spells and curses, and divine the future—is said to be a written and pictorial accounting of the First Fool's journey through the stages of magickal development, from novice to ascended master, which he then bestowed upon his family members and fellow tribesmen, essentially choosing them to become emanations of the Major Arcana. So, as he became the First Fool, his son became the First Magician, his wife the First High Priestess, his cousin the first Hierophant, and so on. Many historians consider these Major Arcana emanations as gods and goddesses, while the Minor Arcana were said to have evolved into the elemental affinities magickal practitioners identify with today. Together, the Major and Minor Arcana are said to represent both the magickal-spiritual as well as the mundane journeys and challenges of all human life."

"And here I thought it was just a deck of cards," I tease.

"Maybe at Madame Zelinski's House of Whimsical Wonders in Los Angeles, yours for the bargain-basement price of just $19.99, all sales final." Kirin laughs. "But it's a little more complicated than that for us."

I rise from my chair and pace the floor, an excited buzz running through my veins. The more I learn, the more I *want* to learn—the legends, the facts, the hypotheses, all of it.

I'm starting to understand why Kirin devotes so much of his life to research. Being a Tarot magick nerd is kind of badass.

"Okay." I stop pacing, tap my lips. "So we've got the First Fool, a brief and sordid history of the Tarot... When does the Dark Arcana creepshow start?"

Kirin holds up a finger, then rifles through his stack of books. "Damn, I guess I didn't grab that one. It's in Arcana Mythology, one level up. I'll go find it."

"Hey, I'm coming too! You promised me some hot action in the stacks, and so far I haven't seen a single stack."

Kirin blushes again, his smile nearly overtaking his face. "You're insatiable."

"Just call me your favorite little book slut."

"You're definitely my favorite, Stevie."

With that, I follow him back out through security and up the stairs to the next level. This floor doesn't have the centralized open space where students and researchers can work—just bookshelves. Rows and rows of beautiful, majestic, gleaming oak bookshelves, their polished sheen a stark contrast to the dusty tomes that line them.

We're all alone up here, and I take a deep, lemon-oil-and-old-book-scented breath.

Heaven.

The Arcana Mythology section spans several large shelves, and I follow Kirin as he runs his finger along the bottom of each row, searching for the book he wants. It's taking all of my bodily resistance not to start grabbing random books off the shelf to take back to my suite; my to-be-read list is already out of control, and I've only been here a week.

"Eureka!" Kirin says, which is pretty much the cutest, dorkiest thing ever. "Son of the Fool: The Rise and Fall of the Magician in Modern Arcana Mythology."

"Sounds like some real light reading," I say with a laugh. "Is there an H.E.A.?"

Kirin's brow furrows, his glasses sliding down his nose.

"Happily," I say, pushing them back up, "ever after."

SARAH PIPER

He grabs my finger, offering an apologetic frown as if my question was serious. "It isn't that kind of story, Stevie."

"You think?"

"Tell you what. After we figure all this out, I'll make you a reading list of my favorite books—the ones with an H.E.A. Sound good?"

"Sounds amazing."

"In the meantime, we've got the Dark Magician." He releases my finger and flips open the book, paging through to whatever section he wanted to share.

"Let me guess," I say, peering over his shoulder. "Broody emo boy, lots of Daddy issues, too much free time on his hands?"

"Pretty much," Kirin says. "Remember, we all honor the First Fool for his sacrifice, but he was still just a man—a tribal elder who left behind not only his tribe, but his family. A wife and three children, including his eldest son. Listen to this." He runs his finger down the page, then reads, "The tribesmen drank the blood and tears of their elder, and then held a feast honoring him—a man whose great sacrifice would grant them power beyond their wildest imaginings. But this young boy, no more than sixteen years of age at the time, was in no mood to celebrate. What others saw as heroic, he saw as desperate and irresponsible, a selfish father who'd abandoned his entire family in pursuit of magick and glory. The boy had watched helplessly as the source emissaries carved and desecrated his father's body, wringing every last bit of life force from it and assuring—in accordance with the predominant belief at the time—that the family would never be reunited in the afterlife.

"When the spirit of the First Fool made his son the First Magician, the boy developed a new appreciation for power, though not in the way his father had intended. Instead of serving witches and mages on their magickal paths, the Magician vowed to take his vengeance. He claimed that because his father had abandoned his responsibilities to his family in exchange for the gift of magick, then it stood to reason that the gift of magick was, in fact, the boy's inheritance. The other Arcana did not see it this way, and assassinated the boy before his plans for vengeance could be executed. For this reason, while practitioners honor the Fool on April 1st, we devote Winter Solstice to the Dark Magician, thanking him for his family's great sacrifice and leaving elemental offerings to mollify his spirit—tobacco or herbs from the earth, wine to represent water, a candle for fire, incense for air."

"And that's supposed to keep him at bay?" I ask. "Doesn't sound like a fair trade for his father's life—or for his own."

"No, which is why his soul remains restless, reincarnating many times over." Kirin glances at the page again. "Sometimes, he carries on his duties as the Magician was meant to, helping witches and mages become the masters of their own magick and manifestation. But according to some legends, every five thousand years or so, he rises in darkness, embarking on a quest for the sacred objects forged of his father's flesh and blood—the pentacle of iron and bone, the chalice of blood and sorrow, the sword of breath and blade, and the wand of flame and fury." Kirin skims down the page, muttering through the details, then reads, "It is said that he who is in possession of these objects, along with the blood of the world and an arcane spell of indeterminate origins—wait, there's a footnote." He flips to the back of the chapter, shakes his head. "They don't really know much about the spell. But you get the point, right? Whoever has all of that stuff gets to claim magick for himself. Control it, basically."

I lean back against the bookshelves and cross my arms over my chest, my mind working through the stories, automatically looking for connections. There's something we're not seeing—something so close and obvious, I can practically feel it taking shape, like my hands are holding a lump of clay, desperately trying to make an ashtray.

"So in these old stories," I say, "the Dark Magician—when he incarnates—bends his will toward acquiring the sacred elemental objects and reclaiming the true source of magick, which he believes is his unequivocal birthright."

"Precisely." Kirin closes the book and slides it back into place on the shelf. "What we're still trying to figure out, though, is how these legends connect with your visions, and what the larger meaning is. Symbology? Metaphor? Some other context we're just not seeing?"

"Kirin, seriously?" I pop my hands on my hips. "You know that saying—the simplest explanation is usually the right one?"

"I'm familiar with the saying, sure, but statistically

speaking, that's not true. There are so many variables to every situation, and explanations can vary widely from—"

"Kirin!"

Kirin shuts his mouth.

"Here's a thought," I say. "A simple one. A *possible* explanation, if you don't mind hearing it."

"I'm listening."

"What if it's not a legend? What if the stories of the Dark Magician are real?" I step closer and lower my voice. "The passage from the notebook the other day?"

Kirin nods, and I repeat it softly:

> *Between the space where black meets white*
> *Betwixt the woods of dark and light*
> *A mirror flat reveals the sky*
> *But turn it 'round to know the why*
> *Zero begets the next, the One*
> *Innocence lost, magick undone*
> *Beware the rise when darkness falls*
> *For magick corrupts, and blood trumps all.*

"Zero is the number of the Fool in the Major Arcana," I say. "One is the Magician. Zero begets the One—The Fool is the father, the Magician is his son. Innocence lost—that's also the Fool, right? And magick undone—that could mean the magician reversed. Basically, the Magician going dark."

"Beware the rise when darkness falls," Kirin repeats. "The rise of the Dark Arcana, when that darkness falls upon us. Trump is another word for the Majors. Blood trumps all

—that could also mean the bloodline itself—the Fool's and the Magician's, or something else entirely…" He gazes up at the ceiling. "This is totally insane."

"It's all connected. All of it." I turn and grab Kirin's forearms, the ideas crashing into my brain so quickly, I know if I don't get them out, I'll lose them. "We keep looking for the bad guy in all of this, like some crooked, high-level mage making deals with humans and other crooked mages to wipe out the magickal population, maybe leave those few crooked mages in power positions, or pay them off. But that doesn't really make sense, does it? Why would any high-level mage willingly give up power to humans?"

"He wouldn't," Kirin says. "He might play along though, plan a double-cross in the end."

"This is bigger than a few crooked mages. Bigger than an inside job. This is a legend come to life."

"What are you saying?"

"I'm saying we might just be standing here at the five-thousand-year mark—time for the next dark rising. And maybe that motherfucker is coming to take his toys back."

Kirin opens his mouth to debate, but there are no facts and figures to argue, no readily available statistics to disprove my theory.

"And if that's true," I continue, "then what I saw in my vision was probably just a *glimpse* of what he's got planned. Death, mayhem, an eternity of darkness…"

I lean back against the shelf again and close my eyes, the enormity of our revelations weighing heavy.

Kirin has gone silent, and when I finally open my eyes

again, I find him standing before me, watching me with an intensity that makes my heart stutter. His pale green eyes are wild, his cheeks dark, his breath coming in short bursts, warm and gentle on my cheeks.

"What is it?" I grip the shelves at my sides, preparing for the worst.

Kirin takes a step closer, erasing all the space between us.

"We're standing here talking about death and mayhem and horrible legends that might actually be true," he says softly, "and if they *are* true, a lot of people are going to die, including us, and all I can think about is… is…"

"Is what?" I whisper, my heart thumping, my own breath turning ragged.

Kirin reaches out and brushes his fingertips along my jaw. "All I can think about is how badly I want to kiss you."

FORTY

STEVIE

My back hits the bookshelf, cracked leather spines pressing against my shoulder blades, the smell of old parchment and lemon oil swirling through my senses.

"I've been dreaming about your lips since the first time I saw you smile," Kirin says, tracing his fingertip across my bottom lip. "Since that first day I walked into Kettle Black—when you made me the almond tea with pepper."

"Toasted almond peppercorn," I remind him, touched that he remembered the moment. I'll never forget it either. The first day he walked into the café, everything about my life changed, as if my memories and future plans and everything in between were already rearranging themselves to make room for this moment, right here in the library in the Academy I swore I'd never, ever set foot in.

I couldn't explain it at the time.

I still can't explain it now.

But Kirin's touch is driving me wild, sending cascades

of shivers rolling down my spine.

"That's the one," he says, smiling. "Toasted almond peppercorn."

He slides his fingers along my chin, then into my hair, cupping the back of my head.

Suddenly, I'm stretching up on my toes to get closer.

Kirin's eyes blaze with new heat.

We both smile—an invitation, an acceptance—and Kirin slowly lowers his mouth to mine.

His kiss is sweet and tender, savoring, tasting me in the same way he used to sip my teas at the café—with slow, deliberate appreciation. My lips part gently, and he deepens our kiss, a soft moan reverberating through his chest.

I slide my hands beneath the hem of his T-shirt, gliding over the smooth, hard muscles of his back, his skin warming at my touch. The strong, steady beat of his heart thuds through his skin, and I pull him closer, wanting more.

He hesitates for no more than five rabbit-quick beats of his heart, then slides his other hand in my hair, guiding me into a deeper kiss, the intensity building between us.

We're walking on a precipice, both of us scared to fall off, to ruin the friendship we've been building since those first days at Kettle Black. There's the translation and research work to consider, too—so much at stake. So much resting on us.

But right now, with his sweet mouth teasing and tasting me, his strong hands tangled in my hair, I'm ready to jump.

His chest brushes against my nipples, and I gasp, trying to steal a breath without breaking our kiss. Kirin pulls back, his gaze sweeping down my face, then leans in again, kissing my neck, my throat, working his way down the front of my shirt. He tongues my nipple through the fabric, then bites, making me gasp again. I reach out and grab the edge of the bookshelf behind me, and Kirin continues kissing and biting, his glasses falling to the floor, his mouth eager and hot, his hands roaming along my curves.

Then he drops to his knees.

A pulse of white-hot desire floods my core, and I close my eyes, focusing on the feeling of his nimble fingers as he undoes my jeans.

His hands are trembling, but his mouth is urgent, insistent.

He presses it to the top of my pink panties, dragging his lips along the edge, tracing his nose down the front. His tongue darts out, teasing my clit through the lace.

I open my eyes with another gasp.

"Kirin," I breathe, sliding a hand into his hair, sinking back against the bookshelf.

He looks up at me with so much admiration in his eyes, so much tenderness, I nearly melt. It's the kind of look that could make me go supernova, the kind that could make me start to feel things… To fall…

I close my eyes again and arch my body closer, showing him how much I want this.

He presses another kiss to the triangle of lace, then slides my jeans down over my hips, letting them pool around my ankles. Warm, rough palms glide up my calves, my thighs, my ass.

He kisses my thigh, then traces a path to my hipbone with his tongue, taking the edge of my underwear between his teeth.

My core is throbbing for him, desperate for his mouth, his fingers, anything to relieve this mounting ache...

Reaching up with his hands, he guides the underwear down, leaving me bare and exposed.

I lift my foot to step out of the pants, but Kirin grabs my leg, holds it steady. I let him take control, trusting my body to him, my pleasure, all of it.

His mouth lingers at the apex of my thighs, the tip of his tongue swirling just out of reach, driving me wild. I try to spread my legs, to give him room, but the jeans and his firm grip hold me in place.

Hot breath ghosts over my clit, and he curls his hands around the back of my thighs, fingertips teasing my entrance. When he feels how wet he's made me, he leans in closer, moaning softly against my bare flesh.

Slowly, maddeningly, he guides my thighs apart, teasing me with deeper strokes as he presses a hot kiss to my clit, then tongues me. I fist his hair, the fire building between my thighs, the tingling already starting in my belly, my leg muscles trembling. Kirin continues to tease me, slow and savoring, just like everything he does, pulling back and then moving close once again, another kiss, the ghost of a breath, and I'm writhing in pure agonizing pleasure, willing him to take me harder, faster, more, and then suddenly he's pressing his face between my thighs and sliding two fingers deep inside, sucking and nipping, stroking, and suddenly I'm falling headfirst over the edge.

I clamp a hand over my mouth and let out a stifled cry as the orgasm rushes through me, my shoulders hitting the shelves again, a few books toppling to the floor.

And here between the stacks of Arcana Myths and Legends and Astrological Correspondences for the Major Arcana, a bright flash of light explodes before us, the ground shaking, books tumbling from the shelves, glass breaking in the distance, a fire raging across the walls, devouring every book in its path…

"Kirin! The lightning!" I shout, and he's on his feet in an instant, cupping my face, whispering that everything will be okay, that he's sorry, that he shouldn't have done this…

"Come back," he says. Begs. "It's okay, Stevie. You're safe. I'm so, so sorry."

I follow the sound of his voice, the feel of his hands on my face, the summer-storm scent of his skin. The library slowly comes back into view, and I look around to assess the damage. The shelves are still standing, most of the books where they should be, save for the couple that fell out during my grand finale.

It was another vision. Just a vision.

"Okay?" Kirin whispers, and I nod, but my heart is still raging, my legs trembling in a way that has nothing to do with Kirin's mouth.

"I don't understand," I whisper, terrified that anything louder will unleash another vision. "What's happening?"

Kissing Kirin, kissing Baz, even those mental games

with Dr. Devane... I always seem to get pulled into some sort of vision with them. Is it always like this for witches and mages? Or does it have something to do with the true form thing they were talking about at their meeting?

Kirin's eyes are wild, his mouth glistening, and he's looking at me like he doesn't know whether to run, cry for help, or grab me in another breathless kiss.

I decide for him, leaning in and capturing his bottom lip between my teeth, grazing the tip of it with my tongue. I taste the salt of my own desire and slide a hand down over the front of his jeans, feeling the bulge of his hardness. Kirin shudders, his hands tightening on my hips.

But then he pulls back again, resting his forehead on my shoulder and letting out a deep breath. His grip on my hips loosens, and I know in that moment he's letting me go.

"Kirin?" I whisper. "What is it? What's wrong?"

His cock is hard, straining against his jeans in a way that tells me he wants this as much as I do. But then he lifts his head and looks at me with so much sadness and regret in his eyes, I almost fall into them and die.

"It's... it's the library," he says randomly, clearly casting about for an excuse. He crouches down and picks up his glasses, then the books that fell, sliding them back into their right places on the shelf. "Someone might see us, and it's probably against the rules, and I just... I'm sorry. I have to go."

And there, in the space where commanding hands and a passionate, devoted mouth worshipped my flesh mere minutes ago, a cold emptiness echoes.

FORTY-ONE

STEVIE

"Light some more sage," Isla says from my living room couch, sipping her whiskey-spiked chocolate lavender tea, which is only about half as disgusting as it sounds. "And shuffle the deck again. Must be some stuck energy."

"Isn't it bad luck to keep asking the cards the same question and hoping for a different answer?" Jessa asks. It's our inaugural Friday Night Witch-'N-Bitch Happy Hour, and we've got her on video chat on my laptop, propped up on the coffee table. On her end, she's got a margarita, just like old times.

"It's definitely bad luck," I say, but I'm already lighting another sage bundle, passing it over my cards anyway. At this point, I'll try anything to change the outcome of this dumb story.

"Maybe the crystals are in the wrong positions." Nat rearranges them. Again. "Or maybe we need different ones. I think rose quartz is supposed to be good for love."

SPELLS OF IRON AND BONE

"I'm not in love with him," I clarify.

"Which him?" Isla teases, and I reach over and smack her foot.

"*Either* him. As far as I'm concerned, they're both crazy and destined for eternal bachelorhood and celibacy."

All three women shoot me the same mischievous, knowing glances.

After that insane night at the library last week, I haven't seen or spoken with Kirin at all—not even about the Dark Magician legends we were working on. Every time I went to the library this week, his office was locked, and he wasn't in the archives. Professor Phaines popped in to help with Mom's translations once, but when I tried to casually ask about Kirin, all he said was that Kirin was working on another high priority project this week.

As if saving the world from the Dark Arcanapocalypse isn't high priority enough.

On top of that nonsense, Baz is being chilly, too. He's not ignoring me outright—he always says hi in class, jokes around a little bit, but it's nothing like before. He never runs to catch up to me after class, or makes any more comments about rescheduling our little "makeoutus interruptus" session.

I'm even starting to miss his damn innuendos.

The only good thing about Baz sidelining me is that I'm basically off Carly's radar now, so that's going in the "win" column.

Dr. Devane is actually being nice to me, which is a mindfuck in the other direction. Pretty sure it's only because he's worried I'll get myself worked up and fall into another acid trip down undead-army lane, and none of us wants that.

The only one being totally normal is Ani, and if it wasn't for him and my witchy-bitchies here, I'm pretty sure I'd be looking for the escape hatch on this Academy right now.

"Okay, try again," Isla says.

I take a deep breath, shuffle my cards, and ask the question of the hour:

"What is Kirin Weber's dumbass, bumble-fucking problem?"

"Suggestion?" Nat raises her hand, then smiles. "Maybe reword the question without so much rage?"

I blow out a breath. "Okay. Why is Kirin being such a dickhead?"

"Not exactly what I had in mind," Nat says. "One more time?"

"Fine. What kind of asshole gives a woman a mind-blowing orgasm with the tongue of a master cunnilinguist, then bails on her, leaving her shoved between bookshelves like a dusty old book with her pants literally down around her ankles?"

Nat doesn't offer any more helpful suggestions this time. Just passes me the bottle of whiskey, which at the moment feels like an even better suggestion.

I take a swig, then turn over three cards.

The Tower—the one with all the fire and brimstone, people jumping out of burning buildings, all that fun stuff.

Three of Swords, which is basically a big heart with

three swords run right through it. *Subtle, Universe. Real subtle.*

Finally, The Star, my mysterious lady at the lake, endlessly pouring out her urns of water.

"Maybe she's pouring out her tears for her lost lovers," Isla says.

Nat glares at her. "Not helpful, Isla."

"Stevie doesn't need help right now," Isla says, fingering her teardrop pendant. "She needs tough love."

"I think she just needs to get laid," Jessa pipes in, and we all crack up.

"Yeah, I don't need the cards to confirm that." I take another swig of whiskey. "Okay, next question. Why do I have a stupid crush on Baz?"

I shuffle all the cards again, then lay down my next three:

Cernunnos, my old horned-god friend. The Lovers, which is ironically the card Professor Nakata joked about using to enhance your sex life. And The Star. Again.

"I can't believe you keep getting the same cards every time for each question," Jessa says. "Is that even statistically possible?"

The mention of statistics reminds me of Kirin, and I get up and head to the kitchen in search of something more palatable than whiskey to drink.

"See, this is why I have rules in the first place," I say, putting my company kettle on to boil. "Even though I keep forgetting to follow them. Who else wants tea?"

"I'll have a warmup," Isla says. "Nat, you good?"

But Nat's buried in her phone, her eyes wide, her hand covering her mouth.

"What's wrong?" I ask, heading back in to check on her.

"Text from my mom," she says. "Apparently, there were two more arrests last night—a mage in San Francisco accused of poisoning the food in his own restaurant. No one died, but a bunch of people got really sick. And another —a witch in Portland, Oregon. My mom used to work with her—she lives about half an hour from our house." Her face goes slack, her eyes filling with tears. "Goddess, they're saying she tortured her husband and her mother-in-law to death with a clothes iron."

"What the fuck?" Isla whispers. "No way."

"The city of Portland is declaring a state of emergency," Nat says, still scrolling through the message. "Since the story broke, people are starting to protest on both sides. They're asking for federal assistance to help deter any riots. They're... Holy shit. They're sending in military."

"To Portland?"

Nat nods, and in the silence that follows, a sliver of fear cracks through my heart.

Things are getting worse.

FORTY-TWO

CASS

"Two more attacks. Two more wrongful imprisonments. Towns falling under martial law, military presence on the rise in every major U.S. city and a good deal of Europe as well." I pace in front of the classroom, looking at each of my students—my responsibilities—in turn. "The news is becoming more grim by the day. I don't tell you this to frighten you, but to inspire you."

Twenty-one faces stare back at me, including my bonded brother and another who's come to mean more than just a responsibility to me.

Stevie raises her hand, and I fake a cough to hide my smile.

Never a dull moment with this one.

"Yes, Miss Milan?"

"I was just thinking… I mean, you're the professor, so don't take this as gospel or anything. But as far as inspirational pep talks go, maybe we could focus on something a little more... I don't know. Inspiring? Peppy?"

"I was getting to that."

"Oh! Good. Carry on."

"May I?"

She gives me two thumbs up, flashing her heart-stopping smile.

It's good to see her smiling again, her cheeks pink, her eyes bright. After that snake bite incident, I never want to see her so close to the brink again. Her body healed quickly, but I won't soon forget the wild, crazy look in her eyes, as if she'd gotten a glimpse of her own death.

In so many ways, she had.

I look at her again now, taking in the sight of her, reminding myself that she's whole and alive and beautiful, just like always.

That she's safe.

"Mental shielding magick may seem complicated," I continue, practicing some shielding of my own, lest I be sucked into another one of those visions of her by the lake. "But it's actually quite simple, and fairly easy to practice. I want each of you to become adept at these techniques and to feel confident in your abilities. The more confident you are in the face of danger, the less likely you'll be to suffer an attack of this nature."

I cross to the other side of the room, deftly avoiding Stevie's gaze.

"Fear is a powerful weapon. All it takes is a single doubt, a single crack in your armor, and the enemy will find

SPELLS OF IRON AND BONE

it and exploit it to the fullest extent. But here's something the enemy doesn't want you to know—fear itself isn't real. Danger may be real, but fear is just an emotional response to that perceived danger. First, there's a stimulus—say, a lion prowling around your cave. Then your brain forms a thought about that stimulus—lion wants to eat me! Danger, Danger!"

Some of the students chuckle.

"From that thought, your emotions respond accordingly —danger! I feel fear!—and then you have another thought about what to do—run? Fight? Next, your brain tells which-ever parts of your body are involved to get moving—feet, make haste! Or hands, pick up that shotgun! It's a long chain of events that happens in mere seconds, but the part we want to focus on is that initial thought formation after the stimulus. We're going to learn how to essentially hack our brains—hijack those thoughts before they have a chance to produce the fear response, or to linger there too long. The key to all this starts with presence and awareness, and that's what we're going to practice today."

I pair them off, giving them a series of exercises to test each other's awareness, telling myself it's a good start.

But in the face of everything Kirin and Stevie have postulated so far, it feels futile. Though they've made progress on her mother's prophecies and the Dark Magi-cian legends, we still have no way of knowing who the Magician is, what form his or her rise will take, when it will happen, and what—if anything—we can do to prepare. And none of us has any ideas how this is all connected to the arrests in the wider community—only that it *is* connected. It must be.

I rub my eyes and take a deep breath, trying not to let my own fear consume me. Tucked away in my bottom desk drawer, the whiskey bottle calls.

I ignore it, looking out at my students once again. This *is* a good start, I remind myself. And start we must.

By the end of the class, I'm fairly confident at least half of them would survive a lion attack, and possibly even a dark mage possession, which at this point is the more pressing danger.

The chime announces the end of class, and I assign them two pieces of homework—one, practice their presence and awareness exercises with their roommates. And two, stay safe and alert, especially at night.

Then I send them on their way.

Not sure I'll ever get used to that—the emptiness that creeps in next. The fear—one that no amount of presence and awareness—or whiskey, for that matter—has ever allayed.

When they're here in my classroom, safely ensconced inside these four walls, I can protect them. Stevie. The other first-years. Even Baz, who still insists he doesn't need protection.

Shaking off the old ghosts, I glance down at my desk, trying to get things in order for my next class.

But it seems not all the students have left.

A shadow falls over my desk, and I look up to see her

standing before me, her eyes lidded, brow furrowed with some new worry.

"I need to speak with you, Doc," Stevie says, and my heart melts a little bit.

I love when she calls me that, but still, professional boundaries and all. I turn my attention back to my paperwork, shuffling and reshuffling. "Stevie, you know the rules."

Ignoring me, she blurts out, "What's going on with Kirin?"

I look up, try to think of a quick answer. But there isn't one.

"Kirin is… He's going through some personal challenges right now."

"What challenges?"

"That's not something I'm going to share, Stevie. But I will tell you that it's not your fault, and Kirin is okay. He'll be back at work with you soon."

"No," she says, adamant.

"No?"

"No, I don't buy it." She sets down her bag, crosses her arms over her chest.

Shit. We're in it for the long haul, then. Prepare for battle.

I rise from the desk, cross to the other side to meet her.

"Stevie, I'm not going to delve into Kirin's personal business with you. I'm sure you can appreciate the need for privacy and personal boundaries, though I know you struggle with the latter."

"*I* struggle with the latter?" She steps closer, her eyes

blazing, heat and anger emanating off her body in waves so strong they nearly knock me down.

Jabbing a finger into my chest, she says, "You know what drives *me* crazy? I'll tell you. You warned me not to trust anyone, yet you seem to want me to trust you in everything. You guys are always asking me to give this a chance, to respect the rules, to respect privacy. And I think I've done a pretty damn good job of all that, considering I signed onto this project with zero upfront information and have rolled with the punches—punches that keep on coming, mind you—and you and Kirin, who insist that you're here to help me, basically stonewall me every chance you get. Now Kirin has gone AWOL, and you're stonewalling me again."

"Stevie, there are things—*delicate* things—that require—"

"Don't give me that bullshit, Doc, unless you want *your* delicate things to end up in a jar."

Instinctively, I cover my crotch—an excellent example of the stimulus-thought-response mechanism at work.

"Kirin needs his privacy right now," I say firmly. "I will respect that, and so will you. End of discussion."

Stevie's anger spikes so high, her hair practically crackles.

"So it's okay to keep me in the dark?" she asks. "To stay in total control, leaving me hanging out here in the breeze by myself? What about *my* privacy?"

"If the situations were reversed, I would afford you the same courtesy," I say.

And then I realize my mistake.

Stevie smirks, hands on her hips, her eyes laser-focused on mine. "Really? So... What's my true form? You all seem to know it, yet none of you thought to clue me in."

I'm falling off a cliff, scrambling to hold on to something, but she's got me right where she wants me. I knew this would come up again after that day in her bedroom, after the delirious snake-bite conversations, but now is not the time.

There's absolutely nothing I can say in response. All I can do is close the classroom door, hope like hell no one else is listening in.

"One more chance," she says, lowering her voice and leaning in close—so close her honeysuckle sweetness tickles my nose. My heart lodges in my throat—I have no idea what she's going to say next, only that it's going to hit hard.

I steel my nerves, slap on my poker face.

"Who are the Keepers of the Grave?" she whispers.

I choke out a sputtering cough. So much for the poker face.

"Nothing to say?" she presses. "Cat got your tongue? What about the Book of Shadow and Mists? Hmm, drawing another blank?"

"Stevie, how do you... This isn't..." I grab her shoulders, desperate. "I don't know how you see the things you see, and yes, there are a great many of them I've kept from you. Not out of secrecy or betrayal or a desire to keep you beholden. But because it's dangerous for you to know. There is so much you have yet to learn, so much we haven't even delved into yet with your mother's prophecies, and now we have a possible dark uprising, the consequences of which you've seen with your own eyes, and..."

I close my eyes, take a deep breath.

Get a hold of yourself, Devane—before this situation spirals so far out of control, you lose everything you've ever cared about.

Mustering all the authority I've got left, I open my eyes and shoot her a firm glare. "Stevie, now is not the time or the place. I've got a class to prepare for. And you need to get to your potions class before Professor Broome writes you up for tardiness."

"Professor Broome won't write me up. *She* isn't an egomaniacal control freak."

"Are you saying I am?"

She glares at me, her smart mouth twisted in a smirk, her anger still simmering. "What else would you call a professor who drones on and on about fear magick, too scared to face his *own* fears and trust someone once in a while?"

"Drone on?" I shout, knowing that's not what we're arguing about but seizing on it anyway—anything to avoid the raw nerve she just scraped. "Do you have any idea how important it is to learn proper defense against mental manipulation? Clearly not, or you wouldn't be so damned stubborn and insolent."

"Clearly not," she says, imitating my voice. "Or I'd be able to defend myself against your boring-ass lectures!"

Mere inches separate us, and despite the ridiculously immature turn this argument has taken, all I want to do is kiss her. It's completely inappropriate, totally unethical, absolutely forbidden by Academy policy, but it's taking a good deal of mental magicks of my own—thoughts of icy rivers, of puppies, of wrinkly old grandmothers and hot garbage and other things that make my cock shrivel on command—to stop me from claiming her right here.

Instead, I turn my back on her, return to the safe harbor of my desk.

"Go to class, Stevie. And I meant what I said about staying safe," I tell her, shuffling through my paperwork. "I don't want you wandering around campus at night without an escort."

"I'm perfectly capable of assessing situations and handling them accordingly, Dr. Devane."

She grabs her bag and huffs toward the door.

Not before I see her eyes glaze with tears.

Shit.

I set down my papers. "Stevie, wait. Can you just—"

"Just what?" She calls over her shoulder, refusing to turn around. "Just trust you?"

I lower my head. Point made.

And then she's gone, every last one of those damnable old ghosts rushing back in to fill the space.

I slide open the bottom desk drawer, reach for the bottle.

And hope that one of these times, the booze will chase away those ghosts or erase the lingering pain or infuse me with all the courage I lack.

Hope that one of these times, it will do something other than burn all the way down.

FORTY-THREE

STEVIE

The archive drawers containing Mom's research seem to go on forever, packed not just with her notebooks, but with books and scrolls from all over the library.

Professor Phaines told me she was working on many different things, all of them connected to her prophecies, many of them considered blasphemous by some of the elder administrators. He didn't mention Trello by name or offer much detail beyond that—and I still don't feel comfortable asking him about it—but something tells me Trello played a big role in my parents' downfall.

For all her rah-rah-rah, we're-here-to-help talk on that first day, I haven't seen her once.

Professor Phaines also told me that when Mom left the Academy, some of the other researchers wanted to destroy her work, but he fought to keep it all in place. Despite her tarnished reputation, he had a hunch the Academy might eventually glean something from the prophecies.

"After all," he told me with a wink, "Melissa Milan was a talented seer, and many of us never stopped believing that."

I'm glad at least Professor Phaines falls into that camp. At this point, he's the only one involved in this project that I still trust.

I haven't spoken to Dr. Devane since my outburst on Monday. In today's class, we were content to ignore each other. And Kirin? Still a no-show. I haven't seen him in almost two weeks now, and he isn't responding to my texts —not about our work or anything else.

Ani told me that he, Kirin, and Baz have plans tonight, which means Kirin's not dead in a ditch—the only acceptable excuse, as far as I'm concerned. And as much as I'd love to fly on over to their super-secret Keepers of the Grave cave again, I haven't heard a peep from my avian familiar.

So that's it. Kirin's officially ignoring me.

And I'm officially heartbroken.

"Everything okay, Stevie?" Professor Phaines asks, and I look up from my spot at the archive table, startled.

"I didn't mean to scare you," he says, then takes the seat across from me. "You look a bit melancholy. Are you all right?"

I force a smile, even as my throat tightens at his kindness. "I'm good. Low blood sugar. I should probably eat a candy bar or something."

He glances around, making a show of inspecting the room, even though we're clearly alone. Then he presses a finger to his lips and retrieves a Snickers bar from his pocket, passing it over.

"Professor Phaines! I thought there was no food allowed in the archives?"

"It's my one weakness."

"Guess that explains the chocolate fingerprints I found in Plant and Animal Symbolism in the Major Arcana."

"Page nineteen?" He chuckles. "I won't tell if you won't."

"My lips are sealed." Laughing, I tear into the candy bar with gusto, grateful for the sugar rush. "Now we're officially co-conspirators. Mmm, perfect. This is all I needed."

He nods, but I can tell he's not convinced. "Are you sure you're okay?"

Sometimes when he looks at me like that, he reminds me not of a grandfather, but of my dad, who was always the best listener, patient and soft-spoken, never rushing a conversation or talking over anyone. Basically, the opposite of me.

But Professor Phaines is not my dad, and he doesn't need to be burdened with the lovesick melodrama of a twenty-three-year-old student who's supposed to be putting forth an image of abject professionalism and dedication.

"I'm fine. Just getting a little lost in these old books." I rest my hand on the most recent one I've been reading—a particularly dense tome with gilded pages and a cream-colored leather cover, cracked and peeling. There's no author name, and the contents are all hand-written.

"Journey Through the Void of Mist and Spirit." Professor Phaines peers at the title over the top of his glasses. "I don't think I've read it. What do you make of it?"

"Still trying to work that out," I say. "None of the pages seem to be missing, but it reads as if half the contents were either removed at some point, or never written at all."

"But you say there are no pages missing?"

"It doesn't look like it. They're numbered consecutively, and the binding looks intact. But on each individual page, the sentences themselves seem unfinished. Like someone had a thought, and just gave up halfway."

I shake my head. You'd think I'd be used to that style by now—Mom's grimoire is the same way. Most of her spells sound half-baked, and her journal entries are just as confusing. I wonder if she was inspired by this book—some hot minimalist trend in spellbooks.

I laugh at the thought. "All part of the mystery, right? Part of the fun of cracking the code."

"Indeed, Stevie." He smiles at me, his eyes twinkling. "The more time you spend with these books, with your mother's prophecies, the more comfortable you'll become at understanding their meanings. Every witch and mage develops their own personal language—you will too, in time. Maybe someday a couple of eager researchers will be sitting in these very chairs, reading over *your* prophecies."

"If that's the case, I hope they don't scare easily."

Professor Phaines chuckles, but then his eyes turn serious. "Any more progress on connecting the Dark Arcana legends with your mother's work? With the larger threats?"

"Not yet," I tell him. I might have a different answer if Kirin were around to help, but that ship has clearly sailed, and I'm on my own. "I'm still trying to connect all the dots. And there are a *lot* of dots."

"As many as the stars in the sky." He taps the book, meeting my gaze across the table once more. "Stevie, I want you to know that I'm here for you if you need help. Especially with Kirin otherwise occupied, you can lean on me anytime."

I return his kind smile. "I know. And I appreciate that. But you have your own research, too."

"We all need each other, Stevie. Community, family— that's how we survive. Especially witches and mages."

"And candy sneakers." I wink, then take a deep breath, deciding to take him up on his offer.

Besides, it's not like anyone else has been particularly forthcoming on this matter.

Looking at you, *Dr. Devane.*

"Professor Phaines, have you ever heard of something called the Book of Shadow and Mists?"

"Oh, yes," he says, his brow furrowing, transforming his face from wise old grandpa to serious professor in an instant. "It's part of the deeper legends of the Dark Arcana. It's said that the Book of Shadow and Mists will unlock the arcane spells protecting the sacred objects, thereby making their secret location known."

I bite my lower lip, trying to remember what Kirin and I had learned about that spell. "Kirin and I read something a little different."

"That's to be expected. The legends all differ, which is part of the reason the truth is so hard to pin down. What did you read?"

"Well, it didn't mention the Book of Shadow and Mists by name, so I didn't even think about it at the time. But in terms of the spell itself… It sounded like whoever had the objects in his possession already—along with something called the blood of the world—could then use an arcane spell to somehow claim magick for himself. Basically, to take control. But the version you mentioned makes it sound like you'd need the spell first, in order to find the objects."

"Yes, that was always my understanding of the legend. But like I said, there are often many, many versions, passed on through generations and translated with many twists and turns along the way."

"Do you think they're talking about the same spell?"

"I do," he says thoughtfully. "There are enough similarities in the story to suggest it could be one and the same."

"Something to consider, I guess." I make a note to ask Kirin about it later, but then cross it out, and make a note to myself instead.

"Tell me, Stevie," Professor Phaines says. "Where did you read about the Book of Shadow and Mists, if not in the research you found with Kirin? The old scribes were notoriously superstitious—it's rarely ever mentioned in the accounts by name. Most of what I know about it comes from oral tradition—in fact, I'm working on my own transcription as part of my research, but it's slow and painstaking, as you might imagine."

SARAH PIPER

"If it's anything like this job, I understand, and you have my sympathies."

"It's a labor of love," he says. "Well, and now one of urgency, perhaps, if your visions are any indication."

I take a breath to tell him where I'd first heard the term, but then change my mind. I'm not sure why exactly, but I don't want him to think I'm basing my scholarly research on the rantings of a dream visit from my dead mother. My so-called visions about the apocalypse are crazy enough.

As with so many things lately, I need more information first.

"I'm not sure," I hedge. "I must've come across it in my research, or maybe in my mother's notes. At the time, I guess I just figured it was another name for a witch's grimoire—like a book of shadows. But now that I'm getting more comfortable with the Tarot symbols, I'm starting to go back through everything again with a fine-toothed comb, see if there are any details Kirin and I missed the first time."

"An excellent scientific approach," he says confidently. Then, checking his phone, "Oh! I'm afraid I've got another matter to attend to. Headmistress Trello is quite demanding —don't tell her I said that."

"All of your secrets are safe with me," I say.

Professor Phaines chuckles, then rises from his chair, bending across the table to place a kind hand on mine. "Great work, Stevie. Keep digging, keep questioning, keep exercising that beautiful, magickal mind of yours. We are making excellent progress."

"Thank you—I agree. And if I come across the reference

to the Book of Shadow and Mists again, I'll be sure to let you know."

"Yes, I'd be interested in hearing if there's any connection to your mother's readings. Regardless, if you have any other questions, don't hesitate to ask me."

Questions? I almost laugh.

Where the hell has Kirin been, and why is he avoiding me? Why did he make me feel literal sparks and lightning, only to disappear on me like that?

"Will do," I say with another forced smile, watching him leave.

Wiped out from all the brainpower—not to mention the obsessing about Kirin—I pack up my notes for the day and head home, hoping to catch Isla and Nat for an early dinner.

Whatever happened between me and Kirin in the library that night—whatever sparks kindled between us this summer at Kettle Black—I have to let that go. He doesn't want that with me, and I never should've let things go as far as they did.

With this in mind, and a newfound appreciation for the rules of my heart I so blatantly disregarded, I take all of my previous feelings for Kirin, fold them into a little stack, and stick them in the very bottom drawer of my mind, a dusty old book of myths and legends better left forgotten.

FORTY-FOUR

BAZ

I can't get her out of my head. Not ideal, circumstances being what they are.

I wish I could tell her as much. Wish I could wrap her up in my arms, kiss her until she can't see straight.

I wish we could finish what we started out on the rocks that day, before Emory showed up and blew my life to shit.

Well, not my whole life. But the Stevie part of my life, which I was just starting to enjoy.

Now Carly's got me locked into this bullshit deal with her parents...

And there she is. Walking down the path toward Flame and Fury, probably meeting up with Ani. At least she can still count on him, which is more than I can say for the rest of us fucking degenerates.

Brotherhood, my ass. She's one of us. We should be sticking together.

"Baz?"

Fuck, she saw me. No use trying to play it off now.

I step out of the shadows, give her a smile. Shove my hands into my pockets to keep myself from touching her.

"Hey," I say, real fucking smooth-talker. I try to maintain eye contact, try to feign polite disinterest, but she's wearing tight black leather pants that hug her delicious curves, and a silky low-cut number with sequins on it that's basically a death trap for my eyes.

One look, and I'm about to fall in headfirst.

"What are you up to tonight?" I ask, because if I don't say something inane, I might just say something real, and then we'll all be up a river of shit.

"I'm supposed to meet those guys for karaoke. Ani and them," she says, but her heart's not in it. I can see it in her eyes, staring up at me with the same deep well of desire I feel in mine.

Talk me out of it, she seems to be saying. *Give me a reason to bail.*

"I thought you couldn't sing," I say.

"How'd you hear that?"

"You told me the first day we met."

"Oh, right. I'm surprised you remembered."

"I remember everything about you, Little Bird."

She's smiling now, a soft blush creeping into her cheeks. But then it fades, and she frowns like she just got a whiff of something unpleasant.

Fucking Kirin.

Fucking me.

"Where have you been, anyway?" she asks. "I haven't seen you outside of class much. We haven't... hung out."

"Yeah. Just... busy."

Disappointment flashes in her eyes. Maybe a little hurt.

Or maybe that's just wishful thinking on my part. Not because I want to hurt her, but because it would mean she thought of me. *Wanted* to hang out.

So I'm standing there with my dick in my hand, trying to figure out one decent thing to say to the woman, one thing that isn't *fuck all this shit, just come back to my room with me and we'll start over,* when out of nowhere she grabs the front of my jacket.

"If you don't tell me to stop right now," she says, "I'm going to kiss you."

And I'm looking down into those eyes, the deep well of them, and remembering the taste of her creamy skin, the feel of her nipple on my tongue, and I'm so hard for her I'm about to lose it right here.

Fuck it.

I lean in close to meet her. Her breath hitches. My heart's doing double time.

My lips brush against hers for the briefest instant, fucking bliss, and then there's a dark shadow looming over us both, and I look up to find Carly.

She rolls her eyes at me, then comes around and grabs my arm, putting on her innocent face.

"Oh, hey, Stevie. You look... available." Then she looks up at me and goes, "Come on, Baz! We have reservations, remember?"

I feel Stevie's sigh, the weight of her frustration settling over my shoulders as she waits for me to send Carly away, or make some pithy comment.

But Carly's got her arm around me, holding me close, and this time, there's not a damn thing I can do about it.

A deal is a deal.

If her parents weren't so powerful, and mine weren't so deplorable…

Wishes and dreams. Ashes and dust.

But we can't choose the families we're born into any more than we can choose our magickal affinities. Sometimes you hit the lotto. Other times you hit rock bottom.

Your only choice is to figure out what to do from there. Both can be opportunities, both can be death sentences.

Right now, I'm still trying to decide where I fall.

"Have fun at karaoke," I tell her, holding her gaze for just a little too long. "Maybe we'll see you there later."

She's holding my gaze, too. And when Carly turns around, I stay focused on Stevie, just one more second.

"I kind of hate you sometimes," she whispers.

"I know." I offer a sad smile. "I kind of hate me, too."

FORTY-FIVE

ANSEL

"So you hate Baz, but you also kind of like him? And you like Kirin, but he's driving you crazy?"

"Exactly." Stevie passes me the carton of veggie lo mein. "See, this is why you're so perfect, Ani. *You* get it. You don't try to overcomplicate things. *You* don't make excuses. *You* don't think with your dick."

"No, my dick has much better things to do."

We've just hiked to the top of the Cauldron of Flame and Fury for a Saturday picnic, and now we're sitting on a blanket on the rim with a breathtaking view of the canyon below, the pool of red water at the bottom sparkling in the sunlight.

Everything about the day is pretty much bang-on perfect—I can't think of anything I'd rather do than run around outside with a cute girl who laughs at my corny jokes and kicks my ass all the way up the trail.

Except for maybe run around outside with a cute girl who *isn't* obsessing over my best friends.

Not that I blame her. Kirin and Baz... hell, if I swung that way, they'd be tops on my list too.

But right now, I kind of want to toss both their asses into this canyon for the mind games they're playing with Stevie.

And I hate violence of any sort, so that's definitely saying something.

"Sorry I was such a downer at karaoke last night," she says, probably for the fifth time today. "I really did want to sing *I Will Survive* with you. I just didn't want that jerkface to think I was singing about him."

"I told you, stop worrying about it. One day, when you least expect it, I'll spring a new song on you, and you won't be able to say no. I'm thinking... rap."

"I won't let you down. Make your ears bleed, maybe, but I won't bail out on you."

I open up the beef and broccoli, let her have the first few bites.

"I don't know what I'm doing," she says, passing it back to me. "Okay, I have this personal rule. I don't get romantically involved with anyone I really like."

"Um. Okay, that makes basically *no* sense, but hey—you do you, boo."

"I'm just risk-averse with stuff like that—relationships or whatever. Which makes Baz the perfect candidate, because there's no way I could possibly like him, unlike Kirin, who I can't seem to stop liking, no matter how hard I try. But with

Baz, I knew right from the first time I met him. I thought, hey, here's a guy you *definitely* don't want to get involved with. Except now I think I kind of do. And also, still with the Kirin obsessing..." She lies back on the blanket and covers her face with her hands. "What is *wrong* with me?"

"Wait. Slow down." My head is spinning, and it's not from the exertion of the hike or the overdose on Chinese food. "First of all, perfect candidate for what? You just said you don't do involvements."

"For... you know. Non-involvements."

"Friends with benefits," I clarify. "Fuck buddies, booty calls, midnight marauders."

"Thanks, walking sex thesaurus."

I set aside the food and lie down next to her. "Serious question: How does one declare his candidacy for something like that, anyway? Is there a nomination process? An early vote? Can I get on the ballot?"

"Ani!" She smacks me on the arm, her laughter swirling around me like a warm bath. I swear, being near her makes me want to write poems about birds or run barefoot through a field of flowers.

Completely mental.

"My Tarot cards keep telling me to run far, far away. Like, every time I ask lately, I draw the standard He's Just Not Into You starter pack. Ten of Swords, Three of Swords, Eight of Cups, The Tower. If Professor Nakata ever reads my journal..." She does a mock shudder. "I don't think I've written so much emo word vomit since high school. *Early* high school. And I'm still completely torn."

"Over Kirin and Baz?"

"Told you I'm crazy. What should I do, Ani?" She turns over on her hip, facing me, looking at me like I'm the wise older brother with all the answers.

It's a kick in the balls, to be honest. That look says it all. I'm in the big-brother zone, which is even worse than the friend zone, because at least friends have a chance at evolving into something else. Big brother? Nowhere to go from there.

"Stevie, first of all, you're not crazy. Maybe you should just… I don't know. Date both of them? Why does it have to be a big drama?"

"What? That's so shady! You guys are all basically best friends. And even if they were total strangers… no. I can't sneak around like that."

"I'm not saying you should sneak around. I'm saying— brace yourself, super cutting-edge concept here—talk to them about your feelings and see what happens from there. Maybe you can come up with a casual arrangement. They might surprise you."

Why am I encouraging this? I should tell her to listen to her cards, run far away from both of them. And me. And Cass.

But the truth is, she's always going to come back. The five of us are bonded, whether she knows it or not.

"Ani, if you think any guy would be okay with sharing —even casually—you're even more optimistic than I thought. Which is something I totally love about you, so don't go changin' or anything. But seriously."

Which I totally love about you…

Okay, I'm an idiot. I know it. I can feel the idiotness rising up inside, consuming me whole, yet I'm powerless to stop it.

I'm crushing hard on this woman, and she's so caught up in Kirin and Baz, she can't even see it.

And I'm too much of a chicken shit to admit it. Talk about your feelings? Yeah. Great advice, Ani.

She's probably right about the sharing thing, but I can't help but think it'd be different for Kirin and Baz. For me, too, if the opportunity ever presented itself. We're brothers, after all. Maybe not by birth, but in all the ways that count.

I close my eyes, cutting off my daydream before that bus veers any closer to crazytown than it already has. Brothers or not, none of us have any business getting mixed up with Stevie like that. Yeah, she's part of this thing too, but romantic entanglements—casual or not—have a way of complicating everything.

I kind of see her point about not getting involved with people you like.

"Stevie, listen. If you really—"

Both of our phones ding at the same time—a chime that's reserved for emergency Academy correspondence.

We exchange a worried look, then pull out the phones. It's an email from Anna Trello.

Esteemed Witches and Mages of the Academy,

It is with a heavy heart that I'm reporting this grim news. Danika

Lewis, the witch arrested in Taos two weeks ago for allegedly murdering her own children in a blood sacrifice, has been sentenced without trial to die for those crimes—crimes she most certainly did not commit.

Moreover, for the first time since magick became known in the wider world and our community fell under close public scrutiny, the authorities have decided to broadcast the execution on live television.

It is scheduled for this evening at 6:00 PM.

She will be hanged, as the officials wish to make a bold statement about the dangers of witchcraft by stoking long-buried but not forgotten embers into the raging fires of corruption and control.

To say this is a horrible, damnable offense is a gross understatement. But at this time, we are nearly powerless against such reckless, sanctioned hatred.

I say nearly *powerless, because even at our lowest moments, the fight is far from over. I do not want any of us to take this as the final word of law, or as proof that we are somehow tainted, evil, or inhuman. We can reclaim our power—slowly, perhaps—but great change often moves in seemingly imperceptible increments. The strides we make now will ensure our children and grandchildren can openly embrace their magick and live their lives without fear of retribution.*

To that end, I'm asking all students to recommit to your studies with renewed passion and determination. I'm asking all faculty members to recommit to our students with renewed promise to guide them through these difficult times, and all the difficult times still to come.

And I'm asking our entire Arcana Academy family to come together now, to support one another, to hold tight to the magick that connects and bonds us all as witches, mages, and gifted humans.

A vigil will be held in the Hall of Remembrance tonight during the broadcast. I realize this will be a difficult thing to observe, but it is our hope that by doing so together, we may draw strength from one another and weather this storm, as our kind has always weathered such travesties.

Attendance is not required, of course. We encourage all students and faculty members to practice good self-care and decide for yourselves whether or not you'd like to participate in the group ritual or even to watch the broadcast at all.

If you are able to join us, please meet at the Hall entrance by 5:45 PM. Black candles will be provided to all who wish to light one for Danika, or for anyone else you may wish to remember at this time.

As many of you know, one of our first-year witches, Amelia Weatherby, is Danika's niece. Not only has she suffered the death of three of her young cousins, but her beloved aunt will now be executed. We ask that you keep Amelia and her family in your hearts.

Counselors will be available during the broadcast and for the rest of the academic year for any students or faculty members who wish to talk about the tragedy or about any anxieties or emotional difficulties you may be struggling with.

Please know that you are not alone. We will get through this together, as a community and a family.

Sincerely,
Anna Trello, Headmistress
Arcana Academy of the Arts

FORTY-SIX

STEVIE

There is only one Tarot card drawn today, in my bedroom and in all the rooms and suites across campus.

Death. Literal and figurative, for as Danika loses her life tonight, humanity loses something too—itself, a day of reckoning that will forever separate our time into its distinct before and after.

The Hall of Remembrance is a large chapel and museum on the south end of campus, dedicated to honoring the departed as well as the Academy's past. Carved statuary depicting the Academy's first professors lines the wall, and in the back, a separate chamber includes a huge scale model of the entire campus, including a working replica of the fountain. With high vaulted ceilings, stained-glass windows, and the scent of incense permeating the air, it immediately inspires reverence and peace.

Tonight, the chapel is packed with witches and mages, all of us sitting shoulder to shoulder, some standing in the back, everyone holding a single black candle, a sea of flames flickering in the darkness. Headmistress Trello makes no announcement or welcome; she stands somberly at the front with the other professors, including Dr. Devane.

There is no talking, no whispers, no fidgeting. Only the quiet hush of those gathered in mourning.

In fear.

At 5:55 PM, a large screen rolls down at the front of the room. Five minutes later, the broadcast begins, the news ticker scrolling beneath.

It's on every channel.

The skies in Taos are overcast, a light mist rolling across a green field. Many people have gathered before a large wooden platform that looks hastily erected, a lone man in a dark gray suit standing in the center. In the distance, the square, nondescript buildings of a prison loom, barbed wire curled along the top, armed snipers positioned at intervals.

Beside the man on the platform, the noose swings, a terrifying silhouette against the gray sky.

Among the assembled crowd, someone is selling popcorn, another selling beer.

My stomach churns inside, and next to me, Nat sniffles, knowing her family friend in Portland may soon face the same fate.

Seated on Nat's other side, Isla puts an arm around our friend, and together we squeeze in close.

On the screen, an armed guard escorts a bound woman down a path across the grass, and up a small set of stairs leading up to the platform. Members of the crowd—fellow humans—shout and curse, throwing rotten fruit and beer cans and dolls tied with nooses.

"Dead witch walking!" they shout and spit. "Burn in hell, wicked cunt!"

I can't help but remember my brief time in prison, the way the other inmates—fellow humans—would chant and throw things at me, too.

Camera flashes pop, the media jostling for better angles.

I take a shuddering breath, keeping the tears at bay.

From the row behind me, Ani reaches out, squeezes my shoulder. I touch his hand and the first few tears escape.

The man on the platform glances out over the crowd. Once the woman is led to the noose and the rope is slipped around her neck, he begins.

"Danika Beth Lewis," he booms into a microphone clipped to his lapel, his voice echoing across the field. "You have been convicted on multiple counts of public witchcraft, magickal malicious intent, magickal abuse by a person in a position of trust, and murder. There is no atoning for these crimes. Let your sentence be a warning to all who seek to follow in your dark footsteps: rest assured, those footsteps will lead them right here."

The man then launches into a half-hour-long sermon on the dangers of witchcraft—a sermon I tune out, focusing my attention instead on Danika, on her face, on her eyes, still fierce despite everything she's endured.

Her children are dead.

Soon, she will join them.

When he's finally finished extolling the dangers of

magick and all who practice this tool of the devil, he turns to Danika, his voice laced with contempt.

"Danika Lewis, do you have any last words?"

At this, she looks into the cameras, tears streaking silently down her face, and makes her final mark on this world.

"Fucking *fight*!"

The man—judge, jury, and executioner—turns away from her and presses a button on a remote in his hand. The part of the platform beneath her feet collapses.

And Danika Beth Lewis, mother and wife and witch and human being, falls to her death.

It's not quick. It's not painless.

When she finally stops kicking, when her body stills and her eyes bulge wide, when her bladder empties, we know it's finally over.

Here in the Hall of Remembrance, candles flickering in the darkness, our souls connected by our shared pain and shared determination, all of us release a collective breath.

And though no words are uttered, I know we've all just made the same silent promise.

We will honor her life. Remember her words.

Fucking fight.

Back home, my suite has never felt so empty, so sad. I turn on all the lights and set out candles for Danika, then set the kettle to boil, returning to that one familiar comfort.

There's no problem a proper cup of tea can't fix.

But just before the water boils, there's a chime at the door.

I peer into the security monitor and see an unexpected visitor, and I immediately open the door.

"Dr. Devane?" I whisper, as though he's not really here at all, as though I can't trust my eyes.

"I thought maybe you shouldn't be alone tonight." His eyes are bloodshot, his hair disheveled, the faint but unmistakable scent of whiskey lingering on his breath, and my heart melts. A tear tracks down my cheek, and we stand there in awkward silence, my mouth unable to form the words I feel inside.

"Perhaps I misjudged." Doc offers a sad smile, then lowers his eyes. "If you'd rather I—"

"No." I take his hand and pull him inside, close the door behind him, and wrap him into a hug.

He stiffens at first, then slides his arms around me, holding me tight. He presses a kiss to the top of my head and breathes in my scent. I don't want to let him go, and I'm pretty sure he feels the same way. We stay like that for several silent moments until the door chimes again.

This time when I open it, Kirin, Baz, and Ani stand before me.

"None of us wanted to be alone tonight," Baz says, and I stand aside and invite them all in, hugging Baz first, and then Ani.

Kirin is last. He closes the door behind him and holds

out a bouquet of pink-and-white stargazer lilies wrapped in cellophane.

Ignoring the flowers, I wrap my arms around him, holding him close, fighting the raw emotion bubbling up inside. It's the first I've felt his warmth since that night in the library—the first I've even seen him—and as he slides his arms around me, cellophane crinkling against my back, I press my ear to his chest and listen for the strong, steady beat of his heart—the beat I felt when he kissed me in the library. When he made the world explode before my eyes.

The guys settle in on the living room sofa and chairs, and I put Kirin's flowers in water and swap out my single-size kettle for the company one.

I don't have to ask what kind of tea to make tonight. Vanilla chamomile, with a dash of cinnamon and a spoonful of wild honey—soothing and comforting, something that feels like the hug we all so desperately need.

As horrifying and depressing as it is, we can't seem to turn off the news coverage, the five of us gathered in front of the television like voyeurs peering in on a reality no one wants to believe exists.

"Officials in New Mexico tonight made grim history when they carried out the first live broadcast of an execution for the crime of public witchcraft," the newscaster says. "Danika Beth Lewis, age thirty-seven, was hanged for her alleged crimes today—crimes for which she was arrested just two short weeks ago. No trial was held."

Cut to the platform, still standing in the field with the prison looming behind it. Gruesomely, her body was left as a warning, now drenched in rain. Four men stand guard as revelers mill around at the platform, drinking and taking selfies.

A journalist is already speaking with one of them—a woman who looks about the same age as Danika, dressed in a T-shirt that reads *Hell is for Witches*.

"People claim that twenty witches were executed during the Salem Witch Trials, an additional four dying in prison," the woman says, like she's some kind of expert. "But that's not strictly true. It's important to remember that twenty *people* were executed—regular people accused of witchcraft by religious fanatics. Perhaps some of the accused practiced the dark arts, but we can't know that for sure. The difference now is that we *know* witches exist. We *know* how dangerous they are—for a fact. We have no need for fanciful testimony and fanaticism. Witches and mages are the greatest threat our country faces at this time."

"More than terrorism?" the journalist asks. "War?"

"Witchcraft *is* terrorism," she insists.

"Plenty of witches and mages live peaceably in our communities," the journalist says, "and have done so for long before we knew they existed. Surely they can't all be terrorists."

The woman's jaw ticks, her face turning red and blotchy. "The only way to ensure our children will be safe is to completely eradicate magick from this world. Since none of us knows how to do that, the next best thing is to eradicate those who wield it. Unfortunately, we can't just go around shooting them on sight." She laughs, as though we should all be in on this joke.

The journalist says nothing.

Cut back to a closeup on the execution site, the black silhouette of her body swinging from the gallows like something out of a seventeenth-century Puritan nightmare.

Baz changes the channel.

It's the same show on every one—revelers celebrating her death. Mocking her. Talking heads extolling the dangers, debating the legalities, speculating.

No one defends us.

No one dares.

Finally, Dr. Devane turns it off, and we all let out a sigh of relief.

I wash the teacups, including Doc's Bugs Bunny mug, and Baz tries to make us something to eat with whatever randomness he finds in my fridge. But in the end, no one is hungry.

No one has much to say, either. We all seem to understand that ours is a temporary truce, a reprieve on our fighting and misunderstandings, on all the secrets and unsaid words.

Eventually, we fall asleep together on the living room rug, our legs all tangled up, my head on Ansel's chest, Baz's arm draped across my waist, Kirin stretched out on the couch above, his hand skimming my shoulder. Even Dr.

Devane stays with us, perched on a chair by the window, keeping silent watch.

And in the hours that follow, I sleep soundly, my secretive, imperfect, infuriating—and yes, compassionate, thoughtful, and kind—mages a protective shield keeping the nightmares at bay.

Keeping my heart safe.

Maybe it's just for tonight, but I'll take it.

FORTY-SEVEN

STEVIE

Classes are canceled for the next week, the administration deciding we need the time for mourning and reflection, for gathering our strength.

Amelia has officially dropped out of the Academy to be with her family. No one knows if she's planning on coming back next year, or ever.

I don't blame her.

The horrible murder of Danika Lewis gives new meaning to my work, and even on these days set aside for rest and contemplation, I find myself in the library archives with my own Tarot cards, scrutinizing Mom's research, comparing my translations, asking the cards for guidance.

Sometimes I wonder if this is how Mom felt, frantically scribbling notes, flipping cards, desperate to make a connection, to find the single unifying thread that would finally explain all the crazy visions.

Today, after a quick break for lunch, I return to the

archives and set out the notebooks I'm working on, along with Journey Through the Void of Mist and Spirit, the authorless book I still can't figure out. I feel like the answer is right before me, hiding in plain sight among these seemingly unfinished words. But no matter how long I stare at them, they just keep eluding me.

I pull out my Tarot cards, give them a good shuffle. Since I started using this deck in earnest, my old randomly vanishing cards haven't appeared. It seems these have taken their place, which is fine by me. I prefer getting the messages when I'm ready for them rather than, say, waking up in a bathtub full of scary-ass cards of doom.

"What am I missing here?" I turn over three cards.

Two of Swords, Two of Cups, Two of Wands.

Curious about the repetition, I turn over two more.

Two of Pentacles and the High Priestess, the Major Arcana whose corresponding number is also two.

I record the reading in my Tarot journal. Two. Something with twos. Balance? A decision? Two pathways? I look at each card in turn. The High Priestess is telling me to look within, to search my own hidden depths for the answer, but nothing comes.

I don't know how long I'm in there, poring over the cards, poring over the notes, my eyes going blurry. I've got my face buried in the middle of the Journey book when a familiar scent drifts to my nose—storms in the summer, clean and electric.

I look up to see Kirin standing at the end of the room, his eyes red, his hair a wild mess.

It's the first time we've been alone since that time in the stacks—the first time he's held eye contact for more than a few seconds.

"Danika's death… The news… I can't stop thinking about it." He comes to join me on my side of the table, kneeling before me, taking one of my hands into his.

My heart runs up into my throat, making it hard to breathe.

"None of us can, Kirin," I say.

"No, I mean… Okay." He drops his gaze and blows out a breath, then looks up at me again. His glasses are smudged. I don't think he's slept much lately. "I just kept thinking, what if that was me? Or one of the guys, or… or you? What if it was you?" His voice cracks at the end, and despite my rules, I run a hand through his hair, stroking the back of his neck.

"We're doing everything we can to make sure that doesn't happen," I say, but I'm not certain he even hears me.

"I just kept thinking," he continues, "I just kept thinking over and over… What if something happened to me or to someone I cared about, and I never even told them how I feel? I'm running away, I'm hiding, I don't even know what I'm doing anymore. Where I'm going. Why."

"Kirin, slow down," I say softly. "What's wrong?"

He starts to respond, then closes his mouth and shakes his head, still hesitating. Still lost.

"Do you remember our time at Kettle Black?" I ask.

"You used to say, 'Stevie, you're the queen of leaves, and I trust you implicitly.'"

A slow smile dawns on his face.

"Tell me," I say. "I'm right here with you. And you *can* trust me implicitly. I promise."

"I know. I *do* trust you. It's not... I just... I think I'm... I'm falling..." He squeezes his eyes shut, shakes his head again as if he's still trying to talk himself out of this confession.

Then he looks up at me again and drops the bomb.

"I'm falling in love with you, Stevie." His eyes glaze with emotion. "And I can't let myself do that. I just can't."

My heart skips, my stomach tossing and turning like a clothes dryer. "But... why?"

"Why? Are you kidding me?" Kirin laughs nervously. "Because you're smart, and you make me laugh, and I love the way your mind works, the way you question every-thing, the way your eyebrow does that thing when you're thinking." He reaches up, smooths his fingertips over my eyebrow. "I love how you throw yourself into everything you're learning, and how you devour books, and how you always know how to make the perfect tea blend—I've always loved that about you, my queen of leaves. And you're beautiful, Stevie. Every time I look at you, my heart breaks a little more, knowing I'll have to close my eyes at some point and miss your face. I just... I'm falling and..."

"Kirin," I say through the tightness in my throat, and when I speak again, my voice is no more than a whisper. "I

432

meant—why can't you do that? Why can't you fall in love with me?"

He cups my face, thumb grazing my cheek. His smile turns sad, his eyes haunted and pained, and when the wave of his energy hits me, it's so desolate and bleak it makes me gasp.

A tear rolls down his cheek, vanishing at the edge of a broken smile.

"Because everything I touch, I destroy."

FORTY-EIGHT

STEVIE

The execution is never far from anyone's thoughts, but by the end of October, a small ray of light begins to pierce the shroud of darkness, and the first few pumpkins are carved and placed on the steps of the main hall.

Soon after, the dorms begin to transform, too. Iron and Bone becomes a pumpkin patch, complete with jack-o'-lanterns, scarecrows, and ravens perched along the windowsills. Breath and Blade is a haunted house, with intermittent moans and spine-chilling music emanating from the windows. Blood and Sorrow is now a vampire den, coffins popping out of the ground and bats hung from the eves, Count Dracula swooping down over the front door on unsuspecting visitors. Flame and Fury took inspiration straight from the depths of hell, with billowing flames made out of red and orange sheets and demons crouching on the rooftop.

By All Hallows' Eve, every pathway is lined with

glowing jack-o'-lanterns, the water in the fountain is spelled to look like blood, and the entire campus is decked out in full-on, spooky gothic glory—including the students. Foundations of Tarot Magick this morning was packed with witches, ghosts, skeletons, vampires, sexy vampires, slutty vampires, and more than a few slutty Disney Princesses. Even Dr. Devane got into the spirit, dressing up as a cranky old professor.

Okay, maybe *that* wasn't a costume, but still. He wore it well.

It's the witch's new year, a time for fresh starts, as well as a time to honor the dead, and before I head out to meet Ani at the Flame and Fury bar Hot Shots, I take a moment to honor mine.

The altar is small, set up on a table in my bedroom with three black candles and a fresh pot of vanilla mint tea. Mom's three-legged ceramic pig sits before the candles, along with their Yosemite carabiner. I also found a photo of my parents from the last Halloween celebration they attended here, the two of them posing in a pumpkin patch near the river, stars glittering overhead. Dad is dressed like a scarecrow, with overalls and a red flannel shirt and a floppy hat, a stuffed crow perched on his shoulder. Mom is a sexy black cat, her leg curled seductively around his, her head thrown back in laughter.

They looked happy that night.

Next to the photo, I placed the Death card.

Kneeling before it now, I light the candles—one for each of us—and close my eyes, picturing them in my mind. Not

in the rushing water, as I last saw them, but in Kettle Black, Mom baking scones, Dad sorting through herbs and leaves, sniffing every bag. A typical Sunday. Happy. Content.

I tell them about my first month at the Academy, about the friends I've made here—Isla and Nat, the guys. I tell them about my professors and my favorite subjects, my Tarot cards, the journal I've been diligently keeping for Professor Nakata's class. I tease Mom about her cryptic prophecies—how she always liked to make me work a little harder than necessary, but that I don't mind, because it means I get to spend more time in the library. More time with her.

After a few minutes, a deep peace settles over me, and I release a long breath, my last remnants of guilt about attending the Academy finally evaporating. It feels as though I've been holding all of this back for far too long.

"I will always honor you," I whisper, picking up their photo and letting the tears fall freely. "Maybe not exactly how you wanted me to, but in the best way I know how."

I kiss the photo, then put it back in its place of reverence.

A breeze floats through my bedroom, snuffing out the candles. In its wake, I catch the unmistakable scents of roses and spicy Mexican chocolate, and I feel their energy embracing me—a hug from the great beyond.

I wrap my arms around myself and smile. "I love you, too, guys. Take care of each other, okay?"

FORTY-NINE

STEVIE

Dressed in sparkly devil's horns and a silky blue spaghetti strap dress that hugs every curve, I point my pitchfork at my reflection in the mirror and make the official declaration:

"Girl, you are one hot-ass bitch!"

It had to be said. Claim your truth, right?

Satisfied that everything is as perfect as it can be, I snap a selfie for Jessa, then head downstairs to go meet Ani at Flame and Fury. Hot Shots is doing a Major-Arcana-themed costume gathering—I refuse to call it a party, lest I go back on my vow to never attend a party with Ani again—and it's just what I need tonight. Fun with friends, a few drinks, eye candy.

No confusing feelings. No dreams about Kirin's declaration and disappearing act. No fantasies about Baz's filthy mouth on mine. No esoteric occult books and Tarot readings and nonsensical rhymes predicting our doom.

No nightmares about witches being hanged for crimes they didn't commit.

Just a fun Halloween night.

Holding my tail in one hand, my pitchfork in the other, I'm just rounding the stairwell on the third floor when I run into Baz. He's on his way up, his arms loaded with grocery bags.

His eyes bulge when he sees me, making no effort to hide the fact that he's totally checking me out.

"Hot *damn*, girl. You trying to send every man at the Academy to an early grave?"

I cock an eyebrow. "Not a bad idea, but... No. Just going to the thing over at Hot Shots."

"Oh right, the Major Arcana party. So you must be—"

"The Devil," I say proudly, sticking out my chest a little bit. Okay, maybe a lot, but Baz deserves to know what he's missing out on. "Devil in a blue dress. Get it? I thought about going as The Star, but she's naked, so..."

"That sounds like an even more amazing costume. Hey, if you ever need someone to model for, to give you an honest opinion about your costume dilemmas..." He smiles, a look that could definitely turn into a slow death for me—*if* I let it.

Which I won't.

Not a chance.

I lift a bare shoulder. Yep, that's me, artfully elegant, totally nonchalant. "I've got Ani, so I'm good."

Baz nearly drops his groceries. "You and Ani? You guys are a thing? When the hell did that happen?"

"You need help with those?" I ask brightly, ignoring the question and reaching for one of the bags.

Baz offers no resistance, surprising the hell out of me.

Fuck. Now I have *to help him. Now I have to take this into his room—at least as far as his door.*

So much for nonchalance.

I turn around and head down the third-floor hallway, knowing Baz is totally checking out my ass. I put a little swish in my step.

I've never been to his room, so I finally step aside to let him catch up. We walk all the way to the end, a corner room on the opposite side of where my room is, and he scans us in.

I try to pass him the groceries, but he doesn't take them.

"Come on in," he says, flicking on the lights.

Against my better judgment, I follow him inside.

His suite is not at all what I expected.

It's slightly smaller than mine—seems like just one bedroom—but it's laid out similarly, with a cozy living room and open kitchen. But that's not what surprises me.

Framed black-and-white photos line nearly every wall and shelf, each one more heartbreaking and breathtaking than the last. There are shots of the guys, of hikes and camping trips they must've taken together. Shots of wildlife —birds of prey, lizards, even a rattlesnake, coiled on a sun-warmed rock. There are the Towers of Breath and Blade, the pool beneath the Cauldron of Flame and Fury, closeups of the Petrified Forest. A dog. An elderly man. There's even one of Headmistress Trello, caught in what I imagine was a rare moment of candid laughter, her eyes closed, her smile wide.

There are a couple of portraits of Baz, too, looking out the window in different positions, the light illuminating one side of his face, the other falling into darkness.

There's so much humanity and raw emotion in the photos they damn near bring tears to my eyes.

"Are all of these yours?" I ask, finally finding my voice.

Baz, who was busy emptying out the groceries on the kitchen counter, shrugs.

"My dad gave me a camera for Christmas one year—a real one. I guess I was about fifteen, sixteen? Pretty much got hooked after that."

Seeing the photos humanizes him in a way I can't explain, and suddenly it's like his hard, tough-as-nails, quick-with-a-joke shell falls away.

"Baz, they're beautiful. Seriously."

He stares at me for so long, I almost think I've said something to upset him. But then he smiles again, cocky and confident as always. "Yeah, I know. But thanks."

My phone buzzes against my body, jolting me. I retrieve it from between my boobs.

His jaw drops. "Um, want me to get that next time?"

I shoot him a warning glare, then check my text messages. "No, thanks."

Baz grabs a beer bottle from the fridge. After a beat, he goes, "Everything okay? You look like someone knocked you down and stole your candy."

"It's Ani." I sigh. "He's not feeling well tonight. Guess I'm on my own for Hot Shots."

Baz shrugs and pops off the beer cap, passes the bottle across the counter. "Blow it off."

I look at the beer, considering the offer. As much as I was looking forward to the Arcana thing, I really don't want to go to Hot Shots alone.

"Your middle name is Temptation," I say, taking the offered beverage. "Either that or Bad Influence."

"Both, actually. Baz Temptation Bad Influence Redgrave. My parents had a sick sense of humor, what can I say?" He opens a beer for himself, then we head into the living room. "You want the tour?"

"Why not?"

He makes a show of walking me around the small living area, but I'm more focused on the photos, anyway. They're just so incredible—like they should be in a magazine.

It makes me wonder what else I don't know about him. Enough to fill volumes. The entire library, perhaps.

He walks into the bedroom, standing aside to let me enter.

"And this is where the magick happens," he says, then laughs. "Well, not really. I do most of my spellwork in the kitchen. Easier cleanup."

There are more photos in here, and I take my time exploring them. There's a really captivating shot hanging over his dresser, black-and-white like the others. It's the back of a woman's shoulder, the line of her chin just barely visible in the frame, a thin black strap slipping down her skin. It's a picture that's worth a thousand words, that tells a thousand stories.

"Is that Carly?" I blurt out like a fucking idiot.

"What do you think?"

I turn around to face him. He's right behind me, so close I can smell that damn sexy masculine scent—pepper and earth. Woodsmoke. Danger.

"I told you," he says, "I'm not with her. Not like you think."

I glare at him, trying to find the lie in his words. But when I reach out for his energy, I find only sincerity. Intrigue. Lust.

"Who is she, then?" I whisper.

"Dunno. Just a model in a photo class I took in high school. You and Ani?"

"Not a thing. Not like you think." I swallow hard. The bottle in my hand is turning warm.

Baz leans in close, takes away my beer. He sets both bottles on the dresser.

"No coasters?" I ask.

"Stevie?"

"Yes?"

"You look fucking hot in that dress." His eyes blaze, and he lifts a hand to my shoulder, fingertip tracing the thin strap.

Goosebumps erupt on my skin.

I swallow again, blood rushing to my head, heat rushing to my core.

"This is a bad idea," I whisper.

"Terrible."

"The worst."

"Obviously." His mouth crashes into mine, insistent, demanding, and I melt into his kiss, wrapping my arms around his neck as he slides his hands down to cup my backside.

We bump into the dresser, knocking over the beers, but Baz doesn't care. Doesn't stop. His hands are everywhere and his mouth is everything and when he sucks my bottom lip between his teeth and moans, I feel the last of my resistance crumble into dust.

"Are you sure this is what you want?" he asks, panting between kisses.

A spike of panic hits my gut. "Did you change your mind?"

"Not a chance."

"You *have* to know how much I want this, Baz."

He cups my face, looking into my eyes with that intense, red-brown gaze. "I need you to say it, Little Bird, or this ends here."

God, I'm already so wet for him, so hungry for the hot slide of his cock. But the fact that he's actually making sure?

My body is going to burn if he doesn't put his mouth on it.

Reaching up for the zipper at my back, I give it a tug and let the dress fall to my feet, pooling on the floor like water. The black lace bra and panties follow.

Baz stares at me in wonder. "You're lucky my camera's not close by right now."

I smile, then reach up to remove my devil horns. "I want this, Baz. I want *you*."

That maddening, slow-burn grin slides across his mouth. "Leave the horns. They're sexy as fuck."

I do as he asks, then wait for him to strip out of his jeans and henley.

He stands naked before me, his cock hard and smooth, his lean muscles like a work of art in the moonlight. If I had a camera, I'd be taking *his* picture right now.

I'm practically drooling, but Baz just laughs and shakes his head.

I cross my arms over my chest. "What's so funny?"

"Just remembering that time you called me... What was it? The guy who cops attitude to compensate for a small dick?"

"I've been known to be wrong a time or two before. But for the record, you *do* cop attitude."

"Mmm-hmm." He smiles at me again, and before I say another word, he leans in and feathers his lips across mine —gentle, soft as a breeze—then spins me around, facing his bed. His hand wraps around my hair, lifting it off the base of my neck, tugging just right.

Goddess, I love a man who knows how to pull my hair...

He licks a path up the back of my neck, then pushes me gently onto the bed, falling on top of me, kissing my neck, my back, taking his time covering every inch of flesh as I writhe against the sheets.

Holy. Fuck. Can shoulder blades come? Is that a thing? Because I'm pretty sure mine are about to, his tongue swirling in hot patterns along their edges, his kisses devouring me. His mouth moves down along my spine, his hand stroking my thighs, sliding between them.

"Please tell me you have a condom," I breathe.

After what feels like an eternity of slow, torturous kisses, he finally reaches for his nightstand drawer, pulls out a package. I hear the wrapper tear, then he's kneeling behind me and gripping my thighs, guiding them apart.

I arch my back, giving him access.

"No conditions this time?" he teases, hands trailing down my thighs. "No one-time-only, never-talk-about-it-again, don't-tell-a-soul?"

"Just... just make me forget how to form words," I say, remembering what he said that day at the rocks.

It's cute that you think you'll still be able to form *words while I'm fucking you...*

But Baz is way ahead of me, teasing my clit with the tip of his cock, my core aching with need.

Sure, some guys are just good at sex—they know all the tried-and-true techniques, always making sure their partner finishes happy—but this goes well beyond just being generically good at sex.

This man? He knows my body so perfectly, it's like we were born to do this.

He leans forward, kissing my neck again, tracing my skin with his nose, inhaling my scent.

And then he's plunging inside me, sinking in deep as I arch to meet him, taking him in. He pulls out slowly, running his hand up my back and fisting my hair, tugging

445

gently as he slides back inside, and I'm pretty sure he's going to keep his promise, because suddenly I can't remember how to speak.

He moves slowly, deeply, then speeds up, thrusting harder and faster, but it's not hard enough.

I find my voice, forcing out breathless words as the heat crests between my thighs.

"Harder," I breathe. I want him fast and furious, unleashing the rush of pleasure that's already building to dangerous levels inside.

He plunges in harder this time, and I push back against him, taking it, demanding it. He grabs my hips and slams into me, and I feel his energy—all of his pent-up rage, all of his bitterness, all the hidden darkness swirling inside him, begging for a way out—but then it's evaporating, chased away by a wave of pleasure, relief, and the raw desire I know he feels.

Baz moans my name, his cock growing thicker inside me. My body tightens around him, and suddenly it hits me, the orgasm exploding in a starburst of white-hot pleasure I feel clear down to my toes.

"Baz," I breathe, digging my nails into his pillow, one hand braced against the headboard as I ride out wave after wave, and Baz lets out a possessive growl, shuddering against my backside as he comes.

He collapses on top of me, nuzzling my neck, and there we remain. Minutes? Hours? I'm not sure. He's breathing deeply, but everything is sticky and hot, and I need to go.

Didn't Baz warn me he's not the cuddle-afterward type?

As gently as I can, I extricate myself from the tangle of his limbs and sneak into the bathroom to clean up.

When I come back to the bedroom, I see him watching me, smiling in the darkness.

I feel the babble queuing up inside, all the things I want to say. *That was amazing, thank you, holy shit can we please do this every day and twice on Sundays?*

But, you know. Dignity.

I hunt around for my clothes, then step into my underwear.

"Um. What are you doing?" he asks, narrowing his eyes as I pick up the dress.

"Um. Getting dressed?"

"Why?"

"I can't walk up to my room naked, Baz. Even if it *is* Halloween."

A low growl rumbles up from his chest, and it takes me a beat to realize it's not a growl at all.

It's a laugh. Baz is laughing at me.

Okay, granted, I'm balancing on one foot, my boobs hanging free, half-dressed in a blue gown, a devil's tail trailing behind me. But I still don't see the humor here.

"And what," he says, rising from the bed and prowling toward me like a panther, "gave you the impression that I was finished with you, Little Bird?"

"The big orgasm, for starters."

"Orgasm? One? And you think that's it? I'm just warming up."

"One is a respectable achievement, especially one of that

magnitude."

"For amateur night." He kisses my collarbone, slowly dragging his mouth down my sternum, pulling the dress off as he goes. Dipping his head, he closes his lips over my nipple and sucks hard, making me gasp.

"But lucky for you," he says, leading me back to the bed, "it's *not* amateur night. It's Halloween, and I'm not done handing out treats."

It's the middle of the night, still dark outside, and someone is banging on the door.

I bolt upright in my bed, quickly realize it's *not* my bed, and commence the epic freakout.

"Shit. Shit, shit, shit!" I'm on my feet in a heartbeat, darting around Baz's room in search of my underwear and my dignity, neither of which can be found.

The devil himself is just leaning back against his headboard, my devil horns perched on his head, looking sinful as hell with his sleepy eyes and sex-hair.

"I'm glad you think this is funny," I say, "but someone's at your door, and they're not going away."

"Fuck off!" he shouts toward the living room, then laughs. "Now they'll go away."

"*Excuse* me?" the voice on the other side snaps. Definitely female. Definitely not going away.

Baz goes, "Oh, fuck."

Yep. Definitely Carly.

He gets up, pulls on his jeans.

I cross my arms over my bare chest. "Seriously?"

"I need to deal with this. Just wait, okay? Don't go."

Like I'm going anywhere with that harpy outside the door.

Baz goes out into the hall, leaving me inside to stew. Quickly, I pull on my clothes. Through the door I hear their muffled arguing—Carly's shrill voice, his deep one.

A few minutes later, he's back, darkness seeping into his energy.

"What was that about?" I ask.

"Stevie…" He shakes his head, blows out a breath. "I can't tell you. But it's not—"

"Look," I say firmly, trying my best to hold on to my anger. "I know we're not exclusive. And it's none of my business who else you're seeing. But if Carly thinks you guys are together, I can't—"

"There's no one else. Only you. Okay?"

"I don't want to do this if I'm going to have to fight off the Claires every time I want to see you. I'm still holding my breath, waiting for those pictures to turn up."

"They won't. I deleted them off Emory's phone."

"She might've made copies."

"They *won't*," he says again, adamant. He crosses the room, reaching for my face, but I step back.

"Stevie, just… Trust me, please. Can you just trust me?"

I offer a sad smile, plucking the devil horns from his head. "Sorry, Baz. That was the wrong favor to ask me tonight."

FIFTY

STEVIE

Despite the late hour, the campus is still crawling with revelers, all of them happy and laughing, an endless parade of drunk skeletons and empresses and other sparkly-horned devils, too.

I don't want to go home. But I don't feel like partying, either.

So at three in the morning, I find myself heading to a familiar place.

And there, on the steps of the library I've come to love, I run into a familiar face.

"Stevie? You're out late," Kirin says, swallowing hard as he takes in the sight of me. I've still got the dress and the horns, but my hair is pulled in to a careless bun, my makeup left behind, all over Baz's pillowcase. "I mean, you look nice," he says. "Are you... did you have a good Halloween?"

Oh Goddess... Please don't see it in my eyes. Please don't ask me anything else about my night. Please just… just go.

"I was just… I felt like doing a little work," I say.

"Me too. I mean, I came here to work. But now I'm going home."

Silence. Awkward, heavy silence that presses in on me from all directions.

I'm so mixed up inside, so twisted and tangled over him and Baz and everything I'm supposed to do to figure out the prophecies.

I look into his eyes, letting him see the hurt in mine.

The love.

I have to tell him.

"Kirin," I say, "the other night, when you said you were falling? The truth is, I think I'm—"

"I should get home," he says dismissively, and even though I feel the regret in his energy, the pain, and yes, the love, it still stings. He reaches up to touch my shoulder, but just gives it an awkward pat instead.

And then he disappears down the path, leaving me with a head full of questions and a heart full of swords.

* * *

Up in the archives, I throw myself completely into the work, blocking out all other distractions. All other pains.

I keep going back to the authorless book—Journey Through the Void of Mist and Spirit. There's something here, I'm certain of it, but I can't seem to crack the code. I flip through each page, noticing again how the odd, broken language is written a lot like my mother's grimoire, with thoughts that go nowhere, as if the sentences are literally chasing their conclusions off the page.

Frustrated, I flip back to the original translations Kirin and I worked on our first few days here, reading one of them aloud—the one from my dream.

> *Book of shadow, book of mists.*
> *What magick draws, you won't resist*
> *Death to those who shun its call*
> *Where one shall rise, the others fall*
> *Book of shadow, book of mists*
> *The truth emerges from the myths*
> *Flame and blood and blade and bone*
> *What starts with zero ends with one.*

Book of shadow, book of mists. Book of shadow, book of mists. I look through my notes, my journal, scanning over my Tarot reading again. All those twos.

Book of shadow, book of mists.

Book of shadows. A witch's grimoire. My mother's grimoire.

Two.

The broken, missing-pieces language.

Two.

Book of shadow, book of...

Wait. That's *it*! Two! It's two!

My heart hammers in my chest, and I flip through my

notes once more, the idea taking shape, excitement and adrenaline flooding my limbs.

I'm out of my chair, racing back through security and back downstairs, back to my suite.

All along, I kept thinking it was one book—the Book of Shadow and Mists. Even Professor Phaines indicated as much—*It's said that the Book of Shadow and Mists will unlock the arcane spells protecting the sacred objects, thereby making their secret location known…*

Those were his exact words.

But it's not one book.

It's two.

Book of shadow, and book of mists. A coded reference to a witch's book of shadows and possibly the Journey Through the Void of Mist and Spirit. A long shot, maybe, but the books are written so similarly… I have to try.

Back in my suite, I grab my mother's grimoire from the dresser drawer where I've kept it, kiss her photo, then race back to the library. Up the stairs, through security, then I'm sitting at the table in the archives once again, my hands trembling.

Kirin. I need to text Kirin.

I grab my phone, and suddenly it buzzes in my hand. My heart hammers, hope already rising…

But it's not Kirin. It's Carly, of all people, texting through the student directory app.

Stevie, where RU? she demands.

Library, I text back, leaving off the rest of my thought,

which is basically—what the fuck is it to you, and why the fuck are you bothering me?

I watch the three dots, see her next message pop up. *Get out of there. NOW. Something bad's about to happen.*

I send her the eye-roll emoji.

Immediately, my phone rings. What the hell does she want?

"Carly," I snap, "I'm busy and it's late, so—"

"Stevie, listen. I'm fucking serious. You need to get out of there right now before—"

The line goes dead.

Fucking Carly. It's bad enough she barged in on my night with Baz. No way will I let her barge in on my work.

I decide to hold off on texting Kirin. Instead, I bring Mom's grimoire to the table, open it to the first page.

Next to it, I open Journey Through the Void of Mist and Spirit.

My hands begin to tingle, the books emanating a faint glow. With both books open to the same page, I run my fingers along the passages, just like I did with my mother's notebooks.

Nothing happens.

On a hunch, I tip her book up on its side, forming a right angle with the Journey book.

Suddenly, new passages illuminate both books, writing before my eyes between the lines of the old words, filling in the missing pieces.

"Ha!" I press my hand to my chest, my heart thudding, tears blurring my vision. "Holy shitcakes!"

"Stevie? What are you doing here at this hour?"

I look up to see Professor Phaines entering the archives, his eyes wide with excitement. "Have you found something?"

"I couldn't sleep, and I had a thought, and there were all those twos in the Tarot cards and the books and I just…" I force myself to take a deep breath, then try again. "Professor, the Book of Shadow and Mists isn't a legend. And it isn't one book, either. It's two. At least, that's how the magick is activated."

"Whatever do you mean?"

"Look." I wave him over, then show him one of our original translations from Mom's notebooks.

> *Between the space where black meets white*
> *Betwixt the woods of dark and light*
> *A mirror flat reveals the sky*
> *But turn it 'round to know the why*
> *Zero begets the next, the One*
> *Innocence lost, magick undone*
> *Beware the rise when darkness falls*
> *For magick corrupts, and blood trumps all.*

"The first part—between the space where black meets white, betwixt the woods of dark and light? She's talking about the pages—literally, paper made from wood—and reading between the lines—the black text. The Book of Shadow and Mists—she mentioned it to me in a dream. Remember I said her grimoire is written a lot like the

Journey book? Like, with half missing? Well, when I put her grimoire next to the other book, tilt it upright, and touch the pages, I can see the other verses. The missing text! Spells and symbols, so many new lines!"

He stares at me, astonished.

"Remarkable," he whispers.

"The mirror part? She's talking about her own grimoire. Turn it round to know the why." I tip the grimoire onto its side again, forming a right angle to the other book. The pages illuminate with new spells.

"I don't see anything," he says.

"No, it's like that with all her notebooks. Only I can see them. But now I can start translating!"

"That won't be necessary, Stevie." Professor Phaines smiles, but suddenly his energy shifts.

Gone is the grandfatherly warmth, the sneaker of Snickers bars, the supportive pats on the shoulder. Now, his energy is cold and prickly and dark, a wave of pure evil washing over me.

Carly's warning echoes. *Stevie, listen. I'm fucking serious. You need to get out of there right now…*

My heart drops to the floor, my hands trembling all over again.

Professor Phaines is a fucking traitor.

I whip out my phone, try to get a text out to Kirin, but the phone flies out of my hands.

"Young people these days have no respect," Professor Phaines says, the phone levitating before him. "Always texting, chat-snapping. But Kirin can't help you now, can he? Just the two of us at this late hour, I'm afraid."

He closes his fist and the phone bursts into flames, melting into a twisted mass of metal, glass, and plastic before finally dropping to the floor.

"Lovesick children," he says. "That's all you are. Paying more attention to your libidos than your research. Such a waste of a beautiful mind." He dusts off his hands, still sneering at me. "Let's go, Miss Milan. Bring your books."

I snatch up the books and back up against the wall. "I'm not going anywhere with you."

"I think we've had just about enough of your attitude problem for one night." He holds out a Tarot card I can't identify and mutters an incantation, the card glowing red, then vanishing.

Just like that, I'm boneless.

That's how it feels.

I drop to the floor like a bag of water, unable to coordinate my limbs, to move my mouth, to scream. It's a wonder my heart still beats, my lungs still breathe. I can't even blink or move my eyes.

I've got one view now—Professor Phaines crossing the room, his robes swishing over the tops of his boots.

Then he's right in front of me, a boot rising like a dusty black sun.

And the kindly old professor I once trusted, once cared for, once promised that all his secrets would be safe with me, stomps hard on my face.

FIFTY-ONE

STEVIE

Spells of Iron, Spells of Bone
Bind now her magick to mine alone
Spells of Earth, Spells of Old
Through my will and my way, the truth shall
*   unfold*

Phaines repeats the chant, lifting the chalice to his lips, gulping down the contents like it's the most exquisite wine he's ever had.

It's not wine, though. It's my blood.

I'm tied to a petrified tree in the Forest of Iron and Bone, blood running down my naked body in warm rivulets and pooling darkly at my feet.

I still can't move my limbs, but I can speak now, shift my eyes. I can feel pain.

Not from the boot to the face—no, those injuries have already healed.

But now, every time he cuts me, drains me, the wound seals up, and the process begins again.

And every time my blood touches his lips, an image sears my mind—a bearded man in a red tunic and tartan. He's sitting on a throne, a sword and chalice on a table beside him. His hand is raised in the symbol of the horned god, and I know instinctively he's the High Priest of the Tarot, the Hierophant. But in this version, the one I see when Phaines drinks my blood, the Priest has turned dark, his eyes full of hatred, blood dripping from the chalice, running down the blade.

"Spells of Iron, Spells of Bone," he repeats. "Bind now her magick to mine alone."

I swallow past the pain in my throat. "Has it occurred to you, *Professor*, that your spell game is weak as fuck?"

"Spells of Iron, Spells of Bone," he continues, louder now, holding the chalice up to the moonlight, then taking another gulp.

I kind of want to puke.

But I need to keep it together.

First rule of survival: don't freak out.

"Has it occurred to you, *witch*," he says, wiping his mouth on the back of his hand, "that you could make this easier on both of us if you'd give me the translation?"

He can't read the books without me—I'm the only one who can see the secret spells. Somehow, he thinks that drinking my blood will give him access to my magick—to bind it to his so he can read the spells for himself.

I really hope that's not the case. Because while Professor

Phaines is not the Dark Magician, it's clear he's at least working for the douchebag.

"Hmm," I say. "How about… Not a chance in hell?"

"Then ritual sacrifice it is. In the name of the One Whom All Darkness serves…" He shoves his blade into my side again, holds up the chalice for a refill. The world sways before me.

Come on, girl. This is no different than being caught on El Búho Grande in that storm. No different than any number of close calls you've had hiking in the desert.

I close my eyes and take a deep breath, bringing my heart rate down.

Second rule of survival: use what you have, use what you know.

Professor Nakata says a witch's sharpest tool is her mind, and thankfully the professor hasn't put a bind on that yet.

So think, girl. Fucking think.

"I do hope you're not waiting for your familiar," Phaines says casually, and my eyes fly open, my face twisting in a terror I can't hide. "Oh, yes. The poor snowy owl. He made an appearance earlier, but you were unconscious, of course, and I had to make an executive decision." He mimes slicing the blade across his throat. "Too many cooks in the kitchen —you know how the saying goes." He gives me an exaggerated frown. "I'm afraid he won't be returning."

Phaines retrieves something from his robe—a handful of white tissue, soaked in blood.

No, not tissue. Feathers. Owl feathers.

Tears fill my eyes, but I bite back a howl of pain. I won't give him the satisfaction—not now.

"Any time you'd like to share that translation..." he says. "Perhaps the One will show you mercy."

"Fuck off," I tell him. "I'll die first."

"Yes," he says confidently. "But not quite yet."

He's puffing up like a peacock, but inside, I can tell he's starting to unravel. To doubt.

He goes back to his chanting.

I close my eyes and go back to my thinking.

What do I have? No weapons. No clothing. Severe blood loss. No magick owl power. No use of my limbs.

The list of "haves" is thin.

Moving on. What do I know?

I know Phaines isn't going to kill me—at least not yet. He needs me for this, and if the ritual doesn't work, he'll come up with some other torture first, some other threat to get me to translate the spells. So I've got a little bit of time on my side—though probably not much.

As for magick, I'm not strong enough in any one element to make something big happen, and at the moment, I can't even call up my witchfire.

Fuck.

Okay, no panicking. *Think, Stevie. Fucking think!*

Another jab of the blade in my gut, and I gasp, my eyes flying open. Phaines is turning wild with rage, his mouth and chin dark and shiny with my blood.

"Give me the translation!" he shouts. "Give me the spells of Shadow and Mists!"

Healing, I remind myself, ignoring his rants. I can heal others, in a way. I can read their emotions. My empathy isn't just about reading energy, it's about knowing what's *missing* from those energies.

It's a hole I might be able to exploit.

I cast out for his energy, letting it wash through me.

Beneath the dark bile of his hatred, his desperation, I sense the utter lack.

Phaines needs to feel powerful, but he doesn't. He's not the man in charge—just a soldier in the brewing dark war. And he knows Kirin and I have already started putting some of the pieces together.

He needs control, but he's losing it quickly, panicking. Something tells me he doesn't want the power of the spells to serve the One—he wants it for his own ends. He wants to find the sacred objects.

To possess all magick for himself.

It's a double-cross, and he's afraid of being caught. Afraid of someone finding us out here before he gets what he wants. His career at the Academy is over now—he's got no choice but to see this through.

And he's afraid he won't be able to.

Afraid. Fear. What did Dr. Devane say about fear?

I cast my memory back through his classes, his lectures, searching for something I can use...

Fear is a powerful weapon. All it takes is a single doubt, a single crack in your armor, and the enemy will find it and exploit it to the fullest extent…

I go back even further, back to that day in the car right after my prison break…

Fear is our most primal, most powerful emotion. It leaves an imprint—almost like a ghost in the room…

Your fear of death by gunshot was completely sincere and left an intense imprint that my spell was able to amplify…

That imprint, combined with the power of suggestion planted in the rich soil of a soft mind, was enough to make the guard truly believe that I killed us…

I'm not skilled in mental magicks—not like Dr. Devane. But I know what Phaines is afraid of. And if I can somehow plant a seed in his weak mind and amplify that fear…

It's worth a shot.

"Professor Phaines," I say, steadying myself, making my voice as authoritative as I can. I gaze into his eyes, unblinking. Try to rearrange my features until I'm no longer Stevie Milan, first-year witch, daughter of the infamous seer. I'm beyond that form now, a mere vessel for darker forces.

A deadly smile curves my lips.

"A message from the Dark One," I announce.

Phaines looks back at me, uncertain. He worries this is a trick, but what if it's not? His courage is wavering.

> *Across the span of space and time*
> *I come to you, dark priest of mine*
> *What ruinous fate you cast tonight*
> *When dark deception tests my might?*

Not the most epic rhyme, but not bad for a freestyle, all things considered. I stare at him unblinking, my smile firmly in place.

And there in his eyes, I see it. *Fear*. A single doubt. A crack in his armor.

If Phaines had attended Mental Magicks class, he'd know what *else* Devane said about fear—that it isn't real. But Phaines *doesn't* know that. And I've got my opening.

It's a dangerous thing, knowing a man's weakness.

I recall one of the phrases from Mom's earlier work, one I didn't share with Phaines. Still holding his gaze, I recite:

> *Hexed and cursed, bruised and broken*
> *What comes first, the dark words spoken*
> *The veil is torn, the spells diminished*
> *Mage firstborn, the final finish.*

Phaines drops to his knees before me, holding up his hands. Wow, these guys really respect the power of the rhyme.

"You have betrayed me," I say to him. Calm. Collected. Commanding.

"Never. I am only trying to claim the spells in your name. For you, always!"

"They are not yours to claim, Priest." My eyes go wide, and I raise my voice. "Usurper, divider, betrayer, betrayed! All who deceive me shall be repaid!"

Phaines trembles, holding his hands in front of his face.

I'm trying to think up another creepy sounding chant, but movement in the distance distracts me—a shadow gliding in front of the moon.

My owl. My powerful, beautiful, gleaming-white owl. He's alive. Searching for me.

Phaines sees him too.

He glances at me once more, weighing his odds. Fear radiates from his body, the fucking coward. He grabs the books, the chalice, his blade. Pulls a Tarot card from his robe. And with a simple spell, he vanishes into the mist.

My head slumps forward, all the adrenaline leaking out of my broken body.

Third rule of survival: deal with the most pressing problem first.

Phaines is gone, no longer bleeding me. But he's got the books. The real Dark One *is* out there, biding his time. My healing has slowed, my energy completely drained, half of my blood soaking into the dusty ground below, and I still can't move my damn arms or legs.

The owl has vanished once again. Maybe he was never here at all.

No one knows where I am.

I laugh. *Ah, life. What a fucking joke.*

Guess it won't be Mother Nature taking me out after all.

* * *

"Over here! Hurry!" A flurry of voices, all talking at once.

"She's bleeding!" This from Baz. "Fucking hell, there's so much—"

"Cut her down," Kirin orders.

"On it." Gentle hands cutting my binds, Ani's perpetual warmth pulsing over me, a promise that things will turn out okay. "Hang in there, Stevie. We've got you."

My body slumping into a pair of strong arms, a blanket wrapped around me as someone lays me on the ground.

Water held to my lips.

Gentle hands in my hair, stroking my face.

"Come on, baby. Come back to us. Come on, Stevie."

I open my eyes, take in some of the water. Wait for the images before me to solidify. Flint-colored eyes. Dark hair touched with gray.

"Doc?" I whisper, and he nods, eyes glazing with emotion. "You were right," I croak out. "Mental manipulation—acceptable form of self-defense."

Doc smiles. "You were listening."

"Always."

"What do you need?" he asks, brushing the hair from my face. "Tell me how to heal you. How to fix you."

I manage another weak smile. "A wise woman once said, 'There's no problem a proper cup of tea can't fix.'"

His eyes fill with relief. "That can be arranged."

He stands up, holding me close against his chest. Kirin, Ani, and Baz gather around us, linking arms.

"Let's go," Doc says.

Baz holds up a hand, whispers an enchantment that

brings the Petrified Forest of Iron and Bone to life. Sparkling purple magick scoops us up, deposits us back home.

One day, he's going to have to teach me that trick.

FIFTY-TWO

STEVIE

"That was Trello," Baz says, putting the phone back in his pocket. "No sign of Phaines, but she's got her best mages out tracking him."

Devane squeezes my hand. "We'll find him, Stevie. Don't worry."

"He's got the books," I say, probably for the hundredth time. "If he figures out how to read them, the spells will lead him straight to the arcane objects."

No one responds to that. There *is* no response for that.

We're sitting in my living room a day after Halloween, the last rays of sunlight warming my face. The mages are all gathered around me, refusing to leave my side.

I'm mostly healed from the ordeal—the physical parts, anyway. But despite what Dr. Devane says, fear *is* real—at least for me, at least right now. Every time I close my eyes, I see that boot stomping down on my face, the blood slicking over the mad professor's lips, the crazed look in his eyes as he demanded the translations.

Professor Phaines betrayed me. Betrayed us all.

I still can't believe it. With all the secrets and hushed whispers floating around me at the Academy, all along I thought *he* was the safe bet. The sure thing.

"I trusted him," I say, closing my eyes against a fresh onslaught of violent, gruesome images. "What a fool."

I formed my impression of him that first moment in Trello's office, and that impression took root, solidifying with every act of kindness, every encouraging word. That was *his* form of mental magicks—finding the void my parents' death left in my heart, exploiting it to the fullest extent.

I let him do it, too. He didn't even obfuscate his intentions or try to block his energy from my empathic senses. From our first meeting that day, I made my assumptions, and that was that. I never even bothered to question them—not until it was much too late.

"It wasn't just you, Stevie," Dr. Devane says. "He had us all fooled—for years. Decades. Even the Headmistress."

"Even the Claires," Baz reminds me.

I nod, reminding myself to call Carly later and thank her. Turns out those "special sessions" she mentioned at the river party? Phaines was just trying to tap into their psychic skills, to manipulate them into helping him find the spellbooks. After her argument with Baz out in the hallway last night, Carly had an actual premonition about me. She really *was* trying to warn me.

After our call got disconnected, she called Baz, told him what she'd seen. It wasn't long before the guys stormed the library looking for me, but by then I was already unconscious, bleeding, and tied to a dead tree.

It was my owl that finally led them to me. He was injured—Phaines hadn't lied about that. But he wasn't dead. After Phaines attacked him, he must've flown hard and fast back to campus. He showed up outside the library window, clawing at the glass.

I haven't seen the owl since, but I can sense him now. He's always with me, our souls connected. Eventually, I'll learn how to call him. To communicate.

"About the objects," Kirin says now, removing his glasses and polishing them on his Chewbacca T-shirt. "I've been doing some research this morning."

"Of *course* you have." I smile.

He smiles back.

Life is… getting better.

"According to the legends," he continues, "after the Magician vowed his revenge, the other Arcana feared the sacred objects would be forever hunted, so they divided them up, hiding them in four different places around the globe, all at undisclosed sacred magickal sites."

"Magickal sites like where the Academies were built?" I ask, a new spark of excitement flickering in my chest. I wouldn't have thought it on my first day here, but researching the prophecies, digging into the old legends— it's become one of my favorite activities.

Turns out I'm pretty good at it, too.

"That's one theory," Kirin says. "That the Arcana Academies were actually built later on those same sites, specifically to help keep the objects hidden. But another theory postulates that the Majors, figuring everyone would expect them to divide up the objects, did the exact opposite."

"Hid them together?" Ani asks.

"That's the theory. Either way, now that Phaines has the books, we have to assume he'll eventually crack the spell. We have to get ahead of that."

"You think we should look for the objects," I say. It's not a question. "Why not leave them hidden? Maybe they're safer that way."

"No," Devane says. "Kirin's right—we need to find them. We can't risk it on a *maybe*. If Phaines believed in the legends, we have to assume others do as well—that other witches and mages are already scouring the old books for clues, searching the Academy campuses for the objects."

"A lot of them are just treasure hunters," Baz says. "Rich assholes who enjoy pilfering priceless antiquities and impressing their friends with all the creepy stories around them."

"And the rest?" I ask. "The ones who *aren't* just treasure hunters?"

Baz clenches his teeth, the muscle in his jaw ticking. When he finally glances up at me, his eyes are fierce, his protective energy rushing out in a wave. "You had a front-row seat to how that played out, Stevie."

We fall into silence once again, each of us lost in our

own thoughts. I get up and stretch, then head into the kitchen and put on the kettle for—what else?—more tea.

When I rejoin them in the living room, Kirin looks up at me, his gaze serious.

"You don't have to stay for this, Stevie. We can talk to Trello. Relocate you, set you up with a new identity. That was part of the original offer."

"Yeah?" I smile like I'm actually considering it, then narrow my eyes. "You think you can get rid of me that easily? Well guess what, dickheads. I'm not going anywhere."

The guys crack up—some much-needed levity breaking through the thick air.

"Told you she was one of us," Ani says, tossing an arm over my shoulder and pressing a kiss to my temple.

"Yes, but with better boobs and a cuter ass," I point out.

Their smiles evaporate.

Damn, rough crowd. I really thought that would go over better.

"Stevie," Devane says, his energy turning dark and serious. Well, more dark and serious than usual. "When Ani said you're one of us, he meant that literally."

I roll my eyes. "More dark brotherhood stuff?"

No one responds.

They all stand up now, gathering around me. Closing ranks.

I look into each pair of eyes—Dr. Devane's, stern and gray. Ani's, warm and sunny like melted caramels. Baz's, the red-brown eyes of the devil that can make me weak with a single glance. And Kirin's, my sunset behind the saguaros, the gaze of a man I started to fall for long before I ever set foot inside the hallowed halls of Arcana Academy.

"Who *are* you guys?" I whisper, the question as ominous as the mood.

"We are the Keepers of the Grave," they reply in unison.

"Who *are* you?" I ask again, my eyes filling with tears, everything about this moment heavy and terrifying and real.

Very, very real.

It's Ani who answers now, picking up the novelty deck from the table. He turns one card over and passes it to Baz —Cernunnos, The Devil, the lovers sleeping in the meadow before the horned god. The next card goes to Dr. Devane— The Moon, a full moon shining down on the ocean, a wolf and a dog howling before a stone gateway guarding a path to the unknown. The next card is for Kirin—the Tower, a bolt of lightning striking a stone tower, people jumping to their deaths, fleeing the sudden destruction. Ani keeps the next card for himself—The Sun, a child riding a pony, a harp at his side, the sun shining bright overhead.

Then he hands a card to me. I know what it is before I even glance at it.

"The Star," I whisper, a tear sliding down my cheek as I turn it over and confirm.

"We are the Keepers of the Grave," Dr. Devane says. "Four emanations of the Major Arcana, sworn to protect magick and its many secrets from all who seek to destroy it. The Grave is a reference to the Fool's Grave, an honorary site our forebears designated in the Forest of Iron and Bone, the place that symbolizes our connection to the First Fool."

"The Majors are… are real," I say, my mind whirling at the possibility, all the pieces clicking into place, forcing me to truly accept all that I've experienced. Seen. Felt. The secrets, the mystery, the magick, the darkness. "You guys are the… and I'm… and that means Phaines…"

"From what you saw when he drank your blood, we believe he's the Hierophant, or High Priest. Trump Five." Ani removes that card from the deck, turns it upside down. "Gone dark, just like Trump One." He pulls out the Magician.

He then removes two more cards, turning them both upside down—Seven, the Chariot. And Twenty, Judgment.

"Based on your vision of the undead army," Devane says, "we believe these have also turned dark, all in service of the Magician's quest."

I recall my words, spoken through the haze of my fever. *One, five, seven, twenty. Arcana devours, all and plenty…*

Ani puts the Dark Arcana back into the deck, but the mages are still holding their cards. I look at each one in turn.

The Devil, Trump Fifteen.

The Tower, Trump Sixteen.

The Moon, Eighteen.

The Sun, Nineteen.

Then, glancing down at my own, I shiver.

"Seventeen," I whisper, gazing at my lady of the lake, pouring her sacred urns. "I'm The Star."

"You are the center holding us all together." Kirin's voice is thick with emotion. In his eyes, I see his true feelings for me, and I feel his walls start to break down, despite his best efforts to keep them in place.

"But... how do you know?" I ask. "About any of this? About your own gifts and about each other's? About mine? Is this why I'm spirit-blessed? Are all of you the same?"

"No," Dr. Devane says. "Your elemental gifts are special and unique to you, Stevie. I'm simply water-blessed, Kirin is air, Baz is earth, Ani is fire."

He puts a hand on my shoulder, and I feel the ocean at my toes, the cool, salty breeze tickling my skin.

"As for how we know about the Majors? It's something you come to learn over time," Dr. Devane continues. "It's different for everyone. We believe the four of us found our way to this Academy for this very purpose—to form our Brotherhood, to serve our cause. When you started having visions of our true forms—and we of yours—we suspected you were one of us, too. But some Majors—like Phaines—they actively shield themselves. It's possible he knew about us, but we didn't know about him."

"This is... I still don't understand," I say.

"We are the Keepers of the Grave," Dr. Devane repeats, then heads to the spare bedroom. He returns with his briefcase—the same one he had at the prison. He pops it open and retrieves a large black book, setting it on the coffee table.

Chills erupt across my skin, and a wave of nausea makes my knees wobble.

I sit on the couch, the others gathering around me.

"I used to think your book was the Book of Shadow and Mists." I tell them about my flight with the owl, how I'd witnessed their meeting. "I thought it was evil."

"This is the Book of the Brotherhood, Stevie," Dr. Devane says. "The Book of Reckoning. It's a record of our accounts, our tasks, our solemn order. It's been marked with the blood of all the Keepers of the Grave at this Academy for generations."

"Why does it make me feel like... like I'm going to be sick, and it's going to drag me right down to hell?"

"It's calling to your blood. It knows you're one of us—it wants the connection."

"You *are* one of us," Ani says again, squeezing my hand.

My mouth is dry, but my eyes aren't. My brain keeps searching for the flaw in their argument, for some other explanation. Majors aren't real—it's all just a legend. The Dark Arcana—they're just crooked mages and witches, bent on power. This is a trick, isn't it? An elaborate prank, the hazing Ani swore they'd never do.

But no matter how hard my mind rails against it, deep down, I know they're telling me the truth. Finally.

"Your very name speaks to your destiny," Kirin says. "A clue lying in stasis your entire life, waiting for the moment of discovery."

"Starla Eve," I say. "My mother used to call me Starlight."

"It's likely she knew," Dr. Devane says. "She was a great seer, after all. And a Major herself."

I gasp, my eyes darting up to meet his. He opens the book, shows me her signature on one of the old pages. *Melissa Milan.*

"Your mother was The World, Stevie. Trump Twenty-One. The end and the beginning. And you are only just starting to understand her legacy. We all are."

"Did... did my father know?"

Devane shakes his dark head. "We are all bound to secrecy. You can never speak of your nature—or of ours—to anyone outside of the Brotherhood."

"But my mother... She's dead," I say. "Does that mean there isn't a World now?"

"No," Dr. Devane says. "There are always twenty-one, along with the Fool, whose essence runs through all of us. When our physical form passes, our spirit finds another. Sometimes we know our destiny from birth. Other times, like I said, we come to that knowledge much later."

"The World," I whisper, still trying to wrap my head around all of this. "Wait—the world... Blood of the world... Kirin, remember that passage from the Arcana Legends book?"

Kirin's eyes light up as he nods, both of us recalling the words.

It is said that he who is in possession of these objects, along with the blood of the world and an arcane spell of indeterminate origins...

"Do you think that's what it means? My mother's blood? *My* blood?"

"It's possible," Kirin says. "We won't know until we do more research."

"We haven't even scratched the surface of those prophecies, have we?"

Kirin shakes his head. "But you've made more progress in a month than the Academy elders have made in a decade, so that's promising."

"Your destiny is bound to this, Stevie," Dr. Devane says, setting an athame on top of a fresh page in the book. "In more ways than one. But you are not obligated to serve the Brotherhood, or to continue this quest any more than you already have. You say you don't want to relocate—okay. But you still have the option of remaining at the Academy and completing your studies."

I nod and close my eyes.

"You don't have to decide right now," Baz says.

"I know. Thank you. I just... Wow, this is a lot to take in." I let out a breath, run my hands through my hair. "I guess... I guess I just have one question."

"Anything," Ani says.

"What is it, Little Bird?" Baz asks, and I hear the hopefulness in his tone, feel the rise of protective, welcoming energy radiating from each of them.

"Okay, here it is." I take a deep breath, calling up the most somber, serious face I can muster. "If I sign up for this gig, do I get one of those creepy black robes?"

"Oh, absolutely," Dr. Devane says with mock reverence. "The secret society aesthetic must be upheld at all costs."

My laughter crests, then fades. I take another deep

breath, looking at each of the friends gathered around me. At the brothers.

The Dark One *is* rising—it's not a legend, and it's connected to the crimes against the broader magickal community in ways we can only guess at. Professor Phaines has disappeared, and he's no doubt in league with those trying to bring the darkness to power—a loose cannon bent on stealing magick for himself. At least two other Majors have gone dark, and they may be joining forces. We've lost the Books of Shadow and Mists, and my mother's prophecies still loom large in the distance— mysteries we've yet to solve. I still have so many unanswered questions about my mother, about her time here, about what happened to make her and Dad turn their backs on magick for good. And now, we've got four sacred objects to hunt down before someone else finds them first.

And if that's not enough excitement for a lifetime? The five of us have some *serious* interpersonal issues to work through, because I'm pretty sure this bond we share goes a *lot* deeper than just brotherhood.

But when I look at the mages surrounding me now, when I feel their energy and see the loyalty and friendship in their eyes, I know Ani was right.

I *am* one of them.

Without another moment's hesitation, I reach for Doc's athame, prick my palm, and sign the book in my blood.

Starla Eve Milan.

The five of us rise as one.

"Who gathers here as bonded brothers?" Dr. Devane asks, taking on his official tone.

"We, the Keepers of the Grave."

"Who spills his blood as a symbol of our commitment to one another and in the service and protection of the First?"

"We, the Keepers of the Grave."

"Who vows, by his life or his death, by his silence or his words, in this and all incarnations henceforth, to protect the one true source?"

"We, the Keepers of the Grave."

"We, the Keepers of the Grave," Dr. Devane says reverently, holding my gaze for an eternity.

"We, the Keepers of the Grave," I repeat.

Finally, he closes the book, puts it back in the case.

Our ritual is complete, and the guys let out a collective sigh.

"It's official," Ani says. "Welcome to the Brotherhood, Stevie."

"Thanks," I say, a grin stretching across my lips. "Now, which one of my dashingly handsome brothers is buying dinner?"

It's not over yet! This story continues in book 2, Spells of Breath and Blade!

Stevie and her sexy, secret-keeping mages are safe for now, but the quest for the sacred objects—and for Stevie's heart

—is only just beginning! Find out what happens next in **Spells of Breath and Blade!**

* * *

Are you a member of our private Facebook group, <u>Sarah Piper's Sassy Witches?</u> Pop in for sneak peeks, cover reveals, exclusive giveaways, book chats, and plenty of complete randomness! We've got a great community of readers and fans (and fellow Tarot lovers too!), and we'd love to see you there!

XOXO
Sarah

SHADOW KISSED EXCERPT

Paranormal romance and urban fantasy fans, do you know I've got more sexy reverse harem series ready to steam up your Kindle? The Witch's Rebels is a complete series about a witch outrunning her past, five smoldering-hot supernatural guardians, and the dark secret that could destroy them all. Read on for a taste of book one, **Shadow Kissed!**

* * *

CHAPTER ONE

Survival instinct was a powerful thing.

What horrors could we endure, could we accept, could we embrace in the name of staying alive?

Hunger. Brutality. Desperation.

Being alone.

I'd been alone for so long I'd almost forgotten what it was like to love, to trust, to look into the eyes of another person and feel a spark of something other than fear.

Then *they* came into my life.

Each one as damaged and flawed as I was, yet somehow finding a way through the cracks in my walls, slowly breaking down the bricks I'd so carefully built around my heart.

Despite their differences, they'd come together as my protectors and friends for reasons I still didn't fully understand. And after everything we'd been through, I had no doubts about who they were to me now. To each other.

Family.

I didn't know what the future held; I'd given up trying to predict it years ago. But I didn't need my Tarot cards or my mother's old crystal ball to know this:

For me, there was no future without them. Without my rebels.

"Gray?" His whisper floated to my ears.

After several heartbeats, I took a deep breath and opened my eyes.

I heard nothing, saw nothing, felt nothing but the demon imprisoned before me, pale and shattered, fading from this realm.

"Whatever you're thinking," he said, his head lolling forward, "don't."

Looking at him chained to the chair, bruises covering his face, blood pouring from the gashes in his chest, I strengthened my resolve.

His voice was faint, his body broken, his essence dimming. But the fire in his eyes blazed as bright as it had the day we'd met.

"Whatever horrible things you've heard about me, Cupcake, they're all true..."

"Please," he whispered, almost begging now. "I'm not worth..."

His words trailed off into a cough, blood spraying his lips.

I shook my head. He was wrong. He was *more* than worth it. Between the two of us, maybe only one would make it out of this room alive. If that were true, it had to be him; I couldn't live in a world where he didn't exist. Where any of them didn't exist.

This was my fate. My purpose. My gift.

There was no going back.

I held up my hands, indigo flames licking across my palms, surging bright in the darkness.

The demon shuddered as I reached for him, and I closed

my eyes, sealing away the memory of his ocean-blue gaze, knowing it could very well be the last time I saw it.

* * *

2 Weeks Earlier...

Don't act like prey, and you won't become it. Don't act like prey...

Whispering my usual mantra, I locked up the van and pushed my rusty hand truck down St. Vincent Avenue, scanning the shadows for trouble.

It'd rained earlier, and mist still clung to the streets, rising into the dark autumn night like smoke. It made everything that much harder to see.

Fortunately it was my last delivery of the night, and I'd brought along my favorite traveling companions—a sharp stake in my waistband and a big-ass hunting knife in my boot. Still, danger had a way of sneaking up on a girl in Blackmoon Bay's warehouse district, which was why most people avoided it.

If I hadn't needed the money—and a boss who paid in cash and didn't ask questions about my past—I would've avoided it, too.

Alas...

Snuggling deeper into my leather jacket, I banked left at the next alley and rolled to a stop in front of the unmarked service entrance to Black Ruby. My hand truck wobbled under the weight of its cargo—five refrigerated cases of O-positive and three AB-negative, fresh from a medical supplier in Vancouver.

Yeah, Waldrich's Imports dealt in some weird shit, but human cops didn't bother with the warehouse district, and the Fae Council that governed supernaturals didn't get involved with the Bay's black market. The only time they cared was when a supernatural killed a human, and some-times—depending on the human—not even then.

Thumbing through my packing slips, I hoped the vampires weren't too thirsty tonight. Half their order had gotten snagged by customs across the bay in Seattle.

I also hoped someone other than Darius Beaumont would sign for this. I could hold my own with most vamps, but Black Ruby's owner definitely struck me as the shoot-the-messenger type.

No matter how sexy he is...

Wrapping one hand discretely around my stake, I reached up to hit the buzzer, but a faint cry from the far end of the alley stopped me.

"Don't! Please!"

"Settle down, sweetheart," a man said, the menace in his voice a sick contrast to the terrified tremble in hers.

My heart rate spiked.

Abandoning my delivery, I scooted along the building's brick exterior, edging closer to the struggle. I spotted the girl first—she couldn't have been more than fifteen, sixteen at most, with lanky brown hair and the pale, haunted features of a blood slave.

But it wasn't a vampire that'd lured her out for a snack.

The greasy dude who'd cornered her was a hundred percent human—just another pervert in dirty jeans and a sweat-stained henley who clearly thought runaway kids were an easy mark.

"It'll all be over soon," he told her.

Yeah, sooner than you think…

Anger coiled in my belly, fizzing the edges of my vision. I couldn't decide who deserved more of my ire—the asshole threatening her now, or the parents who'd abandoned her in the first place.

Far as I was concerned, they were the same breed of evil.

"Well now. Must be my lucky night." The man barked out a wheezing laugh, and too late, I realized I'd been spotted. "Two for the price of one. Come on over here, Blondie. Don't be shy."

Shit. I'd hesitated too long, let my emotions get the best of me when I should've been working that knife out of my boot.

Fear leaked into my limbs, and for a brief instant, I felt my brain and body duking it out. *Fight or flight, fight or flight…*

No. I couldn't leave her. Not like that.

"Let her go," I said, brandishing my stake.

He yanked the kid against his chest, one meaty hand fisting her blue unicorn hoodie, the other curling around her throat. Fresh urine soaked her jeans.

"Drop your little stick and come over here," the man said, "or I'll break her neck."

My mind raced for an alternative, but there was no time.

I couldn't risk going for the knife. Couldn't sneak up on him. And around here, screaming for help could attract a worse kind of attention.

Plan B it is.

"All right, big guy. You win." I dropped the stake and smiled, sidling toward him with all the confidence I could muster, which wasn't much, considering how hard I was shaking. "What are you doing with a scrawny little kid, anyway?"

He looked at the kid, then back at me, his lecherous gaze burning my skin. The stench of cigarettes and cheap booze lingered on his breath, like old fish and sour milk.

"I've got everything you need right here," I purred, choking back bile as I unzipped my jacket. "Unless you're not man enough to handle it?"

His gaze roamed my curves, eyes dark with lust.

"You're about to find out," he warned. "Ain't ya?"

He shoved the kid away, and in one swift move, he grabbed me and spun me around, pinning me face-first against the bricks.

He was a hell of a lot faster than I'd given him credit for.

"So you're an all talk, no action kind of bitch?" He wrenched my arms behind me, the intense pain making my eyes water. His sour breath was hot on the back of my neck, his hold impossibly strong, my knife impossibly out of reach. "That ends now."

A few blocks off, an ambulance screamed into the night, but it wasn't coming for us. The kid and I were on our own.

"Mmm. You got some ass on you, girl." He shoved a

hand into the back pocket of my jeans and grabbed a handful of my flesh. "I like that in a woman."

Of course *you do.*

After all these years making illegal, late-night deliveries to the seediest supernatural haunts in town, this wasn't my first rodeo. The one-liners, the threats, the grabby hands... Human or monster, guys like this never managed to deviate from the standard dickhole playbook.

But this was the first guy who'd actually pinned me to a wall.

At least he'd ditched the kid. I tried to get her attention now, to urge her to take off, but she'd tucked herself behind a Dumpster, paralyzed with fear.

The man pressed his greasy lips to my ear. "No more bullshit, witch."

You don't know the half of it, asshole.

He didn't—that much was obvious. Just another dude with a tiny dick who tossed around the word "witch" like an insult.

My vision flickered again, rage boiling up inside, clawing at my insides like a caged animal searching for weak points.

It wanted out.

I took a deep breath, dialed it back down to a simmer.

God, I would've loved to light him up—spell his ass straight to oblivion. But I hadn't kept my mojo on lockdown for damn near a decade just to risk exposure for *this* prick.

So magic was out. I couldn't reach my knife. And my top-notch negotiating skills had obviously failed.

Fuck diplomacy.

I let my head slump forward in apparent defeat.

Then slammed it backward, right into his chin.

He grunted and staggered back, but before I could spin around or reach for my knife, he was on me again, fisting my hair and shoving my face against the wall.

"Nice try, little cunt. Now you eat brick."

"Don't!" the girl squeaked. "Just… just let us go."

"Aw, that's cute." He let out a satisfied moan like he'd just discovered the last piece of cake in the fridge. "You'll get your turn, baby."

Okay, she'd saved me from a serious case of brick-rash —not to mention a possible skull fracture—but now she was back on his radar. And I still couldn't get to the knife.

Time for plan B. Or was this C?

Fuck it.

"Hey. I've got some money," I said. "Let us go, and it's yours."

"Yeah?" He perked up at that. "How much we talkin'?"

"Like I said—some."

Lie. At the moment, I was loaded. Most of the $3,000 I'd already collected tonight was in the van, wrapped in a McDonald's bag and shoved under the seat. I also had $200 in a baggie inside my boot and another $800 in my bra, because I believed in diversifying my assets.

My commission depended on me getting the cash and van back to the docks without incident. I couldn't afford incidents. Rent was due tomorrow, and Sophie had already covered me last month.

But I couldn't—wouldn't—risk him hurting the kid.

"It's in my boot," I said. "Left one."

"We'll see about that, Blondie." He yanked me away from the wall and shoved me to the ground, wet pavement biting into the heels of my hands.

With a boot to my back, he pushed me flat on my stomach, then crouched down and grabbed my wrists, pinning them behind me with one of his meaty hands. With his free hand, he bent my leg back and yanked off my boot.

Bastard.

"I hope you feel good about your life choices," I grumbled.

Another wheezing laugh rattled through his chest, and he coughed. "Choice ain't got nothin' to do with it."

Whatever. I waited until he saw the baggie with the cash, let him get distracted and stupid over his small victory.

The instant he released my wrists and went for the money, I pushed up on all fours and slammed my other boot heel straight into his teeth.

The crunch of bone was pure music, but his howl of agony could've called the wolves.

I had just enough time to flip over and scamper to my feet before he rose up and charged, pile-driving me backward into the wall. The wind rushed out of my lungs on impact, but I couldn't give up. I had to keep fighting. Had to make sure he wouldn't hurt the girl.

I clawed at his face and shoved a knee into his groin, but *damn it*—I couldn't get enough leverage. His hands clamped around my throat, rage and fire in his eyes, blood pouring from his nose and mouth as he spit out broken teeth.

He cocked back an arm, but just before his fist connected, I went limp, dropping to the ground like a pile of rags.

The momentum of his swing threw him off balance, and I quickly ducked beneath his arms and darted behind him, crouching down and reaching for the sweet, solid handle of my knife.

"You can't win," he taunted as he turned to face me. Neither his injuries nor the newly acquired lisp diminished his confidence. "I'm bigger, stronger, and I ain't got no qualms about hurting little cunts like you."

Despite the tremble in my legs, I stood up straight, blade flashing in the moonlight.

"Whoa. Whoa!" Eyes wide, he raised his hands in surrender, slowly backing off. "Hand over the knife, sweetheart."

"Not happening."

"You're gonna hurt yourself, waving around a big weapon like that."

"Also not happening."

"Look. You need to calm the fuck down before—" A coughing fit cut him short, and he leaned against the wall, one hand on his chest as he gasped for air.

I held the knife out in front of me, rock steady, finally

getting my footing. Chancing a quick glance at the girl, I jerked my head toward the other end of the alley, willing her to bolt.

Her sudden, panicked gasp and a blur of movement beside me were all the warning I had before the dude slammed into me again, tackling me to the ground. My knife clattered away.

Straddling my chest, he cocked back an arm and offered a bloody, near-toothless smile. "Time to say goodnight, witch."

"Leave her alone!" No more than another flash in my peripheral vision, the kid leaped out from behind the Dumpster, flinging herself at our attacker.

She scratched and punched for all she was worth, eyes blazing and wild. I'd never seen anyone so fierce.

But he simply batted her away like she was nothing. A fly. A gnat. A piece of lint.

She hit the ground hard.

I gasped, heart hammering in my chest, shock radiating through my limbs. She *wasn't* a fly or a gnat. She was a fucking child in a unicorn hoodie, lost and scared and totally alone, and he'd thrown her down.

Just like that.

Still pinned in place, I couldn't even see where she'd landed.

But I would never forget that sound. Her head hitting the pavement. The eerie silence that followed. Seconds later, another ambulance howled into the darkness, nowhere close enough to help.

"What did you do?" I screamed, no longer caring who or what might've heard me. "She's just a kid!"

I clawed at the man's chest, but I was pretty sure he'd already forgotten about me.

"No. No way. Fuck this bullshit." He jumped up to his feet, staggered back a few steps, then took off without another word.

Still trying to catch my breath, I crawled over next to the girl, adrenaline chasing away my pain. Blood pooled beneath her head, spreading out like a dark halo. Her breathing was shallow.

"Hey. I'm right here," I whispered. "It's okay, baby."

She was thin as a rail, her wet jeans and threadbare hoodie hanging off her shivering frame.

"Jesus, you're freezing." I shucked off my jacket and covered her body, careful not to move her. "He's gone now. He can't hurt you anymore."

I swept the matted hair from her forehead. Her skin was clammy, her eyes glassy and unfocused, but she was still conscious. Still there, blinking up at me and the dark, cloudy sky above.

"What's your name, sweet pea?" I asked.

Blink. Blink.

"Hon, can you tell me your name?"

She sucked in a breath. Fresh tears leaked from her eyes. That had to be a good sign, right?

"Um. Yeah," she whispered. "It's… Breanne?"

"Breanne?"

"Sometimes Bean."

"Bean. That's a great nickname." I tucked a lock of hair behind her ear, my fingers coming away sticky with blood. "Hang in there, Bean. I'm going for help."

"No! Don't leave me here. I—" She reached for me, arms trembling, skin white as the moon. "Grape jelly. Grape—"

Grape jelly grape, she'd said. And then her eyes went wide, and I watched the spark in her go out.

Just like that.

"Bean!" I pressed my fingers beneath her jaw, then checked her wrist, desperate to find a pulse.

But it was too late.

Here in the middle of vamp central, the sweet kid in the unicorn hoodie—the one who'd ultimately saved *my* life—was dead.

* * *

Ready for more? Dive into the sexy supernatural world of The Witch's Rebels! **Grab your copy of Shadow Kissed now!**

ABOUT SARAH PIPER

Sarah Piper is a witchy, Tarot-card-slinging paranormal romance and urban fantasy author. Through her signature brew of dark magic, heart-pounding suspense, and steamy romance, Sarah promises a sexy, supernatural escape into a world where the magic is real, the monsters are sinfully hot, and the witches always get their magically-ever-afters.

Readers have dubbed her work "super sexy," "imaginative and original," "off-the-walls good," and "delightfully wicked in the best ways," a quote Sarah hopes will appear on her tombstone.

Originally from New York, Sarah now makes her home in northern Colorado with her husband (though that changes frequently) (the location, not the husband), where she spends her days sleeping like a vampire and her nights writing books, casting spells, gazing at the moon, playing with her ever-expanding collection of Tarot cards, binge-watching Supernatural (Team Dean!), and obsessing over the best way to brew a cup of tea.

You can find her online at SarahPiperBooks.com, on TikTok at @sarahpiperbooks, and in her Facebook readers group at Sarah Piper's Sassy Witches! If you're sassy, or if you need a little *more* sass in your life, or if you need more Dean Winchester gifs in your life (who doesn't?), come hang out!